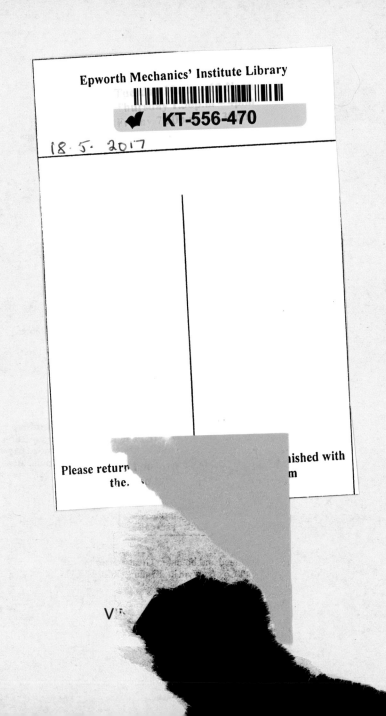

Published by Vintage 2011

4 6 8 10 9 7 5 3

Copyright © Robert Masello 2011

Robert Masello has asserted his right under the Copyright, Designs
and Patents Act 1988 to be identified as the author of this work

First published by Great Britain in 2011 by Vintage

Vintage
Random House, 20 Vauxhall Bridge Road,
London SW1V 2SA

www.vintage-books.co.uk

Addresses for companies within The Random House Group Limited
can be found at: www.randomhouse.co.uk/offices.htm

The Random House Group Limited Reg. No. 954009

A CIP catalogue record for this book
is available from the British Library

ISBN 9780099554295

The Random House Group Limited supports The Forest Stewardship
Council® (FSC®), the leading international forest certification organisation.
All our titles that are printed on Greenpeace approved FSC® certified paper
carry the FSC® logo. Our paper procurement policy can be found at:
www.randomhouse.co.uk/environment

Printed and bound in Great Britain by
CPI Cox & Wyman, Reading, RG1 8EX

THE MEDUSA AMULET

Robert Masello is an award-winning journalist, television writer, and the author of many previous books. His most recent supernatural thriller, published in nine languages, was the critically acclaimed *Blood and Ice*. His other novels include *Vigil* (which appeared on the *USA Today* bestseller list) and its sequel, *Bestiary*. His articles and essays have appeared often in such publications as the *Los Angeles Times*, *New York Magazine*, *People* and *Parade*, and his non-fiction book, *Robert's Rules of Writing*, has become a staple in many college classrooms. Among his produced television credits are such popular shows as *Charmed*, *Sliders*, *Early Edition*, and '*Poltergeist: the Legacy*'. A longstanding member of the Writers Guild of America, he lives in Santa Monica, California.

ALSO BY ROBERT MASELLO

Blood and Ice

In memory of my parents,

Tom and Sonia

The

Medusa Amulet

Prologue

[From *La Chiave Alla Vita Eterna* (The Key to Life Eternal) printed in Florence, Italy, c. 1534. Attributed to Benvenuto Cellini. Anonymous gift, donated to the Permanent Collection of the Newberry Library, 60 W. Walton Street, Chicago, Illinois.]

To venture into the Colosseum at night is not for the faint of heart, and in following the lead, and the lantern, of Dr. Strozzi, I wondered if I had not cast my fortune unwisely. Although the old man was learned, I could not help but see his hand shaking as we came near to the great and ancient stadium itself.

Long abandoned, and in much need of repair, it was surrounded by pens and stables and fenced yards, which had once held the lions and crocodiles, bulls and tigers, elephants and leopards, that had been imported from all corners of the Empire and then pitted against each other in the arena. Thousands of them, it has been said, were slaughtered in a single day's entertainment.

Men, too, of course. As Dr. Strozzi carried the lantern past the barracks of the Ludus Magnus, where the gladiators had trained, I could still detect the scent of sweat and leather and iron.

But like all young men of talent and industry, I did not allow fear or superstition to bar my way. On my back, I carried the burlap sack containing the necessary ingredients for the unholy work that lay ahead. In preparation for that night, Dr. Strozzi, a man whose skills in necromancy were famous from Palermo to Madrid, wore the robes of a dead Franciscan friar, and I wore the clothes of a murderer, hanged at a crossroads on the outskirts of the city.

"To call upon the dead," Dr. Strozzi had informed me, "it is necessary to become *simpatico* in every way. We must take on the odor of decay." For that purpose, we had not bathed for a period of nine days and had eaten no salt, as that was a preservative. Our meat was dog, the companion of Hecate, goddess of the dark moon. Nor had we engaged in any carnal intercourse. As I said to Strozzi in answer to his many warnings on that matter, "Who would have me in such fashion as this?"

In further deference to the spirits that we hoped to summon that night, we entered the Colosseum through the Emperor's Gate. The bronze clamps that had held the marble in place had long since been stolen, and the marble itself had been plundered for its quicklime. As an artisan, I mourned the loss of such skilled work. The world, as I have often remarked, is overrun with barbarians.

With rain coming soon, we did not hesitate once inside. Under the gaze of the ancient gods, whose broken statues stared down at us from every column, we descended into the *hypogeum*—the labyrinth of tunnels and ramps and stairs that had once been concealed by the dirt and sand of the arena floor. Now, the maze lay exposed, and at its very center, we found a holding cell where part of the roof still afforded some protection from the gathering storm. Rusted manacles hung from the walls, and a flogging post provided me a hook on which to hang the sack.

Moving always in a left-handed direction, as that is the direction of all things occult, the aged sorcerer made a circle of chalk in the dirt, marking it with the symbols of Earth, Air, Fire, and Water. This would keep the demons and spirits at bay. As he did so, I prepared the fire from the kindling in the bag. Once Dr. Strozzi was done, he directed me to feed the flames with the herbs we had also brought. Myrtle, sage, asafetida. The wood had been soaked in tar, and between that and the stench of the herbs, I thought my senses might give way at any moment. My eyes wept, my nostrils burned, and more than once sparks from the fire threatened to burn the filthy tunic I wore. I would not have mourned its loss.

But even as the doctor made his incantations, and raindrops began to splatter the stones around us, I lowered my head and made my own invocation. Despite his reputation, the doctor, I feared, would not succeed. His motives were impure. He sought out the dead only to ask them where great treasures might lie hidden in the earth, while I sought them out in order to fathom the depths of genius, and thereby procure my own immortality. And so it was that as the night wore on, and the doctor's supplications yielded no result, my own did . . . in the form of a pale figure, flickering like a wax taper, just beyond the limits of our circle.

Dr. Strozzi, upon seeing it himself, fainted dead away, but my resolve was only strengthened. This figure, with its long nose and pointed chin and sharp eyes, was the very spirit I had wished to summon. It was the shade of the greatest poet the world had ever known, a fellow Florentine by birth (though he had denied it by character), Dante Alighieri.

"I honor you," I said.

"And still you trouble me? Am I to be your dog?"

I sought the right words to explain myself, but the shade simply turned away, its winding sheet trailing on the wet stones. "I know what you seek," it said.

Armed with only the short sword I carried at my side, I stepped across the holy circle and followed. But the path soon became confusing, and I felt that we were descending farther into the earth, beneath the Colosseum itself, and into another region. Here, although there should have been no light at all, there was instead another sky, with clouds that looked like banks of glowing coals and a yellow moon the color of a rotting tooth. The shade led me on over ground that crackled like bread crust under my boots. In the wind, I could hear voices murmuring and lamenting, but I could see no one other than my silent guide. At the end of a promontory, he stopped and, pointing a lean finger toward a marshy hollow below, said, "There. Take the water, if you can."

I saw a green pool under a rocky ledge, surrounded on all sides by bulrushes waving in the hot wind. And though I carried no cup or bowl, I thought perhaps that he meant for me to drink. And so I descended into the bulrushes, which came and went like the wind. When I sought to part them, they vanished, and when I did nothing, they clung to my garments, obscuring my way so that I stumbled over several blocks of stone. Or so I thought. It was only upon a closer inspection that I discerned these had once been human shapes, now cast in stone, their arms still upraised, their faces twisted in horror. I clutched the handle of my sword, but I had not come so far to turn back now.

Wading into the pool, I cupped my hand to drink of the water, but even as I did so, the water seemed to shrink away. I put my hand yet lower, and again the water receded. *Then I shall simply plunge my face in,* I thought, *and drink whatever I can catch.* But my lips were less than a *braccia* from the surface when I saw a face reflected there. Its glowing eyes were shaped like almonds and its hair was made of writhing serpents. I could hear their hissing and I knew that the Gorgon, whose gaze could turn a man to stone, was crouched on the ledge above me. I drew my sword, and watching its image in the water, I saw it spring from the rock. My blade swung round and caught the creature in its scaly breast.

But it was not a deadly blow, and while averting my eyes, I held its head beneath the water. The tiny snakes bit at my hands, and when I could hold on no more, I lifted the head enough to hew at the neck as if it were a stump of wood. It came away in my hand like a melon cut from the vine.

Even to this day I cannot say how I escaped this infernal region. My guide was gone, but my boots, half-filled with water from the pond, somehow retraced their steps to the Colosseum floor. Of divine help, I'm sure there was none, not in such a place as that. Crossing again into the circle, I hurled what sticks remained upon the smoldering fire and left Dr. Strozzi to lie in peace, his whiskers blowing in the wind and his limbs twitching in the throes of his dream.

It was many hours till dawn, during which I kept watch, but when it broke, Dr. Strozzi awakened and, rubbing his eyes, said, "My thoughts remain cloudy."

"As do mine," I said. Indeed, my head hurt as much as if I had drunk a barrel of wine.

"Did we raise the dead?"

A pair of crows landed in a puddle of mud, squawking.

"And what is that in the bag?" he said, pointing at the sack swinging back and forth on the flogging pole. Water had leaked from its bottom, and the few blades of grass below it had withered and died.

When again I did not reply, the doctor said, "Whatever prize it may be, I promise that you will receive your share."

But this was no treasure to be divided like coins, and when Strozzi saw that I was not in the giving mood, he wisely busied himself with other things. The trophy was mine, and no man would ever take it from me.

[Translated by David L. Franco, Ph.D., Director of Acquisitions, Newberry Library Collections, Chicago, Illinois. All rights reserved.]

Part One

Part One

Chapter 1

As the guests began to take their chairs, David Franco felt that little flutter of anxiety that he experienced whenever he had to make a speech of any kind. Somewhere he had read that public speaking was one of the most commonplace fears, but that wasn't a lot of help right then. He glanced at his notes for the hundredth time, told himself that there was nothing to be nervous about, and straightened his tie again.

The room itself—the exhibit hall of the Newberry Library—had been nicely appointed for the event. Lighted display cases held a selection of the rare manuscripts from the library's collection, and a classical ensemble, playing antique instruments, had only just stopped playing. A computerized lectern was set up on a dais at the front of the hall.

"It's showtime," Dr. Armbruster, the matronly chief administrator, whispered in his ear; she was dressed in her usual gray skirt and jacket, but she had enlivened it for the occasion with a rhinestone brooch in the shape of an open book. Stepping out to the lectern, she welcomed everyone to the event. "And thanks, especially," she added, "for coming out on such a freezing day."

There was an appreciative murmur, followed by a bit of coughing and rustling as the thirty or forty people present settled into their chairs. Most of them were middle-aged or older—well-heeled and successful book lovers and friends of the library. The men were generally white-haired, and wore bow ties, Harris tweeds, and flannel pants; their wives were in pearls and carried Ferragamo handbags. This was Old Chicago money, from the Gold Coast and the suburbs of the North Shore, along with a smattering of academic types from Northwestern or Loyola. The profs were the ones in the rumpled corduroy trousers and jackets. Later, they'd be the first to hit the buffet line. David had learned never to stand between a professor and a free Swedish meatball.

"And on behalf of the Newberry," Dr. Armbruster was saying, "one of Chicago's landmarks since 1883, I want to thank you all for your continued support. Without your generosity, I don't know what we'd do. As you know, we are a private institution, and we rely upon our friends and associates to sustain the library in every way, from the acquisition of new materials to, well, just paying the electric bill."

An elderly wag in the front row waved a checkbook in the air, and there was some polite laughter.

"You can put that away for now," Dr. Armbruster said, then added with a laugh, "But keep it handy."

David shifted from one foot to the other, nervously awaiting his cue.

"I think most of you know David Franco, who's not only our youngest but one of our most industrious staff members. A summa cum laude graduate of Amherst College, David was the winner of a Fulbright Scholarship to Italy, where he studied Renaissance art and literature at the Villa I Tatti. Recently, he completed his doctorate at our own University of Chicago, and all this," she said, turning toward David, "before the age of what? Thirty?"

Blushing fiercely, David said, "Not quite. I turned thirty-one last Friday."

"Oh, well, in that case," Dr. Armbruster said, turning back toward the audience, "you'd better get a move on."

There was a welcome wave of laughter.

"But as you can see," she continued, "when we received, as an anonymous gift, the 1534 copy of Dante's *Divine Comedy*, printed in Florence, we knew there was only one person to hand it over to. David has supervised its physical restoration—you would never guess what its binding looked like when we first acquired it—but has also entered its entire text, and its many illustrations, into our digital archive. That way, it can become available to scholars and researchers the world over. Today, he's going to show us some of the most beautiful and intriguing images from the book, and also, I think," she said, glancing encouragingly at David, "take us on a brief tour of the poem's nature imagery?"

David nodded, his stomach doing a quick backflip, as Dr. Armbruster stepped away from the microphone. "David, it's all yours."

There was a round of subdued applause as he tilted the microphone higher, spread his papers on the lectern, took a sip from the water glass that had been left for him, and thanked everyone, again, for coming. His voice came out strained and high. Then he said something about the freezing weather outside, before remembering that his boss had already commented on that, too. He looked out at the room of expectant faces, cleared his throat, and decided to cut the small talk and just launch into his lecture.

As he did so, the lights went down, and a screen was lowered to his right.

"Dante, as you might know, had originally titled his book *The Comedy of Dante Alighieri, A Florentine by birth but not in character*. The title *Divine Comedy* only came later, when the book became regarded as a masterpiece. It's a work that can be approached in a thousand different ways, and over the centuries it has been," he said, his voice gaining strength once he was on firm and familiar ground. "But what we're going to focus on today is the use of natural imagery in the poem. And this Florentine edition which was recently donated to the Newberry collection—and which I think most of you have now seen in the central display case—is a particularly good way to do that."

He touched a button on the lectern's electronic panel and the first image—an etching of a deep forest, with a lone figure, head bent, entering a narrow path—appeared on the screen. "'In the middle of the journey of our life,'" he recited from memory, "'I came to myself in a dark wood where the straight way was lost.'" Looking up, he said, "With the possible exception of 'Jack and Jill went up the hill,' there is probably no line of poetry more famous and easily identifiable than that. And you will notice that right here, at the very start of the epic that is to follow, we have a glimpse of the natural world that is both realistic—Dante spends a terrible night in that wood—and metaphorical."

Turning to the etching, he elaborated on several of its most salient features, including the animals that animated its border—a leopard with a spotted coat, a lion, and a skulking wolf with distended jaws. "Confronted by these creatures, Dante pretty much turns tail and runs, until he bumps into a figure—who turns out of course to be the Roman poet Virgil—who offers to guide him 'through an eternal place where thou shalt hear the hopeless shrieks, shalt see the ancient spirits in pain so that each calls for a second death.'"

A new image flashed on the screen, of a wide river—Acheron with mobs of the dead huddled on its shores, and a shrouded Charon in the foreground, pointing with one bony finger at a long boat. It was a particularly well-done image and David noted several heads nodding with interest and a low hum of comments. He had thought there might be. This edition of the *Divine Comedy* was one of the most powerful he had ever seen, and he was making it his mission to find out who the illustrator had been. The title pages of the book had sustained such significant water and smoke damage that no names could be discerned. The book had also had to be intensively treated for mold, and many of the plates bore ineradicable green and blue spots the circumference of a pencil eraser.

But for David, such blemishes and signs of age only made the books and manuscripts he studied more precious and intriguing. The very fact that this book—nearly five hundred years old—had passed through so many unknown hands, and through so many different places, only lent it an air of mystery and importance. When he held it in his hands, he felt connected to that chain of unrecorded readers who had turned its pages before . . . perhaps in a *palazzo* in Tuscany, a garret in Paris, or a country seat in England. All he knew of the book's origins was that it had been donated to the Newberry by a local collector, who had wanted to be sure it would be properly restored, studied, and its treasures made available to all. David had felt honored to be entrusted with the task.

As he talked, he became not only more relaxed, but positively excited by the opportunity to share some of the discoveries he had made about the methodology that Dante had employed in his use of natural imagery. The poet often included animals in the text, but he also made regular use of the sun (a planet, according to the Ptolemaic system of the time) and the stars, the sea, the leaves of the trees, snow. Though the hall was dimly lighted, David did his best to maintain some eye contact with the audience as he elucidated these points, and midway through he noted a woman all in black, with a small black hat and a veil across her face, slip into the room and take a seat close to the door. The veil was what struck him. Who wore such things anymore, even in mourning? For a second he lost the thread of what he was saying and had to glance down at his notes to remember where he was.

"The meaning that Dante attaches to these natural elements changes, as we move from the *Inferno* to the *Purgatorio* to the *Paradiso*." He continued with his thesis, but his eye was drawn periodically to the mysterious woman in back, and for some reason it popped into his head that she might be the donor of the book, there to see what had become of it. As the images passed by on the screen to his right, he found himself explicating them as if he were talking chiefly to the woman concealed behind the veil. She remained completely still, her hands folded in her lap, her legs in black stockings, and it was all but impossible for him to figure out anything about her . . . most notably her age. There were moments he felt she was in her twenties, dressed up as if for a grim costume party, and other times when he suspected she was a more mature woman, perched primly, almost precariously, on the edge of the chair.

By the time he had shown his last illustration—a whirlwind of leaves, containing the Cumaean Sybil's prophecies—and wrapped up the lecture with Dante's closing invocation to "the Love that moves the sun and the other stars"—he was determined to meet her. But when the lights came up in the exhibit hall, a bunch of hands went up with questions.

"How will you go about determining the illustrator of this volume? Have you got any leads already?"

"Was Florence as prominent a publishing center as Pisa or Venice?"

And, from an eager academic in back, "What would you say about Ruskin's comment, concerning the flux of consciousness essential to the 'pathetic fallacy,' as it pertains to the *Comedy*?"

David did his best to field the queries, but he also knew that he'd been talking for over an hour, and that most of the audience would be eager to get up, stretch, and have another drink. In the lobby area just outside the exhibit hall, he could see waiters in black tie balancing silver trays of champagne glasses. The smell of hot hors d'oeuvres wafted in on the central heating.

When he finally stepped down from the dais, several members of the audience shook his hand, a couple of the older gentlemen clapped him on the back, and Dr. Armbruster beamed at him. He knew she'd been hoping he would hit one out of the park, and he sort of felt that he had. Apart from his initial anxiety, he hadn't missed a step.

But what he really wanted to do was find the lady in black, who had apparently escaped the exhibit hall already. In the lobby, long trestle tables had been set up with damask tablecloths and silver serving dishes. The profs were already lined up elbow patch to elbow patch, their little plates piled high.

But the lady in black was nowhere to be seen.

"David," Dr. Armbruster was saying, as she took him by the elbow and steered him toward an elegant, older couple holding their champagne flutes, "I don't know if you've met the Schillingers. Joseph is also an Amherst man."

"But way before your time," Schillinger said, shaking his hand with a firm grasp. He looked like a tall and ancient crane, with a beaked nose and white hair. "I quite enjoyed your talk."

"Thanks."

"And I would love to be kept apprised of your work on the book. I lived in Europe for quite a while, and—"

"Joseph is being modest," Dr. Armbruster broke in. "He was our ambassador to Liechtenstein."

"And I started my own collection of Old Masters drawings. Still, I never saw anything quite like these. The renderings of the rings of Hell are especially macabre, to say the very least."

David never failed to be impressed at the credentials and the backgrounds of the people he met at the Newberry functions, and he did his best to stay focused and courteous to the Schillingers. The former ambassador even pressed his card on him and offered to assist his research in any way he could.

"When it comes to getting access to private archives and such," he said, "I still have some strings I can pull on the other side of the pond."

But the whole time they were talking, David kept one eye out for the lady in black; and when he could finally break away, he found Dr. Armbruster again and asked if she knew where she might have gone, or who it might have been.

"You say she came in midway through your talk?"

"Yes, and sat all the way in back."

"Oh, then I wouldn't have seen her. I was off supervising the food."

A waiter passed by, carrying a tray with one lone cheese puff left.

"I wonder if we'll have enough," she said, before excusing herself. "Those professors eat like locusts."

David shook a few more hands, fielded a few more casual questions, then, as the last guests filtered out, he slipped up a back staircase to his office—a cubbyhole crammed with books and papers—and hung his sport coat and tie on the back of the door. He kept them there for those rare occasions, like the lecture, when he had to dress up. Then he pulled on his coat and gloves and went out by a side door.

Ex-ambassador Schillinger and his wife were just getting into the back of a black BMW sedan as a sturdy, bald chauffeur held the door. A couple of professors, deep in conversation, were still huddled by the stairs. The last thing David wanted was to have them spot him and come up with some other arcane question, so he put up the hood of his coat and set off across the park.

Long known as Bughouse Square because of its appeal to soapbox orators, the park was understandably deserted just then. The late-afternoon sky was a pewter gray and the wind was nearly blowing the big fake candy canes off the lampposts. Christmas was just around the corner, and David had yet to do his shopping. Not that he had much to do. There was his sister, her husband, his niece, and that was about it. His girlfriend, Linda, had moved out a month ago. At least that was one less present to worry about.

Crossing Oak Street, he walked north to Division, and as he approached the El station, he heard a train screeching to a stop overhead. He raced up the stairs three at a time—he'd been on the track team in high school and could still keep up a pretty good pace—and made it through the sliding doors just in the nick of time. He flopped onto the bench feeling victorious, then, as he unzipped his coat and waited for his glasses to defog, wondered why he'd been in such a hurry. It was a Saturday, and he had no plans. As the train picked up speed, and the conductor announced the next stop over the garbled intercom, he reminded himself to put a Post-it note on his computer on Monday morning, reading: "Get a life."

Chapter 2

Even for someone as jaded as Phillip Palliser, it had been a strange day so far.

A car had been sent to his hotel, and the driver—a Frenchman named Emil Rigaud, who looked as if he had spent more than a few years in military service of some kind—had whisked them off to a private airfield just outside Paris, where they had boarded a helicopter and flown south toward the Loire Valley. Palliser, a man who spent a good part of his life flying around the globe, still harbored some reservations about helicopter flight. The din in the cabin, even with the headphones on, was excruciating, and as part of the floor was transparent, he could not help but see the landscape rushing by below his feet. First, the outlying suburbs of the city—a hideous jumble of concrete blocks and crowded highways, much like the wastelands surrounding most metropolitan centers—blissfully followed by snowy farms and fields, then, an hour later, deep, dark forests and valleys.

As they had passed above the town of Chartres, Rigaud had leaned in, and, over his headset, said, "That's the cathedral, right under us. I told the pilot to ring the bells."

And when Palliser looked down, it did indeed seem as if the chopper's rails were about to clip the cathedral's twin spires. He felt a sinking in the pit of his stomach and closed his eyes. When he opened them again a few seconds later, Rigaud was looking at him fixedly, with a smile on his face.

The man was a bit of a sadist, Palliser thought.

"Not much farther," Rigaud said over a burst of static. But his tone conveyed less comfort than regret . . . at the ordeal coming to an end.

Palliser looked away and concentrated on taking deep, steady breaths. For nearly ten years, ever since leaving the International Art Recovery League, he had undertaken private commissions such as the one he was on now. But none was going to be as lucrative as this. If he could find what his mysterious patron had asked him to find, he could finally take that retirement he dreamt of and even, perhaps, begin his own art collection in earnest. He was tired of being the expert instead of the owner, the detective hired to track down the valuable objets d'art to which other people—most of them philistines—held some spurious claim. It was time to set up shop for himself.

As they approached the steep, rugged walls of a cliff rising from the river, Rigaud's voice again crackled in his headphones.

"The Chateau Perdu is due south. You will see it soon."

In all his years, and all his travels, Palliser had never heard of this Chateau Perdu—or lost castle—but he had been sufficiently intrigued by the note left at his hotel to undertake this journey.

"I understand that we share certain interests," the note had said. "I have long been a collector of art, from all over the globe, and would be delighted to have someone with your discerning eye appreciate, and perhaps appraise, some of it." Palliser picked up the scent of a commission down the road. But it was the conclusion that sealed the deal. "Perhaps I can even help you on your present mission. After all, even Perseus did not prevail over the Medusa without the help of powerful friends."

❧

It was that last comment—about the Medusa—that had piqued his interest. The man who had signed the note—Monsieur Auguste

Linz—must know something about the assignment Palliser was on. How he'd found out was anyone's guess, as even Palliser had never met his actual employer on this job. But if this Linz actually knew something about the whereabouts of *La Medusa,* the ancient artifact that he was seeking, then enduring the helicopter ride would have been well worth the trouble.

Rigaud's arm lifted, straight from the shoulder, and he pointed past the pilot's head at a ridgeline where towering old oaks gave way to a grim chateau with pepperpot towers—five of them, Palliser counted—rising from its walls. The day was fading, and here and there lights had come on behind the slitted windows.

A dry moat, like an open grave, surrounded it on three sides; the fourth was just a sheer drop-off to the river far below. But even from this height and distance, Palliser could see that the chateau far pre-dated most of its more famous counterparts. This was not some frilly cupcake, designed for a royal mistress, but a fortress built by a knight back from the Crusades or a duke with his eye on a crown.

The chopper skimmed above the tops of the trees, their branches nearly grazing the bubble beneath Palliser's feet, before banking slowly and wobbling down onto a sere, frost-covered lawn. A few dead leaves scattered in the wash from the propellers. Palliser removed his headphones, unhooked his shoulder harness, and after Rigaud had climbed out of the hatch, followed him, head bent low, as the blades stopped whirring and the engine died down.

His legs, he discovered, were a tad unsteady.

Rigaud, all in black and his dyed blond hair shining in the late-day sun, strode off, without another word, toward the main gate of the chateau, leaving Palliser, in his cashmere overcoat and his fine Italian loafers, to stumble after him, a leather briefcase holding the facsimiles from Chicago clutched in one hand.

They crossed a drawbridge, under a portcullis, and into a cobble-stoned courtyard. A wide flight of steps led to a pair of doors standing open, and Palliser passed through them and into a vast entry hall with a grand escalier sweeping up it on either side. A middle-aged man was just coming down the stairs, dressed in English tweeds as if about to stroll down the lane to his local pub.

"Mr. Palliser," he said warmly, stepping forward. "I am so pleased you could come." His English was good, though it carried a Swiss or maybe Austrian accent.

Rigaud stood to one side, as if he were again on some parade ground awaiting review.

Palliser shook his hand and thanked him for the invitation. The man's skin was both cool and damp, and though his blue eyes were cordial, there was also something in them that made Palliser distinctly uncomfortable. He felt, as Monsieur Linz clung to his hand a moment too long, as if he were being assessed somehow.

"What can we get you after your journey?"

"Perhaps a drink?" Palliser said, still recovering from the helicopter ride. "Scotch, neat?" He could tell already that this place was likely to be a treasure trove of art and antiques. "Followed by a tour of your magnificent home, if you would be so kind? I'm afraid I have never heard of this chateau prior to your note."

"Few people have," Monsieur Linz said, clapping his hands. A servant popped up out of nowhere and was dispatched for the drink. "But that's the way we like it." With his left arm tucked behind his back—was it shaking, Palliser wondered?—Linz strutted off to begin the tour.

"I should start by saying that the house was built in the early 1200s, by a Norman knight who had pillaged his way through the Holy Lands."

Palliser silently congratulated himself.

"Many of the things he brought back are here still," Linz said, waving one arm at a pair of faded tapestries adorning one wall, before ushering Palliser into a baronial hall lined with coats of armor and medieval weaponry. It was a fantastic display, worthy of the Royal Armouries in the Tower of London—swords and shields, bows and arrows, battle-axes, pikes, and spears. Their metal gleamed in the western light flooding through the casement windows. "One can only guess," Linz said, running one hand along the dull edge of a broadsword, "what horrors they witnessed."

Witnessed? Palliser thought. These were the very instruments of destruction.

The servant, breathless, appeared at his elbow with a silver tray on which rested a glass of Scotch.

Palliser put his briefcase down on a table before accepting the drink.

"You may leave that here," Linz said, "I have so much to show you," urging him on.

The tour was a lengthy one, ranging from the many salons to the top of the turrets. "As you no doubt know," Linz said, "there was a royal edict, in the sixteenth century, decreeing that the nobility lower the walls and remove the pepperpot towers from their chateaux. The king wanted no fortresses in France that could withstand an assault by his troops, if it ever came to that."

"But these, apparently, were spared," Palliser observed. "Why?"

"Even then, no king dared to tamper with the Chateau Perdu. The place had acquired, shall we say, a reputation."

"For what?"

"The dark arts," Linz replied, with a hint of amusement. "It has served the chateau well ever since."

From their perch on the ramparts, Palliser could gaze out over the tips of the ancient oaks and down to the river Loire at the foot of the cliffs. The sun was just setting, and the temperature had dropped another ten degrees. Even with the warmth of the Scotch in him, Palliser shivered in his Savile Row suit.

"But come, let's go down to the dining room. We have a marvelous cook."

Palliser was beginning to wonder when they were going to get down to business, but he knew that it was always best to betray no eagerness. Besides, he was astonished at the chateau and the thousand and one works of art it appeared to contain. Every corner held an oil painting in a gilded frame; every cornice was surmounted by a marble bust; every floor was covered with a threadbare, but immensely valuable, Persian carpet. Monsieur Linz, however peculiar he seemed, plainly possessed a great fortune and an exquisite eye. If anyone knew where La Medusa—the silver mirror lost for centuries—was hidden, Linz might be the man.

In the dining hall, a long refectory table had been set, and Palliser was guided to a seat in the middle. At one end, Linz sat down, while Rigaud sat directly across from their guest of honor. The other end was left empty, until Linz muttered something to a servant, and a minute or two later, a pretty blond woman, about thirty, fluttered in.

"I was exercising," she said, and Linz snorted. She was introduced as Ava, but showed no interest in knowing who Palliser was or what he was doing there. Indeed, all through dinner she appeared to be listening to something through the earphones attached to an iPod in the pocket of her blouse.

The courses, many of them, were served silently by an older couple, and several bottles of very old, and very good, wine were poured. Palliser tried to gauge his intake, but the glass was always replenished as soon as he had taken a sip. Eventually, the conversation found its way to the assignment Palliser had undertaken.

"So tell me—what is so priceless about this mirror?" Linz asked, dicing up a roasted potato. Palliser had noticed that even though fish and game had been served, Linz had eaten only soup and vegetables. "Who would want it so badly?"

"That I am not at liberty to divulge," Palliser said, glad for the convenient evasion. His only contact was with a Chicago lawyer named Hudgins, who closely guarded his master's, or mistress's, identity. "But may I ask you a question?"

Linz nodded vigorously, without looking up from his plate.

"How did you know what I was looking for?" He noted Rigaud throwing a glance at his boss.

Linz took a swallow from his wineglass, and said, "I'm an ardent collector, as you have already seen. I have many sources, many dealers, and they all keep me apprised of anything new that comes onto the market. They also tell me about any unusual inquiries. Yours was one of them."

Palliser thought he'd been extremely discreet in his search so far, but now he wondered who had tipped off Linz. Was it that jeweler in Rome? The librarian in Florence? Some rival as yet unknown?

"Tell me what you know of it," Linz said, "and maybe I will be able to help you."

Palliser smelled a rat—a big one—but he suspected that Linz already knew what little he could tell him. Whoever his source was had undoubtedly told him a good deal more about what Palliser was seeking—a handheld looking glass, of sixteenth-century Florentine manufacture, and most probably from the hand of the master craftsman himself, Benvenuto Cellini. One side sported a silver head of the Medusa, her hair writhing like snakes, and the other concealed a mirror. Why his client wanted it more than anything on earth, he could not say.

But when he had finished, Linz speared the last of his asparagus, then said, "A lot of what Cellini made, as I hardly need to tell a man of your experience, has been lost or destroyed over the years. So how do you know it even exists? What proof do you have?"

"None, really, apart from a few papers in my case."

Linz had the briefcase brought to them at the table, and as the servants poured out coffee, Palliser started to enter the combination to unlock the case, when he realized that it was already unlocked. Had he been so careless?

With some reservations, he produced copies of a sketch—in red and black ink—of the mirror, along with copies of some working papers written in Italian, and in a distinctive hand.

Linz studied them intensely, his dark hair, speckled with gray, sweeping low across his brow. There followed a detailed discussion of Cellini's career, and of the Italian Renaissance in general, which bowled Palliser over. A graduate of Oxford, with a doctorate in art history, he knew a genuine connoisseur when he came across one—and Linz was not only a passionate devotee of the arts, but also someone who spoke of them with the intensity of an artist himself, someone who had wrestled with the aesthetic questions on his own terms. Palliser wouldn't have been surprised if Linz had his own studio tucked away in one of the unexplored turrets.

Still, he felt that he had given the game away with little to show for it in return. When he finally ventured to ask his host what suggestions he might have for locating the *Medusa,* Linz leaned back in his chair, and after deliberating, said, "A lost cause, I should say. You admit that it hasn't been seen for centuries. I should think it was best left alone."

To Palliser's practiced ear, it sounded like he knew more than he was telling. "I'm afraid I can't do that."

"Some things are meant to be found," Linz said gnomically, "and others are meant to be lost. Everything has its own destiny. As an artisan," he went on, astutely referring to Cellini in the vernacular of his day, "he was unparalleled in his various skills." Although the term "artist" was also employed, and came into greater use over time, it was no insult, Palliser recognized, to be known as an artisan. "But in his own lifetime, even Cellini's greatest work sometimes went unappreciated."

"The Perseus statue was wildly acclaimed," Palliser protested. He did not even mention the artist's other great triumphs.

"But that was not his greatest work."

Now Palliser was puzzled. Not his greatest work? It was one of the most revered works of all Renaissance art, known throughout the world.

As the evening progressed, Rigaud looked increasingly bored, and Ava perked up only when a torte was brought out, piled high with whipped cream and fresh strawberries. She dug in with gusto.

Linz, too, plainly enjoyed the dessert, a moustache of cream forming on his upper lip. But Palliser had lost his appetite. Glancing at his watch—it was well past ten—he said, "And I do hate to end the evening so abruptly, but I should get back to Paris. I still have *La Medusa* to find."

"You sound undeterred," Linz said. "I'm impressed." Wiping his lips with his napkin, he added, "But if you would prefer to spend the night here, Lord knows we have plenty of room."

Little as he relished the idea of the helicopter ride back, in the dark, Palliser was even less inclined to stay the night under such a strange roof. There was something unsettling about Linz, quite apart from the fact that he had provided so little help. All through the dinner, Palliser had increasingly felt as if he was being drained of all his own information, and for nothing in return. He wasn't used to being duped, and he didn't like it one bit.

"Thank you," he said, "but I have an appointment first thing in the morning."

Linz acceded graciously, rising from his chair. That left arm was definitely palsied, Palliser noticed. But then, to his own great embarrassment, he found himself weaving on his own feet from the effects of the wine. Rocking in place for a second, he said, "Your wine cellar is exceptionally well stocked."

"It's the best in the Loire Valley," Linz said. "In fact, you have been such good company, I'd like to offer you a gift—a bottle of whatever you like."

Palliser demurred, but Linz would have none of it. "Emil," he commanded, "tell the pilot to be ready in ten minutes." And then, taking Palliser by the elbow, he escorted him out of the room while Ava called for a second helping of the torte.

Palliser, holding his briefcase, was led back through the armor hall and the salons, then down a winding stair and through the kitchens and scullery. The temperature grew colder and the air grew damp. Linz circumvented an old dusty rack and flicked a switch. A long corridor, carved from the stone itself, was lined with thousands of bottles of wine, as far as the eye could see. Palliser, who had seen the vaunted storerooms of Moldova, could not even guess at the quantity housed here.

"What do you like?" Linz asked, leading the way under a string of dim white lightbulbs. "Bordeaux? Pinot Noir?" He waved an arm at the racks, moving on. "This valley is best known for its dry white wines. Did you enjoy the Sancerre at dinner?"

"I did," Palliser confessed, wishing that he had enjoyed it a little less.

"Then let me offer you one of these," Linz said, stepping farther down the tunnel and taking a bottle from the rack. Blowing off the dust, he said, "Yes, this is a 1936—a very fine vintage."

As Palliser took the bottle, he became aware of a draft under his feet, and the distant sound of sloshing water. He looked down, and in the wavering light saw that he was standing atop a rusty grate.

"This was once a dungeon," Linz explained. "You're standing above the oubliette."

The shaft, Palliser knew, where prisoners were thrown to die a slow death of thirst and starvation.

Instinctively, he stepped back.

"But the chateau rests on limestone, and the river is eroding the cliffs," Linz said, stooping to pull the grate away to reveal the shaft; he appeared rather proud of his oubliette. "You see? The water has already reached the bottom of the pit."

Indeed, Palliser could just make out a surge of water swirling at the very bottom of the funnel, when he felt a steadying hand on his shoulder and turned to see that Rigaud had rejoined them.

"The chopper is ready to go," he said, Palliser's cashmere overcoat draped over one arm.

"Good," Palliser replied, "thank you."

"Let me take those for you," Linz said, relieving Palliser of the wine and the briefcase before he could think to object.

Then, as Rigaud held up the coat, Palliser turned and slipped his arms into the sleeves. He felt warmer already. But as he reached down to button it, Linz patted him on the shoulder, much harder than he thought necessary, and he was thrown off-balance. Before he could quite regain his footing, Rigaud had crouched down and was lifting him by the cuffs of his trousers.

"Stop! What the—"

But he was already upside down, his hands scrabbling at the edges of the oubliette. He tried to brace himself, but the stone was slick and his fingers kept sliding off into space.

"Let go!" he shouted, trying desperately to kick free, even as the coins and keys from his pants and jacket rained onto the stone, and the glasses slipped off his nose. The Mont Blanc pen dropped from his breast pocket, spinning into the black void. One hand was still firmly planted on the stone, but Linz put out a foot and nudged it aside.

An instant later Palliser was falling headfirst, caroming off the edges of the narrow shaft, shredding his clothes and ripping his skin, until he plunged, screaming, into the black water at the bottom of the pit.

Linz waited a moment, listening to the gurgle of the water, then brushed his hands against his jacket and replaced the 1936 Sancerre on the shelf. He nodded at the grate, and Rigaud bent down and pushed it back into place.

On the way out, Linz flicked off the lights and went upstairs to his bedroom. Ava was in the bathroom, removing her makeup. After getting undressed, he put on his pajamas and red silk robe, and began leafing through the pages from the late Mr. Palliser's briefcase. So far, they looked very similar to papers he'd seen before, more's the pity. They could join all the other sketches and journal entries and *ricordanze*, carried by previous, and equally unsuccessful, emissaries. Sometimes he wondered what he would do for amusement if these detectives and so-called art experts ever stopped coming.

"Who was that bore at the dinner table?" Ava called from the bathroom.

"Nobody."

"Will he be coming back?"

"I don't think so," he replied, turning another page. Linz knew that behind them all, there lurked a rich and resourceful adversary—

though nowhere near as rich and resourceful as he was—and while Rigaud had often advised him to cut the tree down at its roots, Linz resisted. A life like his held little enough to savor, and simply knowing that a nemesis existed gave him a special frisson of pleasure. He had always relished having enemies; he'd felt that their animosity directly fed his own power and invincibility.

And as for these futile attempts to recover *La Medusa*? He was the cat playing with the proverbial mouse.

Ava bounded back into the bed, nude as usual, and yanked the covers up to her neck.

"Tell me again why you won't install central heating?"

"Tell me why you refuse to wear the nightgowns I buy you."

"They're not healthy—they constrict the limbs in sleep."

It was a discussion they had had a thousand times.

"Heating ducts would destroy the integrity of the chateau walls," Linz said. And he had always been terribly superstitious about any alterations to the Chateau Perdu.

She burrowed deeper, pulling the blanket up to her eyeballs. "You and your integrity," she snorted.

Linz slipped the papers into the bedside drawer, right under the loaded pistol he always kept there, and turned out the lights. In the darkness, as he rolled onto his side, he fancied he could hear the cries of his dinner guest, echoing from the oubliette.

Chapter 3

For David, Sunday night had always meant dinner at his sister Sarah's house in the suburbs. And for years, he had looked forward to it.

But those simple, happy days were gone. For the past year or more, it had been an increasingly fraught occasion.

Sarah had been battling breast cancer, just as his mother had done, and like his mother, many years ago, she was losing the war. She had been through endless rounds of radiation and chemo, and even though she was only four years older than David, she looked like she was at death's door. Her wavy brown hair, the same chestnut color as his own, was entirely gone, replaced with a wig that never sat quite right. Her eyebrows were penciled in, and her skin had a pale translucence.

And he loved her more than anyone in the world.

Their father had gone AWOL when he was just a toddler, and after their mother succumbed to the disease, it was Sarah who had pretty much raised him. He owed her everything, and there was nothing he could do to help her now.

Nothing, it seemed, that anyone could do.

He was just stamping the slush off his boots when she opened the door. Around her head, she was wearing a new silk scarf in a wild paisley pattern. It wasn't great, but anything was better than that wig.

"Gary gave it to me," she said, reading his mind as always.

"It's nice," David said, as she smoothed the silk along one side.

"Yeah, right," she said, welcoming him in. "I think he hates the wig even more than I do."

His little niece, Emme, was playing tennis on her Wii in the den, and when she saw him, she said, "Uncle David! I dare you to come and play me!"

She reminded him of Sarah when she was a little girl, but he sensed that Emme didn't like it when he said that. Was she just showing her fierce independence, or was it a sign of some subliminal—and justifiable—fear? Was she aware of the terrible ordeal her mother was going through and trying to separate herself from a similar prospect? Or was he imagining the whole thing?

Eight-year-old girls, he recognized, were beyond his field of expertise.

A few minutes later, right after David had lost his first two games, Gary came in from the garage, carrying a bunch of flyers for the open house he was holding the next day. Gary was a real-estate broker, and by all accounts a good one, but in this market nothing was selling. And even when he did get an exclusive listing, it was usually with a reduced commission.

He was also carrying a pie he'd picked up at Bakers Square.

"Is it a chocolate cream?" Emme asked, and when her dad confirmed it, she let out an ear-piercing squeal.

Over dinner, Gary said, "It's the Internet that's killing the real-estate business. Everybody's convinced they can sell their houses themselves these days."

"But are there any buyers out there?" David asked.

"Not many," Gary said, pouring himself another glass of wine and holding the bottle out toward David, who passed. "And the ones that there are think no price is ever low enough. They want to keep making counteroffer after counteroffer until the whole deal winds up falling apart."

"Is it time for pie yet?" Emme asked for the tenth time.

"After we're done with the meat loaf," Sarah said, urging David to take another piece. There were dark circles under her eyes that the overhead light only made worse. David took another slice just to make his sister happy.

"Save room for the pie," Emme said in a stage whisper, just in case anyone had forgotten about it in the last five seconds.

When dinner—and dessert—were over, and David was helping to clear the table, Gary disappeared into the garage again. By the time he came back in, he was dragging a six-foot-tall tree.

"Who wants to decorate a Christmas tree?" he announced.

"I do! I do!" Emme shouted, jumping up and down. "Can we do it tonight?"

"That's why your uncle David is here," Gary said. "To help us get the lights on. You mind?" he asked, and David said he'd be glad to help.

"Hope you're not starting to feel like a hired hand," Sarah said, taking a plate David had just scraped clean and putting it in the dishwasher.

"I've got to earn my keep somehow."

"You do that every day," Sarah said sincerely. "Without your help, I don't know how any of us could have gotten this far."

David gently rubbed her shoulder, wondering not how they'd gotten through this far but if it would ever end. She'd been through the mastectomy, and all the rest . . . but what happened next? He knew that when their mother had been diagnosed, things had gone downhill rapidly—she was dead within eighteen months—but that was then, and this was now. Surely the odds and the outcomes must have improved since then.

Gary hauled out a box of Christmas tree lights and ornaments, and while David held the tree straight, he positioned it in the stand, screwing in the bolts from three sides. Emme was already trying to attach some ornaments, and her dad had to tell her to wait until the lights were on. Gary had the old-fashioned kind of lights that David liked, big thick bulbs that were green and blue and red and shaped like candle flames—none of those fancy little twinkling white lights—and the two of them wrapped the strings around the tree, handing the cord back and forth. Once they were done, Gary said, "Go for it!" to Emme, and she started sticking the ornaments on as fast as her fingers could get the hooks around the boughs.

Sarah, watching from the sofa, sipped a cup of herbal tea and offered the occasional instruction. "Spread them out, honey. You've got a whole tree to cover."

David and Gary took care of the upper limbs, and when David took a silver papier-mâché star out of the box, he stopped and showed it to Sarah. It was the star she had made in grade school and that they'd always put on the very top of the tree. It was a little bent now, and he straightened it gently before putting it in place.

"I made that in Mrs. Burr's class," she said.

"And I had her four years later, but what happened to my ornament?"

"A mystery for the ages," Sarah said. It was the same conversation they had every year, but it wouldn't have been Christmas without it.

Once the ornament supply was exhausted, and the tinsel flung, Gary said, "Are we ready?" and Emme raced around the room, turning off all the lights except those on the tree. The evergreen sparkled in the dark, its boughs giving off a rich, outdoorsy scent. David sat down next to his sister, took her hand, and intertwined their fingers.

"You know how many years we've been recycling that star?" Sarah said.

David did a quick calculation. "Twenty-four years."

"Next year we should celebrate its silver anniversary."

"Yes, we should," David replied, eager to endorse any implicit hope for the future.

"When do we put out the presents?" Emme asked eagerly.

"That's Santa's job," Gary said, and Emme made a face.

"I like it better when Santa comes early," she said, in such a way as to indicate that the Santa bit wasn't working for her anymore.

"They get so cynical, so fast," Sarah said, with a rueful smile. "I believed in Santa until my senior prom."

"Remember the time you got up on Santa's lap at Marshall Fields' and wouldn't get off?"

Nodding, she said, "Remember Marshall Fields', period?"

They were both nostalgic about the pieces of Chicago history, such as its flagship department store, which had disappeared over the years. Fields had become Macy's, and as far as David and his sister were concerned, the magic was gone.

But the magic of a lighted Christmas tree, festooned with home-made ornaments and strings of tinsel, was as powerful as ever, and Gary flopped down in his armchair with a sigh. Even Emme lay down on the wall-to-wall carpeting, with her chin in her hands, gazing at the tree. Taking off the glasses she'd just started wearing that year, she said, "Oooh, this is even prettier. All the colors get kind of blurry. Try it, Uncle David!"

He took off his wire rims, said, "Yep, it's way better," then cleaned them on the tail of his shirt.

"You'll scratch them," Sarah said.

"Only the finest Old Navy fabric," David said.

"I gave you handkerchiefs for your birthday. What did you do with them?"

David couldn't answer that one. Presumably, they were some-where in his dresser, under the pajamas he never wore, or the old track jerseys he had retired. But he liked having Sarah ask, probably as much as she liked nagging.

When Sarah finally told Emme it was time for bed, David helped her up off the sofa. Sarah had always been tall and slender, like her brother, but it was like raising a wraith now. She hugged David with frail arms. "We never asked about your work," she said. "Weren't you giving a lecture soon?"

"Yep, and it went fine."

"Oh, I wish I could have come," she said.

"Next time," he said, though the very thought of having family there made him more nervous than ever.

"What was it about?"

"We got a new copy of Dante, very old and very beautiful. I talked about that." He never went into much detail about his work; he knew that Sarah was proud of his accomplishments, and that was enough. While he had always been the dreamer, the scholar, she had been the practical one. She hadn't had much choice.

"I'll drive you back," Gary said, stretching his arms above his head and rising from his armchair. "You'll freeze to death waiting for the El."

"I'll be okay," David said, though he suspected Gary wanted the chance to talk in private; he often used these car trips to confide in David about what was really happening with Sarah.

They got into his Lexus SUV, with all the trimmings, and even though David knew the car was politically incorrect—a flashy gas guzzler—he had to admit the ride was great and the heated seat was mighty comfortable. Gary had once explained that he needed to lease a new one every year or two because he shuttled clients around in it, and a real-estate broker who looked like he was down on his luck soon would be.

"You ever going to spring for another car?" Gary joshed as they headed south on Sheridan Road. It was a running joke that David had no wheels.

"Maybe," David said. "Especially since it looks like I might get a promotion."

"Really? To what?"

"Director of Acquisitions." David seldom liked to discuss such things until they were in the bag, but he knew that Gary would mention it to Sarah, and maybe it would give her a little pleasure. And after the warm reception for the lecture, he felt that Dr. Armbruster, who had hinted about it already, might come across at last.

"So you'll be swimming in dough!" Gary said.

"Yeah, right. Just as soon as I pay off my loans. And my rent, by the way, just went up."

"I guess it helped to have that girlfriend of yours split it with you," Gary said, fumbling to remove a packet of Dentyne from the console between the seats. "You want one?"

"No thanks," David said. He knew that what Gary really wanted was a cigarette, but he had given up smoking the day Sarah had been diagnosed. Now he tried to make do with gum and Nicorette. "Linda was usually broke, anyway."

"But not anymore?"

It was a sore spot for David, but he knew Gary meant no harm by asking. "No, not anymore. She's going out with a hedge-fund guy."

Gary whistled and nodded. "I know your sister never liked her all that much." He flipped on the windshield wipers to clear some snow. "But if you don't mind my saying so, she was superhot."

"Thanks for reminding me."

"Don't mention it."

They drove in companionable silence for a few miles, listening to a jazz CD Gary put on. As they passed the Calvary cemetery, David said, "When we were kids, Sarah always used to hold her breath when we passed a cemetery."

"That's funny. She says you're the one who used to do that."

"I guess we did a lot of things alike."

"Still do," Gary observed. "Two peas in a pod."

There were times, David thought, when he sensed that Gary was just the tiniest bit jealous of the bond that David and Sarah had, the history that only they shared, the ability they had to read each other's minds and instantly understand each other's feelings. Gary was kind of a regular guy, a hale fellow well met—somebody who followed the Bears and the Bulls, who played in a weekly poker game and liked to barbecue bratwursts in the backyard. His father had owned the real-estate company, and Gary had just sort of fallen into it, but what used to be an easy living wasn't so easy anymore. David knew that the family's finances had been stretched . . . and that was before all the medical bills had started pouring in.

"Emme's growing up so fast," David said, looking out at the icy, empty streets. "I swear she's grown a couple of inches taller in the last six months."

"Yeah, she's gonna outstrip her mother one day," Gary said, "and maybe me, too. But this whole . . . situation has been taking a toll on her."

"I'm sure it has."

Gary exhaled, like he didn't want to talk about it, though David knew he did. "She's got a look in her eye," he mused out loud, "especially when she's watching her mother. Like she's afraid of what's going to happen next. Like she doesn't want to let her out of her sight. I get the feeling that Emme thinks she's supposed to protect her somehow, but she doesn't know how."

"I know how she feels."

"So do I." He lowered the window, spat out the gum, then stuck a fresh piece in his mouth. "And last night she had another nightmare, one of those doozies where she wakes up screaming."

David hadn't heard about the nightmares. "She gets nightmares?"

"Sometimes."

"Have you thought about taking her to a therapist, somebody who specializes in dealing with kids?"

"I have," Gary said, "and I will. But Christ almighty, I don't know where the money is going to come from . . ."

"Let me help. Remember, I'll be swimming in dough." He was so sorry that he'd even mentioned his own precarious finances.

"Forget about it. That's not why I said anything."

"I know that. But she's my niece, and I want to help."

"I can handle it," Gary said. "This market's gotta bottom out soon. Stuff will start selling again."

"That's right, and then you can pay me back," David said, though he knew he'd never accept a dime.

"Yeah, well, we'll see," Gary said, just to drop the subject. "If I need to, I'll let you know."

Pulling up at David's apartment building—a dreary brownstone in Rogers Park—Gary said, "Home sweet home. Now find yourself another girl. Al Gore's full of it, it's going to be a cold winter and you're going to need something to keep you warm."

"I'll see what I can do," David said. "Thanks for the ride."

Gary waved it off, but then, as David started to walk away, he called out, "Hold on," and pulled something out of the pocket of his coat. It was a plastic bag, with something wrapped in foil inside. "Sarah wanted me to give you this."

"What is it?" David said, though he could pretty much guess.

"A meat loaf sandwich. She says you're too thin."

David took the baggie.

"How come she never tells *me* I'm too thin?" Gary said, rolling up his window again.

David watched as the Lexus did a three-point turn to head back toward Evanston, then went into the foyer, got yesterday's mail out of the creaky metal box, and trudged up the stairs. Apart from the low buzz from the fluorescent light fixture on the landing, the building was as quiet as his own little apartment would be.

But as he put his key in the lock, he was overwhelmed, and not for the first time, by the thought of the world without his sister in it. To him, it was as sad and terrifying a prospect as anything from Dante—but more so, as this one could prove to be all too real.

Chapter 4

Mrs. Van Owen—Kathryn to her close friends, of whom there were almost none—had hoped it wouldn't come to this. She had hoped that no one else would ever have to be sent.

But her lawyer, Mr. Hudgins, had just informed her that Phillip Palliser was dead. His body had been found floating in the Loire, several miles downstream from a little French town called Cinq Tours.

"And what does the coroner say was the cause of death?" she asked, her eyes already straying to the huge windows that looked out over Lake Michigan from her penthouse apartment. "Drowning?"

"Probably," Hudgins replied. "But there were considerable abrasions to the body and face. The injuries might have been postmortem, or they might have been caused by . . . a violent attack first. It's unclear."

Another one, Kathryn thought, *caught in the spider's web.*

He lowered his gaze to the stack of folders and papers arrayed on her glass-topped coffee table. The afternoon light filled the spacious, expensively appointed room, and after he had waited a suitable amount of time, he said, "So what would you like to do?"

She touched a finger to a stray brunette hair, putting it back in place.

"Do you wish to go forward?" he asked.

Did she? What choice, really, did she have? "Yes." It was all like moving another chess piece into play. "Of course I do."

"Then it would be this young man at the Newberry," Hudgins said, glancing at a paper. "This David Franco?"

"Yes." She had always cultivated the next candidate before his predecessor had failed.

"And you think he has done a good job on the Dante volume?"

"A very good job." She had been impressed with his credentials before she had seen him at the library, and she was even more impressed after hearing him speak.

"Then I'll go ahead and make the arrangements for us to meet with him," Hudgins said. "How soon would you like to do so?"

"Tomorrow."

Even Hudgins seemed a bit surprised. "Tomorrow? Well, then, I will leave it to you to assemble the materials you wish to share with him."

Kathryn nodded, almost imperceptibly, but she knew his eyes were riveted on her. Men's eyes generally were, and it was something she had grown accustomed to over the years. Hers was a sensual face, with high cheekbones, arched brows, and full lips, unaided by collagen. But it was her eyes—a remarkable blue, tinged with violet—that made the most striking impression. One ardent admirer had even proclaimed her beauty to be "timeless," and it had been all she could do not to laugh out loud.

"Now, in respect to your late husband's estate," he said, shifting gears and moving a separate folder to the top of the pile, "I've been in contact with his family."

Randolph Van Owen had died a month earlier, but when it happened, one of his sisters had been on a world cruise she was loath to interrupt and the other was recovering from a face-lift.

"They have agreed to come to Chicago and hear the reading of the will this Friday."

"That's fine. The sooner, the better."

"But they have asked if the service could be . . . less private? As one of Chicago's most recognized families, the Van Owens were hoping for a more public expression of your late husband's importance to the fabric of the city. In fact, they had suggested—"

"No," she said. "Randolph would have wanted a very small, private ceremony, and nothing more."

In actuality, she had no idea what he would have wanted, any more than she understood what he was doing racing his new Lamborghini through Lake Forest in the middle of the night. He'd hit a slight bump in the road. But at the speed he was traveling, the car had become airborne and wrapped itself around a stone gatepost. It wasn't that she didn't love Randolph—love was barely in her vocabulary—but theirs had been a marriage of . . . what? For him, she had been the ultimate trophy, a woman whose beauty made men stop in their tracks, and for her, he had been just another refuge. He had provided her with a new identity, in a new place, and a new time. She needed these anchors now and again in order to feel connected to the rhythms and the texture of ordinary life.

And now that that connection was broken—yet again—she was searching for a way out, once and for all. A way out of everything. For most people, it would be easy. But for her, it was a challenge so immense she could take no chances with the outcome. No chances at all.

After Hudgins had cleared up a few other matters, he gathered his papers, and she escorted him to the door. Then, leaving the plates and glasses for Cyril to clean up, she dimmed the lights and mounted a corkscrew staircase to a portion of the apartment accessible only to someone with the silver key she wore around her neck. Once inside, she flicked on the wall sconces, and it was as if she had entered another world. Even Randolph had not been allowed in her private sanctum.

Unlike the rest of the apartment, which was flooded with natural light, this was like entering a catacombs, thirty-five stories in the air. The floors were made of dark tile, and the walls were decorated with oil paintings of religious scenes. An ivory crucifix hung at the end of the short hall, with one room on either side. On the left, a tiny chapel had been erected, with a stained-glass window—artificially backlit—depicting Jesus raising Lazarus from the dead. There was a simple pew set before the altar, on which rested as many as two dozen small urns—some of them ornately carved of marble or porphyry, others cast in silver or steel. The low hum of an air-filtration system was the only sound.

On the right, a slightly larger room was lined with mahogany bookshelves packed with everything from old books in cracked threadbare bindings to memorabilia from around the globe. Egyptian candlesticks, bronze inkwells, carved totems, an ivory saltcellar. There was little furniture—just one armchair, an end table, and a torchère, which she turned to its highest wattage. Atop the table, there was a bundle of papers, as yellow and crackly as parchment, tied with a frayed string. Kathryn sat down in the chair and took the stack into her lap. She carefully undid the string, which nearly disintegrated, and lifted the top sheet of paper; even now, so many years after it had escaped being burned, it gave off an ashy odor.

But the black scrawl was still entirely legible. *La Chiave Alla Vita Eterna*. The Key to Life Eternal.

Scanning the pages, hastily scribbled in Italian with a sharp quill, she could imagine their creator at his desk, head down, brow furrowed. She could envision him filling one page, then tossing it aside and, without so much as a pause, starting on another. Each paper was crammed with words and sometimes drawings, all a testament to the ferment and the fecundity of his thoughts.

But when she came to one page in particular, she stopped.

Its center was dominated by a fierce scowling visage, its hair a mass of writhing snakes. Written beside it, in a florid hand, were the words *La Medusa*. She stared at the creature's grim face and traced the lines with the end of one nail. She had to remain strong, she told herself. At least a little longer. She had to have hope, however tenuous. If she, of all people, did not know that anything was possible, who did?

Closing her eyes and turning out the lamp, she sat in the perfect darkness, hearing only the hum of the air-filtration unit . . . and allowing her thoughts to transport her backwards into an age-old dream, of another place—the city of Florence—and another time, centuries ago, when the Medici ruled . . . and a woman then known as Caterina had been the most sought-after artist's model in all of Europe.

It was an indulgence she rarely permitted herself. But after the bad news about Palliser, she needed it. And the pictures were quick to come. . . .

∽∾

. . . the woman is lying on a straw pallet, in a moonlit studio. It is a hot summer night, and she is waiting to be sure that her lover has fallen asleep.

He is snoring soundly, one arm slung across her naked shoulders. With infinite care, she lifts his arm, well muscled from years of hard work, and lays it to one side.

How relieved she is when the artisan does not stir.

But in putting one foot out onto the floor, she very nearly knocks over one of the silver goblets that had held their wine. The workshop is filled with silver and gold, and a casket of precious jewels, some of which, she knows, have come all the way from the Pope's coffers in Rome.

Cellini is making a scepter for the Holy Father, and the diamonds and rubies are reserved for its handle.

But much as she might have been inclined to steal some of it from any other studio, Caterina does not even consider doing that here. For one thing, she would never betray her lover, and for another, there are three apprentices asleep downstairs, along with a mangy mastiff.

No, it isn't larceny that motivates her. It is simple, but irresistible, curiosity.

Caterina prides herself on knowing all there is to know about men. In ten years of plying her trade, she has seen and learned plenty. But that was only by keeping her eyes open and her wits about her at all times.

Earlier that day, she had been due to model for a medallion Cellini was casting, but she had arrived only at dusk. She knew that coming so late would make him angry, but she rather liked that. She liked making the great artist stew, liked knowing that without her he was unable to proceed with his work; he had once told her so—in front of all his apprentices—and she occasionally liked to wield the power that it gave her.

Still, he had his own ways of showing his displeasure.

As soon as she had come through the door, he had ordered her to strip off her clothes, without so much as a word of greeting; then, when he was posing her, his hands had been rough. But she didn't say a word. She would not give him the satisfaction of complaining—or a reason to withhold the six scudi he would owe her at the end of the session.

When the light was utterly gone, and even the candles were not enough to work by, he had tossed his tools down on one of the worktables and rubbed the back of his hand across both sides of his thick moustache.

That, she knew, meant he was satisfied with what he'd done, for the moment. She dropped her pose—oh, how her limbs ached—and stepped down from the pedestal, then went to fetch her clothes.

"Time for dinner," he said, thumping his foot three times on the wooden floor; a cloud of dust and plaster lifted into the air. She had barely pulled her dress on over her head before one of his workers knocked on the door.

"Come in already," Benvenuto called out, and the apprentice—a swarthy young man called Ascanio, whom Caterina had seen looking at her appraisingly more than once—brought in a wooden tray laden with a bottle of the local chianti, a chicken roasted on a bed of figs and almonds, and a plate of sliced fruits. As Cellini filled two silver cups (destined one day to grace a nobleman's table), Ascanio set the food out on top of a seaman's chest, which held, among other things, the first proofs and rare copies of the artisan's own writings. When Caterina had asked him what they were about, he had waved a hand dismissively.

"Your head is too pretty for such stuff."

Oh, how she wished she could read, and write, better than she did.

As they ate and, more to the point, drank, his mood improved. Caterina had to admit that, when he was in good humor, he could make her laugh like no other man, and his dark eyes could hold her in their thrall just as powerfully as his broad hands did. They were getting along famously until she made the fatal mistake of demanding her wages.

"I'm not done working yet."

"Not done?" she said. "Now you can work in the dark, I suppose?"

"I can work anywhere. Who needs light?" From the way he was slurring his speech, and the empty wine bottle now lying between them, she could tell he was tipsy. She had deliberately held back on her own drinking, waiting for the wine to overtake him.

"I can see in the dark, like you," he said, "*il mio gatto.*"

He often referred to her this way, as his little cat. Another creature known for its stealth and its cunning.

Staggering to his feet, he dragged her not to the pedestal, but toward the bed, tumbling on top of her like a pile of bricks.

"Oof," she said, trying to push him off. "You smell like a barn!"

"And you," he said, kissing her lips, "taste like wine." His hands fumbled under her dress before, in exasperation, he simply ripped it off her shoulders and tossed it aside.

"You'll pay me for that!" Caterina cried.

"I'll buy you a silk dress first thing in the morning," he promised. "And a hat to match!"

She would hold him to it. Benvenuto could be coarse, but he could also be contrite. She knew how to play him.

But then, he knew how to play her, too. As a lover, he made her feel like no other man ever had. There was something about the two of them, a spark that ignited when their skin touched, that she had never known before. His hands felt as if they were molding her flesh, and his eyes studied her face and her body as he turned her this way and that, using her in any way he chose. In his arms, she felt at once compliant, ready to do whatever he wanted, and utterly uncontrolled, free to indulge any impulse of her own.

Was this, she thought, what people meant when they prattled on about love?

When the act was done, and he had dropped like a stone into his habitual slumber, she lay there, her own heartbeat slowly subsiding, her breath returning, the night breeze cooling her limbs.

The moonlight slanting through the shutters fell on the loose boards of the opposite wall.

It was there, behind one of those boards, that she had seen him conceal an iron casket large enough to hold a honeydew. He had thought she was sleeping, but Caterina had kept an eye open—her mother had warned her never to shut both eyes in life—and watched as he covered over the hiding place.

Whatever was in there, she thought, she had to see. She had the curiosity of a cat, too.

And now that he was snoring loudly enough to wake the whole town, she crept, naked, across the creaking floorboards. His worktable was littered with the tools of his trade—chisels and hammers and tongs—along with the waxen model for the medallion he was fashioning for the duke. Often, she marveled at the miraculous things that came from his hands—the silver candlesticks, the golden saltcellars, the rings and necklaces, the coins and medals, the statues in marble and bronze—and at her own small role in their creation. For all his fury and willfulness, she knew she was his muse, the inspiration to one of the greatest artists in all the world. She had often heard him described so . . . and truth be told, he often declared it himself.

The loose board was flush with the wall and would never have been noticed by anyone unaware that it was there. Caterina used her long fingernails (men liked long fingernails, to rake their backs) to pry it open, and it swung down on a concealed hinge. That was just like him, to make everything mechanically precise. The iron casket fit neatly into the space, with only an inch or so to spare. She drew it out—it was heavier than she expected—and carried it over to the window, where the moonlight was the brightest. The sound of snoring suddenly stopped, and she stood as motionless as one of his sculptures, until she heard him roll over on the pallet and grumble in his sleep.

Sitting down on the floor, she put the strongbox between her legs, and was not at all surprised to find it locked. Nor was she surprised to find no keyhole. He was ingenious that way—but so was she. When he was deeply absorbed in his work, he thought nothing of letting Caterina riffle through his many sketches and notebooks—he was always writing, writing, writing; she had once joked that he must be trying to outdo his idol, Dante.

But among all the papers, she had noted a rectangular design just like this box, and there was a series of circles with many small numbers and lines and letters surrounding them. Circles like the ones embossed on the box. And the letters G and A and T and O—as in her nickname. She had memorized the placement of the letters, and thought that if she turned the corresponding circles—and yes, she discovered, they did indeed turn—so as to spell out the word, the box would undoubtedly open.

She smiled at surmising that she had outfoxed the master.

The first circle, where the G had been noted, was in the upper left corner of the lid. She turned it easily, then turned the A on the upper right. The T was at the lower left—she turned it twice around—before finishing with the O. Then waited for the box to click open.

It did not.

She hated risking her fingernails again, but she had to, and tried to find a little crevice that she could use to pry the lid up.

But it was perfectly sealed.

She tried the whole ritual again, turning all the circles, feeling for a latch, but again there was nothing. The master artisan had made another foolproof mechanism.

She wanted to drop the damn thing on his snoring head.

She studied it again, wondering if the box could be opened with a simple use of force. To do that, she would have to find another time, a time when she could finagle her way into the studio when Benvenuto was gone; but even then, it would be well-nigh impossible. The iron was welded so firmly, the hasps so tight, it was like a solid block. She would not have known where or how to strike it.

Outside, in the Via Santo Spirito, she heard the slow clip-clopping of a horse's hooves. A woman's voice called out an invitation to the passing rider: "It's late," she said. "Shouldn't you be in bed?"

Caterina grimaced. *Never,* she thought. Never would she let herself be reduced to that. She hadn't come all the way from France to wind up as some common whore.

But then she almost laughed at the picture she presented instead—a naked model, on the floor in the dark, her legs spread on either side of a locked iron casket she was unsuccessfully trying to break into.

A faint breeze stirred the hot summer air, raising goose bumps on her arms and shoulders.

She could put the box back and forget the whole thing, but when, she wondered, would she ever get another chance like this? *Think,* she told herself. *Think like he did.*

In the quarters below, she heard the dog bark, followed by one of the apprentices throwing a saucer at it.

Benvenuto rolled over again, onto his other side, and for a moment it looked as if his hand was groping for her. But then it fell slack off the side of the pallet.

And she knew the answer.

He was always quoting the late master, Leonardo, and more than once he had mentioned that da Vinci could write backwards, so that the best way to read his writing was to hold it up in a mirror. Benvenuto had tried the trick himself, but to no avail. "It is a gift that God bestows, and alas, in this one thing, He has forgotten me." He was forever comparing his own talents to those of his friends and rivals—Bronzino, Pontormo, Titian—and of course Michelangelo Buonarroti. In fact, he was such an admirer of Michelangelo's that he had once come to blows in his defense. "Of all the men in Italy," he declared, "Michelangelo is the one chosen by God to do His greatest work!" His marble statue of *David*, in Cellini's view, was the testament to that.

But even if Benvenuto couldn't write backwards, he could do other things in reverse, such as setting a lock. Carefully, she turned the circles in reverse order, and at the last one she heard a satisfying little click as the interior gears released. She nearly shouted in triumph.

Raising the lid, she saw that its underside was mirrored. A good sign. But just as she tilted the box to catch the moonlight, a cloud passed across the moon. She ran her fingers along the sides of the box and felt the plush velvet lining he had made for whatever it was constructed to protect. Another promising sign. He wouldn't have done that if it were just a strongbox for coins, or documents. Her fingertips grazed a cold metal band that she withdrew and held up to the light.

It was a silver garland, and made to look as if it were fashioned from gilded bulrushes. It was admirably done, but the metal, she could tell, was thin. It was a nice piece, one that would make a handsome present for some aristocrat, but nothing to rival the riches lying around the studio.

There had to be something more.

She put her fingers back in the box and found the interior mount, where a circular object, the size of a woman's palm, was neatly settled. Waiting for the cloud to pass, she glanced over at the bed again to make sure Benvenuto had not been awakened by the sound of the latch releasing. But apart from the rhythmic rise and fall of his burly chest, he lay still.

The night sky cleared, and suddenly the thing beneath her hand glinted dully in the moonbeams. She withdrew it from the box, expecting to find the richest ornament she had ever seen—a brooch or bracelet fashioned from a dazzling array of sparkling gemstones.

Emeralds, sapphires, diamonds, all embedded in beaten gold. His other claims notwithstanding, Benvenuto was universally acknowledged to be the finest goldsmith in Florence, a city acclaimed for that art. But this medallion on a simple silver chain was almost as utilitarian as the iron chest it came from.

It depicted, though quite skillfully, the head of the gorgon, Medusa—she whose gaze could turn any mortal to stone. Her hair, a writhing mass of serpents, coiled around the edges of the piece, while her fierce eyes and gaping mouth comprised the center. It was done in the niello style, very fashionable just then. The image had been engraved into the silver with a sharply pointed burin—Caterina had often seen such work done—and then the hollows had been brushed with a black alloy made of sulfur and copper and lead. As a result, the design appeared in starker, bolder relief, though Caterina preferred her own silver—what little she had—to shine more brightly.

Still, this was a finely wrought piece, like the garland. Indeed, nothing that came from Benvenuto's hand was not finely made. But why all the fuss? There were a dozen things in the shop that had to be more valuable. Idly, she turned the medallion over, and found, interestingly enough, a stiff black silk backing, neatly anchored by several silver clasps. These she turned, until the silk fell free, and she suddenly saw her own inquisitive face staring back at her.

It was a small circular mirror, with finely beveled edges. Now *that* was something out of the ordinary. She held it higher in the moonlight, angling the glass to capture her own face. There was something about the curvature of the glass, a swelling outward of its surface, which captured her features in a ruthlessly clear fashion, while simultaneously, and subtly, distorting them. It was as if the more she looked, the more deeply she was drawn into the glass, and the more she wanted to look away, the more she could not.

She drew the mirror closer to her face—close enough that her breath clouded its lower half, close enough that she could see her own bright eyes, looking back at her as if she were not looking *into* the glass at all, but was inside it instead, and looking out. It felt as if the thing had come alive, as if it were beating with a subtle pulse. The moonlight flooded across the glass like a silver tide, washing over her image, eclipsing her . . . and that was the last thing she remembered.

When she awoke, she found herself lying flat out on the floor, with the morning sun pouring through the window. A rooster was crowing on the rooftop.

And Cellini himself—in nothing but a pair of loose cotton drawers—was kneeling above her.

"What have you done?" he said, his expression a complex mixture of fear, anger, and concern. "What did you do?"

She looked around, but the mirror, the garland, and the iron box were gone.

Benvenuto helped her to her feet, throwing a sheet around her naked shoulders, and she stumbled, as if she had been at sea for weeks, across the studio. There was a pewter basin and pitcher on the bureau by the bed, and she filled the bowl with water. Her skin felt as if it had been scoured with sand. But when she bent down to throw the cold water on her face and saw her reflection, the breath caught in her throat. Her lush black hair, one of her most prized assets, had turned as white as snow—as white as if the Medusa herself had terrified her beyond imagining.

She whipped around to look at Benvenuto, praying for an explanation. "What have *I* done?" she exclaimed. "What have *you* done?"

But he simply stood there, silent.

"Is this one of your silly pranks?" she demanded. "Because if it is, I don't think it's very funny."

But shaking his head, he came to her and put one of his rough hands to her cheek. "If only it were, *il mio gatto* . . . if only it were."

Chapter 5

⟨◦◦◦⟩

David had barely hung his coat on the back of his office door before his phone rang with a call from Dr. Armbruster.

"Guess what we received by courier this morning?"

She was not normally this playful, and it took David a second to say he had no clue.

"A generous check for our library restoration fund from Ambassador Schillinger and his wife. It seems he was very impressed by your lecture last week."

"That's great," David said, wondering how this might affect his chances of clinching that spot as the new Director of Acquisitions.

"And I have some other good news, too."

At last.

"Another of the audience members would like to come in today and meet with you in person."

As quickly as his hopes had been raised, they plummeted again. He prayed it wasn't just some frustrated academic who wanted to debate Dante's indebtedness to Ovid.

"Who is it?"

"Her name is Kathryn Van Owen."

Anyone who lived in Chicago knew the Van Owen name. At one point, the family had owned much of the Loop. And Kathryn, the recently widowed wife of Randolph, was a prominent, if rather reticent, figure in local society.

"Up until now," Dr. Armbruster continued, "she had asked to remain anonymous, but as you may have figured out already, she was the donor of the Florentine Dante."

For some reason, David instantly knew that she was also the Lady in Black—the one who had come in late, wearing the veil.

"She's arriving here this afternoon, with her lawyer. Apparently, she's bringing along something else for your opinion. I don't need to tell you that it, too, could wind up in our collections."

"Do you want me to prepare anything in advance?"

"I can't think what it would be. Are you wearing a decent shirt?"

"Yes," he said, quickly looking down to check. "Do you have any idea what she's planning to give us this time?"

David could almost hear her shrug. "Her late husband's family is as rich as Croesus—though you probably know that already—but frankly, he never showed much interest in culture or the arts. He built that car museum in Elk Grove, but I think it's really Mrs. Van Owen herself who's donating these things, from her own collection. And she's what you would call," she said, plainly pausing to find a neutral term, "an unusual woman. You'll see what I mean when you meet her. Be in the conference room at a quarter of three."

Hanging up, David ran a hand around his jawline—he should have put a new blade in his razor that morning—and reopened the Dante files on his computer, checking online for any other libraries or archives that might have something that shed some further light on it. He thought it would be cool, when meeting Mrs. Van Owen for the first time, if he had something new to share with her about the book, something he hadn't already discovered and mentioned at the public unveiling. But he also hoped that she could tell him something more about its origins than he already knew. The text, by and large, was the standard, written in the Italian vulgate. Up until the early 1300s, when the *Comedy* was composed, Latin was the only choice for such an epic work, but Dante had changed all that. By writing his poem in the spoken language of his day, and in his inimitable terza rima stanzas, he had thrown down the gauntlet, making a clear break with the verse of the ancient Greeks and Romans and conferring a legitimacy upon the demotic tongue used by his own contemporaries.

But what really intrigued David about this edition, of which he could find no other record, were its illustrations. There was a life and a vigor to them that was unparalleled. They were unlike any other illustrations he had seen, in countless other printings, in a dozen different languages.

At two thirty—and having turned up nothing new and earthshaking—he took his emergency tie and sport jacket off the back of his office door and went down to the men's room to put them on. As he adjusted the knot of his tie, he noticed that his hair, thick and brown and starting to curl up over his collar, could definitely have used a trim. He did his best to get it under control, then headed off to the conference room for his meeting with the mysterious Mrs. Van Owen.

Dr. Armbruster was supervising the setting out of a tea service. The room was wainscoted and warmly lighted, the back wall dominated by an oil portrait of Mr. Walter Loomis Newberry, its founder, in a black suit coat and hanging silver watch fob. Dr. Armbruster glanced at David—he felt like he was being inspected for flaws—and said, "Be appreciative, by all means, but don't enter into any negotiations or comment in any way on the terms of her gift. We leave that to our own lawyers."

"Got it."

At three o'clock on the button, Mrs. Van Owen and a man she introduced as her attorney, Eugene Hudgins, were ushered into the room by the receptionist. The lawyer, a stolid guy with a red complexion, took a seat at the head of the table, as if so accustomed to it that no one would challenge him, and Mrs. Van Owen sat to his right. Dr. Armbruster took a seat on the other side, next to David. The receptionist took care of pouring out the tea, and David took those few minutes to study their benefactor.

Today, she had no veil on, and her face was the most captivating

David had ever seen. Her skin was a creamy white, so flawless and unlined it was almost impossible to assign any particular age to it. Was she younger than he'd been led to believe, or was this the miracle of that Botox stuff he had heard about? He knew she had recently lost a husband—the news of his crash had been carried in all the papers—but David could see no sign of grief. Her hair was jet-black, and sleekly gathered into a tight chignon. She had a regal and vaguely foreign look about her . . . but not so much foreign to this place as to this era. A look that was further accentuated by her most striking feature of all—her eyes.

They were a violet blue. David had never seen eyes of such a color. Maybe that was why she'd worn the veil the day before. Maybe she took advantage of every occasion she could, even if it was to wear mourning attire, that allowed her to keep people from staring. When David found that he was doing just that, he took off his wire rims and pretended to be cleaning them.

Hudgins had opened a bulging valise and taken out a bulky sealed envelope, along with a legal-sized binder imprinted in big block letters with the name of his law firm, HUDGINS & DUNBAR, LLC.

"That was a very interesting talk you gave," Mrs. Van Owen said, and when David looked up, she seemed to be amused by something. "I learned a great deal about Dante." There was a slight smile on her lips, but her words, like her features, carried a distant air. She had a faint trace of an accent, but even David, who was very good at placing them, wasn't sure where this one came from. Definitely European, that much he knew, but it could have been French, or Italian, or even Spanish in origin.

"Thanks very much," he replied. "Coming from the donor of such a beautiful book, it means a lot. And now that you're here, I can't resist asking where the book came from."

"Florence. But you know that."

"I meant, how did it come to be yours?"

"Oh, it had been in my family for many years, and I thought it was time the world was able to enjoy—and study—it."

"But the illustrations," he persisted. "Do you know anything about who executed them? I've consulted dozens of sources so far, and checked archives online all over the world, but I still can't find a match to any known edition."

"No, I shouldn't think you would."

"Really? Why not?"

"Because it is one of a kind."

"You know that? You know that it's the only extant copy?" David could hardly keep the excitement out of his voice. "How?"

But instead of answering, she resorted to an airy dismissal. "That's what I've always been told."

David visibly deflated. All sorts of myths and legends clung to family heirlooms. This copy of the *Divine Comedy* was undoubtedly rare and valuable, but it was possible, even likely, that somewhere in the world, perhaps buried in the bowels of the Vatican library, another copy existed.

But it was unlikely to be a more intact one than this.

"Now that that's been settled," Mr. Hudgins interrupted, as if uncomfortable with this unmediated conversation, "we should really get on with the business at hand. We have some additional material to be transferred," he said, nodding at the bulky envelope on the table and making it plain that David should open it.

As David drew it close, Hudgins continued. "Mrs. Van Owen has graciously decided to leave these manuscripts and drawings in the care of the Newberry Library, for further examination and study. She wishes to know as much about them as the curatorial staff is able to discover and is prepared to underwrite the costs of all such work."

Although David was happy to hear that she would bear the expenses, he was already concerned that something very old and valuable had been transported in such a casual manner as this. He grew even more concerned when, after unsealing the envelope, the unmistakable scent of smoke emanated from inside.

"Their final disposition, however, remains an open question," Hudgins said. "Much will depend on how the completion of the work goes and whether it yields success. If it goes as well as we hope, the Newberry can expect to receive these materials on a permanent basis, along with a very generous and unrestricted gift to support the library. If not . . ." He trailed off. "Other arrangements may be made."

David had just removed the packet of papers, as deftly as he could, from the padded envelope, and already he was astonished at what he saw. Just from the feel of the paper and the ink, he could tell that these papers were hundreds of years old. Fifteenth or sixteenth century, if he had to guess. They reminded him of the many *ricordanze* he had studied over the years—the memoirs and diaries of Italian businessmen, documents that provided a fascinating glimpse into everyday life during the Renaissance.

This handwriting was in Italian, too, and though faded by time, still more than legible. The edges of the papers were singed here and there, accounting for the smell of smoke, and there were dots of mold and decay, like age spots on an elderly hand, sprinkled throughout. But as he turned one page over and glanced at the next, and the next, he could see that they were a virtual treasure trove. These weren't mundane records of grain purchases or wool deliveries. This was a rough draft, with many crossouts and markings, of something called *La Chiave alla Vita Eterna*. The Key to Life Eternal. And in its margins, and in some cases on the backs of the pages, there were drawings and schematics, and references to smelting processes and glassblowing. There was a sketch on one sheet that could only have been the plans for a kiln—a large kiln, big enough to cast a mighty statue. David's heart was hammering in his chest, and he distractedly removed his glasses and wiped them clean on his tie before exploring an underlying page, a page that had been folded over. His fingers paused above it, until Mrs. Van Owen herself said, "Unfold it."

Still, he paused, afraid of doing it some damage—normally he'd be doing this on a lab bench, with some cotton and tweezers, under a dim and indirect light—but Dr. Armbruster, her own curiosity piqued, said, "Go ahead, David. Somebody has to."

Standing up, he unfolded the sheet of paper, maybe two feet square, then simply stood there, stunned.

It was an elaborate drawing, in red and black ink, of the Medusa—the mythological Gorgon whose gaze could turn an onlooker to stone. It was circular, and a reverse view—largely blank, or unfinished—was drawn at its lower right. Although he could not tell what artist had done it, David could see that it was the work of a master—a Raphael, a Verrocchio, or a Michelangelo. And because of its shape, it must have been the design for a medallion, a coin, or the cope on a cloak.

"It was a looking glass," Mrs. Van Owen said, answering his unspoken question. "*La Medusa,* as you can see it was called."

Indeed, the words were written on the page. And of course—that made perfect sense. The back was simply a mirror. "But do you know whose design it is?" He scanned the page for a signature, but there was nothing. Nor had there been one on any of the previous pages.

"I do."

He waited.

"Like all of this, including the copy of Dante, it is from the hand of the greatest and most versatile artisan who ever lived," she said, her violet eyes holding firmly on his. "Benvenuto Cellini."

He sat down quickly, the sketch still spread before him on the table. He could hardly believe his ears. Cellini? One of his heroes ever since Amherst, when he had read every word of his celebrated autobiography in a Renaissance art course? The rebel spirit who had created some of the greatest sculptures of his day, works that had played a role in David's very choice of career? For several moments, he was dumbfounded, before asking, "And what do you want me to do?" Already he was itching to start in on his research. "Verify the drawing somehow?"

She frowned at the very suggestion. "There is no question of its authenticity."

David could see that she was not someone who brooked argument easily, and he was sorry he'd crossed her already. Even Dr. Arm-bruster looked cowed.

"Then what *would* you like me to do?"

With one long, lacquered nail tapping the sketch, and her foot tap-ping the floor impatiently, she said, "I want you to find it."

"The actual mirror?" he asked uncertainly. What did she take him for, Indiana Jones? Dr. Armbruster, too, looked surprised at the na-ture of the request, though she was not about to start raising any ob-jections. "Wouldn't a gemologist, or a specialist in antique jewelry, be your best bet?" he said, but she grimaced in disgust.

"I have tried that route. They found nothing. It needs a scholar to find it; I am sure of that now."

"Is it possible," he said, almost afraid to complete the thought, "that they didn't find it because it does not exist?"

"*La Medusa,*" she said, in a tone that brooked no dissent, "exists."

Looking into those violet eyes, boring into his like a pair of icicles, he didn't doubt it. Nor would he have dared.

"And I need you," she concluded, "to get it for me."

Chapter 6

The knock that had just sounded on Benvenuto's door was not a friendly one, and the voice that called out his name was equally peremptory.

His hands were coated with warm wax, and he was in the middle of making a model of Caterina, who stood in the nude holding a wreath as if offering it up to the Heavens. It had taken him half the day just to calm her down, and it was bad enough that she insisted on wearing a scarf over her white hair.

"Who is it?" he bellowed, his eyes still trained on the girl. "What do you want?"

Cellini had already had to send his assistant Ascanio to the apothecary's shop for a hair dye made of boiled walnuts and leeks—Caterina said she would not set foot outside until her hair was made black again—and now there was no one there to answer the damn door.

"It's Captain Lucasi, and I am here at the behest of his lordship, Cosimo, the Duke de'Medici."

The duke was the immensely wealthy ruler of Florence and patron to all of its greatest artists—Cellini among them. As for this Lucasi, Cellini knew from previous run-ins with the man that he was an officious prig, terribly impressed with the colored balls—the Medici insignia—adorning the front of his uniform.

"Damn it to Hell!" Cellini exclaimed, wiping his hands on a rag and throwing it on the worktable. "Let him in."

Caterina wrapped herself in the bedsheet and, after making sure no wisps of white hair were escaping from under the scarf, opened the door.

Lucasi took her in slowly, looking from head to foot with a sly smile on his lips. "Shouldn't you be wearing a yellow veil?" he said, referring to the garment prostitutes were required to wear in the streets of the city.

Caterina scowled and walked away.

Lucasi stepped into the room, looking all around. "What have I interrupted?" He poked his nose into the fireplace, where a pot of white beeswax was being kept warm and malleable, but when he ventured to touch it with his finger, Cellini shouted, "Get away from that, you dolt!"

The captain pretended to take no offense, but turned, with the smile still on his lips, and said, "You need to come with me."

"Where? What for?"

Captain Lucasi shrugged. "The duke pays for everything you've got here," he said, gesturing widely at the silver cups on the floor, the gems still loose on a table, and finally at Caterina, who had planted herself on top of the seaman's chest, "and when he says come, you come."

Cellini was within a hair of refusing, but even he knew better. When the Medici summoned, you answered their call, or wound up in a cell in the notorious Stinche. He had been there before, for public brawling, and had no wish to return.

"Give me a minute," he growled, roughly scrubbing the wax off his hands and wrists with a bar of lye soap before pulling on a fresh shirt and blue tunic. Beneath them he wore the *Medusa,* which he had sworn to himself he would never again remove. "Take the charcoal from the hearth," he said to Caterina, "and put a lid on the wax." Marching toward the door, he said to Lucasi, "Let's go then."

The captain glanced down at his pants and shoes, still spattered with bits of wax, and said, "You don't want to change those, too?"

"I thought you were in such a hurry," Cellini replied, starting down the wooden stairs. If the duke thought his finest artist should live at his constant beck and call, then he'd better get used to seeing the signs of his toil.

Outside, the narrow street was relatively quiet, the heat having driven everyone indoors hours ago. The sun was lower in the sky, and the shadows of the other workshops fell over the cobblestones. A stray dog lay panting under the eaves of the ironmonger's across the way, a grocer's cart slowly rumbled along behind a swaybacked donkey. From a third-story window, an old woman beat a carpet against the balcony rail.

With Cellini leading the way, and Captain Lucasi doing his best to make it look like the artisan was in his custody, they marched to the Ponte alla Carraia, the ancient bridge where the wool carts from as far away as Flanders and France brought their wares to be sold and dyed and spun. The dyers, whose hands and arms were stained blue and green, used the Arno River below to rinse and wash the wool. But at this time of year, there wasn't much to work with; the water level had fallen so low that dying fish were flopping on the banks. Dante called the river, which neatly divided the city in two, that "cursed ditch," and Cellini would not have argued the point.

When they reached the Piazza della Signoria, the broad public square where some of the city's greatest statuary was on display—Michelangelo's unrivaled *David,* and Donatello's *Judith and Holofornes*—Cellini slowed down, as he could never help but do, to admire the workmanship, and Captain Lucasi gave him a shove on the shoulder. Cellini whirled around and barked, "If you do that again, you'll regret it."

"Just keep moving," Lucasi retorted.

"Barbarian."

The duke's palazzo, a huge fortress of pale stone topped by a crenellated tower, sat on the square like a great brooding giant, a fitting symbol of the Medici power and influence throughout Tuscany and beyond. Cellini had been there countless times before, but he never failed to notice the immediate hush that fell the moment he passed beneath its arched doorway, the sense of leaving the ordinary world and entering a far more rarefied precinct. Not that it instilled in him any trepidation. Since the day he was born and his father had christened him Benvenuto—or Welcome—he had felt at home anywhere. He was proud to say he was cowed by no man, and with only a few exceptions—his friend Michelangelo, the painter Masaccio—considered himself the superior of anyone he met, even dukes and princes and popes.

He would bend the knee, he often said to himself, but never the head.

The footmen recognized him, and even before the captain had announced their arrival, Cellini was mounting the marble steps to the salons that surrounded the central courtyard. He had powerful legs and moved like a bull with his head down, always plowing through any obstacle that might present itself. His shoulders were broad and strong, conditioned by years of sculpting and metalwork; his hands and fingers were knotted and hard from bending gold and silver to his wishes. He was thirty-eight years old but looked younger and could handle himself in a fight with men half his age.

"Where do you think you're going?" Captain Lucasi complained when Cellini turned left at the top of the stairs and took his usual shortcut through the duchess's suite of rooms. Everywhere, on walls and ceilings, in niches and on plinths above the doorways, there were remarkable works of art—frescoes by Benozzo Gozzoli, statues by Mino da Fiesole, paintings by Uccello and Pollaiuolo. Cellini never missed an opportunity to reacquaint himself with the past masters whose work he strove to surpass.

"Benvenuto! Is that you?" he heard, and stopped in one of the galleries. Perhaps this hadn't been such a good idea, after all.

The duchess herself—Eleonora de Toledo—swept out from one

of the antechambers, in a full-pleated *gamurra* and white satin cap, and he greeted her as pleasantly as he could. When she was cordial to him, it was always for a reason—and this proved to be no exception.

"I want you to look at these pearls," she said, "and tell me what you think they're worth."

She held out a rope of seed pearls strung between her fingers.

"Are you planning to sell them?" he asked warily. He could already see that several were losing their luster.

"No, I want to buy them, and Messer Antonio Landi is asking six thousand scudi."

"That's a lot more than they're worth."

From the immediate frown on her face, he knew he had said the wrong thing.

"Are you sure? I think they're quite beautiful." She held them up to her neck, so that they caught the light from the windows.

"Pearls are not gemstones, my lady. They do not hold their color, as a diamond or a sapphire does. They are the bones of a fish"—this alone had always predisposed him to devalue them—"and as a result, they deteriorate. Look, these have already begun to do so."

Her face hardened, and she concealed the necklace in her closed fist. "If I come to the duke to ask him for the money to buy them, and he asks for your opinion —"

Which was likely, Cellini thought.

"—you will take a more favorable view."

Captain Lucasi, hovering at a discreet distance, coughed, and for once Cellini was glad of his prompting. "You will have to excuse me, Duchess," he said, moving on, "but you know how I hate to keep the duke waiting."

Even before he saw Cosimo himself, he saw the crate, resting on a Persian carpet. The duke was at his desk, attending to piles of papers. In a city that boasted over seventy banks, the Medici were the premier financiers; single-handedly, they had made the gold florin the most trusted currency on the Continent. Lucasi announced their presence, and the duke, his black hair hanging down on either side of his long face like the ears on a basset hound, glanced up. "Forgive me," he said, "I didn't hear you come in." He was dressed in crimson velvet, and still had his riding boots on. He raised his chin in the direction of the crate. "That just arrived from Palestrina, and I wanted you to be the first to see what's inside."

Just from its provenance, Cellini could guess what the box contained. A town just south of Rome, Palestrina was a treasure trove of antiquities. Every time a farmer dug a new well, something turned up.

"With your permission . . . ?" Cellini said, and the duke nodded.

Tossing the lid aside, his fingers burrowed into the straw filling the crate, until they felt the hard contours of cold marble. With infinite care, he lifted out the torso of a classically modeled boy. Its feet were missing, its arms were gone, there was no head, but the trunk had been exquisitely executed. It was not more than a couple of *braccia* long, the length of a horse's head, but oh, how Cellini wished he could have seen it whole.

"What do you think?" Cosimo asked.

"I think its maker was a great artist," Cellini said, cradling it in his arms like a baby. "And although restoring such antiques is not my trade, I would be honored to undertake this work."

The duke laughed with pleasure. "You think that highly of it?"

"With the right piece of Greek marble, I could complete it. I could not only add the missing parts, but an eagle, too. We could make it a Ganymede," he said, referring to the beautiful Trojan prince carried up to Heaven by Zeus's eagle.

"You could make what a Ganymede?" Cellini heard from the doorway, where he now saw Baccio Bandinelli, perhaps the most prosperous of the Medici court sculptors, loitering.

After asking pardon for his intrusion, Bandinelli cast a cursory eye over the broken statue and scoffed out loud. "A perfect example, Your Excellency, of what I have often told you about the ancients. They didn't know anything about anatomy—they hardly looked at a human body—before taking the chisel to the stone. And what you get in the end is things like this, full of faults that could easily have been corrected."

"That's not what Benvenuto says. He was quite impressed."

Waving his fingers in the air, Bandinelli sought to dismiss his rival's claims, and it was all Cellini could do to keep from strangling the man with his own long beard. Bandinelli, in Cellini's view—a view shared by nearly every artist in Italy—was an overrated hack whose work disgraced every pedestal it stood on. What made matters worse was that one of his commissions—a dual statue of Hercules and Cacus, the fire-breathing giant the hero had slain—spoiled the Piazza outside the Medici door. Every time Cellini saw it—cheek by jowl with the works of the divine Donatello and Michelangelo—it made him cringe.

"Perhaps that is why, when my own Hercules was unveiled," Bandinelli declared, "there were those who did not understand or appreciate it."

Did not *understand* it? Did not *appreciate* it? Cellini was floored at the man's conceit. As was the custom when any new statue was unveiled, hundreds of Florentines had spontaneously written sonnets about it, but they had unanimously excoriated its shoddy shape and execution. Cellini had written one himself, lamenting the fact that Pope Clement VII had originally awarded the marble to Michelangelo before inexplicably changing his mind. What a waste of fine stone!

"Benvenuto, what have you got to say for the torso now? It's not like you to hold your tongue." A smile was playing around the duke's lips. He knew about the enmity between the two men—and knew, too, that it was a struggle for Cellini to control his temper.

"When it comes to bad workmanship, Your Excellency, I have to yield the floor to Messer Bandinelli. No one knows more about it than he does."

The duke laughed and clapped his hands together, while Bandinelli pasted a condescending smile on his lips. "Joke all you want," he said. "You could never have made my Hercules."

"True enough," Cellini retorted. "I'd have to be blind first."

"Your Eminence," Bandinelli protested.

"If you cut the hair off of its head," Cellini declared, "what would you be left with? A potato. And has it got the face of a man or an ox?" It felt good to let go, and he saw no reason to stop. "The shoulders look like the pommels on a pack saddle, and the chest looks like a sack of watermelons. The arms? They hang down without any grace at all, and at one point, unless I'm mistaken, both Hercules and Cacus appear to be sharing the same calf muscle. You have to wonder—I know I do—how they manage to stand up at all."

Through all of this, Bandinelli fumed and writhed, while the duke listened intently, absorbed and amused. But when Bandinelli challenged him to find fault with the *design* of the statue, of which he was inordinately proud, and Cellini proceeded to demolish that, too, Bandinelli could take no more and he shouted, "That's enough out of you, you dirty sodomite!"

A hush fell over the room, and the duke scowled, perhaps expecting Cellini to launch a physical attack. And the artisan was sorely tempted.

But he knew that if he did, he risked offending Cosimo, too. Instead, mustering all his resolve, Cellini replied, in a cold and ironic tone, "Now I know you've gone off your head. Although that noble custom you just mentioned is reputedly practiced by many great kings and emperors—even Jove himself was said to have indulged in it with young Ganymede—I am a humble man of natural tastes myself, and so I don't know anything about it."

The duke looked relieved, and even Bandinelli, perhaps aware that he had gone too far, shrank back. Out of the corner of his eye, Cellini spotted the duchess coming, wearing the rope of pearls, and lest he get into yet another fracas, he quickly tried to extricate himself.

"I thank Your Lordship for this opportunity to see the antique torso, but I would like to return to my studio now. There is still a good deal of work to do on the medallion."

As the duchess and one of her ladies entered the chamber, and

Bandinelli bowed so low his beard nearly grazed the floor, Cellini made his escape. Eleonora threw him a look, as if to say *I was counting on your support,* but he pretended not to notice and didn't even break his stride to study the Giotto fresco mounted above the staircase. Only when he was out in the Piazza again, standing before the Loggia dei Lanzi, with its pantheon of statuary on display, did he stop and bend over, his own hands on his knees, to breathe deeply and try to calm himself. If Bandinelli had had the nerve to fling such an accusation at him anywhere but the Duke de'Medici's office, he'd have knocked his head off. His heart was pounding so hard that he could feel the cold metal of *La Medusa,* on its thick silver chain, bobbing under his shirt.

"Benvenuto. Are you feeling all right?"

He glanced up and saw the jeweler, Landi, no doubt heading to the Medici palace to sew up the sale of the pearl necklace.

"Yes, yes, I'm fine," Cellini replied.

"Do you happen to know if her ladyship is receiving?"

"She is."

Landi narrowed his eyes and smiled. "And is she in a buying mood?"

"When isn't she?"

Landi laughed, said "God bless her for that," and swaggered on. Cellini hoped that the duchess would keep his appraisal of the pearls to herself. He hardly needed to make another enemy in Florence.

It was dusk already, and the monumental sculptures in the square threw long shadows on the stones. Donatello's Judith stood, sword raised above the head of the Assyrian general, Holofernes. Michelangelo Buonarotti's David, armed with slingshot, gazed confidently across the courtyard. And Cellini, already an acknowledged master in so many arts, longed to make his own contribution to their august company. What the piazza needed, and what he knew he could provide, was a bronze more perfectly modeled and chased and refined than any such statue ever done.

Its subject?

The hero Perseus . . . in the winged sandals given to him by Hermes, and holding the sword—forged by Hephaestus himself, to defeat the Gorgon—bestowed on him by Athena.

What could be more fitting, more dramatic, and more likely to make Bandinelli hang himself in envy?

With that happy thought in mind, he headed off to the Ponte Vecchio, so that he could stop at the artisans' shops that lined both sides of the bridge and pick up some much-needed supplies. He thought it also might be nice to buy some little gift for Caterina, perhaps a bit of lace, or maybe an amber comb. She was undoubtedly attending to her hair, and he was confident that as it grew out, it would return to its lustrous black.

But as for Caterina herself . . . that was another question completely. When would she realize the full import of what had happened? When would she discover the full effect of the moonlight striking the glass? A year? Five years? When would she know?

Or when should he tell her?

He had been a fool to have left the schematics for the iron box out on his worktable . . . but she was more ingenious than he'd suspected, first finding the casket and then figuring out how to open the lock. And it was that very cunning, he had to admit, which gave her such a powerful hold over him. She was not only the most beautiful woman he had ever seen, but the most clever. He had first spotted her on the arm of an aristocrat at Fontainebleau, when he had gone there to design a fountain for the King of France, and he had known from that very first moment that he had to have her . . . as model, as muse, as lover.

After picking up some odds and ends—wire and wax for his armatures—he found a perfect small sapphire at a jeweler's shop, poorly set in a pendant necklace. The foil behind it, meant to bring out its brilliance, was instead dulling it, and he thought that, with a little work, he could reset it. The jeweler, another friend of his, gave him a good price, but as he stepped out of the shop, thinking about his dinner, he caught a whiff of smoke in the air. Several other people had smelled it, too, and they were all looking toward the southern side of the Arno, from which the wind was blowing.

Cellini's step quickened as he crossed the rest of the bridge, and quickened even more as he entered the Borgo San Jacopo. The smell of smoke was stronger here, and it was blowing from the west, the direction of his studio. A gypsy boy was sprinting past, and Cellini snagged him by his arm. "Where's the fire?" he asked and the boy, yanking his arm loose, said, "Santo Spirito."

Cellini broke into a run, the smell getting stronger all the time, and passing people who were also heading in the direction of the fire. By the time he rounded the corner, and saw the fire wagon outside his workshop, with Ascanio and a dozen other men throwing buckets of water at the blaze, he had dropped all but the necklace.

He pushed his way through the onlookers and rushed to Ascanio's side. "Is everyone safe? Is Caterina safe?"

Ascanio, his face smeared with soot, shouted "Yes!" over the crackling of the flames. "We threw what we could out the windows!" Indeed, some loose books and sketches and even a few medallions still littered the street. "I've got the jewels in my pockets!"

"And the rest?" Cellini said, knowing that Ascanio would take his meaning.

"They are safe."

Cellini was so relieved that his most prized treasures had been saved, and Caterina spared, that the loss of everything else hardly mattered. He grabbed an empty bucket, filled it from the barrel on the wagon, and hurled the water through a burning window frame. But he could see, through the billowing smoke, that nothing would stop the fire. The residents of the neighboring houses were already emptying out their own homes, for fear the conflagration would spread, and in all the confusion, a man with a sword at his side suddenly slapped a firm hand on his shoulder and said, "Benvenuto Cellini?"

Before he could even answer, someone else had slipped a black sack over his head and jerked a leather cord to tighten it around his neck.

He heard Ascanio holler, and the sounds of a street brawl, and he swung the bucket at whoever was holding him. It hit something brittle, he heard a groan, then the cord was yanked tighter. He couldn't breathe, and he was knocked off his feet by what might have been the hilt of a sword. Still kicking, he was dragged into an alleyway, then manhandled into a waiting carriage. He heard the crack of a whip and felt the wheels begin to roll. As he struggled to get up again, a knee was pressed to his chest, and a voice close to his ear hissed, "Call on your demons now."

Chapter 7

David was poring over the lab reports when he suddenly became aware that he was being watched.

The moment the analyses had arrived by special courier, he had raced into the Newberry's book silo—a large research space containing the Newberry's precious collections of codices, maps, and manuscripts—to comb through them. Microscopic samples of the ink and paper had been sent off to Arlington, Virginia, where the FBI submitted its own materials, and from what he had ascertained so far, everything about the documents given to him by Mrs. Van Owen checked out. In terms of age and provenance, they were completely authentic. And he'd have been delighted to bring her that news himself if she had not already been standing on the steel catwalk above him, studying him like a bug in a jar.

He had not heard her come in, nor did he know how long she had been silently observing, but the hairs on the back of his neck prickled nonetheless.

"What are you reading?" she asked, her voice muffled and absorbed by the thousands of volumes stored in the cylindrical shelves that rose all around them.

"Ink and paper analyses from the sketch of *La Medusa*," he said, waving one hand over the cluttered desktop.

"I told you there was no need to waste time on that."

With one gloved hand on the railing, she descended the stairs. She was dressed all in black, as appeared to be her custom, and as she left the gloom of the stacks and entered the pool of light in which David was working, several pieces of diamond jewelry sparkled at her throat and ears. The heady scent of her perfume filled the air as she drew out a chair and sat down, crossing her legs, enhanced by a pair of sheer black stockings and sharply pointed heels.

David doubted that the book silo had ever seen anyone quite like her.

"So tell me what you've learned."

For a moment, David could think of almost nothing other than her dark, but oddly forbidding, beauty.

With languid fingers, she turned a page around, glanced at the heading, and said, "Iron-gall extracts?"

"It's a good way of dating ancient inks," David said, still trying to recover. "The Egyptians started using ink on papyrus around 2500 B.C, and the Romans used sepia—the black pigment secreted by the cuttlefish." He was babbling, he knew, but decided to go with it until he'd fully regained his composure. "But by the time of the Renaissance, iron-gall extracts, which were made by mixing bark and tree galls with other ingredients, had pretty much replaced them." He expounded further on the tests that had been done on the ink and the paper, while Mrs. Van Owen appeared to be listening with half an ear. "There's an unusually high degree of logwood extract in these tannins, and that will help us to track down other documents Cellini might have written, or sketches he might have made, from the same period. And those, in turn, may provide some clues as to the present-day whereabouts of the *Medusa*."

What he didn't say was that he thought it all was highly unlikely; he still wasn't convinced that the thing had ever even existed. Cellini was famous for his plans that never came to pass and his designs that never reached fruition. It wasn't for want of trying, but the man led an eventful life, in a turbulent time, and when he wasn't running from a pope, he was dodging a king. His commissions were major undertakings—fountains for the gardens at Fontainebleau, or twelve life-sized silver figurines of the gods—but he seldom lived in one place, under one prince's patronage, long enough to see things through. (Of the twelve figurines, only one—Jupiter—was ever made, and it, like so much of Cellini's work, had been lost, destroyed, or melted down over the centuries.) It was a miracle that his bronze statue of Perseus slaying the Medusa, which had taken shape over a period of nine years, had ever been completed at all, much less survived to become one of the greatest masterpieces of Western art.

"And where are these other documents you would need to consult?" she asked, though he felt, from her tone of voice, that she was simply leading him along.

"Most of them?" he said. "They're housed in the Biblioteca Laurenziana in Florence."

"So?"

He paused, unsure what she was getting at. She leaned back in her chair, falling out of the penumbra of light, but her eyes glowing all the same. "So why are you here," she elaborated, "and not in Italy?"

The question took him off guard on several scores, chief among them the implication that he was working exclusively for her.

"I have a job, right here," he fumbled.

"You are officially on sabbatical now."

David almost laughed. "I'm afraid that only Dr. Armbruster can make that decision."

"I've just spoken to her, and she has."

David was dumbfounded. And if he was thinking about how his absence might affect his chances of getting the job as Director of Acquisitions, Mrs. Van Owen had anticipated him there, too.

"If you were to succeed at something like this—something that would bring such credit to the institution—I don't see how she could not reward you with the directorship. She doesn't see how she could refuse it, either."

David felt as if his whole world was being turned upside down. Suddenly, he wasn't working for the Newberry but for this very rich and very strange lady in black, whose money and power seemed to bend everyone's wills to her own. Now, his very career seemed to depend upon carrying out her orders. He wanted to call Dr. Armbruster's office and see if any of it was true.

"Go ahead," Mrs. Van Owen said, guessing his thoughts. "Call her and see. I can wait."

The offer alone was enough to convince David she was telling the truth. "But are you aware," he said, scrambling, "that the Newberry's budget doesn't allow for—"

"I thought I made this plain," she interrupted, a note of exasperation in her voice. "Money is not an issue. I will pay any and all expenses, without limit. Your boss has no objection to your leaving as soon as possible. If you're successful, the library will profit—enormously—and so will you." She took a gold Cartier pen from her tiny clutch purse, and on the back of a card embossed with her name, wrote something down. She laid the pen on the table and flicked the card in his direction.

"That's our private contract," she said.

David picked it up and saw, just above her signature, "One million dollars."

He did not know what to make of it—it was as if he were looking at an Egyptian hieroglyphic. When he looked up again, she was staring fixedly into his eyes.

"I know you need that money," she said. "If not for you, then for your sister."

Up until then, he'd felt like the ground had been systematically cut away beneath his feet, but with that it was as if she had kicked him in the gut. "What does my sister have to do with this?"

"Her medical expenses have to be immense."

"How do you know anything about that?" he persisted. "My family is none of your business."

"It isn't?"

"No."

"Well, I intend to make it my business." She leaned forward again, her long, tapered fingers spread like talons on the lab reports. "If you get me what I want, I'll get you what you want."

"What I want is a cure for cancer. Are you trying to tell me that you can get that?" Now he was convinced that the woman was as batty as she was rich. She must have been reading Cellini's *Key to Life Eternal,* and mistaken his alchemy and magical formulae for scientific fact.

Coolly surveying him, she said, "You think I'm out of my mind," and he remained pointedly silent. "I'd think so, too, if I were in your shoes. But believe me, I'm not. I cannot go on living without the *Medusa,* and, to be frank, neither can your sister. Let's not deceive ourselves. Get it for me, and I can promise that your Sarah will live to a ripe old age . . . just like me."

To David, that didn't seem like much of a promise; despite the weird aura she gave off, the woman couldn't be much older than his sister at all.

"Or are you prepared to just sit by and watch her die?"

With that, she got up in one fluid motion, floated up the stairs, and was gone, leaving the powerful scent of her perfume lingering in the air where David sat, with her card in one hand, stunned beyond words.

⌘

Mr. Joseph Schillinger, former U.S. ambassador to Liechtenstein, was just finishing the crossword puzzle in the *Times* when his driver and general factotum, Ernst Escher, said, in his thick Swiss accent, "Look who's coming out now."

It was the woman in black, the same woman he'd glimpsed at the Dante lecture. But there was no veil, and he had had time for Escher to run her license plate. It was indeed Randolph Van Owen's widow. But was she the mysterious donor of the book?

"And it gets better," Escher said, turning his shaved head and thick neck to grin at his employer.

It did indeed, because just as she got back into her waiting car,

David Franco, the young man he'd come here to track, came bounding down the steps after her. He was holding out something gold—a pen, perhaps?—in his hand. Her window rolled down, she took it, and after they'd exchanged no more than a few words—and what wouldn't Schillinger have given to know what those words were?—the car rolled off down the snowy street.

"What would you like me to do?" Escher asked, always on the lookout for action and preferably of the violent kind.

"Nothing. Just sit still." The man was like a hand grenade with the pin pulled out.

As Schillinger kept watch from the backseat, Franco, wearing no coat against the bitterly cold wind, stood rooted to the spot. Even from this distance, across the width of Bughouse Square, he looked dazed, and Schillinger wondered what had transpired inside the library. Had he discovered yet what Schillinger had guessed the moment that the book had been revealed? That the illustrations were from the hand of the master artisan—and necromancer—Benvenuto Cellini? No one but someone steeped in the occult could have depicted the scenes so powerfully, or in such a distinctive style.

For years, ever since meeting Monsieur Linz at an auction on Lake Como, Schillinger had been a part of the man's web, keeping his eyes and ears open for anything that might be of value to someone of such dark and rarefied tastes. And now he had it. The small favors that Linz had done him in return—parceling out word of a long-lost Vermeer drawing, or a Hobbema landscape, about to emerge onto the black market—could now be repaid in spades.

Schillinger reached for his phone and placed a call to France.

"*Oui?*" the voice on the other end snapped. "*Que voulez-vous?*"

Every time Schillinger had to speak to Emil Rigaud, he had to swallow his bile. To think that a former United States ambassador could be treated so contemptuously by a decommissioned French army captain, was infuriating, to say the least. But keeping his temper, he explained what he had just learned.

"But how much do you think he knows," Rigaud asked, "this David Franco?"

"He's a very intelligent young man," Schillinger said, vaguely proud that they shared an alma mater, "but he's just getting started. At this point, I suspect he knows only a bit less than I do."

Rigaud sighed, as if he'd heard this veiled complaint before. "We keep it that way for your own benefit, Joseph. If you knew more than what we tell you, if you took it upon yourself to start nosing around where you are not wanted, dire consequences could ensue."

Schillinger, insulted, went silent.

"Comprendez-vous?"

"Je comprends."

"Good," Rigaud said. "Now call Gropius in Antwerp. Ask him about the small Corot oil that has just come to light."

Schillinger had always coveted a Corot. How did they know that? "Thank you, Emil." Maybe he wasn't such a bad sort after all. "But what would you like me to do about this David Franco? I have Ernst Escher with me here, and something," he said, in a more sinister tone of voice, "could be done."

"Do nothing. When we have to, we will take care of things from our end."

"And Mrs. Van Owen? We move in similar circles. Her husband recently died. Perhaps I could become her friend and learn something more that way." He felt absurdly like a young flunky, trying to ingratiate himself with the boss.

"Monsieur Linz has the situation well in hand," Rigaud replied, as if lecturing a schoolboy.

"I'm sure he does, but I thought—"

"Stop thinking, will you? Monsieur Linz is a Grand Master, and you are playing at tic-tac-toe. Call Gropius." And then the line went dead.

When the ambassador looked back toward the library, Franco was trudging up the steps like a man with the weight of the world on his shoulders. What did he know that Schillinger didn't? There were times, and this was one of them, when Schillinger felt that he was playing for penny antes when great stakes were being wagered all around him. Perhaps if he pursued his own interests a bit more strenuously, he would not only gain in the material sense—and his acquisitive instincts had not lessened with age—but he might find himself in a position to command some respect from that toady Rigaud and his mysterious master.

"Well?" Escher said, eagerly, from the front seat.

"Home," Schillinger replied, and he could see his driver's shoulders fall with disappointment. He had so hoped for a confrontation. As Escher pulled the car back into the city traffic, blasting his horn at a slow-moving school bus, the ambassador put in the call to Antwerp.

Chapter 8

The hood was left on his head until the coach had rumbled over the last bridge leading out of Florence and taken to one of the bumpy rural roads. After another hour or so, a pair of rough hands loosened the cord and yanked it off. Cellini gasped for a breath of the fresh country air.

One of his captors leaned back in the opposite seat and surveyed him with a crooked smile. The other two, he presumed, were up on top, driving the horses.

"They said we'd need ten men to subdue you," the man said, glancing at the ropes binding his prisoner's hands and feet. "And now look at you, trussed up like a prize pig."

Though there were black muslin curtains in the open window, the moon was bright, and Cellini was able to see enough of the countryside to know what road they were on and to guess where they must be going.

Rome.

Which meant that these men, prepared to abduct a man of Cellini's stature—a man in the current employ of the Duke de'Medici, the ruler of Florence—could only be in the service of the Pope himself, Paul III. No one else would have dared.

But for what offense? Cellini had served the Papacy well for years. He had fashioned the elaborate cope, or clasp, for the ermine gown of the previous Pope, Clement VII, and made a dozen other jeweled ornaments, silver ewers and basins, coins and medals, for the leaders of the Church. And when the Duke of Bourbon, and his army of mercenaries, had invaded and sacked Rome in 1527, who had been its ablest defender? It was Cellini who had manned the gun batteries of the Castel St. Angelo, where Clement had taken refuge for seven long months from the marauding troops—if those savages could be dignified with such a term. Indeed, it was Cellini to whom Clement had turned when all seemed lost and the hoard of papal treasures threatened to fall into enemy hands.

And now this new Pope, Paul III, had sent his ruffians to set fire to his studio and carry him off by force?

"Don't you want to know who we are?" the man in the carriage said. He was an ugly brute, whose teeth had all grown in sideways so that his words came out with a whistling sound.

"You're the scum the Pope sends to do his dirty work."

The man laughed, clearly unoffended. "They said you were smart," he conceded, digging at something in the corner of his mouth with a long, filthy fingernail. "I see that now. I'm Jacopo." He flicked the offending particle to the floor.

"But why like this? If the Pope wished to see me, he had only to send a request."

"We are the request. He requests that you throw yourself at his holy feet and beg him not to hang you from the Torre di Nona."

"For what?"

Ignoring his question, Jacopo lifted the curtain and stared out at the rolling hills of Tuscany. "It's nice up here," he said. "I've never been this far from Rome." He wiped some spittle from his chin with the back of his hand—a gesture Cellini imagined must be routine.

"Well? Are you going to answer me?"

"You'll find out soon enough," he said, before settling his head against the rocking wall of the cabin and dropping into a deep, snoring sleep.

And there he was right. Most carriages would have put in for the night, but this one, with lighted lanterns swinging from the four corners of its roof, managed to drive all night, even at the risk of running off the road or injuring the horses. At dawn, they pulled into a post house, and though Cellini was allowed some bread and wine and a chance to put a cold compress on his head, he was bundled back into the carriage as soon as the new horses had been harnessed. Jacopo took the reins, and one of his accomplices—a wiry fellow with a huge, livid bruise on one cheek and a blackened eye—assumed his place inside the cabin.

"What happened to you?" Cellini said, knowing full well. "You look like you got hit with a bucket."

The man spat in Cellini's face. "If I wasn't under orders to deliver you in one piece, I'd break you in two."

"And if my hands weren't tied, I'd give you another black eye to match the one you've got."

The carriage rolled on for several days, until Cellini felt that his back would break from the constant jouncing. With his hands and feet tied—these scoundrels must have been expecting a good bounty for his safe delivery—there was little he could do to make himself comfortable, and the prospect of whatever awaited him in Rome was hardly encouraging. As they finally approached the Eternal City, the roads became smoother and better paved, but they also became more crowded, with shepherds bringing their flocks to market, and rickety wagons carrying barrels of wine from Abruzzo, wheels of cheese from the Enza Valley, and loads of the distinctive blue-gray marble from high in the Apennines. Cellini could hear the driver—right then it was Bertoldo, the one with the sword who had first clapped him on the shoulder in Florence—shouting, "Make way! We come on order of His Holiness, Pope Paul! Get out of the way!"

From the oaths and epithets he heard in reply, there were many who didn't believe him. But the *contadini* were like that, Cellini mused. They worked the farms and fields all day, sometimes not speaking to a soul, and when anyone did speak to them, they were instantly suspicious of his motives—especially if it was a stranger with a sword, driving a fancy black carriage and ordering them around.

Jacopo, sitting inside again, couldn't resist parting the curtains and holding his ugly mug in front of the window. Cellini had the impression that he hoped to be spotted traveling in such style by someone— anyone—he knew.

The streets of Rome, unlike Florence, were a mess. In Florence, the streets were narrow and often dark, but the people knew how to behave. They did not throw their offal into the gutter, they did not empty their chamber pots out the front windows, and they did not leave dead dogs or cats or birds to rot in the sun. But these Romans, they lived in a cesspool and didn't even seem to mind. Every time he had come to Rome, Cellini had marveled at the state of chaos, the teeming confusion all around, where the greatest masterpieces of the ancient world were surrounded by tanning yards and the classical temples overrun by pig markets. As the carriage passed through the Porta del Popolo, the tomb of Nero's mother appeared on their right, a crowd of beggars littering the steps. The tomb of the Roman emperor Augustus fared no better, pieces of its marble façade having been torn down and burned for the lime they would yield. The Campo Marzio was cluttered with workmen's shops, some of them tucked into the ruins of once-glorious mansions. The Temple of Pompey had been turned into an unruly hotel, where scores of families had carved out spaces for themselves, with open fires and hanging laundry, beneath the enormous and dilapidated vault. If Florence was an elegant ball, Rome was an untamed circus.

And Cellini feared that he was about to become its main attraction.

Passing through the Borgo, as the bustling area between the banks of the Tiber and the mighty Vatican City was called, Cellini could not help but recall his first trip to Rome, when he was only nineteen. He and another goldsmith's apprentice, Tasso, had often talked about leaving their hometown of Florence; Rome was the place where fortunes and names were truly to be made. And one day, on a long ramble, they had found themselves at the San Piero Gattolini Gate. Benvenuto had jokingly said to his friend, "Well, we're halfway to Rome. Why don't we keep on going?" Tasso had looked a bit dubious, but Cellini had bucked him up.

Tying their aprons behind their backs, they had set out on foot. In Siena, they had the good fortune to find a horse that needed to be returned to Rome, and so they were able to ride the rest of the way, and once they'd arrived in the city, Cellini had quickly found work at the studio of a successful goldsmith named Firenzuola. He took one look at a design Cellini had executed for an elaborate belt buckle and hired him on the spot to execute a silver vessel for a Cardinal, modeled on an urn from the Rotunda. Tasso was not so lucky, and homesickness got the better of him. He returned to Florence while Cellini stayed on in Rome, changing masters, and making objects, from candlesticks to tiaras, of such great beauty and ingenuity that he had soon become the acknowledged master of his craft.

But the hands that had made rings and miters for popes were now so chafed and numb from the ropes binding them that he could barely move his fingers.

At the main gate of the Vatican, the carriage was stopped by several members of the Swiss Guard, in their green-and-yellow uniforms and plumed helmets. They were young—these days they were always young, as nearly all of their predecessors had been massacred during the sack of the city—and there was some haggling over papers. The leader of the Guard poked his head into the cabin to see who was inside. He wrinkled his nose at the smell, and said, "You'll want to give this one a wash before taking him to the Holy Father." The portcullis was lifted and the carriage passed through into the main piazza. Cellini ached to be out of the carriage, even if it was only to mount the steps of the papal palace and face an unknown fate.

Bertoldo appeared to have taken the guardsman's suggestion to heart, and he stopped at a fountain, where he let Cellini dismount. Unbinding his hands and feet, he allowed him to scoop some of the cool water with his cupped hands onto his face and neck. The water felt so good that Cellini dropped to his knees and ducked his whole head into the fountain. When he lifted his head back out again, he shook his long black curls like Poseidon rising from the deep. The water coursed across his broad shoulders and chest, and over the *Medusa* that still hung below his shirt. The sun was hot and bright, and he held his face up to it, not knowing how much longer he might be able to enjoy such a simple pleasure. A pair of friars, in long brown cassocks, stopped to watch, muttering behind their hands.

Bertoldo and his confederates hauled Cellini to his feet, bound his wrists again, and with the water still dripping off him, marched him up the steps of the palace and through the smaller throne room, where dozens of men—merchants, aristocrats, city officials—milled about, waiting anxiously for an audience with the Pope. Some clutched papers in their hands, others were carrying gifts (one had a squawking green parrot on his arm), but all of them fell silent when Benvenuto was briskly escorted past them. Clearly, none of them wished themselves in his shoes.

In the greater throne room, another crowd was gathered, but this one was made up of priests and cardinals, ambassadors and their secretaries. The Pope himself, draped in a red velvet cape, sat on a high-backed purple throne, giving orders and directives, and apparently carrying on ten conversations at once. He had a long face with a long nose, and a bushy white beard with a dark streak down its center. As Cellini boldly approached the throne, Bertoldo and his men fell away. Benvenuto recognized many of the courtiers—some were prelates who had begun their rise in Tuscany, and some were foreigners whose kings and princes he had worked for—but there was one he knew well. Signor Pier Luigi had recently been made the Duke of Castro, and if he had to guess why he had been brought here under such duress, he'd guess it had something to do with him.

"And look who it is," Pope Paul exclaimed. "The wandering artist." There was no malice in his voice, which temporarily puzzled Cellini.

"I came as quickly as I could, Your Holiness . . . and would have done so willingly."

The Pope only now seemed to take notice of his bound hands and gestured at Bertoldo to undo them.

Bowing his head nervously, Bertoldo unknotted the rope and stepped backwards toward the rear of the room. Cellini shook his hands to get the blood moving again and straightened the damp collar of his shirt.

"Forgive me, Your Eminence, but my traveling companions—fine fellows all, but a bit lacking when it came to conversation—failed to tell me the reason for this visit."

The Pope laughed. "You haven't changed a bit, Benvenuto."

"Perhaps it was time he did, Father," Signor Luigi put in, and Cellini smiled wryly at his form of addressing the Pope. In this case, calling him "Father" was more than symbolic; Luigi was in fact his bastard son—which accounted for the heap of titles and monies bestowed upon him—and Luigi liked to subtly remind people of his paternity. He was a dark, scowling man, with thick black eyebrows, a drooping moustache, and black beard. And now, as always, he wore his armored breastplate. He had enough enemies, Cellini reflected, to make that precaution wise.

"Perhaps Messer Cellini would like to turn into an honest man," Signor Luigi added.

Cellini felt the blood rise into his face, but he held himself in check, simply saying, "I have never been anything else."

Signor Luigi strode between the papal throne and where Cellini stood in order to look him in the eye. "Really?" he said scornfully. "Then isn't there something you'd like to tell us about?" he asked. "Something you'd like to confess in this holy place after so many years of concealment?"

Cellini was as honestly confused as he had ever been in his life. "You will have to enlighten me. As always, when Signor Luigi speaks"—he purposely avoided using any of his grander titles—"there is a lot of noise, but not much music."

The Pope quietly guffawed, which only made his son angrier.

As if he were speaking in the Colosseum itself, Signor Luigi raised his eyes and his voice and even his arms, as he moved in circles around Cellini to declaim his charges. "Would it surprise you to know that your confidences have been breached? That certain confessions you once made, in your usual boastful manner, have reached the Holy See?"

"Confessions? To whom?" Cellini had not visited a priest for that purpose in years.

"A certain apprentice from the town of Perugia."

Ah, so that was it. He must have been referring to Girolamo Pascucci, a lazy thief who had broken his contract with Cellini and still owed him money. But a confession? Much less to someone he'd never trusted?

"We know, Messer Cellini—we *know*—what happened during the attack on Rome, sixteen years ago."

"Ah, then you know that I commanded the artillery that defended Pope Clement VII when he was under siege in the Castel St. Angelo?"

"We do," Signor Luigi said sarcastically, annoyed at having his peroration interrupted.

"And that I was the one who kept the three beacons burning every night, to prove that we had not surrendered?"

"But that is not—"

"And that it was a shot from my arquebus that brought down the Duke of Bourbon himself?"

"We know," Luigi boomed, "that the Pope, in his hour of most desperate need, with the barbarians battering at the very doors of his sanctuary, entrusted you with the jewels belonging to the Holy Apostolic Chamber."

At last Cellini could see where this was going. "That he did. I would never deny it. Pope Clement, may his soul rest in peace, came to me one night and said, 'Benvenuto, we must find a way to preserve these treasures. What can we do?'"

"So you admit to this concealment?"

It was all Cellini could do not to thump the idiot on his fancy breastplate.

"With the help of the Pope himself, and his servant Cavalierino," Cellini explained, more to the Pope on his throne than his insulting bastard son, "we removed all the precious stones from his tiaras and miters and crowns and sewed as many of them as we could into the folds of the robes that he and his servant had on. In order to move the gold more easily, we melted it down." Cellini remembered well the small blast furnace he had hastily built in his quarters. He had tossed the gold into the charcoals and let it drip down into the large tray he had placed beneath the brick.

"And where are those jewels now? Where is that gold?"

"Where it has always been. In the coffers and vaults of the Vatican."

"All but eighty thousand ducats' worth!" Signor Luigi trumpeted.

"Is that what you are accusing me of? Stealing the Pope's jewels?"

Signor Luigi rocked on his heels, his thumbs hooked beneath the corners of his breastplate. "If you didn't, who did?"

Cellini hardly knew where to start, but he knew that he had to be careful; Signor Luigi was a dangerous enemy. Even if Pope Paul knew him to be a bit slippery, the man was still his son—and blood was thicker than water. Cellini never forgot that.

"First of all, even if I had committed such an unthinkable offense, I would never have confessed it to a man like Pascucci; the city of Perugia never gave birth to a bigger liar and thief. And as for the missing stones, I suggest you consult the account books. Have you done that?"

Signor Luigi didn't answer.

"I didn't think so. Everything—every ring, every diamond, every ruby, even every garnet—was recorded in the accounts as soon as the siege was lifted. While Pope Clement was negotiating the settlement, a small diamond ring, worth no more than four thousand scudi, fell from his finger, and when the imperial ambassador bent to pick it up, the Pope told him to keep it. Apart from that, you will see that not a ducat's worth—much less eighty thousand ducats' worth—is missing." Cellini scoffed, to indicate the absurdity of the charge he had just addressed.

And though Pope Paul appeared mollified, Signor Luigi was not. Indeed, his brow was more furrowed than ever, and rather than let it go, he said, "The account books will be looked at." He snapped his fingers and waggled them at a retainer, who scuttled out of the room to get started. "But that still leaves us with an equally grave charge."

"Another?" Pope Paul said, sounding a bit put off.

"Yes, Father . . . a charge of heresy."

The room fell utterly silent, and the Pope leaned forward on his purple throne, his long white beard brushing his knees.

Signor Luigi, pleased at having recaptured everyone's attention, said, "In his workshop in Florence, Messer Cellini has experimented with forbidden texts and arcana that are in direct contravention of Church teachings. My sources tell me—"

"What sources?" Cellini broke in. "Pascucci again?"

"No," Signor Luigi replied dryly, "other apprentices you employed. And they tell me you have employed various grimoires"—the black books of magic banned by the Catholic Church—"to fashion objects of an occult nature. Objects that may give you powers properly reserved for God alone."

Pope Paul fell back in his chair. A foreign ambassador—French by the look of his finery and lace—gasped and held a handkerchief to his face, as if to avert a contagion. Cellini felt the temperature in the room fall by several degrees.

"I don't know how to answer such baseless accusations," Cellini said, "especially as I don't know who's making them."

"That's for me to know," Signor Luigi declared.

"Is it true?" Pope Paul asked.

And here Cellini paused. He would have to continue his denial, but lying to the Pope himself was a sin of a magnitude he could hardly contemplate. And Signor Luigi must have noted his hesitation because, before Cellini could think of what to say, he had swooped forward, reached under Cellini's shirt collar, and lifted the chain out.

The *Medusa* lay in the palm of his hand, her face glaring up at the throne.

"The proof, Father, the proof! An unholy object, whose true purpose only the Devil can know."

The Pope indicated that he wanted to see it, and one of his priests came forward and lifted it over Cellini's head. When it was placed in the Pope's hand, he studied it closely, then turned it over, rubbing his thumb on the black silk backing.

"What is it?" he asked.

"A looking glass, Your Holiness."

The Pope twisted the latches and the silk cover slid away. Cellini inadvertently glanced toward the long windows giving onto the Vatican gardens. Blessedly, the sun, and not the moon, hung in the sky above the grove of orange and lemon trees.

"It's not a very good one," the Pope said, eyeing the convex, and distorting, glass.

"No, Your Eminence, it did not meet my own expectations, either. It was designed for Eleonora de Toledo, but as it came out imperfectly, I kept it for myself and made another—a perfect copy, with ruby eyes—for the duchess."

"Rubies from the Vatican's casks?" Signor Luigi threw in.

Cellini's fists clenched—he had taken all the insults he could—and Luigi, backing away, ordered Bertoldo and his henchmen to grab him.

"You will have all the time you need to contemplate your imperfect workmanship," he said, "in your old home—the dungeons of the Castel St. Angelo."

Cellini started to protest, but the Pope, reluctant to thwart his son any longer, handed the glass to one of his retainers as if it were a piece of spoiled fruit from his garden, and conspicuously turned away.

Chapter 9

"One more time, Uncle David! One more time!"

David was about to get off the ice—he hadn't been skating in years and he considered it a miracle that he hadn't taken a fall yet— but in deference to his niece, he agreed to go around the rink with her for one more lap. After all, it was Christmas Eve.

It was cold, but still bright and sunny out, and as they skated past Sarah, sitting on the bench and wrapped in a long down coat and a woolen cap pulled down tight around her ears, David shouted, "You hanging in there?"

Sarah nodded and gave him a thumbs-up.

"Then we'll be right back!" And still holding Emme by her mittened hand, David sailed back into the crowd of kids and teenagers weaving their way around the rink to the tinny, amplified sound of "Frosty the Snowman." It was a picture out of Currier and Ives—the frozen pond in the park, the skaters in their stocking caps and colorful leggings, their breath fogging in the air.

And it felt good to be out and exercising in the open air, especially as he had felt trapped in the whirlwind of his own thoughts ever since Mrs. Van Owen's visit to the library. It had been the single most surreal moment in his entire life, and even after he'd run outside to return her pen—and she'd assured him that she meant every word she'd said—he'd been consumed by her promises. On the one hand, he knew it was insane—how could she possibly guarantee to save his sister's life? No one could do that. But on the other, there was that business card, with the one-million-dollar offer on it. What kind of treatments or care or special attention could a million bucks bring? Plenty, he thought. He kept the card tucked away in his wallet, but he was never unaware of its being there. It just didn't feel right—and he wondered if it was the kind of thing he should divulge to Dr. Armbruster . . . although he noticed, guiltily, that he hadn't.

In an effort to forget about the distractions and just get on with the work, he had thrown himself into reading through the remaining pages of *The Key to Life Eternal,* presumably written in Cellini's own hand. And as the secrets of the manuscript revealed themselves, he had come to understand what was driving Kathryn Van Owen and her search for *La Medusa.*

She believed in it.

She believed that the book was true, and that the glass truly held the power of immortality. As she had told him outside the Newberry, she had never entrusted this particular document, in its entirety, to anyone but him.

"Guard it carefully," she had said. "You are the first person that I believe can make sense—and use—of it in your search. Do not disappoint me."

As it turned out, the *Key* was not only an account of Cellini's experiments with sorcery—the disinterment of dead bodies from holy ground, the construction of strange devices designed to nurture *homonculi,* the quest for the Philosopher's Stone—it was also a detailed account of his own obsessive quest for immortality. Not content with the marvelous creations he had already made, or the artistic genius he had been blessed with, he had enlisted the help of a Sicilian magician named Strozzi and gone in search of the greatest gift of all—life everlasting. What he wanted was nothing less than all the time in the world—time in which he could re-create Nature in its most idealized forms, and craft things, from statues to fountains, paintings to glittering parures, of unmatched beauty and ingenuity.

He reminded David of another great, if fictional, figure—Faust—who was prepared to sell his own soul for the knowledge acquired through immortality.

And in perhaps its eeriest passage, he recounted a hallucinatory (or so David had to assume) expedition to the underworld, led by Dante himself. Cellini claimed to have found not only the secret of invisibility—in a clump of bulrushes—but the secret of eternity, too. It lay in the water from the infernal pool, a few drops of which he had preserved beneath the glass of *La Medusa*. The mirror, Cellini wrote, could grant this gift, but only *"se il proprietario lo sa come approfondire"*—or, "if its owner knows how to use it." In his Tuscan dialect, he went on to explain how the mirror must be held—"closely and directly, as if staring into one's own soul"—and graced by the light of the moon, "the constant, but ever-changing, planet above us." He concluded with an admonition: "But it is a boon less simple, less desirable, than may be thought, and I do fear that great anguish and misfortune may ensue."

Tell that, David thought, to Mrs. Van Owen, as he distractedly embarked on one more circle of the rink.

"Amanda!" Emme screeched, before abruptly dropping her uncle's hand and skating off to join her best friend, who was just teetering her way onto the ice.

David took that as his cue to skate over to the edge of the rink and plop down on the bench next to Sarah.

"Looks like she got a better offer," he said, unlacing his skates.

"Don't feel bad. She and Amanda are pretty much inseparable."

"How are you holding up? Should we pack it up and head home?" Her face had the cold translucence of ice, and with her eyebrows gone from the chemo, she looked alarmingly like a glass mask. Only her eyes—as dark a brown as David's—still held any spark of color and life.

"No, Emme's having such a good time, it makes me feel better just to watch. I never know how many more chances like this I'll have," she said matter-of-factly.

It was the very offhandedness of her remark that struck David most forcibly. He tried like hell to keep his sister's mortality out of his thoughts, but of course he knew that the subject was never far from hers. How could it be? For over a year, she had been living under a sentence of imminent death. She had gone from one surgery to another, one treatment to another, one special protocol to another, and while there were occasional respites in her decline, the general direction was unmistakable. Remission, if it came, would not come for long.

"You know what I'll miss most?" she said, musing aloud.

He hated this line of thought, but if she needed to express it . . .

"Getting to watch Emme grow up."

Just then, her daughter whirled by, laughing, and swinging hands with Amanda.

"But you *will* get to see her grow up," David said, meaning the best, even if he knew—and he knew she knew—that any reprieve was temporary. "You're looking better all the time, and Gary tells me that this new regimen they've got you on has shown some real improvements. You are going to get better."

She patted the back of his hand, still following Emme, and said, "Put your boots on, or your feet will freeze." He finished removing the skates and pulled on his boots, which were cold as icicles inside.

"I'd give *anything* to make that true," she added, and David could not help but flash again on his strange conference in the book silo with Kathryn Van Owen.

In a deliberately casual tone, he asked, "You would?"

"Would what?" she said, already having forgotten what she'd just said. The drugs made it hard for her sometimes to follow the thread of a conversation.

"Do anything to . . . keep on going?"

She took a deep breath and looked out across the rink at the laughing, spinning skaters.

"I never thought I'd believe that," she said. "I always thought—as much as anybody who's healthy ever thinks about it at all—that I'd be happy to live my life, and go peacefully, with no complaints, whenever it ended."

She coughed, and raised a gloved hand to her colorless thin lips.

"But that's what you think when things are fine," she said. "That's what you think when there's nothing really wrong. I don't think like that anymore."

A note of bitterness, one he seldom heard, had crept into her voice.

"Now, I'd give anything I could—and do whatever it takes—to live. To get old and gray with Gary. To see Emme play in the all-city orchestra, and go to her high-school prom, then off to college. To find out who she falls in love with, and what she decides to do with her life. To see her become a young woman, and have children of her own. I want all of that, David, all of it," she said, tears welling up in the corners of her eyes. "I never thought I could want anything so much. And I'm so ashamed to be so weak and angry now."

"You have no reason to be ashamed of anything," David said, wrapping an arm around her shoulders and hugging her tight. "You're the bravest person I know, and you've got a right to be angry. You've been through hell." Mrs. Van Owen's offer—"I can promise she'll live to a ripe old age"—rang in his head like a cracked bell.

The tears were rolling down both cheeks, and one or two of the passing skaters threw a glance their way.

"Don't let Emme see me like this," she murmured into his coat.

"Don't worry. She's way over by the concession stand with Amanda," he assured her.

"I just needed to say it."

"You can say anything to me, you know that. You always have."

She sniffled a little and smiled at that.

"Remember how you told me," he said, "back when I was in junior high, that no girl would ever go out with me if I didn't get rid of my dandruff? Or that I was such a bad dancer, I should just sort of stand in place and shuffle my feet around?"

"I told you that?" she said. "I'm so sorry."

"Don't be—you were right. I bought shampoo, and I learned how to dance."

She wiped her eyes on the back of her mittens and straightened up. "I wonder if this is how Mom felt, right about now?"

It was something that David had considered, too. Had their mother, who perished in the same way, felt this same anguish and frustration and—yes—fury toward the end?

"Maybe so," David said.

Sarah just nodded.

Emme was skating toward them very carefully, with a big cardboard cup of hot chocolate in her hand.

"Watch it or you'll spill that," David said, getting up and giving her a hand. Emme looked at her mother, knowing something was up, as she plopped down on the other side of the bench and began to take her own skates off.

"I see you got the whole enchilada," David said to distract her. "Whipped cream and marshmallows on top. What happened to the cherry?"

"Is everything okay?" Emme asked her mother, pulling on her boots.

"Fine, honey. Everything's fine. But did Amanda pay for that? I'll go give her mother the money."

"No," Emme said, reclaiming the hot chocolate. "A friend of Uncle David's bought one for both of us. He said it was his treat."

Sarah glanced at David, just as a puzzled look crossed David's face. "A friend of mine? What was his name?"

"I don't remember. But he had a funny way of talking."

"Is he still here? Point him out, Emme," he said, in a cautiously neutral tone. "I'd really like to go and say hi."

Emme took a big swig of the chocolate while her eyes scanned the rink, then the street beyond.

"That's him," she said, pointing out toward the street, where a stocky man with a bald head was just then unlocking the door of a black BMW.

"Do you know him?" Sarah asked nervously.

But the look on his face told her no.

"I'll be right back," David said, taking off around the edge of the rink.

"David, just call the police if you have to! Don't do anything that could get you hurt."

But David was already hearing nothing but the pounding in his own eardrums. Who was the guy, closing the car door? If he'd really been some friend, he'd have come over to say hello. But he was starting to look vaguely familiar. Why?

"Hey!" he shouted, rounding one end of the rink, with his arm raised and waving. "Hey, you!"

He had to scramble through the line of kids waiting at the concession stand before he actually got out of the park.

The BMW had pulled away from the curb, and David, marooned on the wrong side of the street, had to wait for a bus to rumble by. By the time it did, the car was moving toward him, and David skidded out into the slushy thoroughfare, waving his arms and calling out for the car to stop.

All he could see of the driver, hunkered down behind the tinted windows, was a shaved head, tilted inquisitively to one side, as if the guy was amused at playing a game of chicken.

"Stop!" David shouted, holding up his hands, though instead of slowing down, or even swerving, the car kept coming right at him. "Stop the car!"

If anything, the guy sped up, blasting his horn. Somebody at the bus stop shrieked, and David, his feet slipping on the icy pavement, had to leap out of the way at the last second, landing in a snowbank piled up at the curb. He plunged into the snow up to his elbows, but by the time he was able to turn around again, the black car had zoomed by, horn still blaring, and was turning at the next corner. There was no time to make out any of the numbers on the license plate, or much else.

A passerby suddenly leaned over the snowdrift, extending a hand

and saying, "That was a close call! What the hell were you doing in the middle of the street?"

David took his hand and pulled himself over the snow and onto the sidewalk.

"You hurt?" the man asked.

"No, I'm okay," David said, dusting the snow and ice off his pants and coat. Several people were standing in the park on the other side of the street, and some of the skaters had stopped dead to watch the drama unfold.

"It's all over," David called out. "End of show."

But it wasn't. Above the noise of the passing traffic, and the scratchy sounds of "White Christmas" from the concession stand, David heard Emme's voice, screaming his name.

⸺⸙⸺

The ambulance arrived within minutes, and after hugging Emme and assuring her that her mother was going to be all right, David sent her home with Amanda and her mom. The paramedics said he could ride in the back.

Sarah was going in and out of consciousness, and from the best David had been able to gather, she had run after him in a panic, lost her footing on the ice, and smacked her head on the sidewalk. He hovered above her, holding one hand while the medic monitored her vital signs.

"Anything else I should know about her condition?" the medic asked, glancing up at David.

"She's being treated for cancer," David said, and the medic immediately nodded, confirming his suspicions. It was hard to look at her and not guess it.

"Which hospital?"

"Evanston."

"Good. That's where we were going, anyway."

As soon as they got there, Sarah was rushed through the emergency entrance, and David made a quick call to her husband's cell phone. When Gary picked up, he said he'd already heard from Amanda's mom and was on his way from a real-estate conference in Skokie. When he arrived, the paper name tag was still stuck to the lapel of his sport coat.

Fortunately, her oncologist, Dr. Ross, was on call, and he joined them near the nursing station, with a grave expression on his face.

"This certainly hasn't helped," he said, "but we do have her stabilized again. She's conscious, and she doesn't appear to have suffered a concussion. But we'll keep her in the ICU overnight, just for observation."

"And then?" Gary asked.

"Then," he said, with a slightly more hopeful expression, "I'd like to enter her on a new experimental regimen. We've just gotten the go-ahead on it, and I think Sarah might be a very good candidate. The clinical trials in Maryland were impressive."

For a minute or two, he explained how the therapy might work, and what its side effects might be, then concluded by saying, "But as it *is* experimental, there may be some trouble getting it by your insurance company."

Gary didn't hesitate. "I'll handle it."

"And I can help," David blurted out, thinking of the business card in his wallet.

"That's fine," Dr. Ross said with a nod. "And I'll do what I can from my end. But I just wanted to warn you." And then he left them there, to continue his rounds.

"Why don't we adjourn to the cafeteria?" David said. "I could use a cup of coffee."

Lost in thought, they sat staring into their respective cups. A crooked Christmas tree, decorated with ornaments made by the pediatric patients, stood forlornly beneath the ticking wall clock.

David didn't have to guess what was going through Gary's mind. Apart from the life-and-death question that was forever hanging in the air, there were the money worries. Whether the insurance plan picked up most of this experimental protocol or not, Gary was looking at financial disaster. His business, David knew, had been way down—Sarah had once confessed that he was thinking of quitting and trying something else entirely—and there was no way he could cover any further demands without, at the very least, selling his own house.

But what couldn't a million dollars do?

David would have to go to Florence. And he'd have to go now, while Sarah had been granted this temporary reprieve. There was always a chance that the new protocol would work . . . and there was always a chance that it wouldn't. If he was ever going to take this chance, now was the time.

"You know that promotion I mentioned that I might be getting?" he ventured, and Gary nodded, without lifting his eyes.

"Well, to nail it down, I might have to go to Italy."

"When?"

"As soon as possible."

Now Gary raised his weary eyes. "For how long?"

"It's hard to say," David replied, "though I could come back, on a moment's notice, anytime I had to."

He could see Gary processing the information, just another complication in his already tumultuous life. "I just hate leaving you in the lurch like this, but—"

"Go," Gary said kindly, "go. There's no reason all of us have to live in this damn hospital. And if Sarah were sitting here, she'd be saying the same thing. You know that."

There, David knew, he was right. It only made sense for him to leave immediately especially as he had begun to entertain—against his own better judgment—the nagging, and utterly irrational, notion that Mrs. Van Owen's claims weren't as impossible as they seemed. For one thing, he was beginning to believe that someone else took them seriously. Why else had he nearly been run down in the street? He glanced down at his knuckles, scraped raw from plunging into the snow and ice. Determined as Mrs. Van Owen was, was there some rival out there, equally determined to thwart her?

And for another—and this was the part that troubled him even more deeply—right after she had driven away from the Newberry, he had returned to the book silo and, slumping in his seat, turned the next leaf of *The Key to Life Eternal*. A sketch, one that he had barely paid attention to on his first reading, jumped out at him like an acrobat.

It was clearly an early rendering of the figure of Athena, destined for one of the panels making up the base of the great statue of Perseus. And the likeness to Kathryn Van Owen was startling—the imperious gaze, the haughty posture, the rich mane of dark hair. The words, *Quo Vincas / Clypeum Do Tibi / Casta Sosor,* were faintly legible below it; "I, thy chaste sister, give thee the shield with which thou wilt conquer." Athena was the goddess who had provided the advice, and shield, that allowed the hero Perseus to slay the Medusa. And though David recognized that the woman who had just left the library could not possibly have been the artist's model—that this had to be a mere coincidence, maybe even a trick of his own imagining— there was another part of him that said, *Believe it.* Because at this point, a belief in miracles, in the long-lost secret of immortality, might be his sister's best—and only—hope. How could he dismiss it?

Chapter 10

Father DiGennaro yawned widely and checked his watch again. It was almost midnight, and after that he could lock the massive bronze doors of the Holy Name Cathedral—seat of the Roman Catholic Archdiocese of Chicago—and go to bed. The younger priests would still be celebrating Christmas Eve, with spiked eggnog and pizzas, but all Father DiGennaro wanted was a shot of Maalox and a good night's sleep. At seventy-three, he'd ushered in more than enough holidays.

And the one piece of pizza he'd had was already giving him heartburn.

The archbishop liked to keep the cathedral open late on Christmas Eve, as it was a time when some parishioners came in to quietly reaffirm their faith. And perhaps a dozen or so people had already done that. But Father DiGennaro was alone now, and the interior of the vast Gothic church echoed with his footsteps as he made the rounds. Built in 1874 to replace the previous cathedral, destroyed in the Chicago fire of 1871, Holy Name was large enough to seat two thousand worshippers at one time, and it was richly decorated with red Rocco Alicante marble and a massive granite altarpiece, weighing six tons. The wall sconces and votive candles lent a warm glow to the lower regions of the interior, but the ceiling, 150 feet high, was barely visible. Some work was being done up there, and plywood sheets and tarps were stretched across a portion of the apse. But the red hats of the previous Chicago cardinals—Meyer, Bernardin, Mundelein, Cody, and Stritch—were still hanging, as tradition dictated, until they were reduced to dust . . . a reminder to all that earthly glory is passing.

Father DiGennaro burped, holding his closed hand to his lips, and shuffled slowly toward the double doors, decorated, like the rest of the church, with motifs meant to suggest the biblical "Tree of Life." He was fishing in his trouser pocket for the key ring, when he saw, to his surprise—and if the truth be told, to his chagrin—the doors opening, and a slender woman, in a veiled hat and long fur coat, entering the glass-enclosed vestibule.

Oh, Lord, he thought, *please let her just light a candle and be gone.* The corns on his feet were killing him, too.

But once inside, she stood, as if a stranger, looking all around and hesitant to enter any farther. He had the sense that she was coming to some decision, which did not bode well for him. People in the throes of a spiritual crisis seldom found quick release or comfort.

Approaching her slowly enough not to startle her, he said, "Merry Christmas . . . and welcome to Holy Name."

As he emerged from the shadows of the nave, she took off her gloves, crossed herself, and with a sudden determination, said, "I'm sorry to trouble you at this hour, but I wish to make my confession. Can you do that for me?"

This was going to be worse than he thought. "I was just about to lock up," he replied, slowly, hoping she would take the hint and come back the next day, but she didn't move from the spot. He quickly sensed something else about this woman, too—that she was used to getting what she wanted, when she wanted it.

He let the key ring drop back to the bottom of his pocket.

"Where would we go?" she said, looking around nervously.

The old priest gestured toward several carved wooden booths, with thick red curtains, that stood between banks of flickering candles.

The woman strode off, her heels clicking on the floor, as if she were eager to get this thing over with, and Father DiGennaro wearily followed. Parting the curtains of a booth, she disappeared inside, and he went into the other side, settling into the cushioned chair and folding his cold hands in his lap. Why, he thought, hadn't he just cheated by five minutes and locked the doors early? Right now, he could be taking his shoes off and rubbing the life back into his sore feet.

The woman was kneeling on the other side of the screen, her veil removed—he certainly didn't see many of those anymore—and from what he could tell, a cascade of black hair had washed down onto the shoulders of her fur collar. Her face was lowered as she mumbled, "In the name of the Father, and of the Son, and of the Holy Spirit . . . My last confession was . . . a long time ago."

A lapsed Catholic, he thought. He could be here all night. And then he chided himself for his uncharitable attitude. This is what he was here for, what he'd been doing for well on fifty years. He recited several brief verses from Romans—"For with the heart man believeth unto righteousness; and with the mouth confession is made unto salvation"—as this sometimes seemed to help the penitents unburden themselves, then he waited.

But there was silence . . . except for the very distant sound of some revelers caroling on State Street. He stifled another burp.

"What would you like to tell me?" he finally prompted, and it was then he gathered that the woman was so distraught that she had been silently crying. He saw her lift a handkerchief to her eyes, and he caught the scent of perfume wafting off the fabric.

"I have sinned," she said, before stopping again.

"So have we all," he said, consolingly.

"In a way that no one has sinned before."

He'd even heard that before, too. "I doubt you have broken new ground," he said, hoping to ease her strain with a tiny touch of levity. "Why don't you just tell me what's troubling you and we'll see what's to be done?"

"It's not something you'd ever understand."

"Try me."

"It's not something God would ever understand."

He began to wonder if he had more on his hands than a lonely woman seeking absolution on a lonely Christmas Eve. There was always the chance that this might be someone in need of clinical attention. For just such emergencies, he carried, as did all the confessors, a cell phone in the breast pocket of his jacket.

"Now why would you say that?" he replied as soothingly as possible. "God forgives everyone. If you are truly sorry for your sin, and offer it up to God, He will take that burden from your heart. That's what the holy sacrament of confession is all about."

"But what if you have transgressed against His will? What if you have transgressed against Nature?"

He also wondered if perhaps she might not be a little bit drunk. Maybe she'd come here straight from some holiday bash, tipsy and suddenly overcome by remorse for some youthful crime. An abortion, perhaps? He'd heard that sad story too many times to count.

"I shouldn't be here," she whispered, and though he leaned close to see if he could smell the scent of alcohol, all he got instead was another whiff of the cologne from the handkerchief . . . but with something underneath it.

"The church? You shouldn't be in the church?"

"Alive," she said. "Alive."

Now he knew that this was a deeply troubled woman, not just some conscience-stricken partygoer, and he had to be very careful and alert in what he said. He felt another pang of the heartburn, and sat up straighter in his chair. The air in the close confines of the booth was growing warmer and more redolent of her perfume. He wanted to sneeze but squeezed the tip of his nose to stop it.

"That's a very grave thing to say," he said, "and a very sad thing to be convinced of. I'm quite sure that it's wrong, too. How long have you felt that way?"

At times like this, the line between priest and therapist became perilously thin.

She laughed, a bitter hard laugh, and this time the scent of her breath—cloves and spearmint—did come through the screen, but again it commingled with that same troubling note from before. Was it hers, or his own? He felt himself sweating, and another hot gust of indigestion burbled up in his throat. He longed to open his half of the booth and let some fresh air in.

"How long? I can't tell you *that*," she said, in an oddly coquettish tone, like a woman who'd been asked her age at a dinner party. "I just need to know what happens to people who have committed grievous sins. Is Hell real? Do you really go there? Is it for eternity? Is there any way out?"

"Now, now," Father DiGennaro said, "you're jumping the gun here. We're getting way ahead of ourselves. Let's leave Hell out of the picture altogether and let's just talk about—"

"Why can't you give me a straight answer?" she demanded. "Why can't anyone *ever* give me a straight answer?"

He remained silent, not wanting to throw any potential fuel on the fire. He took the cell phone from his pocket and held it low, so that she wouldn't see its glow.

"I can't go on like this," she said, her face just inches from the screen that divided them. "Don't you understand that? Life is just a . . . a dead tree, with dead leaves that fall forever. They fall and fall and fall, and there's nothing but more dead leaves to fall after that."

Father DiGennaro could not help but be reminded of the Tree of Life motif with which the cathedral was imbued, from its doors made to look like overlapping planks of wood to its two-hundred-foot-tall spire. Was she reacting on some level to that? He would have to tread with extreme caution.

"I'd get out if I could," the woman was saying, "but I don't know how. I don't want to go from bad to worse. You can certainly see why I wouldn't want to do that, can't you?"

"Of course I can," he said, his finger hovering over the phone, not wanting to break the seal or the sacrament of the confessional but wondering if it wasn't time to call 911. "Of course I can." The air in the booth had become cloying. He felt a sheen of sweat forming under his clerical collar, and he hastily undid the top button on his shirt. How he wished he had that Maalox with him now.

"Non era ancor di là Nesso arrivato," she suddenly recited, *"quando noi ci mettemmo per un bosco, che da neun sentiero era segnato."*

Father DiGennaro, who had spent several years in Rome, knew a perfect accent when he heard one.

"Non fronda verde, ma di color fosco; no rami schietti, ma nadosi e 'nvolti; non pomi v'eran, ma stecchi con tosco."

And he also knew his Dante. She was reciting from the *Inferno,* the lines describing the wood of the self-murderers, where the damned souls were tortured forever, bound into gnarled tree limbs studded with poisonous thorns. A chill ran down his spine. *"Non han si aspri sterpi né si folti quelle fiere selvagge che 'n odio hanno, tra Cecina e Corneto i luoghi cólti."*

There was no better indication of her intentions, or her state of mind, than this—she was contemplating suicide. But when he tried to punch the tiny buttons on his phone, his thick fingers, damp with perspiration, misdialed. His left arm tingled.

And the booth, it seemed, had become darker.

He had to get out, and rising from his chair, he was almost overcome by dizziness. He swept the curtain of the confessional aside, and stumbled out into the dimly lighted cathedral. A sudden draft extinguished a bank of candles, and glancing up, he saw a plastic tarp drifting down from the gloom of the apse . . . trailed by the cardinal's red hats, like so many dead leaves.

A rivulet of sweat ran down his back, and he felt himself in the grip of something strange. His left arm was aching, and his breath was coming in short, shallow bursts.

He took hold of the curtain on the penitent's side of the booth, and yanked it open. He had never done such a thing in his life.

Nor had he seen what he saw then.

Her veil thrown back, her fur coat open, the woman stared up at him with a face that was at once as beautiful as any he had ever known—her eyes were wide, and even in the shadows, looked violet—and as terrible, too. Beneath the taut white skin, and for just a split second, he caught a glimpse of a gleaming white skull, and the very air seemed diffused with the scent of corruption. His heart seized up in his chest—it felt like a fist clenching—and his legs crumpled. But even as he fell to the floor, the cell phone skittering across the flagstones, he was unable to tear his eyes away from her awful and implacable gaze.

❧

The cell phone glowed at her feet as Kathryn watched the priest collapse. Snatching it up, she dialed 911, reported the incident, and before the operator could ask her anything more, flicked it closed and gently replaced it in the priest's hand.

But she could tell that he was already as dead as dead could be. She envied him.

Then she descended the steps of the cathedral as fast as her sharp heels and the blowing snow would allow her. Cyril saw her coming and held open the rear door of the limousine.

"Quickly," was all she said.

The moment the door was closed, she raised the interior partition, and the car swerved away from the curb.

Eyes closed, she rested her head against the back of the leather seat. A blast of cold Chicago air buffeted the car as the tires swooshed through the salt and slush. In the far distance, she thought she could already detect the wailing siren of an ambulance.

Take your time, she thought. *Let the man rest in peace.*

The limo was warm and dark and comfortable inside, like a cocoon, and as she reclined there, listening to the siren race past in the opposite direction, she wondered if there was any reason for her to stay in this city any longer. With Randolph dead—and how many husbands, pray tell, had preceded him?—perhaps it was time for her to reinvent herself yet again, to decamp for another country, another continent, under another name . . . as she had done countless times before. There was only one thing she kept constant in her peregrinations, and that was her first name. She always employed some variation on Caterina; it was the only way she could hold on to any identity at all.

But she had grown so weary of life . . . and death. She felt as if she had been marching in this solemn parade forever, with no end in sight. Had she known what that strongbox contained, so many centuries ago in Florence, she would never have opened it, never have risked Benvenuto's wrath, or subjected herself to this . . . nightmare from which there was no awakening. If there was any hope for finishing the dreadful course she was on—for starting life again in its natural course, or ending it fairly, here and now—then that hope lay in *La Medusa*.

And in David Franco's being able to find it.

She had sent others—treasure hunters, mystics, once even an Interpol detective—but all had either given up in frustration . . . or vanished off the face of the earth. Palliser was only the last in a long line. Although she had no way of knowing for sure, she felt that she, too, was caught up in some vast malignant web, and that there was a great evil spider brooding at its edge, sensing any vibration upon the strands.

How long would it be before the spider sensed a new intruder?

The storm outside was picking up, and by the time the limo was approaching her lakefront building, the streetlights were bobbing in the wind, and the snow was swirling in the air.

But pacing back and forth in front of the steps, as if oblivious to the storm raging around him, she saw a young man, his hood drawn, his hands stuffed down in his coat pockets, and she immediately knew who it was.

"Cyril, let me out in front," she said over the car intercom.

"Are you sure? I'm almost at the garage entrance. Whatever you—"

"Let me out!"

Without another word, he pulled the car up at the curb, and Mrs. Van Owen jumped out, gathering her fur coat around her.

David turned around and threw his hood back. With the wind whipping his thick brown hair into a frenzy, the snow sticking to his cheeks and eyelashes, and an absolutely tormented look in his eye, he stared into her face. She had the impression he wanted to grab her by the fur collar of her coat and shake her like a kitten.

"Did you mean what you said?" he demanded.

"You mean about the money?"

"Yes," he said, but waving it away as if it were only a secondary consideration. "I mean the rest of it."

Ah, the promise to save his sister. "I did."

"Every word?"

"Every word."

He was studying her face, as if he were trying to reconcile it with some other image or impression. She could see him wrestling with himself right before her eyes, trying to believe in something that could never, in any rational terms, make sense. She was afraid to say anything more lest she accidentally deter him. The swaying sodium light overhead threw his features into a sickly light, then into deep shadow, and back again.

But the haunted expression never left his eyes.

"I'll hold you to it," he said, as if issuing a threat.

"I'd expect you to."

There was something more he wanted to say—she could see the words almost forming on his lips—but then he must have thought better of it. She suspected she knew what it was—he wanted to demand some further proof, some ironclad guarantee, some assurance that he was not being duped.

But what stopped him was the overwhelming need—and desire—to believe. It's what stopped anyone from questioning his or her faith beyond a certain point. Who wants to burn down the only house they can bear to live in?

"I will leave tomorrow," he said, and Kathryn nodded.

"I'll have all the arrangements made immediately," she said.

And then, raising his hood back over his head, David turned and marched away, leaving a trail of wet footprints on the snowy sidewalk. Pulling her fur collar up around her face, she watched him go, wondering all the while if this was to be her savior . . . or only more bait for the spider?

Part Two

Chapter 11

The moment the plane taxied up to the gate at Galileo Galilei Airport, David was out of his first-class seat and waiting in the aisle. Over his shoulder, he had the black leather valise in which he carried perfect copies of the Cellini papers and the all-important drawing of *La Medusa*. Too irreplaceable to travel with, the originals had been secreted, for safekeeping, in the upper regions of the Newberry book silo.

True to her word, Mrs. Van Owen—or her travel consultant—had made all the necessary arrangements virtually overnight. And while most people were still digesting their Christmas dinners, David was clearing Customs. A uniformed driver was waiting for him, and they drove straight to the Grand—an eighteenth-century palazzo that had been converted into one of Florence's most luxurious hotels. An opulently furnished suite had been reserved in his name, the bedroom walls decorated with faded frescoes of a courtier and his lady wandering through a cypress grove filled with songbirds. The birds, and the grisaille tint with which they were rendered, were plainly a tribute to another of the city's Renaissance masters, Paolo Uccello—whose last name, literally translated, meant "birds"—and it reminded David that he was back in his spiritual home, the cradle of Western art and culture.

Only now it was more than a vast, open-air museum. It was a vault that might hold the key to his sister's very life.

And he couldn't afford to waste a second of his time there.

It was a cold but sunny Sunday, and even though David had once lived and studied in Florence, he still had to reorient himself to the crooked, narrow streets, lined with ochre buildings several stories high. As a Fulbright scholar, he had walked these streets with a crumpled map, a Eurail pass, and maybe fifty bucks' worth of lire in his pocket, and he found it strange to be navigating them again now, under such different circumstances. Several times he passed a café that he remembered having lingered in, or a gallery that he recalled visiting. Waiting for some traffic to pass—the Italians, he could see, still drove like madmen—he spotted the blue shutters of the little pensione he had once stayed in.

The Grand it was not.

Crossing the Ponte Vecchio, the old bridge with its ancient jumble of jewelers' shops and tradesmen's studios, he stopped to catch his breath and watch the Arno River, rushing below. In the summertime, the river was often reduced to a trickle, but at this time of year it was running high, its greenish water churning wildly under the graceful arches. Of all the city bridges, this had always been the most beautiful, and as a result it was the only one spared in the bombings of the Second World War. Hitler, who had always considered himself a connoisseur of art, had made a visit to Florence in 1938 and taken a special fancy to it. The Luftwaffe had subsequently been given his express orders to keep it safe.

It might be the only thing, David thought, which could ever be said to his credit.

The bridge was busy, but not so crazy as it was in the summertime, when hordes of tourists descended on its many shops. The Florentines themselves were a fairly sober and hardheaded lot, at least by Italian standards, and went about their business immune to the rich history in every corner of their hometown. On many of the older buildings, the Medici insignia—a triangle of colored balls—was still incised in the stone above the doorways, and in the main square of the town—the Piazza della Signoria—a plaque marked the very spot where the mad Dominican priest, Girolamo Savonarola, along with two of his followers, had been burned at the stake in 1498. For a few years, in his quest to purify Florence in the eyes of God, Savonarola had held the city in his grasp, murdering and mutilating his critics, pillaging the homes of the high and mighty, looking for anything of worldly value—from "sacrilegious" art to silver buckles and ivory buttons—to feed the flames of his bonfires . . . until the city had awakened, as if from a trance, and thrown off his spell with the same barbarity that he had exercised it.

David's steps took him across the broad expanse of the city square, and toward its most remarkable site—the *Loggia dei Lanzi*, and its pantheon of statuary known the world over. Here, Cellini's own masterpiece, the heroic bronze figure of Perseus, held aloft the severed head of the Medusa. Even the sunshine did nothing to detract from the sinister power of Cellini's sculpture, from its indelible image of the nude warrior, clothed only in helmet and sandals, with his eyes still averted from the deadly visage of his prize, and his feet planted on her corpse. In an especially grim touch, the Gorgon's blood spurted over the lip of the marble pedestal on which the entire statue was raised. As David approached, he saw a tour guide with a purple iris, the official flower of Florence, stuck in the lapel of her overcoat, leading a group of lackadaisical college students to the base of the *Perseus*. Several of them were carrying notebooks, and one held out a tiny recorder as she spoke.

"Can anyone tell me," the guide prompted them, in heavily accented English, "who was this Perseus?" While the students all suddenly dropped their heads and waited, pens poised, David loitered on the fringe of the group. The guide—a slender young woman with black hair pulled back from her face and hastily tied in a ponytail with a thick blue rubber band—took note of him, but she didn't seem to mind his listening in. Maybe she was glad to have someone who looked interested.

"A king?" one of the girls hazarded.

"That is close," she said, "that is close. He was the grandson of a king."

"So that makes him a prince, right?" the girl said, proudly, twirling her pen.

The guide made a wavering motion in the air with one hand. "It is not so simple," she said. "I will explain."

And as David hovered in the rear, the guide told the story of Danaë, the most beautiful maiden in all of Greece, who was impregnated by Zeus, the king of the gods. "She lived in a palace, all of bronze, and Zeus came down to her as a shower of gold."

"I've seen that painting," another girl piped up, "the one by Rembrandt," and the guide nodded encouragingly.

"Yes, you are right," she said. "And this son, he was named Perseus. He grew up with his mother, on a far-off island, where the king fell in love with Danaë, too, and wanted to marry her. But he did not want to keep her son around."

"I know what that's like," one student joshed, and a couple of them snickered.

"And so he said to Perseus, 'I want you to make me a special marriage present,' and Perseus, who was very brave but also foolhardy, said, 'I will give you anything you ask.' And the king said, 'Then you will get me the thing I want most—and that is the head of the Medusa.'"

This turn of events seemed to interest the students even more.

"But no one could kill the Medusa," the guide went on, her voice rising, as if she wanted to make sure that even David could hear. "If you looked into the eyes of the Medusa, you would turn to stone." The Notre Dame kid turned around and gave David a curious look. "The Gorgons were immortal, and the waters from their secret pool, if you could collect it without being killed, offered eternal life."

David suddenly felt as if this woman with the iris in her lapel—a woman he had never even seen before—knew why he'd come to Florence and what he was looking for. He'd been in the city no more than a few hours, but he felt as if he'd already been exposed.

"I guess he did the job," the Notre Damer said, "or this statue wouldn't be here."

"Yes, but how?" the guide said. "Do you know how he killed the Medusa without even looking at her?"

When there was no reply, she said, "He called upon his friends, the gods."

"That would help," another student said.

"Yes, it did. Do you know who is Hermes?"

"The guy on the FTD commercials," Notre Dame said, but the reference seemed to baffle the guide.

"The messenger of the gods," a girl put in. "He could fly, I think."

"*Sì, sì*," the guide said, clapping her hands encouragingly, "and he gave a magic sword to Perseus, a sword that could cut off the head of the Gorgon. Another friend to Perseus was called Athena—"

"The goddess of wisdom," the same girl volunteered, and the guide beamed at her.

"Yes, Athena, she gave him a shield, a very . . ." she searched for the word, then said, "*reflecting* shield, like a mirror, so he would not have to look at her. Also, he had a hat, a helmet, that made him . . . invisible."

And so, according to the myth, the heroic Perseus had journeyed to the distant isle where the three Gorgons lived and, using these strange gifts, had slain the one named Medusa. And, for allegorical reasons that art historians still liked to debate, the Duke de'Medici had commissioned this monument, this retelling of the ancient story, to be erected in the central square of Florence. Originally planned to stand only a couple of *braccia* high, Cellini had increased its proportions in the process of composition, and raised it on a tall marble base adorned with four niches, holding beautifully modeled figures of Zeus, Athena, Hermes, and the young Perseus with his mother. These figures were so stunning, in fact, that when Eleonora de

Toledo, the duke's wife, first saw them as freestanding sculptures, she insisted that they were too exquisitely wrought to be wasted on a pedestal, and announced that they would be better suited to her own apartments in the palace. Cellini, though grateful for the praise, was not about to shortchange his masterwork, so before she had time to claim them, he raced back and soldered them into their assigned niches, where they stood between the sculpture above and the four bronze plaques below, illustrating scenes from Perseus's later adventures.

It was just such maneuvers, David reflected, that had made Cellini, in his own life, one of the most infuriating men in Europe. In the service of his art—and his ego—he was forever crossing swords with princes, popes, and noblemen. And when he wasn't being celebrated for his achievements, he was being hauled into court, or hauled off to jail, on charges of everything from murder (he confessed to several, though claiming self-defense every time), to sodomy (not so uncommon a practice in those days), to failing to pay child support. (The Florentine courts were very progressive for their time.) Perhaps it was this selfsame transgressive nature—the willingness to act boldly, even in plain defiance of secular law and holy authority—that had first endeared him to David. As someone who lived his own life strictly by the rules—working hard, avoiding trouble, winning every academic prize within reach—David had been irresistibly drawn to this figure who took life by the reins and rode it anywhere he chose. Whose art, and writings (he had also authored treatises on goldsmithing and sculpture), revealed a mind that was always in quest of new knowledge, new techniques, new frontiers.

Judging from the *Key to Life Eternal,* he had even searched for a way to cross the line between life and death . . . and claimed to have found it. That was one aspect of his career which the Van Owen papers had revealed in a way that neither David, nor any other scholar, had ever known.

"And who can see the *miracolo* in the back?" the guide was now saying, crooking one finger at the students to draw them around to the rear of the statue. David, tagging along, knew what she was going to point out.

Nodding at David as if to give him permission to join the group, she was calling attention to the fantastically ornate helmet on Perseus's head. Wings sprouted from either side of the visor, along with a crouching gargoyle on the top, but it was in back that Cellini had created his optical illusion. Hidden among the folds and curlicues of the helmet was a stern human face, with a long Roman nose, a lush moustache, and piercing eyes under arching brows. You could look at the back of the helmet and never see it there, but once it had been pointed out, you could never again miss it.

"There's a face, looking out," the girl with the twirling pen announced.

The guide clapped her hands together again. "That's good. Very good. This, I think, is the face of Cellini himself."

And David agreed. Not only was it just like Cellini to bring off such a stunt, the visage also bore a resemblance to the only known depiction of the artist, rendered by Vasari in later life. It was one further proof of his ingenuity, or, in the academic lingo that David had so come to detest, his "reverse iconography and intratextual complexity."

Several of the students dutifully scribbled in their notebooks, and the guide, checking her watch, said, "Come, we must now look at the Palazzo Vecchio," waving her hand at the massive and forbidding wall of the Medici palace that brooded over the square. With the students trudging after her, the guide, whose own enthusiasm never seemed to flag, cast a look back at David, who smiled and raised a hand in farewell. David mouthed the words, *"Grazie mille,"* and the guide tilted her pretty head and said, *"Prego."*

❧

An hour later, after completing his own tour of the piazza, David was sitting inside a nearby café, nursing a cup of cappuccino to stave off the jet lag and making some notes for the next day. The Biblioteca Laurenziana would open its doors at ten, and he planned to be the first one through them. There was a lot of work he wished to do in their archives, and he was drawing up a list of his priorities when, out of nowhere, a cyclone hit his table.

The opposite chair was yanked back, a body dropped into it, and a voice called out to a passing waiter, "*Due ova fritte, il pane tostato, ed un espresso. Pronto!*"

Glancing up, David saw the tour guide unbuttoning her overcoat and scanning the tabletop as if on the lookout for anything she could eat while waiting for her eggs and toast to get there.

"*Buon giorno,*" David said, surprised but amused.

"*Buon giorno,*" the guide replied. "*Lei parla l'Italiano?*"

"*Sì,*" David said, glad to start giving his rusty Italian a tryout. "*Ma sono fuori di pratica.*" But I'm out of practice.

The guide nodded quickly three times, and said, "*Ciò e buono.*" That's okay.

The waiter put a cup of espresso in front of her, and the guide downed half of it in one gulp, snapping her fingers before the waiter could get away and saying, "*Un altro.*"

While the waiter went to get another, David introduced himself. "*Mi chiamo* David Franco."

"Olivia Levi," the guide replied, taking the band from her pony-tail and shaking her hair loose. Olivia—it was the perfect name for her, David thought. Eyes as black as olives, and skin the color of the espresso foam. "And, if you do not mind, we will speak English."

David felt vaguely insulted. Was his Italian so bad that she'd given up already?

"It is for me," Olivia said. "I must use it so that the *studenti* don't have any reason to laugh when I talk."

"I thought you did an exceptional job."

Olivia blew a sigh of disgust. "That is all it is—a job. I must do it for the money. Everything," she said, lifting her hands from the table in resignation, "I must do for the money."

She had all the theatricality of the Italians, too, David thought. "Leading tour groups must keep you pretty busy. Especially in a place like Florence."

"But it keeps me from my work. My *serious* work. I am not a guide; I am a writer."

"Really?" David said intrigued. "What do you write about?"

"What do I write about?" she said, gesturing at the wonders of Florence surrounding them. "The greatest collection of art ever produced in one place, at one time. What other city can claim Michelangelo and Botticelli, Verrocchio and Masaccio, Leonardo and Ghiberti, Brunelleschi and Cellini? They were all here. Their work, it is *still* here. And I do not even mention yet Petrarch and Boccaccio and the immortal Dante!"

"But you Florentines gave Dante a pretty rough time," David said with a smile. "Exiling him forever in 1302, as I recall."

Olivia stopped dead and gave David a more appraising look, as if to acknowledge that this was someone who might know a little something, after all.

"Not *my* people. My people never had a say in anything. They lived on the Via Guidici."

In other words, she was telling him that they lived in the Jewish quarter.

"Even Cosimo, who was supposed to be our friend, he closed the Jewish banks in 1570 and forced everyone, whether they liked it or not, to live in that damned ghetto."

The waiter set a plate and another espresso down in front of Olivia, who lowered her head—the ringlets of her jet-black hair artfully framing her narrow face—and dug in unashamedly.

What amused David about the Florentines—and it was certainly true of Olivia just now—was the way that they spoke of their history almost in the present tense. Olivia dropped the name of Cosimo de'Medici, dead for five hundred years, like he was a personal acquaintance, and as if the removal of the Jews from much of Florence was something that happened just yesterday. In fact, David knew, the Florentine Jews had gradually regained many of their rights, and by 1800 had once again been allowed to live anywhere in the city that they chose. There was even a city ordinance on the books that prohibited malicious references to Jewry from the public stage. The ghetto was gradually eradicated—there was no trace of it remaining—though the undercurrent of anti-Semitism that ran through so much of Europe lingered long after.

An undercurrent that Hitler, in his own time, had brought roiling to the surface.

"Your family survived the war then?" David said hopefully.

Mopping up some yolk with the bread, Olivia said, "A few. Not so many. Many of them, I am told, were sent to Mauthausen."

A concentration camp where thousands of Italian Jews were gassed.

"I'm sorry," David said, and she shrugged her shoulders wearily.

"After all this time, what can you say? Many of the Italians, they hid the Jews in convents and cloisters. But the Pope? He did nothing. And the Fascists? They liked their brown shirts and their boots, and they liked killing shopkeepers and clerks; it was easy. But once that was done, so were they. They were cowards at heart." She scraped the plate for the last of the eggs, as David pictured in his mind's eye Mussolini hanging by his heels from a meat hook.

"Where do you live now?" David asked.

"You know the Giubbe Rosse, in the Piazza della Repubblica?"

"No, I don't."

She shrugged again and said, "It's the best café in Firenze. I have an apartment next door to it." Having cleaned every crumb from her plate, she leaned back in the chair and fumbled in her pocket for a pack of cigarettes. She held them out to David, who declined, then lighted one herself.

"But what are you?" Olivia asked. "You are American. But a tourist?"

David wasn't sure if this was just polite conversation, or if he was being sized up as a potential customer.

"I'm actually here on some business."

"You do not look like a businessman."

David decided he'd take that as a compliment. "I'm researching something. I work in Chicago, at a library."

"I have been to Chicago," Olivia said triumphantly. "It was very cold. And I also lived in New York, for five years." She spread her fingers to emphasize the point. "I was writing a dissertation, at Columbia." She said it like Colombia the country. "Now I work here."

"On a book?" David asked.

A furtive look crossed the tour guide's face. "A very big book," she said. "A history—I cannot tell you more. I have been working on it for seven years."

"So you must be nearly done?" David said encouragingly.

But Olivia shook her head and exhaled a cloud of smoke over one shoulder. "No. I have met with much resistance. And it will cause a lot of arguments." Glancing at her watch, she said, "And now I must go. I have a private client for a tour. Where are you staying?"

"The Grand."

"The Grand?" David could see another reappraisal going on in Olivia's eyes. "And who is it you work for? What library is this?"

"The Newberry. It's a private institution."

"And are you going to work at the university here?"

"No, at the Biblioteca Laurenziana."

It was as if David could actually hear the wheels spinning in her head, like a slot machine that was coming up all cherries. He expected another volley of questions, and was beginning to wonder if he should have been quite so forthcoming. Was it really just by chance that she had followed him to the café and joined him? Or was he being paranoid? Ever since that guy had tried to run him down in the street, he'd been uncharacteristically suspicious.

Olivia stood up, taking one last drag on her cigarette. "I will be late," she said, dropping the butt in her empty espresso cup. "But I thank you for the meal."

"You're welcome," David said.

"You may join another of my tours, anytime. Also for free."

"Careful," David replied, "I might take you up on that."

She smiled and said, "It is possible I could teach you a thing or two."

And then, as he pondered the full import of that, she hurried off across the square, the tails of her old coat flapping around her. He was still looking when she turned her head unexpectedly and caught him. Her laugh rang out across the piazza.

Chapter 12

❧

Damn, damn, damn. What should he do now, Escher wondered, from his vantage point across from the café. The girl was leaving, and David was staying, but he couldn't very well tail both of them.

Who was she? An accomplice of some kind? Or just a tour guide who'd taken a fancy to the guy who'd joined her group?

On Ambassador Schillinger's orders, Escher had followed David all the way from Chicago, never more than a few hundred yards behind. While David flew in the first-class compartment, Escher had squeezed into the last available seat—back by the bathrooms—in coach.

And while David traveled into the city in a private car, Escher had followed in an unlicensed cab.

And as David had checked into the Grand Hotel, Escher had lurked in the lobby. He was still carrying his overnight bag slung over one sturdy shoulder.

On a hunch, he followed the girl. She was good-looking, though with less meat on her bones than he liked. Maybe in her late twenties, she walked with the brisk pace of someone who was intent on getting a lot done. As she passed a trash bin, she pulled the iris out of her lapel and dropped it in. Escher snorted in approval, thinking she must have worn the flower solely for the benefit of the tourists.

A few blocks from the piazza, she ducked into a used-books store and came out half an hour later with a fat volume tucked under one arm. With her other hand, she was fishing in her coat pocket, and when he realized that she was looking for her car keys, he hailed the first passing cab, jumped in, then had the driver wait until she stopped beside a beat-up little Fiat and got in. The thing was more dents than car.

"Follow it," he told the cabbie, tossing some bills onto the front seat.

She drove like she did everything else—fast and direct, cutting through the traffic like a knife, honking her horn, whipping around the traffic circles, taking corners so sharply that pedestrians had to jump back to keep their feet from being run over.

"This woman's crazy!" the cabbie said, doing his best to keep up.

"Just don't lose her," Escher said, tossing another bill.

At the Piazza della Repubblica, she went up and down the local streets a couple of times, apparently looking for a parking spot—in Florence, it was never easy—before someone in front of a busy café pulled out. Another car made a beeline for the spot, but the little Fiat, clattering like a tin can, cut it off at the pass and dove in headfirst, one tire bumping over the curb, the back end sticking out into the street.

Escher could hear a brief shouting match, but the girl grabbed her book, locked the car—who would ever steal that hunk of junk, he wondered?—and marched up the steps of a small, dilapidated apartment building without so much as a glance back.

Once she was inside, Escher got out of his cab and watched the windows. She appeared on the third floor, yanking open some curtains, and when he consulted the apartment roster, he was able to deduce that her name was Levi, first initial O.

He'd have to run it by Schillinger in Chicago and see if it rang any bells. If not, Schillinger could always kick it upstairs.

He waited in the cold for another hour or two before deciding to call it quits for the day. He was damn tired of running around. He hadn't been to Florence in years—the last time he'd been there, he was part of the official Swiss Guard accompanying the Pope—but he remembered where Julius Jantzen, his local contact, lived, and fortunately it wasn't far.

He set out on foot, into the increasingly seedy districts of the city, now inhabited by immigrants and foreign workers. Many of the shops had signs in Arabic and Farsi, and the streets were littered with dirt and refuse. This part of town was definitely off the tourists' maps. There were dozens of cheap hotels, betting parlors, and kebab joints, punctuated, oddly enough, by the occasional ancient church, or—and wasn't it another sign of the times—a makeshift mosque.

On the corner of a dismal street, there was a sliver of a building painted a faded orange, with a tobacconist's shop on the ground floor. Escher brushed past a few young men loitering in front and into a shadowy courtyard surrounding a stagnant green fishpond. At the back there was a sheet-metal door—the only thing in the building that looked new and intact—and dropping his overnight bag on the threshold, he banged on the metal with his closed fist three times.

He eyed the window beside the door and saw two fingers part the dingy blind. Stepping back to make sure Julius could get a good look at him, he heard the locks being turned and the bolts unlatched, and while waiting he noticed one of the young men he'd just passed— they looked like Turks to him—watching him from the street.

"What are you looking at?" Escher called out.

The man didn't answer, but his dark eyes lingered on the overstuffed bag on the threshold. Ernst had half a mind to go back and kick the shit out of him.

But the door opened partway, revealing Julius's hand waving him in. Escher slipped in, and the door slammed closed behind him. After the locks and latches had all been resealed, Jantzen turned around and looked his visitor up and down.

"You shouldn't have come here."

"Nice to see you, too."

"I told them, I'm done. They have already ruined my life."

Looking around the place—one lousy room with a cracked linoleum floor and an unmade bed behind a Chinese screen—Escher thought he might have a point.

"You're never done," Escher said, "You know that."

Julius Jantzen had once been a respectable doctor in Zurich, best known for his work with Swiss athletes and cyclists. He had also been a pioneer in the use of anabolic steroids, blood oxygenation, and other performance-enhancing techniques. Escher had been one of his best clients . . . before it all came crashing down.

"What are you doing here, anyway?" Julius asked, brushing some unruly curls of hair back off his forehead. He looked like a sick little rabbit, with stooped shoulders and a concave chest under a flannel shirt and rumpled trousers. Escher suspected him of using some of his own pharmaceuticals—just not the right kind.

"Running a fool's errand, if you ask me." He threw some newspapers off the couch and sat down. "What are you going to offer me to drink?"

Julius let out a breath of disgust, went into the kitchen, and came back with a cold bottle of Moretti.

"You've gone native," Escher said, raising the bottle, then drinking off half of it at once. A soccer match was playing on the TV, with the sound muted. Escher had grown to prefer American football. More action, more scoring, more physical contact.

Julius sat down in what was clearly his favorite chair, a battered Naugahyde monster next to a side table littered with a full ashtray, a beer bottle, a TV remote, and a scattering of pistachio shells. Now that he looked around, Escher saw that there were pistachio shells all over the floor, too.

"Why don't you get your pistachios already shelled?"

"I enjoy the exercise."

Julius turned the sound back up, and for a while they watched the game in a wary, if companionable, silence. Escher was tired and could use a bit of a boost himself. Back in Rome, Jantzen had visited the barracks once every month or two with a bulging satchel of everything from B-12 to Oxycontin. To stay in the Swiss Guard you had to keep fit, and with the help of some regular injections Escher had always remained ahead of the pack. But judging from the looks of Jantzen now, and the dump he lived in, his dealing days were over. Escher had been sent here for two things—a gun (there was no way to smuggle one aboard the flight from Chicago) and a base to work from.

He would take the gun, but he'd sooner check into any flophouse than try to sleep here even for one night.

Still, he put his head back, closed his eyes, and gradually drifted off. When he awoke with a start, the soccer match was over, and the evening news was on. No daylight at all was slanting in through the front blinds.

And he was alone.

"Julius!" he called out. "Where the hell are you?"

He got up, looked behind the Chinese screen, then went down the short hall, between a galley kitchen and an immense old wardrobe, to the bathroom. But he wasn't in there, either. Nor was there any note lying around.

"Jantzen!" he called out one last time, and as if out of nowhere, the man appeared behind him, in a white surgical apron. The door to the wardrobe was open, and Julius said, "Christ, you snore."

"Where were you?" Escher said, peering around the wardrobe door. There was no back to the thing, and a bright light washed into the hallway from a room tucked away behind the cabinet's false front.

"Working," Jantzen said, stepping back through the armoire, with Escher close behind.

No one would ever have guessed the lab was there. It was spotlessly clean and antiseptic, with bright fluorescent lighting overhead, an examining table, sink, and metal racks well stocked with everything from medical equipment to drug supplies. And suddenly, it all made much more sense to Escher.

"I put out something you might want," Julius said, gesturing at a Glock nine-millimeter, with its silencer already attached to its muzzle, on the counter. Escher was glad to see that Jantzen had followed orders, and he picked up the gun and examined it. "It's loaded, so please be careful," Jantzen said, as he finished counting out a pile of pills into waiting vials. "Are you hungry?"

"Yes."

"There's a decent little place down the street," he said, brushing his hands on his apron, then taking it off and folding it on the examining table.

"Looks like you've got quite an operation here," Escher said, impressed.

"We have a small, but loyal, clientele."

When they were back in the hall, Jantzen slid a panel across the back of the armoire and pulled a bunch of old shirts and jackets across on the rod.

"You can leave your things here," Jantzen said, "and spend the night on the sofa. Tomorrow, I expect, you'll want to find better accommodations."

Escher said nothing though he had no intention of waiting that long. He rummaged in his bag for a pack of cigarettes as Jantzen pulled on an overcoat, stuck a silly Cossack-style hat on his head, and undid the locks. He had no sooner thrown the last bolt and cracked the door open—"The restaurant's run by Spaniards"—when the door flew back and he was hit so hard by a flying tackle that he was carried halfway into the room, with a dark-skinned man in a sweatshirt still gripping his shoulders. Escher looked up just as two more men—the Turks who'd been watching him when he arrived— charged into the room, one with a knife drawn, the other holding a gun.

The one with the knife kicked the door closed while the one with the gun pointed it at Escher, who held up his hands to show he wasn't armed, and ordered him to move away from the bag.

Escher backed off, and the gunman knelt by it, quickly groping through the things inside.

"You can keep the cigarettes," Escher said, "if you get out now."

"Shut up," the man said before giving up on the bag and kicking it aside. Escher figured the Turks must have thought he was making a delivery.

"You've made a mistake," Escher said, and the gunman fired a warning shot into the sofa pillow, six inches from his arm. A plume of feathers erupted into the air.

"Ahmet, put the gun down," Jantzen pleaded, still on the floor.

So he knows him, Escher thought. *A customer. But how much does this customer know?*

"In back," Ahmet said, gesturing with the gun toward the hallway—and the armoire.

Too much.

Jantzen got to his feet, blood trickling from the corner of his mouth, and both he and Escher were herded toward the wardrobe.

Ahmet and the others let Jantzen push the clothes to one side, slide the panel back, and step through. Jantzen flicked the lights on, and Escher moved calmly but deliberately toward the Glock 9 on the counter.

"What are you doing there?" Ahmet said, his view blocked by Escher's back. "Stop now, or I will shoot you."

Escher discreetly picked up the gun, turned slowly with his head cocked to one side as if to signal acquiescence, and shot Ahmet point-blank in the chest. He dropped to his knees, mouth gaping, and the other two looked stunned. Escher took advantage of their shock to shoot the one in the sweatshirt, too, the bullet whipping his head back against a metal rack; but Jantzen was in the way of the third one, who hurled his knife wildly, then rushed from the room, screaming.

"Get out of the way," Escher said, pushing past Jantzen, whose own eyes were bugging out of his head, and followed the last one out into the apartment. He was already at the door, struggling to turn a lock and get it open, when Escher said, "Hold on, I'm not going to hurt you."

The man turned his head, his face twisted in fear, and Escher said, "Step away from the door."

His fingers fumbled at the lock again, and the door was just starting to open when Escher shot him. The bullet caught him in the shoulder, but the man barely reacted. Escher had to leap at him, grab hold of his sleeve, and pull him back into the room.

"No, no, don't shoot!" the man shouted, putting his hands together and crumpling to his knees. "Don't shoot me!"

But Escher knew that some things, once begun, had to be finished.

He pressed the gun to the kneeling man's forehead, fired, and let him drop to the floor like a sack of potatoes.

He heard Jantzen throwing up in the hallway.

That would be just one more thing to clean up, he thought.

Wedging the gun under his belt, he stepped away from the body. Christ, what a mess. He considered calling his boss, the fancy ex-ambassador, but he knew he had a reputation already for a certain hotheadedness. And for all he knew, it was Schillinger who was responsible for this whole fiasco. Had he sent Escher off to Italy in secret, on his own initiative? An initiative that had conflicted with someone else's greater plan?

The pool of blood was widening, and he had to step back again.

If that was the case, then Escher was caught in the gears of a colossal case of miscommunication—a place he always hated to be.

Or was it only what it seemed? A drug robbery gone wrong? Given Julius's clientele, that wasn't so hard to believe, either.

Now he regretted having been quite so hasty. If one of the Turks had been kept alive, he might have been able to get some answers out of him. Next time he'd have to remind himself to be more patient.

"Julius," he called out, rolling up his sleeves.

"What?" Jantzen replied, still doubled over and averting his gaze from the door.

"You ever going to stop puking?"

Jantzen replied with another dry heave before croaking, "What . . . the hell . . . do we do now?"

"Well," Escher said, putting aside his deeper ruminations, "I'd say we start with a mop and a pail. You do have them, don't you?"

Chapter 13

Cellini could tell from the slant of fading sunlight on the wall of the dungeon that it was almost time for his single meal of the day. He slumped in the corner, watching idly as a pair of tarantulas mated in the straw spilling from his mattress. He had grown used to them, along with the rats and other vermin that inhabited his tiny cell. After months of imprisonment, he might have missed them if they'd gone.

There was a shuffling tread outside, a clanging of keys, and the wooden door creaked open. While the guard stood outside with a drawn sword, the jailer, in clothes almost as soiled as the rags Cellini wore, carefully placed a pewter bowl filled with the usual cold gruel on the floor.

"Eat well," he said, stopping to admire the rough sketches that Cellini had scrawled on the wall with cinders and chalk. The centerpiece depicted Christ among a host of angels.

While he gazed with amazement, Cellini's own glance went to the door, and specifically its hinges. He had worked on loosening the real ones and replacing them with facsimiles made out of candle wax and rust since the day he arrived, and he was close to completing his task. When he had been taken to the Castel St. Angelo, he had declared no prison could hold him, and he hoped to prove it soon.

"Oh, and the Duke of Castro asked me to add this, since it's a feast day today," the jailer said, pulling a hunk of fresh bread from his pocket and dropping it beside the bowl.

"Tell Signor Luigi—the duke, I mean—that I look forward to thanking him soon, in person."

"Benvenuto, Benvenuto," the jailer said, shaking his head. "Why do you make things so hard on yourself? A man who can draw like that," he said, gesturing at the sketches, "can do anything. Tell the duke what he wants to know, beg forgiveness of the Pope, and you'll be a free man again."

"I can't confess to what I didn't do. I can't give back gold and jewels that I never stole."

The jailer, a simple soul, shrugged his shoulders. "These things are too much for me to understand."

He turned around and shuffled out, the door slamming closed behind him. The artificial hinges held, and despite himself, Cellini eagerly scuttled toward the food, dipping the bread in the cold slop and shoving it into his mouth with trembling fingers. A rat in the corner watched greedily.

It was only as he scraped up the last of the gruel with his tin spoon that he felt something crunch between his teeth, and he stopped chewing. Studying the bottom of the bowl, he saw an almost invisible shard glistening there, and his heart suddenly sank as the truth of what had just happened dawned on him.

He had been poisoned . . . and by a common enough method among princes and noblemen.

A powdered gem—a diamond—had been introduced into his food. Unlike other pulverized stones, the diamond kept its sharp edges and, instead of passing harmlessly through the body, its tiny pieces—no matter how fine—clung to the intestines and pierced the linings. The result was not only a slow and agonizing death, but one that could be confused with a host of natural afflictions. The duke, who had no doubt hatched the plan, could never be held accountable by his father that way.

Cellini keeled over, his forehead touching the damp floor, reciting a *Miserere* under his breath. It was just a matter of time—hours, or maybe a day or two—before he would begin to feel the effects.

But what then?

The shock of the thought actually brought him back up. What would happen to a man such as he, a man who had manufactured *La Medusa* and gazed into its magical depths? He would not die; he could not die.

But would he, then, be destined to suffer forever?

Suddenly, he had to wonder if his adventures in sorcery were not the making of his own doom. Hadn't Dr. Strozzi warned him?

But when had he ever listened to warnings?

The bulrushes, they had been one thing. The ones that had clung to his clothes in his escape from the Gorgon's pool, he had gathered in a bunch—not an easy task, as they continually appeared and vanished and reappeared—before swiftly twining them together and dipping the garland in a bath of molten silver. Settled upon the brow, like the laurel wreath upon the head of Dante, the finished piece granted the wearer the gift of invisibility.

By the standards of his trade, it was a comparatively simple procedure.

But the looking glass was quite another matter. When he had made it, he had been so intent on its creation that he had hardly stopped to think through its myriad implications. He had focused all his skills, all his cunning, on replicating the fearsome visage of the Gorgon he had slain. Countless hours had been spent in his studio, the midnight oil burning in the lamp, as he made models, then casts, for the front of the mirror. And though glassmaking had not been among his many talents, he had apprenticed himself for weeks to a master blower, who had taught him how to make the beveled glass in back.

And when he thought he had acquired the requisite skills, he made one mirror—just as he had told the Pope—as a gift for the Medici duchess, Eleonora de Toledo. (He was forever having to find ways to stay in her good graces.) To add some luster to its burnished niello finish, he had placed two rubies in the Gorgon's eyes.

And then, satisfied that he could accomplish the work, he had cast another.

This one was for himself, to achieve his lifelong dream.

This one was to award himself the gift of the gods themselves . . . the gift of everlasting life.

He had consulted Strozzi's books, he had pored over the grimoires from France and England, Portugal and Spain, and then, with the greatest care he had ever mustered, he had opened the flask containing the pale green water he had salvaged from the infernal pool. The waters of immortality that had returned with him, trapped in his boots.

With the mirror laid facedown on his workbench, he had poured the glistening liquid into the hollow of its back. The droplets swished and hissed in the tiny, lead-lined basin, moving and coagulating like mercury. It was almost as if they were struggling to get out, but Cellini quickly fixed the glass into place and sealed the edges tight. Under his breath, he recited the Latin incantation from Strozzi's book, the final benediction that would complete his task and forever empower his creation.

"Aequora of infinitio,
Beatus per radiant luna,
Una subsisto estus of vicis,
Quod tribuo immortalis beneficium."

And then, for good measure, he recited his own translation, in the vernacular tongue he preferred.

"The waters of eternity,
Blessed by the radiant moon,
Together stop the tide of time
And grant the immortal boon."

With the talisman made, only one step remained—to see if it would work. If it did, then anyone catching the moonlight in its glass, along with his own reflection, would find himself frozen in time forever, as unchanging as the image trapped in the glass.

Had anyone, Cellini wondered, ever accomplished so much as he? Could any artisan, in his own age or the ages to come, boast of such achievements?

He had sat back on his workbench, the lantern light reflected in the glass of *La Medusa* and felt . . . what? Exultation? Yes, but mixed with the bitter rue that came from knowing he could never trumpet it to the skies.

What he had done, no man could ever know.

If the Holy Roman Church were to learn of it, he would be burned at the stake. If kings and princes knew, he would be captured, imprisoned, and the fruits of his labor stolen. A race of immortal men, no doubt as corrupt and venal as their mortal counterparts, would spring up to overtake the world. No, the only sensible course was to keep *La Medusa* close and secret, its powers bestowed only on its creator, and on whatever worthy soul that creator chose to favor.

The lantern had sputtered, its last drops of oil consumed, and gone out. The workshop had been bathed in the light of the winter moon, full and white and cold as a glacier.

Cellini had slipped the chain onto the amulet, then looped it around his neck. Tiptoeing past Ascanio and the other apprentices, fast asleep downstairs, he stepped into the silent courtyard behind his house. Walls of stone rose on all sides. But high above, like a gleaming coin, the moon hung in a starry sky. His nervous breath fogged in the air.

Was he prepared to put his work to the ultimate test? Was he ready to accept any outcome, whether it be everlasting life . . . or sudden death? No grimoire guaranteed its results.

A shiver rippled down his spine, inspired by the chilly air, or the anticipation. With numbed fingers, he lifted *La Medusa,* the snarling face glaring into his own . . . and deliberately turned it over. The curvature of the glass twinkled in the moonlight.

His own face—with its prominent, hooked nose, coal-dark eyes, and luxuriant moustache—appeared in the mirror, but there was something strange going on, something that it took him a second to realize. It didn't feel like his reflection he was seeing . . . it felt as if he were already inside the mirror, and helplessly staring out.

The amulet itself seemed to come alive, as if the liquid inside had been brought to a sudden boil.

A dog howled from the alleyway and ran for the street.

Cellini could not tear his eyes away. He felt as if he were being drawn down into a whirlpool, around and around, down and down. His scalp prickled, and his skin erupted in a welter of goose bumps. *La Medusa* seemed to twist in his hand like a frightened bird, and before he could even think to let it go, he had felt his mind grow dim and his knees buckle beneath him. The cobblestones of the courtyard rose up like an engulfing wave.

"Are you done with your bowl?" the jailer asked through the iron grate in the door.

Cellini, still mourning over the poison he had just ingested, looked up from the floor, then nodded.

"Then pass it to me," the jailer said, and Cellini picked it up and carried it to the door.

"Tell me," he asked, "did Signor Luigi—forgive me, the Duke of Castro—himself prepare my food tonight?"

"Are you crazy? Of course not."

"Then who did? Anyone unusual?"

The jailer smiled. "Nothing gets by you, Benvenuto. It was prepared by a friend of the duke's."

Cellini waited.

"A man named Landi. He wore one of those loupes around his neck."

Of course, Cellini thought. Landi was the jeweler who'd tried to foist off the bad pearls on Eleonora in Florence; he had subsequently moved here, to Rome. How pleased he must have been to receive this deadly commission from the duke.

"Why do you ask?"

"You will know soon enough," Cellini replied, taking one last look into the bottom of the bowl, and noticing yet another minute splinter. He wet the tip of his finger, removed the shard, then passed the bowl sideways through the bars.

When the jailer had gone, he went to the window and placed the tiny fragment on the sill. How strange to be looking at something so small and yet so lethal. How many, he wondered, had he consumed?

But then, in the last light of the summer sun, he noticed something that made his heart spring up in his chest.

The shard had the tiniest hint of a greenish cast . . . as if it might be beryl, or some other semiprecious stone.

He examined it more closely. The sun had almost set over the Roman hills, but there was just enough light to catch that cast again. His mouth suddenly so dry he could barely breathe, he grabbed his spoon and pressed it down on the shard. There was a pleasing crunch, and when he lifted the spoon, a spot of harmless dust lay on the windowsill.

Cellini crumpled to the floor, knowing that he had been delivered . . . and by the hand of the unscrupulous jeweler. Landi had, no doubt, been given a diamond to complete the task, but had pocketed it instead, thinking a less-valuable gem would do the job just as well.

In that, he was mistaken.

But if Benvenuto had needed any further impetus to escape, this was it. His usefulness was at an end, and so long as it could be made to appear a natural death, his enemies were prepared to kill him now. He dug under his sodden mattress and removed the long ribbon of cloth strips, laboriously tied together, that he planned to use to lower himself over the walls. He had hoped to make it longer, just as he had hoped to wait for a night with no moon, but now that he knew his chances of a papal reprieve were null, it was time to put his scheme into action. When the midnight bell had tolled, he used his spoon to remove the artificial hinges he had placed in the door, crept past the jailer's room, where he was snoring soundly, and out onto the parapet of the Castel St. Angelo.

All of Rome spread out below him, swaddled in night, and with the strength still left in his emaciated frame, he lowered the rope—still too short to reach the ground—and began his slow and perilous descent.

Chapter 14

∽◈∾

Monday dawned cold and gray, but after a hot breakfast delivered to his room, David packed up his leather valise and set out on foot for the Biblioteca Laurenziana, still determined to be the first one through its doors.

Florence could be a forbidding city under the best of circumstances, with its ancient buildings glowering over its crowded streets and squares, but that morning, with a blustery wind keeping everyone's heads down and dust and dirt flying up from the cobblestones, it was especially sinister. On the Via Proconsul, he passed by the Bargello, once the headquarters of the chief city magistrate. For centuries, criminals had been publicly hanged from its tower windows, and if they were foreigners, their bodies had been donated to medical students and "anatomists" such as Leonardo da Vinci for dissection and study.

A few shifty-looking men huddled in the Bargello's doorway, throwing dice, and David instinctively hugged the valise more tightly to his side. Italy boasted some of the greatest artists and inventors of all time, but it was also the home to some of the world's most skillful pickpockets and thieves.

The streets were congested with morning traffic, cars rumbling by and motor scooters whizzing past like hornets. Jumping out of the way of one, David thought he caught sight of a figure in a slouched hat, with a rolled-up newspaper under one arm, dodging into an alcove. But a break in the traffic opened up, and without looking back he darted across the street.

Ahead, Il Duomo, the mighty rose-colored cupola of the cathedral of Santa Maria del Fiore, rose above the surrounding rooftops. Ever since its construction in the 1420s, city law had dictated that no building should ever exceed it in height. Built by Brunelleschi, it was a miracle of both artistry and engineering, soaring over three hundred feet into the air and so all-encompassing that it was, in the words of the Renaissance architect Alberti, "large enough to shelter all the people of Tuscany in its shadow." Mark Twain had said it looked like "a captive balloon," floating over the town.

A bunch of tourists, climbing off their bus and hoisting their videocams, snagged him in their midst, and before he could extricate himself, he thought he glimpsed that same figure, hat pulled low, mingling with the mob; but he could have been mistaken.

He wondered if his near miss with that driver back at the skating rink in Evanston had left him a bit paranoid.

Heading across the piazza, he could see the smaller, but no less captivating, dome of the ancient Church of San Lorenzo; like every major construction project in Florence, the contract had called for the cathedral to be *"piu bello che si puo,"* or in English "as beautiful as can be." It was a stipulation the city fathers had insisted upon throughout the Renaissance, and it had yielded an unparalleled crop of striking architecture. Over the centuries, San Lorenzo—which claimed to be the oldest church in Florence, its original cornerstone having been laid in 393—had been rebuilt and expanded until, gradually, it had become a sort of monastic complex, housing an old sacristy by Brunelleschi, a new sacristy by Michelangelo, the Medici burial chapels, and, in an adjoining cloister, David's destination . . . the world-renowned Laurenziana library.

From the outside, the buildings presented a fairly austere appearance, their walls layered in the dark stone, or *pietra serena,* of their native Tuscany. And although in warmer weather its cloistered courtyard was filled with green leaves and banks of multicolored irises, today it was barren and sere.

David's footsteps echoed across the empty square, a flock of dirty gray pigeons scooting out of his way.

But under the sound of their fluttering wings, he became aware of sneakers squeaking in one of the shadowy arcades. When he stopped, pretending to tie his shoe, the squeaking stopped, and when he stood up and went on, he could hear it again, not far behind. He turned quickly, but saw only one old matron, in hard black shoes, persistently scrubbing a window frame. He waited for another second, peering into the arcade, with its rounded arches and deep recesses, but no one appeared.

Was he being followed? Was it just a pickpocket, and not a particularly good one at that? Was it someone who knew what he carried in the fancy valise?

Or had he just seen too many movies?

He shook his head and climbed the stairs to the second floor of the cloister, where the library and its world-famous collection of books and codices was housed.

But he was no sooner at the top than he heard that squeaking sound again. Was Mrs. Van Owen—rich and eccentric as she was—having him tailed, for God's sake?

For all he knew, that maniac in the BMW had followed him all the way from the States.

He no longer knew what to believe.

But he did know how to waylay his pursuer and find out once and for all.

The vestibule of the library had been purposely designed by Michelangelo to be dim—the windows had been bricked up, in fact—so that the visitors to the library would feel themselves ascending from its gloom into the sudden illumination—in every sense—of the library at the top of the stairs. David pressed himself into a niche that housed a marble bust of Petrarch, and with the valise clutched under one arm, held his breath.

The steps came closer, and paused just outside the vestibule.

Had the tracker decided to abandon his quarry?

And then, squeaking softly, the steps continued. David saw the back of a hat and raincoat, with a newspaper sticking out from under one arm.

Stepping out of the niche, David said in Italian, "What can I do for you?"

The figure whirled around, a copy of *La Stampa* flying out from under one arm, one palm dramatically pressed to her chest.

To his astonishment David saw that it was the tour guide, Olivia Levi, from the day before.

"*Maron!*" she cried. "You nearly killed me! Why did you do that!"

"Not until you tell me why you've been following me!" At least his suspicions had been proven correct—he *had* been followed.

Olivia bent to pick up the scattered pages of the newspaper, just as a heavyset female guard, in a gray uniform and cap, showed up at the top of the steps to see what the sudden commotion was all about.

"Oh no," she shouted, glaring at Olivia, "not you again! You're barred from the library—you know that—so get going!" She slapped her hands together, up and down, to emphasize her dismissal.

"But I'm not done with my research!"

"That's too bad. The director is done with you."

There was a pleading look on Olivia's face and, without missing a beat, she added, "But I am working today! I am this man's assistant. He has hired me to help him with his work here."

She quickly glanced at David, waiting for confirmation, and David didn't know what to do. His normal impulse was to help out a fellow scholar, but there was too much about this woman that he simply didn't know, or trust.

"Is that true?" the guard asked suspiciously. "She works for you?"

But it wasn't going to be that easy. "Why are you barred?" David whispered in English.

"What does it matter?" Olivia whispered back. "It was nothing!"

"Last chance—why are you barred?"

"I had an argument with the director," she said, shrugging. "The man is a Nazi."

From the way she said it, coupled with that weary shrug, David almost laughed. But it still took him several seconds before he decided to take a chance. Looking up at the guard, he said, in Italian again, "Yes, I've hired her."

"And who are you?"

David took his own letter of introduction from his pocket and advanced with it in hand. "Dottore Valetta is expecting me."

The guard studied the paper, glared one more time at Olivia, then turned around and waddled into the library, a nightstick straining in the belt at her side.

"*Grazie mille*," Olivia mumbled to David, who mumbled back, "But we're not done—you'll still have to tell me why you were following me."

"Because you told me you would be working here," she said. "I needed a way back in."

"Why didn't you just ask me?"

"Because you didn't know me."

"And I do now?"

"We are getting there," she said, with a half smile that, despite himself, he found beguiling.

Following the guard, they entered the long and elegant hall that was the library's main reading room. Bay windows, framed by marble pilasters, lined one wall, throwing a bright but diffused light onto the red and white terra-cotta tiles—demonstrating the fundamental principles of geometry—embedded in the floor. Wooden desks lined both sides of the room under a high, beamed ceiling. An old woman, studying some ancient text with a magnifying glass, glanced up as they passed, then quickly buried herself again in her work.

At the end of the hall, the guard turned into a side corridor and rapped her knuckles on a frosted-glass panel. She opened the door, announced them, and before David could even see Dr. Valetta, he heard the director say, "No, that woman is not allowed on the premises!"

"She's working for Signor Franco," the guard tried to explain.

David neatly stepped around her, where he saw the director, in a crisp tan suit with a pocket square, standing behind a desk. When David extended his hand, Dr. Valetta accepted it, all the while keeping a close eye on Olivia, who loitered near the door.

"Greetings, Mr. Franco. We've been expecting you. But how is it that you know Signorina Levi?"

"She's volunteered to help me with my research," David improvised. "She tells me she's quite familiar with the Laurenziana's collections."

Dr. Valetta snorted. "That much is true. But I wouldn't believe anything else she tells you. The signorina has her own 'theories,' and no amount of fact can ever dissuade her."

"What?" Olivia broke in, unable to contain herself. "I have plenty of facts, and I'd have more if people like you weren't forever standing in my way!"

David turned to her and said, *"Basta."* What had he gotten himself into?

Subsiding, she said, "I will wait for you in the reading room," and stalked out.

"Sorry about that," David said to the director.

Valetta looked like he was still wondering what to do, then said, "You will have to be responsible for her, you know?"

"I will."

Determinedly regaining his composure and pinching the crease of his trousers before resuming his own seat, Dr. Valetta invited him to sit down.

David took the chair opposite the desk, resting his valise against his leg. The walls of the office were lined with shelves of books, all perfectly arranged and aligned. More, David thought, for show than for use.

"And you are comfortable if we continue to speak in Italian?"

David nodded and said he preferred it.

"Good. I believe that you have done some research in our collections before?"

"I have. But it was some years ago."

"Then permit me to remind you of our procedures."

David listened attentively, in part to make up for Olivia's transgressions, as the director explained that any manuscript or text that was requested had to be brought to the borrower's assigned desk by a library attendant, and no more than three at any time. Any manuscript being returned also had to be given back to one of the attendants. Any portfolio or briefcase leaving the library had to be inspected by a security guard—assisted by a librarian—at the checkout station. No photographs were allowed, except by special permission. And, to avoid any ink spillage, no pens—only pencils—were allowed for note-taking.

"We have set aside an alcove for your exclusive use," Dr. Valetta said, "for as long as you need it."

"That's very kind of you," David said.

"And I have instructed the staff to be accommodating, if, say, you need more than the usual number of texts at a time."

"Thank you again."

Dr. Valetta lifted his hands and said, "Mrs. Van Owen has been very generous to us. We are only too happy to repay her in any way we can."

Mrs. Van Owen. Was there anywhere, David thought, her reach did not extend? Any move he made that she did not anticipate? For a moment, he wondered if Olivia wasn't one of her plants, sent to keep tabs on his progress.

After a few more minutes of chitchat, during which Valetta seemed to be probing into the focus of David's research—a probing that he did his best to fend off—David stood up to excuse himself.

"I'm on the clock," he said, wondering if the expression would make any sense in Italian. "I'd better get started."

"Of course," the director said, and ushered him out.

In the reading room, Olivia was seated next to the woman with the magnifying glass, pointing out something on the yellowed page she was studying. The woman looked rapt and appreciative, and David had the sense that, for all her eccentricity, Olivia Levi did indeed know her stuff.

A young librarian, in a red vest that David normally associated with car valets, showed them to an alcove with a massive desk, a pair of sturdy oak chairs, and a dual-headed banker's lamp that cast a warm glow around the interior. A faded fresco of the Muses in a garden adorned the wall beneath the window. There was even a silver cup, holding a bunch of sharpened No. 2 pencils, like arrows in a quiver, along with a pad of call slips.

Olivia threw her coat over the back of a chair and broke into a grin. She looked as if she'd won the lottery.

"So, you're some kind of big deal, huh? A private alcove? An audience with the dictator himself? Who are you, really?"

David took off his own overcoat, placed the valise on the desk, and wondered about that himself. Up until now he'd been a Renaissance scholar working in obscurity in a private library in Chicago, but over the past few days he'd begun to feel like a secret agent. And now he had to think like one. He could either dismiss this young interloper, send her off to attend to her own "theories" and hope she didn't create another row, or he could offer some hint about what had brought him there.

Plainly, she could see his quandary.

"You do not trust me," she said. "That's okay. But I would remind you of one thing."

"What's that?"

"It was you who found me in the Piazza della Signoria, not the other way around."

"I'm not the one who tracked me to this library."

"Okay," she conceded, "so I did do that. But maybe I can help you." She glanced at the closed valise with undisguised curiosity.

"Show me one thing, give me one clue, then see if I do not know what I am talking about."

She waited, while David mulled over her offer. Then he opened the valise, took out a few of the papers, and placed them on the table.

Olivia lunged forward in her chair and bent low over the documents. Gradually, her expression became very serious, and, although none of the pages bore a signature anywhere, it was only a minute or two before she whispered, "Cellini." Looking up, awestruck, she said, "These are from the hand of Benvenuto Cellini."

Unless he was still being duped, she was darn good.

"Where in the world did you get them?"

"First you tell me how you knew that."

"Please," she said, with some disdain, "I am not an amateur in these matters. No one wrote quite like Cellini—in the Italian vernacular—and no one was so interested in these—how would you say?—dark matters."

While it was still possible he was being gulled—that she had somehow known in advance what he was investigating—the possibility seemed increasingly remote. Could she really be such a fine actress? There was something in the expression on her face and in the tone of her voice—even in the undisguised scorn with which she had answered his last question—that persuaded him she was on the level.

And if that was true, then she could prove to be of inestimable value.

Slowly, David removed the rest of the papers from the valise—her eyes widened even more—and began to explain how they had been donated to the library by an anonymous (that much he kept to himself) patron. Olivia sat silently, riveted by each page, until she said, "But what is this?" Her fingers nimbly plucked from the stack the sketch of the Medusa's head. "A preliminary study for his famous statue—where we met?" She gave him a quizzical smile.

"It's possible."

But on second thought, she shook her head, frowning. "No, that's wrong—it's nothing like it, really. The Medusa in the piazza is defeated—this one is defiant." Her eye fell on the empty oblong on the same page, the reverse view, and she looked puzzled. "It was a medallion?" she hazarded. "Unfinished?"

"No, it was a mirror, simply called *La Medusa*," David said. "And I have reason to believe that it *was* finished."

Olivia gave it some thought, before saying, "I know a great deal about Cellini, probably more than anyone in Italy—"

Despite himself, David had to chuckle; one thing she had was the artisan's ego, that was for sure.

"—but I've never heard of this thing, this mirror, called *La Medusa*."

"No one has," David replied. "But it's my job to find it."

She flopped back in her chair, her arms hanging down in mock defeat. "And how do you propose to do that? Find something that has been missing for five hundred years?"

"I don't honestly know," David said. "But since the Laurenziana holds more of Cellini's papers than anyplace on earth, this seemed like the right place to start looking."

She cocked her head, uncertainly.

He took a pencil from the silver cup. "Do you have a better idea?"

Olivia studied him, then, leaning forward, said, "Does this mean you are offering me a job?"

Was he? He felt like a diver, standing on the edge of a cliff and about to jump into unknown waters. Should he step back before it was too late, or take the plunge? "Does this mean you are available if I did?"

"I'm not sure. I am very busy, with my tours, and my own research, and—"

"Fine," David said, starting to fill out the call slip and calling her bluff. "It was nice meeting you."

But her hand flicked out and stopped him. "Already," she said, "you are hard to work for." And then she laughed, and the sound of it made David laugh, too. "I want a raise!"

There was a shushing sound from someone in the main reading room, as Olivia snatched the call slip and read what David had been writing there. "The Codice Mediceo-Palatino?" she inquired.

"Yes," he said, wondering if it would meet with her approval.

"A good place to start," she said, nodding. Raising her hand to signal one of the library attendants, she added, "You may not be so bad, after all."

Chapter 15

The wind off Lake Michigan howled around the walls of the Holy Name Cathedral, rippling the tarps where the ceiling was still being mended, and sending a cold draft into the side chapel where the private ceremony was being held. A blown-up photo of Randolph Van Owen at the wheel of his yacht had been mounted on an easel, with a caption providing his dates of birth and death.

Despite the prominence of the Van Owen name, and its long history in Chicago, Kathryn had arranged for this to be a small gathering—just Randolph's sisters, their children, and a scattering of his friends from the yacht club. The young priest, Father Flanagan, was doing his best, but he was nervous and laboring hard to say something true and consoling about a man he'd never met. The Van Owenses had not been churchgoers, and it was clear that a lot of the priest's eulogy had come from a quick search on Google.

Kathryn just wanted it to be over. She wished she had never had to set foot in Holy Name Cathedral again, and glancing at the confessionals on her way in, she had experienced a predictable pang. She had had to step over the very spot where the old priest, Father DiGennaro, had collapsed just a few nights before, the cell phone spilling from his hand. There was nothing to mark it now, nothing to alert anyone passing by that a man had died there. But then, she sometimes thought there was no place on earth that didn't bear that same stain; others might not see them, but she could, everywhere. Live long enough, she thought, and the whole world starts to look like a graveyard.

The onyx urn containing Randolph's ashes rested on a marble pedestal, and from time to time the priest looked over at it with a show of deference, as if it contained some presence, some essence . . . something other than what it did, which was purely dust and rubble. Kathryn had no illusions. For someone in her position, it would have been impossible to feel otherwise.

When the priest intoned his last prayer and the ceremony was over, Kathryn said good-bye to the other mourners from under her black veil. Randolph's sisters, with whom she had never gotten along, trailed out, dragging their spoiled progeny, and the boating pals shook her hand, no doubt heading off to the yacht club to get drunk in his honor.

Father Flanagan came to her side, and after she had thanked him for his words, he said, "No, I must thank you."

"For what?"

Gesturing upward, where the hats of the previous Cardinals had been reattached to the rafters and the ceiling work was again under way, he said, "I was told that you had made a very generous contribution to the church, to cover all the expenses of the roof repair."

That she had done. Out of guilt. If she hadn't given the old priest such a shock, he might have one day died, peacefully, in his own bed, instead of on these cold stones. The next day, she'd written a check. Writing checks was easy.

"May I escort you out?" he asked, but she said that wasn't necessary. Cyril had already taken the urn in his gloved hands and walked her down the aisle to the great double doors with their Tree of Life motif.

The moment the doors were opened, she was hit by a freezing blast and had to navigate her way down the steps carefully. The limousine was still warm inside, and she nestled down in the backseat while the wind and snow battered the windows. It was a half-hour drive, maybe longer in this weather, to the Calvary Cemetery on Clark Street, the oldest Catholic cemetery in the archdiocese, where the Van Owen family mausoleum had been erected more than a century ago. She rode in silence, accompanied only by the sounds of the tires skimming through the slush and the regular beating of the windshield wipers. Cyril knew when she wanted to be alone with her thoughts.

And her thoughts had turned in the direction they so often went of late . . . to David Franco and what progress he might be making in his search for the *Medusa*. He had been in Italy only a matter of days, but Randolph's death—the last in a string of so many—had reinforced in her the need to find the mirror again, and with it, she hoped, the answers to her unending dilemma. But what were the chances? Others had gone before, and they had either returned empty-handed, or, as in the case of a certain Mr. Palliser, been fished out of the river Loire with a grappling hook.

The mission, she knew, should come with a warning, but then who would take it?

All along the lakefront, jagged hunks of limestone and ice were piled up like a jumble of building blocks, and the lake itself was a gray, heaving slab, the wind teasing its surface into whitecaps. The late-afternoon sun was barely visible, and what light it shed was cold, dim, and diffuse. It was not a landscape Mrs. Van Owen would miss. With Randolph gone and no reason to stay, she was determined now to head for some warmer clime . . . and reinvent herself as she had done countless times before. She owned other homes, under other names, all over the world; she would inhabit one of them. The one thing she could never do was stay in any one place too long, lest she eventually arouse suspicion.

And her time in Chicago, plainly, had already worn out.

As they approached the cemetery, Cyril slowed down and turned under a Gothic archway with the Greek letters for Alpha and Omega—Christian symbols, as Kathryn was keenly aware, for God as the beginning and the end—in a triangle above the driveway. Even passing under them, Kathryn felt a sense of trespass. The limousine rolled through the deserted, windswept grounds, past rows of bleak stone monuments and crypts, beneath the barren branches of the trees that Dutch elm disease had so far spared.

"It's around the next bend," Kathryn instructed Cyril, "on the left side."

The Van Owen mausoleum was easily the most ostentatious in the entire cemetery. Designed to resemble a Greek temple, and made of the same white limestone piled up in the breakwaters separating Sheridan Road from the lake, it sat on a slight rise, commanding an unobstructed view of the lake. Not that that did its occupants any good, Mrs. Van Owen reflected. Well over a hundred Midwestern winters had dimmed its luster, and even opened a crack in its roof, where some tenacious vines had penetrated and taken hold. When the cemetery staff had once asked Randolph if he wanted the vine removed, he had said, "Leave it be—it's the only living thing for a square mile."

Kathryn felt the same way.

Cyril stopped the car in the middle of the roadway, since both curbs were banked with snow and ice. Only one other car was even visible, a hearse, its tailpipe emitting a plume of smoke as it lumbered off into the farther reaches of the graveyard.

Kathryn gathered her fur coat around her, and once the door was opened, stepped gingerly out onto the ice. Cyril was holding the urn in the crook of one arm, and she took hold of the other to keep her balance. Together, they stepped over the snowy curb and plowed up the hill through the blustering winds. The door to the mausoleum was nearly ten feet high, and it was made of black iron, filigreed around a thick slab of opaque glass. Kathryn dug deep in the pocket of her plush coat and removed an iron key ring that looked as if it should have opened the wards in Bedlam. She handed it to Cyril, who was unable to insert the key into the frosty, recalcitrant lock.

But he had come prepared, and after clearing the hole with the end of a screwdriver, and then injecting some WD-40, he was able to get the key into the lock then crack the door, as ponderous as any bank vault, open.

"Shall I come in with you?"

"No," Kathryn said, cradling the urn in her arms. "Why don't you just take the car around the loop, so we're heading in the right direction when I'm ready to go? I'll need ten or fifteen minutes."

Kathryn stepped into the vault, and Cyril closed the vault behind her. A pair of casement windows, their glass as occluded as the door, allowed a pale nimbus of light to infiltrate the chamber, which was larger than it appeared from outside. The marble walls at this level were inscribed with various quotes from Scripture, and a bust of Archibald Van Owen, the bearded railroad baron who had founded the family fortune in the late 1800s, glowered over anyone entering.

A few steps down, the chamber opened up, and on the granite slabs to either side rested perhaps a dozen caskets, their brass handles tarnished with age, their once-gleaming wood now dull and covered with a thick film of dust. And on two shelves that ran around the four walls of the crypt, there were a host of urns, in everything from porphyry to porcelain, containing the cremated remains of other family members. The air inside was cold, but not altogether still—the place in the ceiling where the vine had broken through allowed the tiniest hint of fresh air. In the uppermost corner, a spiderweb a yard wide trembled, and the marble beneath it bore a broad yellow-and-green stain from the seepage of rain and melting snow.

A wave of repulsion swept over her, but not from the cold or the dreadful occupants of the place. It was the sight of the black spider herself, scuttling across the fine filaments, reacting no doubt to the unusual air currents in the room and thinking her web might have trapped some unlucky prey; first the spider went one way, then the other, looking in vain. And Kathryn, trapped for centuries in a web from which there was no apparent escape, could not help but feel like prey herself.

Stepping down, she went to the wall and, raising a gloved hand, cleared a space on the shelf, before placing the urn holding Randolph's remains on it. For a few seconds, she let her hand rest atop it, as if in benediction; but in actuality she was simply waiting for some corresponding emotion, some sense of finality or even sorrow.

But there was nothing. It was a scene she had played already, too often, and it had grown stale. Her heart was as dead as the occupants of the crypt.

Instead, she found herself thinking of other times, now long removed. Times when she had genuinely been young and had had an appetite for the things that life had to offer. When artists had begged her to be their muse and aristocrats had showered her with gifts in the hopes that she would become their mistress. But truth be told, in all that time, there had been only one man who had touched—no, taken—her heart. Only one man whose soul she felt had touched her own. Even now, she could imagine his rough hands on her body, turning her this way and that, posing her limbs for yet another of his masterpieces. She could feel the scratchiness of his beard on her face, hear the sound of his bawdy laughter, and smile at the memory of his insolence to lords and ladies who had crossed him. She remembered the nights they slept on the hard pallet in his studio, ate their meals off borrowed silver, and strolled arm in arm along the Ponte Vecchio.

Nor could she ever forget the fateful night she had pried open the iron casket and changed her own destiny forever. Now her only hope was to find the accursed mirror again and hope that by breaking it, she could shatter the spell and free herself from its power. If the *Key* was correct—and everything it had said about the powers of *La Medusa* had proved true so far, so why should she doubt this?—then that might be her one escape from the iron grip of immortality. Once the glass had been shattered, her life would resume again, as if she had only been frozen, and move forward, day by day, like that of any mortal woman. And end, in due course, just as naturally. In the words of the immortal Shakespeare—though when she had known him, no one had treated him as anything more than a prolific scribbler—it was "a consummation devoutly to be wished."

Without her even having noticed at first, hot tears had begun coursing down her cheeks, and she could taste their saltiness on her lips.

She had fled Florence, then the European continent altogether, with the Duke of Castro's men hot on her heels. Her ship had foundered and sunk two days out of Cherbourg, but she had been rescued after several days of clinging to the wreckage, and eventually found shelter under another name, among the gentry of England. It was there, years later, that she had heard news of Benvenuto's death, and his burial beneath the stones of the Basilica della Santissima Annunziata. Had he found a way, she wondered, to cheat the blessing, or the curse, of the looking glass? Or was she the only one on whom the magic had been performed? Could he have made the thing and not employed it himself? It seemed unlike him, but at the same time, perversity was in his very nature. At the news, she had found herself overwhelmed by a wave of loneliness more profound than anything she had ever experienced before.

But she had grown accustomed to it over the years. She was a lone wayfarer, carried along on a cold, inescapable, and unending current.

The cobweb vibrated again, and she saw the fat black spider scuttling across its strands. Hoarse sobs were coming from her throat, and she had to retire to a stone bench beside the caskets. She took a scented handkerchief from the pocket of her coat and dabbed at her tears. A breeze encircled her as Cyril cracked the door open.

"Are you all right?" he asked.

But all she could do was nod. Like anyone else, he would think it was just the release of all those emotions that had been building up since the death of her husband. Let him.

"The car's right outside," he said.

And this time she said, "I'll be there in a minute."

The door groaned shut again, and she took a few moments to

compose herself. Her eyes, inadvertently, went back to the spider, biding its time in the corner of its web. And the sight of it was enough to send a shudder down her spine and bring her back to her feet. When she closed the door of the mausoleum behind her, she knew it was the last time she would ever see this place.

Chapter 16

A butcher shop. As far as Ernst Escher was concerned, that was what the place looked like. And not for the first time, he wondered if he was being paid enough for this job.

Julius Jantzen, in a surgical mask and blood-spattered apron, was just depositing one of the last severed feet into the acid bath. Disposing of three bodies, from the hair on the head to the last toenail, wasn't easy, and Escher and Jantzen had been hard at it for almost two days. Julius had wanted to smuggle the bodies out of the apartment and dump them into the Arno, or even somewhere in the surrounding countryside; but Escher knew from experience that bodies had a way of turning up. Rivers were dredged, fields were tilled, even asphalt parking lots were sometimes broken up for a new development. No, as he had patiently explained to Julius while mopping up the blood in his foyer, it was always best to get rid of the evidence, right then and there.

And who could ask for a better place to do it than Julius's private lab?

Escher had gone out and picked up a hatchet, a bone saw, a steel mallet, gallon jugs of chemical supplies, and everything else necessary for the destruction, decomposition, and disposal of human remains. On the way back from his last trip, he had stopped to pick up several packs of good, German beer—Löwenbräu—so that he wouldn't have to drink any more of that Italian swill. It would be thirsty work, of that he had no doubt.

Even though Jantzen was the doctor, Escher quickly discovered he had no stomach for the dirty work. It was Escher who'd had to lift each of the three Turks onto the examining table and start chopping with the axe and the saw. The human body was neatly divisible into six pieces—the arms, the legs, the head, and the torso—but after smashing the jaw, for instance, the delicate work was extracting every last tooth and making sure it was properly pulverized.

While Escher took care of the butchery, he left the acid immersions, incinerations, and flushing of the remains to Jantzen, who several times stopped to throw up into his surgical sink.

"Good God," Escher asked him at one point, "how did you ever get through medical school?"

"I hadn't murdered the cadavers."

"And you didn't murder these. I did. Or would you rather I'd have let them kill us?"

"Ahmet wouldn't have killed anyone; he was just hopped up and looking for a quick score."

"And that's what you think?" Escher said.

"Why? What else could it have been?"

"I think he was here to see me," Escher said, smashing the skull on the table with the mallet, "and got a bit distracted." Softened by the sulfuric acid, the head squashed like a pumpkin. "Never send a junkie to do a job. That's what I always say."

Every few hours, Escher went out for a meal—the place run by the Spaniards at the corner really was as good as Julius had claimed—but usually he went alone. A couple of times, he brought something home for Jantzen, and though he'd never planned on staying the night, much less two, in such a dump, there was so much work to do he hadn't bothered to find a hotel. He'd simply commandeered the bed.

As for keeping tabs on David Franco, he knew what he was up to—nosing around the Laurenziana library. The moment he'd disappeared inside, Escher had put in a call to Schillinger—the man did know everyone—and within minutes, the library's director, a Dr. Valetta, had gotten in touch and promised to keep him posted on David's doings. Fortunately, no one, to Escher's knowledge, knew anything about this little Turkish incident, and he certainly had no intention of mentioning it to anyone.

He wished he could be so sure of Jantzen.

His cell phone rang in his breast pocket, and he had to snap off his latex gloves to answer it. It was Valetta himself, true to his word.

"He's gone, but she's here," he whispered, as if afraid of being overheard in his own office.

"Where has he gone?"

"How should I know? But Olivia Levi is working alone, in the main reading room. Right now. You said you wanted to know when she was accounted for."

"All right, all right," he said, "thanks for the word."

Turning to look over his shoulder, he saw Jantzen holding the hand hose and washing some ashes and bone dust down the sink. Every few hours, just for safety's sake, they poured in some drain cleaner, too.

"You feel like an outing?" he called out.

Jantzen turned to look at him, a numb expression in his eyes. His whole body, haggard enough to begin with, looked stooped and defeated. Why, Escher wondered, didn't he just prescribe himself some uppers?

"Come on," Escher said, tossing his gloves onto the blood-soaked table. "I'll buy you a *gelato*."

Passing through the courtyard, a squirrelly young man appeared out of nowhere, wringing his hands, and said, "Dr. Jantzen? Dr. Jantzen? I need to see you, sir."

Another one of his friend's fine clientele, Escher thought.

"Not now, Giovanni," Julius said.

"But I need to see you," he pleaded, clearly strung out on some substance and plucking at Julius's sleeve.

"He said not now," Escher intervened, and the man, after taking one look into his hard blue eyes, fell back, silent, nearly toppling into the stagnant fountain.

Julius's car—a Volvo, exactly as Escher might have guessed—was parked outside the tobacconist's, and as Escher waited for him to unlock the doors, he couldn't help but notice that there were several people inside the shop, jabbering excitedly, and a dark, beetle-browed woman, in a headscarf, with a couple of children clinging to her coat. More Turks. As Escher slung his satchel onto the floor of the front seat of the car and got in, the woman in the headscarf came to the shop window, looking fixedly at him, and then—making the bell above the door jingle—came bustling out.

"Drive," Escher said, as Julius started the car.

The woman was shouting in bad Italian—something about her husband not coming home—but Escher's window was up, and when she rapped her knuckles on the glass, her rings clattering, he gave her a level stare but said nothing. The children capered about in the street, as if to impede their escape, but Escher said, "Run them over, if you have to."

"For God's sake, Ernst . . ."

But Escher leaned over and blasted the horn, and the kids jumped out of the way.

The woman spat on the window, and for the rest of the ride— maybe ten minutes in slow, thick traffic—the spittle clung like glue to the glass. Escher told Julius where to go, and once they'd reached the Piazza della Repubblica and found one of the very rare parking spots, he picked his satchel up off the floor and got out.

It was a brisk, sunny morning, and Escher mounted the steps of the apartment building two at a time, with Julius lingering behind. First, he rang the buzzer, to make sure no one else was home— just because Olivia was accounted for didn't mean she had no roommates—and when there was no answer, he rang all the others, until someone buzzed him in. When he heard a door open down the hall, he called out, "Delivery for Levi!" and swiftly climbed to the third floor, with Julius close behind.

The door itself, decorated with a postcard of some ancient sculpture, was easy work—Escher could pick any lock, and this wasn't even a good one—and the curtains were drawn. The place was like a cave. Sweet Jesus, Escher thought, don't any of the Florentines live in decent places? He finally located the light switch, turned it on, and found himself staring into a pair of big, blinking eyes.

An owl, with one mangled wing, was perched on a rickety stand. It was free to fly, if it could, and hooted several times at the intruders.

"This city is *pazzo*"—crazy—Escher said.

The rest of the apartment was also strange. Every sofa and chair, every table and counter, was covered with books and papers. There were cinder-block shelves groaning under the weight of crumbling encyclopedias. The bedroom in back looked like no more than an annex to the library in front. Escher could barely make out the bed.

But it was all in keeping with what Dr. Valetta had reported about Olivia Levi; despite her good looks, he had warned Escher, she was not empty-headed. She was smart. Very smart. She had graduated at the top of her class from the University of Bologna, Italy's oldest and most prestigious school, then traveled to the States to do further research in New York. She had written some provocative papers, published in academic journals that almost no one ever read, and was apparently working on some secret magnum opus while she supported herself leading tour groups around the city. Judging from the look of the place, tour guides didn't get paid all that well.

"So, what are we doing here?" Julius asked.

"You're standing at the window, keeping an eye out for any unexpected visitors."

"All right," Julius said, dutifully taking up his post where he could peek out between the drawn drapes. "But what are you doing?"

"I'm looking for library cards," Escher said, sounding as puzzled as he felt.

"What?"

"I'm looking for call slips, or copies of them, from the Lauren-ziana." Even Escher didn't know why these could possibly be of im-portance to anyone.

But he had more general orders, too. Among other things, he was to scour the premises for anything that looked like a mirror, or a Gor-gon, or a drawing of a mirror or a Gorgon. He was to keep an eye out for any book about Benvenuto Cellini, or black magic, or *stregheria*, the Sicilian strain of witchcraft, or for anything that struck him as oc-cult or unexplainable—most notably, anything that connected such stuff to the Nazi high command during the Second World War. He was to photograph, or take notes on, any such material, and if it seemed particularly unique and rare, simply steal it. It was for Schillinger, whose sanity Escher had begun to doubt, and Dr. Valetta, whom he had only spoken to on the phone, to decide what was sig-nificant. Like any soldier in the trenches, he worried about the wis-dom of his generals.

But Olivia's apartment presented him with a more immediate problem. Even the most cursory review of her books and papers re-vealed dozens of titles—in French and German, English and Italian—on all of those topics and more. Ernst Escher was no scholar, and even though he had a degree in computer science from a technical college in Lausanne—you had to have a bachelor's, even to be con-sidered for the Swiss Guard—he could see that this woman had an ex-traordinarily wide, and bizarre, range of interests. Above her desk she had framed photographs of Mussolini hanging by his heels in 1945, a map of the lost continent of Atlantis, and finally, an official portrait of Mme. Blavatsky, founder of Theosophy. Escher hardly knew where to start.

The owl hooted and stretched its wings.

He began by combing through every desk and dresser drawer in search of the library slips. But he already knew that if they were this important to someone else, Olivia Levi might know that, too, and she would not have left them carelessly about.

Taking his camera from the pocket of his windbreaker, he spent the next hour, as Jantzen kept watch, laboriously photographing her bookshelves, being careful to disturb them as little as possible (though they were such a mess, how would she ever know?) and making sure that all the titles on the spines were legible. Then he took several shots of her desk, where he did have to rearrange several papers to be sure every word on them would be legible. The ones on top had to do with the collaborationist Vichy regime in France. Why was someone like this worrying her pretty head with ancient crap like that? She could have found a rich husband by now and be living *la dolce vita,* as the locals liked to call it. The older Escher got—and he had turned thirty-five on the plane trip to Florence—the less he understood people. Life was a fucked-up affair, and as far as he could tell, the point was to just get through it with the maximum amount of pleasure and a minimum of pain . . . even if that meant inflicting a little damage on other people along the way. If you didn't watch out for yourself, no one else would do it for you.

"Anything happening?" he asked Jantzen as he loaded another flash card into his camera.

"Someone's locking a bike right outside," Julius said from the window. "A young guy."

"Is he tall, with brown hair and glasses?"

"No, he's got black hair, no glasses, definitely Italian."

At least it wasn't David Franco. And he might be coming to any of the apartments in the building. Escher listened for the buzzer, but nothing rang. He noticed a box of books that he'd overlooked under the desk, and was debating whether or not to drag it out when Jantzen urgently whispered, "Someone's coming."

Escher heard it, too, now, the trudge of steps approaching. Jantzen ducked behind the curtains, and Escher swiftly turned out the lights, opened a closet, shoved some clothes to one side and squashed himself inside. The closet was so full the door wouldn't close entirely, and through the crack he heard the rattle of keys, then saw a guy in jeans and a ski jacket, poking his head in.

"Olivia?" he said. "You home?"

Turning on the light, he ventured into the room, a pair of bicycle saddlebags slung over one shoulder.

"Don't get mad—it's just me. Giorgio. Anybody here?"

The owl hooted and ruffled its wings.

"Hey there, Glaucus, I've missed you. You miss me?"

He dropped his bags on the floor and his coat on the couch, then sauntered into the kitchen, where Escher could hear a kettle being filled. He had keys, but he wasn't expected—or perhaps even permitted, which would explain his not ringing the buzzer, and his timid entry. Escher pegged him for an old boyfriend—and when he came back into the front room and started sorting through a pile of CDs on the stereo, and tossing some into his saddlebags, Escher figured he knew what was going on. The old beau had come back, on the sly, to retrieve some of his stuff.

Escher had been in this very spot himself, more than once, but he'd always left a present behind to show he'd been there. Once, it had been a dead rat in the microwave, and oh, what he would have given to see his ex's reaction to that!

The kettle boiled, and Giorgio went to make his instant coffee, or tea. Escher feared that Julius would give himself away, but so far it looked like the boyfriend had no desire to open the curtains either.

And Escher didn't believe he would stick around in the apartment long.

But what if there was something he wanted in the closet?

Escher ran his eye over the clothes. As far as he could tell, they were all dresses and other women's things. It was only when he looked down that he saw the hiking boots, shoved almost all the way to the back—and they were plainly a man's.

The boyfriend came back, and although Escher couldn't see him, he heard him sit down in the desk chair and rummage around in the drawers. Then, he hit the play button on her answering machine and listened to her messages. Escher had planned to do that himself.

But how long was he going to take? Standing in the musty closet was growing uncomfortable, and it was only a matter of time before Jantzen gave himself away somehow.

"You hungry?" Giorgio was saying to the damn owl, and he'd gotten up to feed it something.

Then, as Escher listened carefully, he heard him closing the straps on his saddlebags—was he finally done?—before snapping his fingers, as if he'd forgotten something. It was unmistakable—he was coming to the closet, probably for those fucking boots.

The door opened, and since the boyfriend was already looking down, Escher was able to head butt him, like a piledriver, without much trouble. But because of the bad angle, he ended up catching him not just on the forehead but the bridge of the nose, too. The guy stumbled back, stunned, not knowing what had just hit him, when Escher stepped out of the closet and cracked him under the chin with a swift uppercut.

He was actually lifted off his feet before going down hard, smacking his head for good measure on the edge of a low table. He was unconscious, the blood streaming from his broken nose and split lip, when Julius popped out from behind the drapes and said, "What the hell just happened?"

Escher was already going through his pockets, taking his wallet— he had a faculty card that identified him as Giorgio Capaldi, an assistant history professor—and his BlackBerry.

"Is he dead?" Julius gasped, coming no closer.

"No. But he's going to have a very bad headache when he comes to."

Dragging the body into the bedroom, Escher hoisted it onto the bed, then cut the cord on the bedside phone and used it to tie his wrists.

"Make yourself useful," he said to Julius, who was watching slack-jawed from the doorway. "Find me a scarf, or some stockings." He tied the remaining length of cord to the iron bedstead.

Julius found a silk scarf, and Escher stuck it into the boyfriend's mouth before knotting the ends behind his head. Then, almost tenderly, he lifted the man's head and rested it on the pillow.

"That should do it."

Turning, he ripped open the bedside table, spilling the contents onto the floor. On the dresser, he opened the jewel box and threw the worthless costume jewelry around the room. But just to make things seem convincing, he stuck a couple of necklaces and earrings in his pants pocket.

Jantzen stood mute, as if transfixed, until Escher said, "Let's go," and pushed him back toward the front door. On the way, he swept a few things onto the floor and kicked the owl's perch over. The bird hopped onto a stack of books, hooting and fluttering.

At the top of the landing, he listened for any noise, then gently closed the door behind him and led Julius back down. To add insult to injury, they found a parking ticket on the Volvo.

"I'm not paying that," Jantzen protested, finally finding his voice again.

"Good," Escher said, tearing it up. "Neither am I."

Chapter 17

Too long, David thought. It was all taking him too long. While his sister lay dying, he was stuck here, thousands of miles away, struggling to find an antique looking glass that might, or might not, hold the key to her salvation.

When he'd made his regular call the night before, Sarah was actually back home, but she still sounded so weak. Dr. Ross had gotten her into the new protocol, and while it was too soon to tell if it would work, at least she had not rejected the new drug. "And they say that's a very good sign," Sarah said, doing her best to sound upbeat. "Tolerance has been a problem with a lot of other candidates."

David had done his best to sound enthusiastic, too, and so had Gary, who chimed in on the extension, but sometimes David felt that they were all just acting a part for each other. Gary had asked him if his new promotion had come through, and David had said, "If I'm lucky with my assignment here, I don't see how it wouldn't."

Sarah said she knew it would—she had always been his biggest booster—and when David hung up, he hadn't been able to fall asleep for hours, which might explain why he was having trouble staying awake. The late-morning sun was spilling through the clerestory windows of the reading room in the Accademia di Belle Arti, and taking off his glasses, he rubbed his eyes and yawned.

For the previous three days, he and Olivia had been holed up in their alcove at the Biblioteca Laurenziana, combing over the various drafts and versions of Cellini's manuscripts—his treatises on sculpture and goldsmithing, in addition to the many copies, some in his own hand, of his unfinished autobiography. They were searching for any mention of *La Medusa,* or anything like it, which might point them in the right direction. But there had been nothing so far.

In an attempt to hurry things along, David had left Olivia in charge of the Laurenziana research, while he had taken this ten-minute journey to the Piazza San Marco, and the Accademia library, where the Codice 101, S—yet another draft of Cellini's life—was kept. David knew the director here, Professor Ricci, from his days in Florence as a Fulbright scholar, and though David had thought he was an old man then, Ricci was unchanged, still shuffling around the echoing halls and cloisters of the library—founded by Cosimo de'Medici himself in 1561—in his bedroom slippers, with the bottoms of his pajamas peeking out from under the cuffs of his trousers. His skin was as yellow and crinkled as very old paper.

"So you are going to write about our Benvenuto?" Ricci said, in that proprietary way that Florentines displayed toward their legendary artists as he deposited the original manuscript on the desk in David's carrel. "The Laurenziana, they have some fine things over there," he said, sniffing, "and that Dr. Valetta, he will go on. But they are attached to a church, after all, not a museum."

David had the distinct sense that there was a cross-piazza rivalry here.

"Superstition reigns over there," Ricci concluded, "while reason alone prevails at the Academy."

David had to smile. "Actually, I'm not writing about Cellini himself," he confessed, "but looking for evidence of something he made. A mirror with the Medusa's face on one side."

Signor Ricci scratched the gray stubble on his chin, and said, "I never heard of such a thing. He made the Medusa only once, for the great statue of Perseus." Shaking his head, he said, "No, no, you must be mistaken, my friend."

It was the last thing he wanted to hear. Unless it existed, and he could find it, he would never be able to hold Mrs. Van Owen to her promises. For one thing, he would not be able to lay claim to the money—she had offered no consolation prize—but more important than that, he could never insist that she fulfill her solemn oath . . . to save his sister's life. It was a slim reed to cling to, but he didn't have any other.

As Signor Ricci wished him good luck, and meandered off, David opened the Codice 101, S, with weary hands, and read the all-too-familiar opening invocation: "All men of whatsoever quality they be, who have done anything of excellence, or which may properly resemble excellence, ought, if they are persons of truth and honesty, to describe their life with their own hand. . . ."—but he felt little hope of finding anything new. Although the manuscripts differed by a word or two here and there, they were all close copies, and detailed the same adventures, and the same miraculous acts of creation. Studying them had been a necessary step, but where, David wondered, was he to go next?

He carefully turned another page—the copyist had used a deep black ink that had faded to brown—and let his eye course down its length, looking for anything new, any anomaly, anything to indicate fresh passages to distinguish this copy from all the others. And after working so closely with Olivia Levi, he found it strange to have no one there to consult, or commiserate, with. Although scholarly work was generally solitary in nature, he'd quickly gotten used to having company and exchanging all kinds of ideas. Olivia was open to any suggestion or query, no matter how off-the-wall, and in nearly every case she could top it. She had a vast field of reference—there was almost nothing David could bring up that Olivia didn't already have a firm opinion about—and she was willing to talk all night. He found himself lonely, missing her quick wit, her erudition, and—if he was completely honest with himself—the nearness of her, perched, knees up, in the next chair, her nose buried in a book. Once, she had caught him, lost in thought and simply staring at her, and she'd said, "Don't you have work to do?"

He'd been so flustered, he hadn't known what to say.

Olivia laughed and said, "It's okay. You may be American, but you are also Italian."

She was bringing that out in him more and more each day.

David was about midway through the manuscript at hand, his eyes beginning to glaze over, when he heard the sound of Signor Ricci's slippers and looked up to see him tottering under a stack of loose pages and cracked binders. Just before he almost toppled over, the old man managed to deposit them on David's carrel and steady himself by catching the back of a chair.

"What are these?" David asked.

Ricci, taking a second to catch his breath, said, "Nothing you'll find at the Laurenziana. These are the household accounts of Cosimo de'Medici."

Though he didn't want to appear ungrateful, why, David thought, would Ricci think these would be of any use? Why should he care how much wine or butter or wheat was consumed?

"Including the art and jewelry commissions," Ricci explained, as if reading his mind. "If Benvenuto made anything for Cosimo or his wife or his family—like a looking glass—it would be listed somewhere in here. The Medici kept careful records of everything they spent, and everything they received."

That they did, and for the first time in weeks, David felt a sudden surge of optimism. If nothing else, it was a fresh avenue to explore. Ricci could see that David was pleased, and his face cracked open in a nearly toothless smile. "Go to it," he said, patting David on the shoulder and teetering off. "And be sure to tell people where you found what you needed."

Putting the Codice aside, David cleared a space on the carrel and began to systematically go through the ledgers, skipping quickly over the shopping lists of comestibles and the other household goods, and zeroing in on anything having to do with the purchase of art supplies—marble, brushes, paints, plaster—or metals, such as copper, bronze, silver, gold. Punctuating the lists of raw materials were finished works, separately bracketed, and David was stunned to see the purchase of world-renowned works by Leonardo and Andrea del Sarto, Botticelli and Bronzino, recorded for the first time. On one page, he found a shipment from Palestrina, describing a "stone torso of a boy" that had been unearthed by a farmer's plow. Was this the torso that Cellini had written about in his autobiography, the one that the ignorant Bandinelli had scorned but that Cellini had later refashioned into a Ganymede?

The dates were neatly inscribed, in a spidery but still quite legible script, at the top of each page, and David began to turn to the most promising sections, the years in which Cellini was most regularly employed by the duke. Theirs had been a volatile relationship, and when they were at loggerheads, Cellini had often taken off for Rome, or for the court of the King of France, before coming back to his native town. The *Perseus* statue had taken him nine long years to complete—from 1545 to 1554—and for most of that time he was begging for his pay, or for supplies, and sparring with the duke's accountants, who were forever asking him what was taking so long.

Part of the problem was the constant distractions he had had to deal with. The duke's wife, Eleonora de Toledo, was often peeved with Cellini—his social graces were somewhat lacking—but she recognized his immense talent and was forever pestering him for his opinion on one thing or another; in his book, he'd written about his falling-out with her over a rope of pearls, and the time she'd try to lay claim to some of the figures designed for the pedestal of the *Perseus*. Still, if it was a looking glass that Cellini had made, David figured there was a good chance it had been made for her, and probably before he had ever created the remarkable Medusa now in the piazza. It was hard to imagine an artist like Cellini scaling *down*. Once he had made the definitive Gorgon, he would hardly be inclined to do another, and in reduced proportions besides.

David studied the pile of ledgers and papers that the Academy director had left him, looking for the volumes from the mid-1530s, a period when Cellini had been steadily employed by the duke. Finding a couple, he put the other books on a neighboring table and concentrated on scouring the endless lists for jewelry and other items a duchess might have ordered. And though it was slow work, he did find them—lists of bracelets and earrings, adorned with pearls and precious stones, ornaments for her hair, amber combs and brushes, rings with short descriptions, such as "acanthus motif, sapphire," or "gold band, diamond *pavé*." The duchess was vain, and very particular about the design of everything she commissioned . . . which was one reason David found the idea of a mirror in the shape of the Medusa so strange. It was not, by any stretch of the imagination, a fetching image—far from it—but perhaps that was its purpose. Perhaps it was meant to be defensive. Italians were always wary of *il malocchio*, the evil eye, and a mirror in this grotesque cast might have been considered the perfect way to ward it off.

He was up to June 1, 1538, and about to take a break and call Olivia for an update on her own progress, when his eye happened to fall upon a notation, in that same spidery hand, at the bottom of a page.

But it was listed not as a commission, but simply *"dalla mano dell'artista."* From the hand of the artist.

"Parure," it said, *"in argento."* Or silver. This sort of thing—a matching set of jewelry, usually including a tiara and earrings and bracelet—would surely have been right up Cellini's alley. And though he did not yet see any mention of a mirror, it would have been a likely component. *"Con rubini"*—with rubies—was added to the general description, and though David's sketch of *La Medusa* indicated no such jewels, they might have been destined for any one of the various pieces.

But it was the last words, hastily scrawled in the margin, which made his heart thump in his chest.

"Egida di Zeus motivo." Aegis of Zeus motif. According to classical mythology, the king of the gods carried a shield, or aegis, that had been a gift from Athena. And on that shield, David knew, was emblazoned the head of the Medusa. *"Un faccia a fermare il tempo"* was also

appended there—a face that can stop time—the very phrase that was used in *The Key to Life Eternal* to describe the mirror. Not a face to kill, not a face to turn its observer to stone. A face to stop time.

At last, he felt he had stumbled upon the trail of the thing itself, that he had found some recorded proof—outside of the papers that Mrs. Van Owen had provided—suggesting that *La Medusa* had indeed seen the light of day, that it was more than something Cellini had simply sketched, or claimed to manufacture.

But if that were the case—if he had succeeded in making the *Medusa*—why in the world would he have given it away, much less to a duchess who was no particular favorite of his? *The Key to Life Eternal* claimed that the Medusa could grant the gift of immortality. Cellini would never have given such a creation away.

Nor, however, was he one to waste materials or labor. David remembered a passage from the *Key*, where Cellini had written of the torment he'd endured constructing *La Medusa*, and of the casts he had made prior to hitting on the right one: *"Il bicchiere deve essere perfettamente smussato, il puro argento: un unico difetto, non importa quanto piccola, si annulla la magia del tutto."* The glass must be perfectly beveled, the silver welded; a single flaw, no matter how tiny, will undo the magic of the whole. David was now confronted with two possibilities—one, that Cellini had made the *Medusa* and, after discovering that it did not work, repurposed it as a present to a wealthy patron. Or that he had simply bestowed on the Medici an early cast, a reject, one that he had never intended to imbue with the waters from the sacred pool at all.

And wasn't that just like him, to muddy the trail of something valuable? The same man who had created an optical illusion in his most famous statue, or who had made strongboxes with coded locks, who kept the greatest advancements of his trade to himself, and limited the secrets of his sorcery to the unpublished *Key*, was not likely to leave his most ingenious achievement baldly exposed.

Cellini was a trickster, and David had to figure out how, over the centuries, this particular trick played out.

He quickly turned to the next page, which began with an account of some marble imported for a bathhouse. He jumped ahead several leaves, past some other mundane expenditures, until he found a later annotation, made in another hand, saying, "*Un regalo al de'Medici della Catherine, sul decimo del settembre 1572.*" Or, a gift to Catherine de'Medici, the tenth of September, 1572.

"*Lo sguardo del maggio ottentute proteggere suo da tutti I nemici.*" May the gaze of the Gorgon protect her from her enemies.

Cosimo himself had made the annotation—his initials were boldly inscribed below the note—and he had sent the piece to his niece, who had married into the royal family of France, and become queen. No one at that time in history, David knew, was more besieged by her enemies than the Queen of France, who, facing an insurrection from the Huguenots, had ordered the infamous St. Bartholomew's Day Massacre on August 23 of that same year. In reality, the purge had lasted weeks, during which time thousands of her religious enemies were rounded up and slaughtered all over France. It was later said that the wicked Italian queen had followed the advice of her countryman, Niccolò Machiavelli, who warned that it was best to kill all your enemies in one blow.

David fell back in his chair, trying to sort through it all. If this was indeed the one and only Medusa, then it could not have the powers Cellini had claimed or he would not have given it away . . . unless he'd had no choice. Could the duke have forced his hand? There were a hundred threats and forms of torture the Duke de'Medici could have employed. And perhaps the phrase, "from the hand of the artist," did not so much mean a willing gift as a tribute pried from an artisan unable to refuse or resist.

One way or another, though, this mirror had gone to France— where Cellini himself had spent a good deal of his life, in the employ of the French king—and it was the only one whose trail David could now follow. As a gift to the queen, it would naturally have become a part of the royal jewels. For all David knew, it was still a part of whatever remained of that once-impressive collection. Whether it had the powers it was reputed to possess, or not, it was what Mrs. Van Owen had sent him to find—and find it he would. Shaking it loose, for any amount of money, from the French patrimony, seemed an utter impossibility—even for someone of Mrs. Van Owen's resources—but he would cross that bridge when he came to it. For the moment, he just wanted to share the news with Olivia and get cracking.

With facsimiles of the two pages, produced by a copying machine carefully calibrated to work in low light and heat, tucked away in his valise, he raced back to the Laurenziana. He could have called Olivia on the way, but he wanted the pleasure of seeing her face when he presented his discovery from the Medici account books. In addition to the more personal feelings for her that he could no longer deny, he had also come to value her opinion—and approval—more highly than anyone else's. She was a true eccentric, there was no denying that, quirky and volatile, but she was also one of the most widely read and original thinkers he had ever encountered. Most of her scholarly papers and monographs—and she had shared a few with David—were unfinished and unpublished, but they betrayed a wealth of knowledge on subjects ranging from the philosophy of Pico della Mirandola to the evolution of the early European banking system. It was as if her mind could not be focused on one subject long enough to see it through to its natural conclusion. Instead, she would get distracted and follow some beckoning side path—invariably finding something valuable there, too—without ever bothering to get back to her original argument.

But when David burst into their alcove, Olivia wasn't there. She might have been sleeping late that morning—David knew that she was a night owl—and it was also possible that she was off leading one of her tour groups. David was paying her a stipend out of Mrs. Van Owen's account, but Olivia had plainly stated that she wanted to keep her other sidelines alive. "Otherwise, what do I do when you leave me to go back to Chicago?"

With each passing hour, David found such a thought more distressing . . . and harder to imagine.

But neatness, he would concede, was not one of her many virtues. She had left her yellow notepads, covered with long columns of dates and figures and names, scattered on the table, along with several broken pencils, some crumpled tissues, and a stack of old, leather-bound books that David hadn't ever seen before.

None of them, he discovered, were by or about Cellini.

When David opened the first one, and did a rough translation from the Latin, he was surprised to see that it was called *A Treatise on the Most Secret Alchemical and Necromantic Arts.* Written by a Dottore A. Strozzi, it had been printed in Palermo in 1529.

The one under that—really just a pair of worm-riddled boards, with a loose collection of parchment sheets held between—had no title page at all, but after glancing through some of the text, David could see that it was a manual of *stregheria,* the ancient witchcraft that predated the Roman Empire. As late as the twelfth century, many of the Old Religionists, as the followers of the pagan gods were sometimes called, had dutifully masqueraded as Christians while secretly continuing to worship the ancient pantheon. They had simply accepted the Virgin Mary, for instance, as yet the latest incarnation of the goddess Diana.

He had just picked up the last book on the stack, a vellum-bound treatise, also in Italian, and entitled *Revelations of Egyptian Masonry, as Revealed by the Grand Copt to one Count Cagliostro*—at least this count, a famous mesmerist of his day, was familiar to David—when Dottore Valetta appeared in the alcove, a red silk pocket square blooming from his jacket. "Where is your confederate today?" he sniffed.

"I'm not sure," David replied, scanning the table quickly to see if Olivia had left him any note from the day before. It was then that he noticed the old yellowed cards—clearly the precursors to the same library request cards he and Olivia were using—that had been hidden under the pile of books. The director saw them, too, and before

David could even say a word, he had snatched them up and quickly riffled through them, glowering.

"Her old tricks," Valetta fumed. "Signorina Levi is up to all her old tricks."

"What tricks are you talking about?"

"Wherever she goes, she likes to stir the pot . . . to make trouble. She has tried to make this particular kind of trouble before."

David was utterly baffled. "What was she doing?" David asked. "Checking to see who had consulted these sources before we did?"

Slipping the cards into his pocket, the director looked at David as if he wasn't sure he could trust him anymore either. "She hasn't told you her theory? Or why we have barred her from further use of the Laurenziana?"

"No. She hasn't."

Now the director looked as if he regretted saying as much as he had, or giving her ideas any further airing.

But David wasn't about to let him off the hook so easily. "So *you* have to tell me. If you don't, I'll make sure she does. What's this theory of hers?"

It was clear that Valetta was choosing his words carefully when he spoke. "Signorina Levi believes that my predecessors at the library were Fascist sympathizers and collaborated with the Nazi regime."

David was nonplussed.

"And let me hasten to add, she has never summoned any credible proof of these charges. She simply throws them around," the director said, whisking his hand through the air, "like confetti. And without any regard for the damage such accusations could do to the reputation of this institution."

While it was true that Olivia had never confided to him anything of this nature, David did not have much trouble imagining it. As an Italian and a Jew, whose own family had been decimated by the Fascist regime, Olivia might well have formulated such a theory. And Mussolini had indeed thrown in his country's lot with the Third

Reich. But how this theory of hers had anything to do with the books of black magic that were also sitting on the table, David had no idea.

Nor did he have time to ask Dr. Valetta before they both heard Olivia explode from the end of the long gallery.

"What is he doing here?" she said. "Get out of there!" she shouted, and two or three researchers looked up from their seats in horror at this gross breach of decorum.

Storming into the alcove, her familiar overcoat flapping wide, her dark eyes darted around, swiftly taking in the dismantled stack of books, the loss of the borrower cards, and the look of confusion on David's face.

"I can explain everything," she said to David.

"I already have," Dr. Valetta put in dryly.

"Oh, I'm sure you have." Turning back to David, she said, "This man is just a functionary, another cipher"—she snapped her fingers to indicate what a trifle she was dealing with—"like all the others, who did the bidding of their overlords. Who knows who he really works for? God save us from the bureaucrats who clung to their desks while the Huns sacked the city!"

"All right," Valetta said, "I've heard it all before, and I don't need to hear it all again. Pack your things, Signorina, and get out of my library—"

"*My* library?" Olivia exclaimed.

"—and understand that you will never again receive permission to enter here."

"But I am employed by Signor Franco," she said, holding her hands out toward David.

"I don't care if you are sent here by the Pope himself. You're not getting in." The director turned slightly, to block out Olivia and address solely David. "You are welcome to continue to use our facilities, so long as I believe you are confining yourself to legitimate fields of study. And as long as you are working alone."

David was incensed himself. No one had ever suggested censoring, or even monitoring, his work. "What are you saying? That you plan to approve, or disapprove, of my requests for material from now on?"

"Absolutely. And from that I will know whether or not you're pursuing your own ends, or trying to assist Signorina Levi in hers."

"That's outrageous."

"That's necessity."

"Then you won't be seeing me here again, either," David said, calling his bluff. In point of fact, he had already decided to follow the mirror, copy or not, to France, but it didn't hurt to make a bold stand. "And I'll be sure to tell Mrs. Van Owen that her donations would be better spent elsewhere."

For a second, Dr. Valetta looked stricken. "As I have said, it is only Signorina Levi who has broken—"

"We'll be packed and gone in five minutes," David said, turning his back on him. Even Olivia looked surprised at this turn of events. "Gather your things," he barked at her, and she quickly swept her pencils and pads into a pile on one side of the table.

Once that was all done, they walked in shame, like Adam and Eve being expelled from the Garden of Eden, down the length of the reading room, past the astonished stares of the other occupants, down the steps, and out into the courtyard, where Olivia immediately wheeled on him, and said, "I'm sorry, David. I'm so sorry. It was only while you were at the Accademia. I just wanted to tie up some loose ends on an old project of mine."

"Don't we have enough to do already?" David asked.

"I wasn't going to get another chance."

"To do what?"

"To prove that the Nazis had a special place in their hearts for Florence . . . and why."

On the one hand, David was surprised that this was where she had been going, but on the other, it suddenly made perfect sense and brought together many separate strands of her research and proclivities.

"The Nazis not only looted Florence of its art," she said, as they walked toward the Piazza San Marco, "they also pillaged its books and libraries and monasteries, searching for secrets that would add to their power."

"Like ancient Egyptian rites?"

"Don't laugh," she warned. "Hitler *believed* in the occult. His top officers *believed*. The Third Reich was as mystical as it was military. No one must ever forget that."

But much as David would have liked to stop and explore her theories further, right now he was trying to focus on their next move. "Where did you park your car?" he asked.

"I didn't. It's out of gas."

He lifted his arm and waved for the first cab coming by.

"Where are we going?"

"To your place."

Olivia looked surprised but not displeased.

"You have to pack a bag."

"Why?" she asked. "Where do you think we are going?"

"To Paris."

A white Fiat taxi cut across three lanes and jolted to a stop. She slid over in the backseat, David joined her, and the cabbie took off for the Piazza della Repubblica, the tinny sound of ABBA emanating from his radio. After a minute or two, Olivia couldn't contain herself any longer and said, "What is in Paris that is so important?"

He opened his valise as the cab hung a sharp left, throwing her up against his shoulder, and showed her the facsimile pages from the Medici records. As she scanned the pages, he explained in a low voice how he had come across them, and why he was so sure it was *La Medusa* they referred to.

Olivia's dark eyes absorbed every word and notation before she nodded solemnly, and said, "Then it does exist."

"Or at least it did."

"But what if, as you said, it's just a copy?"

"Without the original to compare it to, who's to say? I was sent to find it, and that's what I intend to do." What he did not say was what he felt in his heart, as surely as he could feel it beating. This was the real Medusa, and returning with it to Mrs. Van Owen would seal their bargain. He believed in it, like so much else now, because he had to. For his own sake, and Sarah's.

"If it went to France," she said, thinking aloud, "then it would have become a part of the crown jewels."

"Exactly," David replied. "Until the Revolution."

"When it was turned over to the citizens of the French Republic."

With Olivia, David never had to finish a thought. As the cab beat a path through the swarming, horn-blaring traffic, Olivia stared silently out her window and David, his mind going a mile a minute, was trying to organize the next leg of his journey and wondering how fast he could get it done. Taking out his phone, he quickly began scanning for flights to Paris. Cost was no object, but timing might be. Olivia would have to collect a few things, he would have to go back to the Grand for his own belongings, and then they'd need to get to the airport.

"How long do you expect me to stay on this job?" Olivia said.

"As long as it takes," David said, concentrating chiefly on his cell-phone screen. Alitalia had a flight at three that they might be able to make if they hurried.

"But why," she said, with an uncharacteristic hesitancy, "do you want me?"

"My French is really rusty," David replied, before thinking.

And he could all but feel her fold in on herself.

And what made it worse was, it wasn't even true. He just didn't know how to tell her what he was really feeling and thinking. Here he was, on a desperate mission to save his sister, and he hadn't confessed even that to her yet. He had so much to tell her that he didn't know where, or when, to start. And in the back of a hurtling cab, it seemed like the worst possible time.

"Olivia," he tried to begin, "I do need your help with this work. If anybody can help me cut through the thicket of the French archives and bureaucracy, it will be you."

"So that's the reason?" she said. "You just need me to help you with your . . . quest?"

God, he had gotten off on the wrong foot again. His French wasn't nearly as rusty as some of his other skills.

The taxi had stopped at a busy crosswalk, but the driver, fed up with the unimpeded flow of pedestrians, leaned on his horn again and to a chorus of jeers, plowed through a narrow opening and sped on. Normally, David would have been appalled at such recklessness, but today he was thrilled.

"And this person you work for—" Olivia ventured.

"Mrs. Van Owen. A widow, in Chicago." He knew he was painting a more staid portrait than was warranted. "Very rich. She'll continue to pay for everything."

"You say she is willing to do anything to get this *Medusa*."

"Yes."

"But you?" She looked at him intently now. "Why do you want to find it so much?"

"I'll get a big promotion," he said, not wanting to get into the whole story yet. *Not here, not now.* "And I'll be well paid."

She frowned, and, shaking her head, said, "No, no, no."

Not for the first time, he felt like she could see right through him.

"You are not someone who works for money."

"I'm not?" Pretending otherwise.

"No, you are like me. We don't care about money," she said. "We only care about knowledge, and truth. If we cared about money, we would do some other kind of work than this. We would be bankers." She said that last word as if she were saying swine.

Overall, he took her point.

"No, what we do," she concluded, "we do for love. There is some love at the root of this—always—and it is personal, too. That is what is pushing you."

It was as if she'd shot an arrow right into his heart. He longed to tell her about the real stakes he was playing for—he ached to unburden himself of the truth about his sister and the strange promise of his mysterious benefactor—but he was afraid he would sound crazy. Even to someone as open-minded as Olivia.

"If we are going to do this thing together," Olivia said, "from now on you are going to have to tell me only the truth." As the cab slowed down to check the street addresses, she pressed him. "Agreed?"

"Agreed."

"On the right," Olivia said to the driver. "Next door to the café."

They got out of the cab, went inside, and climbed three stories of rickety steps with worn carpeting; it made his own place, David thought, look pretty good by comparison. On the third floor, Olivia stopped at a door decorated with a postcard of the Laocoön and put the key in the lock. Something seemed to surprise her, as if the lock had already been turned; but she opened it and stepped inside.

Even with the curtains drawn, David could see the chaos. And when Olivia flicked on the lights and saw her books strewn across the floor and a wooden perch of some kind toppled over, she said, "Oh my God."

It was plain she'd been burglarized, but it wasn't so plain that the thieves were gone.

"Hold on," David said, stepping in front of her and moving cautiously toward the next room. As he approached the half-open door, he thought he heard some commotion inside, and was about to back off when something gray suddenly flew smack into his face, wings fluttering wildly, before careening off into the living room.

"Glaucus!" Olivia cried.

And then David heard another noise—a muffled groan—from the bedroom. He pushed the door wider with one finger and saw a man with a gag in his mouth, half-on and half-off the bed. His hands dangled above his head, tied with a phone cord to the bedstead. Dried blood was caked all over his face and neck.

As David rushed to his aid, Olivia appeared in the bedroom doorway, and said in horror, "Giorgio?"

❧

By the time the ambulance had come and gone, and the police had finished interviewing Olivia, it was too late to make any of the flights

David had hoped for. As far as the carabinieri were concerned, it had simply been a break-in, and the old boyfriend had come back to collect his stuff at just the wrong time. Olivia said she was missing some cheap jewelry, but that was about it. "I'm just glad he didn't take any of my books," she told the cops. "They're the only valuable things in here."

For much of the time, David had sat outside on the stoop, thinking and keeping his own counsel. It didn't seem to have occurred, even to Olivia, that this could be anything more than a burglary gone awry. But to David, who had been nearly run over at the skating rink, it seemed like some very odd things had been happening since he'd gotten mixed up with Mrs. Van Owen. And was this one of them? Or was the strain on his nerves just getting to him? He checked his watch again, recalculating how quickly he could be on his way to Paris.

And when the last police car pulled away, Olivia settled down beside him and said, "Giorgio and I broke up a few months ago. He'd been on a sabbatical in Greece."

"Then you're okay?" David said, draping an arm consolingly around her shoulders.

She sighed, and fumblingly lighted a cigarette.

"You don't need to stay here to look after Giorgio?"

"Him?" She blew out a cloud of smoke in disgust. "Let his new girlfriend do that."

David felt like an immense weight had been removed from his heart. He was ashamed to admit it, even to himself, but ever since Giorgio had turned up in the apartment, he had been wondering where things stood between Giorgio and Olivia. What if she was still in love with him? "So," he said, "does this mean you would still consider going to Paris? There's a TVG, leaving in ninety minutes. We could still make it."

But Olivia didn't answer at first; in fact, it was several seconds before he realized that she was shaking, then quietly sobbing. He hugged her tighter, as the shock of what had just happened at her place sank in. The police were gone, her apartment had been ransacked, her old boyfriend was on the way to the hospital. David, who was so good when it came to talking about an edition of Dante, was again at a loss for words. The lighted cigarette hung, neglected, from her fingertips, before it finally tumbled onto the broken steps. But when she lifted her dark eyes, wet with tears, to his own, he knew— for once in his life he knew—that words weren't what was called for. He pulled her closer and touched his lips to hers. There was no response, and her lips were cool. Her eyes remained open and inquisitive.

"I need you," he said.

"Because I speak French better than you?" she said, with a troubled, uncertain smile. Her shoulders were still quivering.

"*Je vous aide,*" he said flawlessly, "*parce que je t'adore.*"

And now, when he kissed her again, her shoulders were still, and her lips were warm. And they clung to each other, sitting in the middle of the broken steps, saying nothing. For David, burying his face in her dark hair, feeling her arms wrapped around him, it was the sweetest respite he had known for a very long time, and he wished that they could have stayed that way all night.

Chapter 18

Cellini watched from the shadows as the catafalque was carried across the piazza. Four members of the Accademia, of which he had been a founder, bore it on their shoulders, followed by a throng of black-clad mourners. The doors of the ancient Basilica della Santissima Annunziata, in which the tomb was waiting, were held open by a quartet of friars.

He touched the silver garland around his temple to make sure that he was still well concealed by its powers.

Inserting himself into the crowd, unseen and unnoticed, he passed under the narrow archway and into the celebrated Chiostrino dei Voti, or Cloister of the Votives. For centuries, pilgrims to the church, who had come to see its marvelous fresco of the Annunciation, had left their own wax candles and figurines—often of themselves—as offerings here. On that night, February 15, 1571, the whole motley collection, in white and yellow and brown wax, was lighted, along with a hundred torches in the basilica beyond.

The church itself was a simple affair, erected in 1260 by the Oratory of the Servants of Mary. Beneath its dome, there was a single long nave, flanked by altar niches and culminating in a rotunda, where the famous fresco could be seen. Legend had it that the painting had been begun by a member of the Order, a Servite, who had despaired of ever making it beautiful enough. Throwing down his brushes in defeat, he had fallen into a deep sleep, and when he awakened, the painting was done . . . finished by an angel.

At that moment, crowded as the church was, and illuminated only by the flickering torchlight, the painting was almost impossible to see. The casket was placed on a trestle, as monks, chanting and swinging censers, slowly paraded around it. Their voices gradually stilled the commotion, and the family and friends of the artisan, accompanied by his many admirers, filed into the pews, or stood respectfully, silently, in the side chapels, hands folded and heads bowed.

So far, Cellini was pleased with the turnout. Even some of his enemies, he noted, had come to hear the obsequies—though it was possible, he thought, that they just wanted to make sure he was dead.

A young friar, someone he had never so much as seen in his life, stepped up to the altar and began to recite the formal prayers. To be frank, Cellini had never had much use for all the Church's pomp and ritual. He had seen too much of life, too much of men and their venality, to put much stock in it. And he had seen things—*done* things—that no monk or priest or Pope could condone. He had crossed swords with too many, both in the Church and out of it, ever to expect all the acclaim he felt was his due. He had worn out his welcome—not only in Florence, but in the papal court, too—and he knew that if he hoped to keep the dark secret he possessed, there was nothing to do at that point but publicly stage his own interment.

And so he had arranged it, as meticulously as he had constructed and erected his grand statue of Perseus for the central square of the city.

Over a period of years, he had laid the groundwork, letting his beard grow long and powdering it to assume the mantle of age. He had walked with an increasing stoop and pretended to forget things he remembered quite well. He put it about that he was suffering from the pleurisy, and on days when he was expected at the studio, he stayed in bed. His crowning touch had been Michelangelo's funeral—an event that he had largely planned, and which he then did not attend. Instead, he had met the body in private, when it was first transported by mule from Rome. He was shocked to see that it was packaged in a bale of hay, as if it were a crate of pottery—this, the Divine Michelangelo!—and he had personally groomed the body and said his farewells. This was more than a man, this was a force of nature, whose name would still resound long after every preening king and Medici prince had been forgotten.

But speak of the devil . . . there was the Grand Duke himself, in a long black cape and velvet cap, down from his villa in Castello. On his own breast, he wore the silver mirror given to his late wife as a ward against misfortune. An early cast, Cellini had bestowed upon it ruby eyes, which winked in the torchlight.

For the thousandth time, Cellini wondered what had happened to its secret counterpart, a simpler affair, with no bright gemstones but an unimaginable power, ripped from his neck by the Duke of Castro and secreted somewhere among the papal treasures. Would he ever see, or possess, the true *La Medusa* again?

The duke was bowed by age, and his long, sloping face was lined with sorrowful creases. In 1562, on a trip to Pisa, his wife, Eleonora de Toledo, and two of his sons, Giovanni and Garzia, had been struck down by the malaria that haunted the marshlands of Italy. Cosimo had never recovered from the blow. Cellini studied his face, the face of his patron and persecutor, his friend and his enemy, over so many years . . . and, though he knew he could do no such thing, he longed to reach out and touch him, to reveal himself one last time. Cosimo, always a great enthusiast of alchemy and magic, had become even more interested in the unseen world since the deaths in his family. He would be mightily impressed at Cellini's feat.

But the artisan, huddling beside a marble column, restrained himself. How could he think of undoing what he had so painstakingly planned?

The young friar, his own face as unlined as fresh calfskin, was reciting his eulogy, and doing an admirable job. Cellini wondered who had coached him. Giorgio Vasari? No, not Vasari—the encomiums were too grand. His old companion, Benedetto Varchi, would have done it right, but Varchi had been gone for years. Occasionally, as if he were speaking to the corpse itself, the Servite's eyes fell to the gleaming lid of the casket and Cellini had to smile at the notion of such high praise and sorrowful remembrance being directed at its occupant, the most insignificant of men, a destitute wretch whom Ascanio had found in the gutter a month ago and brought home in a wheelbarrow.

"What do you think?" he'd said proudly, displaying the beggar as if he were a prize heifer. "He's about your height, he even looks a lot like you."

At this, Cellini had objected, and his apprentice laughed.

"And if you listen to his cough," Ascanio said, "you'll know he's not long for this world."

The beggar, slurping a bowl of hot stew by the hearth, paid no attention.

"We can lodge him in the stable," Ascanio went on, "until nature takes its course."

Cellini had moved closer to inspect the man, who looked up at him with rheumy eyes while clutching the rim of the bowl, like a dog protecting its few scraps of food.

"What's your name?"

"Virgilio."

An apt one, Cellini thought. Like Virgil leading Dante, this poor impostor could precede him into the next world. But would he be received there with the special considerations due the artisan himself?

The arrangements were made, and in return for staying out of sight, Virgilio was promised a berth in the hayloft, bread and stew and wine every day—he was especially insistent about the wine—and for the next several weeks, as the beggar's cough grew worse, and his strength flagged, Ascanio kept a close eye on him. When his apprentice came to Cellini's workroom one night, shaking his head, and saying, "He won't live to see the dawn," Cellini knew the time had come. The book of his own life—the life of Italy's most famous living artisan—had to be closed . . . and another, newer book begun.

And this one would be lived in another land, under another name.

By then, the friar had given way at the pulpit to various members of the Accademia, who had begun their own eulogies and remembrances. Several sonnets were read aloud, and Cellini could not help judging them against what might have been his own contribution. Despite the name he had made for himself as an artist, he fancied himself a fine writer, too, and regretted that he had stopped writing the story of his own life so abruptly, several years ago. There was so much more to tell, so much to confess; but incomplete copies had already begun to circulate, hand to hand, among other artists and gentry. How could new chapters be expected to appear from the pen of a dead man? Only saints could perform miracles, and Benvenuto knew that he was a saint in no man's estimation.

When the obsequies were done, a select group of Academicians and Servite friars accompanied the casket through the adjoining Chiostrino dei Morti, or Cloister of the Dead, and into the Chapel of St. Luke, where the tomb in the floor lay open. Cellini, careful to touch no one or to have his presence suspected in any way, slipped between the columns, close enough to gaze into the black maw that was even now receiving the casket. The box was lowered on braided ropes, and once it had settled, the ropes were dropped in. A pile of dirt and rubble, concealed beneath a tarpaulin, had only to be shoveled back in.

How many men, Cellini wondered, had ever lived to see their own funerals? It was an unnerving sight, even for someone of his own bold temperament . . . and a grim reminder of the immense transgression he committed with every passing day.

A painter who had studied under Bronzino, another of Benvenuto's great and long-standing friends, stepped to the edge of the grave and, after wishing "eternal peace to this immortal master, who has brought glory to Florence and beauty to the world," let fall a spray of purple irises.

Immortal master—Cellini liked that. If only this painter knew how fitting it was.

The head of the Order, Abbot Anselmo, lifted the tarpaulin, draped it back, and taking a fistful of dirt, cast it into the grave. A painfully shy old man with a terrible stammer, it was he who had agreed to reserve for Cellini this burial spot . . . in return for a magnificent marble crucifix Cellini had made and donated to the Order. As the other mourners stepped up to take their own handfuls of dirt and rubble, the faint strains of a laubade drifted in from the rotunda. Played on a harp, a pair of flutes, and a five-stringed *lyra da braccio,* the composition—both words and music—was also Cellini's creation. As the melody filled the chamber, Cellini felt his fingers twitch involuntarily, as if playing the notes on a flute, and his eyes filled with tears. Not with regret—he had done what he had done in his life, and he made no apologies—but with nostalgia. His father, a musician himself, had longed for his son to become a famous flutist, and though Benvenuto had made a brilliant start, it had never been his first love. Music was too ephemeral; it was lasting monuments that he had always wanted to build.

But listening to the solemn tune, and its equally solemn lyrics—based on the closing words of the divine *Paradiso*—he wondered if he had been right about that. Stone could shatter, gold could be melted down, but the very airiness of this creation—a sequence of notes, a few words and phrases—might that not be more enduring, after all? Who could destroy it? Who, for that matter, could truly possess it? It belonged to anyone with an instrument to play, or a voice with which to sing. Benvenuto wished that his father, with whom he had had so many bitter quarrels, were standing in front of him now, so that the artisan could bend his head—as he did to no one else—and beg for his forgiveness.

Instead, he turned away from the grave, where a long line of mourners waited to pay their last respects, and moved silently, surreptitiously, invisibly, down the long nave of burning torches and out into the gloomy piazza.

Ascanio, who awaited him in the shadows of the loggia, was

nonetheless startled when, with a low cough, he made his presence known.

"Are we alone?"

"Yes," Ascanio assured him, looking again in all directions. "There's no one in sight."

Cellini made his own survey, then carefully removed the wreath, fashioned from the infernal bulrushes, from around his temples. It had been a tight fit—it was a relief to have it off—and seconds later, like a figure shimmering into view as it stepped from behind a waterfall, he once more became visible to the mortal eye.

"You look no worse for wear," Ascanio commented, his eye traveling up and down his master's body.

But Cellini wasn't so sure of that. Watching your own burial was a sobering sight.

"And now that you're dead and gone, have you given some thought to who you are going to be?"

"Royalty, I think. Perhaps a marquis."

Making a grand bow, with one arm folded behind his back, Ascanio said, "And where will the marquis live?"

Cellini had given it much consideration, and in the end he could think of nowhere better suited to his new life than the birthplace of his one great, and long-lost, inamorata. Throwing the hood of his cloak over his head, he strode off into the night, saying simply, "France."

Part Three

Part Three

Chapter 19

Even racing along at almost two hundred miles per hour, the train hardly rocked or swayed at all. A far cry from the Chicago El, David thought, as he gazed out at the rolling hills of the Italian countryside. Dusk was falling, and off in the distance he could just make out the sloping walls of another medieval town. On any normal occasion, he would have been relishing every minute of the trip to Paris.

But this was no normal occasion.

Having tried three times to put a call through to Chicago, he snapped his phone shut and decided to wait until later. The last time he'd spoken to Gary, Sarah had been at the hospital, receiving treatment, but "so far, so good," Gary had said. "Her counts have either improved or held steady. We're just hoping there's not a reaction."

David hoped for more—much more—than that. And he was determined to make it happen.

He heard the latch of the en suite bathroom unlock, and Olivia came out in a black turtleneck and jeans, still brushing her hair back. She looked as sleek as a seal.

But everything had changed for them in the past few hours. Ever since their first embrace on the steps of her building, it was as if all the walls had come down between them. Whatever suspicions he had ever harbored about her were gone, along with whatever reservations he had entertained. In all but deed, they were lovers—and before the night was over, even that, David suspected, might change.

"I just thought of something," she said, pulling the brush one last time through her hair.

"What's that?"

"I haven't eaten since dawn."

Now that he gave it some thought, he hadn't had anything since morning, either.

"And maybe it would be nice to have some wine?" she added.

David needed no more persuading. Taking his valise with him, he locked the cabin and followed Olivia down the long corridor, into the next car, then the one after that, with the smell of food—good food—getting stronger all the time. A steward in a blue uniform smiled at them as they passed and said, "I recommend the trout. Just caught."

The dining car was set with small tables on both sides of a narrow aisle, with white linen tablecloths, gleaming silverware, and little lamps that gave off a rosy glow. A waiter in a white jacket seated them and David ordered a cold bottle of Bordeaux. The last time he'd eaten on a train, it had been on an Amtrak to Detroit, and he'd had a bag of barbecue chips, a stale sandwich, and a lukewarm Coke.

There was something to be said for European transit.

After the waiter had poured the wine and taken their order for trout almondine with asparagus, a sort of awkward silence fell over them. For days, they had been working together, side by side, but now they were having an undeniably romantic dinner on the night train to Paris, and in the warm glow of the table lamp, David couldn't help but focus on her dark and shining eyes and the sensual curve of her full lips. Glancing up at him over the rim of her glass, she caught him staring, just as she had done once before, and said with a sly smile, "What are you wondering about now?"

"Nothing," he said, embarrassed. "It's just been . . . a hell of a day."

"Yes," she said, nodding, "it has. But I wish there had been time, at my apartment, for me to show you something."

"You mean your owl?" David joked. "We met."

"No. It was something not so obvious. Library request cards."

That wasn't what he had been expecting. "Call slips?" No wonder Dottore Valetta had been so incensed at the sight of them.

"I keep them hidden in the stove."

He topped off both of their glasses and said, "The stove? Don't they catch fire?"

"Oh no, I had the gas turned off years ago. I don't know how to cook."

He was learning more about her every minute. "And these cards would be from the Laurenziana, I presume?"

She smiled, and her lips glistened. Was it gloss, he wondered, or simply the wine?

"You wouldn't believe it," she said, and before he could even ask what he wouldn't believe, she leaned forward, her arms crossed on the table and said in a low voice, "I have them all—some of them the originals—from 1938 to 1945."

The elderly couple just across the aisle from them called for their check. The old man winked at David, conspiratorially.

"Could this have something to do with why Dr. Valetta has banned you from the library?" David asked.

"All I wanted was to see who had asked for certain books."

"And what did you expect to find? Adolph Hitler's personal request to see a book about raising the dead?"

"You are mocking," she said, slightly indignant, "but you are not so far off. What do you know about the Nazis and the occult?"

"Only what I see on the History Channel, late at night." He hadn't meant to upset her.

"I do not know what you mean by saying that. What is the History Channel?"

"Nothing," he said, dismissing it. "I just meant that it's considered kind of . . . speculative."

"It is not," she said, a spark kindling in her eyes. "People would like to think so," she said, waving one hand with the wineglass still in it, "but that does not mean it is untrue. Between the First and the Second World Wars, Germany and Austria—both of them—were filled with mystic lodges and secret fraternities. The Ariosophists, the Thule Society, the Vril Society. Every city, every town, from Hamburg to Vienna, had them. Hitler was even a member of some. And when he started to rise in politics, he made sure that he kept spies in every group to report back to him."

The waiter brought their plates, and if David hoped this might change the direction of the conversation, he was wrong. Olivia dug in without missing a beat.

"Heinrich Himmler, the Reichsführer, he was also a great believer. He paraded his troops through the streets of Berlin dressed as Teutonic knights and the people of Germany loved it! The Nazis believed in a super race, an Aryan race, a race that had been pushed aside, or buried in the earth, or corrupted by mixing with impure blood. There were many theories, but they all agreed that this race was going to rise again. It was going to purify itself, and it was going to create a new Reich, which was supposed to last for a thousand years."

David was listening carefully, but given his search for *La Medusa*, he felt his stores of credulity were already sorely depleted. And much as he respected Olivia's scholarship, all of this was still sounding a little too close to those preposterous theories about Hitler possessing the Spear of Destiny, or conjuring up some Satanic power to wield control over the masses. David didn't need any supernatural explanations for evil; as someone who had studied history all his life, he knew it sprouted up as easily as weeds, anywhere. All it ever needed was a little irrigating.

"But what's this got to do with the library cards?" David asked, pouring the last drops of the wine into Olivia's glass, who thanked him, then signaled the waiter to bring them each another glass.

Gulping the wine, but eager to continue her story, Olivia said, "There was one man that Hitler, Himmler, Goebbels, all relied on when it came to the occult. He was a famous professor in Heidelberg, a man who had written books on pagan worship and sun signs and what they used to call the 'root races.' His books were bestsellers, and his lectures were always packed."

"Would I have heard of him?"

"Probably not. His name was Dieter Mainz. And on every one of those borrower's cards," she said, rapping a knuckle on the table with each succeeding word, "I found his signature."

At last, David could begin to see the connection she was making.

"He had requested every one of those books, including the Cellini manuscripts. In certain circles," she elaborated, "Cellini was as famous for his magic as for his art. Just think of the passages from his autobiography, where he describes going to the Colosseum at night, with a sorcerer named Strozzi, and conjuring spirits?"

David remembered it well, but in the published version, the incident had ended rather anticlimactically. After a host of demons had been summoned, Cellini asked for news of a woman he had once loved, and was told he would see her soon. And that was about it. It ended as abruptly as if it had been cut with a sword.

"And think of the journey as he describes it in the book you have shown me, *The Key to Life Eternal.*"

There, he continued the story—in an unexpurgated, and seemingly fantastical, fashion. When Olivia had first read it in the alcove at the Laurenziana, David had watched in amusement as her eyes grew progressively wider.

The waiter returned with their wine. A small man, thin and pallid, had unobtrusively taken the seat at the opposite table and was bent over a book and a bowl of vichyssoise.

"The Nazis knew that there were many drafts, many versions, of Cellini's autobiography," Olivia said, "and they thought the full story might be told in one of them. What they did not know about was the *Key.*"

No one had, according to Mrs. Van Owen. If she was to be believed, hers was the only copy of the book in existence, and judging from the smoky smell that still clung to it, even hers had been barely rescued from a fire.

"But they thought he might have concealed the secrets of his occult knowledge in his art. After all, no one at that time could have conceived of something so grand and so exquisitely made as the *Perseus*. Since he had achieved miracles in his art, the Germans thought he might have uncovered other great secrets, too."

"Such as immortality?"

"Exactly," Olivia said. "Just as he proclaims in the *Key*."

"Immortality," David said again, letting the word roll around his tongue. He had shared so much with Olivia. But he had yet to tell her the real reason he was so desperate to find the mirror. Was this the time?

"If there was one thing Hitler coveted," she continued, "that was it. He didn't just want the Reich to last a thousand years, he wanted to be there—for a thousand years and more—to rule it."

"It must have been a great disappointment to him when the Red Army took Berlin and he had to blow out his brains in the bunker."

Olivia sat back, with an unpersuaded expression on her face. "The body, you know, was never found."

"Sure it was," David said, "along with Eva Braun's. Burned in a ditch." That much he knew.

"*Remains,*" Olivia said. "Only remains were found. By the Russians. And they *claimed* they were the Führer's. But no one else ever had the chance to test them; no one else even had the chance to see them. The Russians said they were incinerated outside a little town called Sheck and the ashes were thrown in the Biederitz River." She drank some more of the Bordeaux. "And we know how trustworthy the Russians are."

The waiter appeared and asked if he could clear the table. David, trying to digest all that he had just heard, not to mention what he'd had to eat and drink, leaned back as the waiter picked up their plates. The man sitting across the aisle was smiling at him through thin lips and gray teeth and said, with what sounded like a Swiss accent, "Forgive me for intruding, but are you honeymooners?"

Olivia smiled, and David said, "No, I'm afraid not."

"Oh," the man said, embarrassed at his faux pas. "Please pardon my mistake."

"No problem," David replied, secretly pleased that they made that kind of impression.

"I had taken the liberty," the man said, "of ordering a round of a special schnapps, made in my hometown, and traditionally used to toast a bride and groom."

"That is very kind of you," Olivia said, beaming at David.

"So perhaps you'll allow me to wish you well, all the same?"

He gestured at the three small glasses, which were lined up on his table. Extending two of them, he said, "It is made from the wild cherries that grow in our valley, and we're quite proud of it. I think you'll see why."

Although another drink was the last thing David needed, it would be too rude to turn it down. Olivia thanked him, too, and after a few minutes of conversation—the man introduced himself as Gunther, a salesman of medical supplies from Geneva—they shook his hand and excused themselves.

David, his valise slung under one arm, was halfway down the aisle when he realized just how much he'd had to drink, and how exhausted he really was. Olivia seemed to be feeling the same way. They were nearly staggering by the time they got back to their compartment, and he fumbled at the lock.

Any dreams David had had of their first night together would just have to wait. Olivia flopped onto the lower bunk without so much as pulling the blanket back, and David tossed the valise onto the upper berth. Stumbling into the tiny bathroom, he looked at his face in the mirror. His expression was weary, almost blank, and the taste of the cherry schnapps was still strong on his tongue.

Turning out the light and closing the flimsy door, he laid Olivia's coat over her. Then he clambered into the upper berth, which, in his present state, felt like the best and softest bed he had ever been in. All he wanted to do was sleep, and the gentle, constant rumble of the train was like a lullaby. One arm rested on the valise, the other dangled off the side of the bunk.

But his thoughts were restless, and he entered into that strange state where he could not be sure if he was dreaming or not. He thought of the salesman with the gray teeth, and pictured him picking cherries and putting them in a basket.

He thought of Olivia's old boyfriend, Giorgio, his face smeared with blood, his mouth gagged, but in the dream he was trying to tell David something urgent.

He pictured a parade of knights on horseback, crossing the Ponte Vecchio in Florence, with Hitler himself leading the procession. Torches were lighted all along the way, and in the fiery glow David saw his sister, standing on the other side of the bridge. Why was she there? Her hair was still gone, and she was dressed in a blue hospital gown. She was watching the knights, a look of horror on her face, and David was trying to run to her. But the horses were in the way and though he kept shouting her name, she could not hear him. The horses and riders kept nudging her closer and closer to the edge of the bridge. She was about to fall off! David was pushing his way through the knights—Nazi pennants were flying from their lances—but he couldn't make any progress. Someone, or something—a horse's muzzle?—was nudging his arm . . . moving it, very gently, to one side.

"Sarah," he cried again, "Sarah."

And his arm was moved again.

He opened one eye. A corner of the pillow stuck up in front of it. But something was stretching over him, reaching into that space between his body and the wall.

He closed his eye, trying to get back to the bridge, trying to get back to his sister before she plummeted over the edge.

But the knights on horseback still blocked the way.

His arm was lifted, and once more he opened his eye. A tiny light, as bright and sharp as a pinprick, was focused on the wall. It reminded him of the light the optometrist used when testing his eyes.

But now the light was directed elsewhere. It was pointed at something under his arm. Something black and firm and smooth as leather.

The valise.

His eye opened wider, and his whole body tensed.

Thick fingers were groping for the handle, and suddenly David knew this was no dream. He could even hear the low breathing of the intruder.

His own arm pressed down on the valise, while he swung himself up in the bed. His head hit the ceiling, and he kicked out a leg that collided with something. He heard a muffled oath, and he shoved the valise out of reach against the wall.

He was suddenly as awake as he'd ever been, and in the dim confines of the cabin he could just make out a bald head and ice blue eyes. He kicked again, and this time his foot caught the man on the chin and sent him crashing backwards onto the floor.

Olivia woke up, shouting his name, but David was already leaping down from the bunk and on top of his assailant. The man's hands flew up against David's chest, so powerfully that David was thrown back against the bed, and there was a cry from the cabin next door and the thump of some other passenger banging on the wall.

"David!" Olivia screamed, "look out!" and that's when he saw the glint of what looked like a knife.

There was nowhere to run and nothing to protect himself with except his duffel. He grabbed the bag and held it to his chest. The first blow was absorbed by the thick canvas, and the blade got stuck in the fabric before it could be pulled loose.

He pressed himself back against the window—railway lights flashing brightly through the glass—bracing himself for another attack when the door to the cabin was yanked open and a steward and a security guard barged in, throwing on the lights and shouting in Italian and French to stop right now! The guard, a burly guy wielding a baton, pushed the bald man away, and said, "What the hell is going on in here?"

"He broke in!" Olivia cried.

But the bald man, an agile and alert fighter a few seconds before, suddenly weaved on his feet and assumed an expression of drunken confusion.

"Broke in?" he slurred. "This is my cabin. Who're they?"

"Who are any of you?" the guard said, demanding to see their passports and tickets.

"He's got a knife!" Olivia said.

But the man shook his head and said, "What knife? I have a flashlight. I don't see so well at night." He held out a silver penlight, then dug around in his pockets to produce a train ticket.

David, his breath only beginning to return to normal, felt a crushing weight in the back of his head, like the worst hangover he'd ever had. The schnapps hadn't helped. It had a medicinal aftertaste he still couldn't shake.

The guard showed the steward the ticket, and the steward, after giving the man a long, hard stare, said, "You are in the next car."

"I am?" the bald man said, putting a hand against the baggage rack as if to steady himself. "Who says so?"

He was doing a good imitation, David thought, of a bumptious drunk.

"I say so," the steward said, taking him by the arm and steering him out of the cabin. Dragging his feet, the man let himself be led away. "Those people are in my cabin!" he shouted from the corridor, and the steward said, "Keep your voice down, people are sleeping."

The security guard gave them back their passports and tickets and said, "He wouldn't have gotten in if you'd locked your door properly."

David was about to retort that they had; but given the state he was in, he couldn't be sure.

The guard looked them both over, as if wondering why they were sleeping in their clothes, and in separate bunks, then shook his head, said, *"Buona notte,"* and pulled the door firmly closed. Through the glass panel, he gestured for David to flip the inner lock and draw down the blind.

David did both, before turning to Olivia, who wavered on her feet for a second before slumping on to the edge of the lower bunk. Holding her head down but pushing her hair back off of her face, she said, "This is not what I expected for tonight." She looked down at her own clothes as if surprised that she was still in them.

"I had something else in mind myself."

The rattling of the train was suddenly muffled as it hurtled through a tunnel in the French countryside.

"So, what do you think?" Olivia said. "Just a thief, and not a very good one?"

"Possibly," David said. He had been pondering the very same question, as much as his aching head would allow him to, but from the look on Olivia's face, she had come to the same conclusion he had. He double-checked the lock on the door and resolved to stay awake the rest of the way to Paris.

Chapter 20

In the winter of 1785, the frost lay on the valley of the Loire like a wrinkled white sheet. The apple orchards were barren, the fields deserted, and the post road, such as it was, had become a twisted ribbon of ice and snow. Anxious as the passengers were to reach the Chateau Perdu before dark, there was only so much the driver of the carriage could do. If he urged the horses on too fast, they could slip on the ice and break a leg, or a wheel could catch in a rut and snap loose from its axle. That had happened once already, and it was only with the help of the two armed guards—one riding in front of the carriage and one behind—that they'd been able to mend it well enough to continue on their way at all.

Charles Auguste Boehmer, official jeweler to the court of Louis XVI and Marie Antoinette, was beginning to regret having made the journey at all. Perhaps he and his partner, Paul Bassenge, reclining in the seat opposite, could have persuaded the queen to order the marquis to come to Versailles instead. It would have been so much easier, and, given the nature of what they were carrying, so much safer. But he knew that the Marquis di Sant'Angelo did only as he pleased, and it did not please him these days to come to Versailles. Boehmer suspected it was the presence at court of the infamous magician and mesmerist Count Cagliostro that was keeping him away. Boehmer had no use for the count, either, but so long as the man provided amusement to the queen and her retinue, he was sure to remain a fixture there.

At a crossroads, the carriage ground to a halt, and Boehmer, throwing his scarf around his neck, stuck his head out the window. The withered carcass of a cow was lying in the middle of the road, and three peasants, wrapped in rags, were hacking away at it with an assortment of knives and hatchets. They looked up at the coach—and its mounted guards—with barely concealed hostility. The whole countryside was starving—the winter had been especially harsh—and Boehmer knew that the rage, which had been simmering in France for years, might boil over into an outright rebellion any day.

He marveled that the king and queen were so blind to it.

"Pardonne, monsieur," Boehmer said to the one in the red stocking cap, who had stood up with his hatchet in his hand, "but can you tell us which of these roads leads to the Chateau Perdu?"

The man didn't answer, but clomped instead, in his heavy wooden shoes, toward the carriage; he conspicuously admired its fine lacquered sheen and the pair of well-tended, black horses that drew it. The horses' breath clouded in the air as they nervously pawed the icy road. Boehmer instinctively drew his head, like a turtle, farther into the cabin, and one of the armed riders spurred his mount closer to the coach.

"You have business with the marquis?" the man said, more insolently than he would ever have dared in years gone by.

"Official business of the court," Boehmer said, to put the peasant on his guard.

The man stood on his tiptoes to survey the inside of the carriage, where Boehmer sat with a cashmere rug across his lap and Bassenge was filling his pipe with tobacco. The man nodded, as if this explained the armed riders, and said, "He is expecting you?"

"I don't see where that's any of your business," Boehmer said, in a voice that he tried to make more forceful than he felt.

"The marquis makes it my business. He likes his privacy, and I help him to keep it."

Bassenge, putting his pipe on the seat, seemed to divine what was going on before his partner did. Taking several francs from his pocket, he leaned toward the window and handed them to the man with the hatchet. "We thank you for your help, citizen."

The man took the coins, rolled them around in his closed fist, then said, "Take the turn to the left. About three more kilometers. You'll see the gatehouse." Glancing up at the darkening sky, he said, "But I'd hurry if I were you."

Boehmer did not know what precisely the vague threat implied, but he did not care to find out. "If you and your friends can clear the road, we would be grateful."

"You would?" the man replied, and Bassenge, shaking his head at Boehmer's slow-wittedness, again handed out a few more francs.

When the carcass had been dragged off the road, and the carriage was again on its way, Bassenge, a tall lean man with a sepulchral voice, chuckled. "To think that you still don't understand what greases the wheels."

"What are you talking about?"

"Money, my dear fellow. Money greases the wheels of the world."

And Boehmer knew he was right. All his life, Boehmer had made it his business to be polite and amiable, open and fair, with everyone he met, and he still found it strange to live in a country where such suspicion and enmity prevailed. Like his partner, Bassenge, he had always been an outsider—a Swiss Jew now living in a French and Christian land—but through his skills and diplomacy, he had procured the office of Crown Jeweller, and he was allowed as many privileges at court as anyone of his background could ever hope to achieve.

As the carriage rattled on, it passed through a tiny town—no more than a tavern, a sawyer's, and a deserted blacksmith's shop— then over a millrace, where the wheel stood still in the frozen water, and on again into the deepening woods, which pressed closer to the carriage on both sides. Often, twisted boughs scratched the sides of the carriage, like plaintive bony fingers, and the wheels screeched as they caught in the icy ruts. The Chateau Perdu—the lost castle—was aptly named, he thought. Though he had never been there before—in fact, he knew no one who had—he was aware that it had been built nearly three hundred years before, by a Norman knight fresh from looting the Holy Land. Hidden away in the most remote corner of a vast estate, and perched on a cliff overlooking the Loire, it had been situated like a fortress, not a palace, and over the years, it had acquired an unsavory reputation—with rumors of terrible and sacrilegious deeds being performed there. Eventually, it had fallen into ruin.

And now it was inhabited by the mysterious Italian nobleman, the Marquis di Sant'Angelo.

As the carriage slowed, Boehmer looked out the window again and saw a stone gatehouse, with a lantern burning inside. A lame old man hobbled out, spoke with the rider in front, then unlocked the gates, and the carriage passed through. There was still no sign of the chateau, only a dense thicket of leafless trees all around, their trunks so closely spaced that they seemed to be fighting for their own room to grow. The twilight sky was filled with crows, swooping and cawing overhead like a flock of heralds. At several junctures the snow was so deep the carriage had to slow to a crawl, lest it fall into an unseen hole. More than once Boehmer saw dark shapes moving swiftly through the woods, tracking the humans' progress with glinting yellow eyes. What, he wondered, could even the wolves find to eat in such a desolate landscape?

The road slowly rose, the trees began to fall away, and here, where the wind had blown the snow away, the wheels of the carriage were able to bite into the hard-packed dirt and gravel. Boehmer was looking out again, and Bassenge, puffing on his pipe said, "See anything yet?"

"Yes . . . but just."

At first, it was only a tiny prick of light, burning as if in midair, but as the carriage rolled on, the light turned out to be a torch blazing at the top of a slender black turret, with its distinctively tapered pepperpot top. The dimensions of the Chateau Perdu gradually took shape in the dusk—a crenellated stone wall, punctuated by five rounded towers, and sitting so high atop the land that anyone approaching it could be seen for at least a kilometer. Even now, Boehmer felt that they were being watched.

The dirt and ice of the road eventually gave way to an evenly laid bed of cobblestones, and the coach clattered toward a drawbridge spanning a wide green moat, also frozen over. The moment its wheels clattered through the postern gate and under the raised portcullis—its sharpened ends pointing down like daggers—the grate dropped again, chains rattling as it fell. The coach and horsemen drew up in a stone courtyard, surrounded on all sides by the gray slate walls and lighted windows of the chateau.

Boehmer straightened his clothes—it had been a long and arduous trip—and said to Bassenge, "Why don't you do the honors?"

Bassenge tamped out his pipe, and reaching into a secret compartment beneath his seat, removed the walnut casket containing their precious cargo.

A footman from the chateau was opening the door and lowering the steps of their carriage as Boehmer stepped out. Night had fully fallen, as swiftly as a curtain might drop at L'Opera Française, and a cold wind was wailing around the courtyard. At the top of a flight of stone stairs, a pair of massive wooden doors, studded with iron rings, stood open, with a beckoning hearth just beyond. With every joint and bone in his body aching from the trip, Boehmer longed to stand before that fire and warm himself.

Other servants scurried out to help unload the coach and take the horses to the stable. The armed riders were led off to the staff quarters, while Boehmer and Bassenge ascended the steps as quickly as safety would allow, and entered the hall. The marquis himself, whom they had sometimes seen at court—more than once on the arm of Marie Antoinette herself—was descending the grand escalier with a pair of wolfhounds on either side. He was dressed, as was his wont, not in court finery, but leather breeches and riding boots. His black eyes sparkled in the firelight, and he appeared as robust as a stonemason. Boehmer, whose considerable girth made him waddle like a duck, envied him his bearing. Not all noblemen struck such an aristocratic pose, he thought. The king himself made an unfortunate impression.

"I was about to send out a search party," the marquis said, his French accented only slightly by his native Italian. "The brigands grow bolder every day."

"No, no, nothing like that," Boehmer said, clasping his extended hand, "but the roads are icy and we threw a wheel."

"I'll have my men make sure of the repairs."

Bassenge thanked him, and while their bags were taken to their rooms, the marquis ushered his guests through the *salle d'armes,* where the walls were lined with medieval weaponry, and into the dining hall, its coffered ceiling gleaming gold in the light of a dozen candelabra. Here, they were served a lavish dinner of roasted boar and fresh pike, accompanied by several bottles of the local Sancerre. It was the best wine Boehmer had ever tasted, and he had tasted many.

The marquis himself was a pleasant enough host, but there remained about him an impenetrable air of mystery. His fortune appeared to be great, but no one at court had ever been able to trace his family or guess where the money had come from. Although he had been received at court by the previous king, Louis XV, he had quarreled with the king's notorious mistress, Madame du Barry—it had had something to do with a portrait—and he'd soon found himself a close ally of the present queen, whose scorn for du Barry was no secret.

Marie Antoinette had come to rely upon this bold Italian's taste in many things, especially questions regarding the fine arts, architecture, furnishings, and, above all, jewelry. It was in deference to his exquisite eye that the jewelers had made their pilgrimage to the Chateau Perdu. If they could procure a recommendation of the piece they had brought—a recommendation written in the marquis's own hand—it would go far toward making up the queen's mind.

Over dinner, the conversation quite naturally turned to the royal jewels—many of which Boehmer had created—and the marquis casually asked, while another bottle of Sancerre was uncorked, if any new trinkets had recently come to light. The royal coffers were deep, and Sant'Angelo evinced a particular interest in antique silver, perhaps with the old-fashioned niello finish. Boehmer was flattered to be asked, but, really, who was more in the queen's confidence than the marquis?

"As you know, the queen favors more . . . glittering fare," he said, nicely paving the way for what was to come.

It was only after the brandy had been served, along with platters of candied fruits and a redolent Feuille de Dreux—a soft, flat cheese topped with a chestnut leaf—that the more abstemious Bassenge caught his partner's eye and laid a hand on the walnut box that had never left his side. The marquis did not miss the signal, either.

"The light will be better in the salon upstairs," he said. "Come."

The marquis led the way up the grand escalier, its two white wings ascending from the main hall, then down a long corridor lined with Gobelin tapestries (Boehmer's eye never failed him) that rippled in the draft from the mullioned windows; a violent wind was blowing outside, rattling the iron frames and whistling through the cracks. At the end of the hall a warm light beckoned, and Boehmer, followed by Bassenge, entered a salon to rival the Hall of Mirrors at Versailles.

The walls were made of molded glass and gilded bronze, each of the mirrors long enough to reflect a man in his entirety, and alternated with bookshelves lined with ornately tooled volumes. The cost of such a room—a pentagon, oddly enough, in shape—must have been extraordinary. An enormous chandelier, its hanging crystals sparkling from the light of no less than a hundred white wax candles, hung overhead. The floor was covered with intricately woven Aubusson carpets, and on an oval table, in a corner of the room, a sturdy serving man was just setting down a silver pot and china cups.

"I thought you might like some hot chocolate," the marquis said. "I've grown very fond of it myself."

Boehmer, too, liked it, though Bassenge, he knew, was never much interested in anything to eat or drink. Already he had drifted over to the books, and with his head tilted to one side was scanning the titles.

Boehmer accepted a cup of the chocolate, thick and aromatic, and took it to the French doors that looked out into the night. He had to put his face close to the glass and shield his face with one hand, but then he could see past the reflection.

They were at the top of one of the towers, and just outside there was a slate terrace; beyond that, he could make out the tops of some very tall and ancient oaks, bending in the wind. Past the trees was a sheer cliff, falling away to the Loire, the longest river in France. Its surface glistened dully in the moonlight, like an enormous black serpent lying across the land. Boehmer imagined that the view might be quite spectacular by day, though right then it was both vertiginous and oddly disquieting.

"Haven't you carried that box long enough?" the marquis said to Bassenge, who was indeed still clutching it under one arm.

Bassenge tore himself away from the books long enough to come to the claw-footed desk in the center of the room, where a bust of Dante had been moved to clear some space. He glanced at his partner to be sure that the time was right, and Boehmer said, "Open it, Paul."

The box was the size of a chessboard and sealed with six brass clasps. Each one clicked as it was flicked back, then Bassenge lifted the gleaming lid, reached inside as delicately as if he were picking up a living thing, and withdrew a diamond necklace of such surpassing brilliance that it rivaled the chandelier above. Boehmer could not have been more pleased with the way the stones caught and magnified the light.

Bassenge's bony fingers held it up by the two ends of its topmost loop—there were three in all—made up of exactly 647 of the most perfect African diamonds, some as large as filberts, culled from the inventory of dealers in Amsterdam, Antwerp, and Zurich. Weighing two thousand eight hundred carats, and accented by several red silk ribbons, it was the single most elaborate and costly necklace in the world—a piece that only royalty could afford to own, or bestow.

Which had been its original purpose. Boehmer and Bassenge had created it for Louis XV, as a gift for his mistress. But the king had died before it was done—before it could be given to Madame du Barry, *and* before it could be paid for . . . leaving it the most valuable, but most bereft, masterpiece in all the world.

Boehmer watched now as the marquis's eye traveled over it, appraisingly, and he wondered if he was as amazed by its audacity and execution as he hoped. Would he be so favorably impressed that he would recommend it to Marie Antoinette? Could he persuade her to purchase the necklace herself? At 2 million livres, it was an astronomical sum, even for the Queen of France. But if she didn't buy it, to whom else could Boehmer and Bassenge hope to sell it?

"Is there a diamond left in the world?" the marquis finally said, and Boehmer beamed.

"Not one to match the quality of these."

"May I?" Sant'Angelo said, and taking it in his own hands, he held the necklace up to the light, gently turning it this way and that and studying the way its thousand facets captured and refracted the glow of the candles. Boehmer noted that the marquis himself wore a simple silver ring on one finger, cast in the shape of the Medusa. Bassenge must have noticed it, too.

"Like Count Cagliostro's," he said to his partner, sotto voce.

"What's that about the so-called count?" the marquis said, his attention still riveted on the necklace.

"He is quite the rage at Versailles these days," Boehmer said.

"So I've been told," the marquis replied disdainfully.

"And he wears a medallion much like your ring," Bassenge explained.

The marquis stopped, as if frozen for an instant, before saying, with affected nonchalance, "Does he now?"

Boehmer nodded his agreement.

"Did you know that I made this ring myself?"

"I had always understood that Your Excellency was proficient in our trade," Boehmer said—which wasn't to say he understood why. A nobleman who was also a silversmith? But then the king himself had a passion for locksmithing. Who could understand all their idiosyncrasies?

"And you say it resembles this Medusa?" Sant'Angelo said, keeping the necklace in one hand while holding out the other that wore the ring, so that they might more closely inspect it.

"Yes. Identical, I would hazard," Boehmer said.

"With ruby eyes?"

"No," Boehmer said, "unless they have been removed. It is really quite plain."

Sant'Angelo's face betrayed no emotion, but he carefully placed the diamond necklace back in its velvet-lined casket, then offered to refresh their hot chocolate from the still-warm pot.

"Why should I simply write a letter?" he said, pouring another dollop into Boehmer's waiting cup. "I will accompany you to Versailles tomorrow."

"And you will personally speak to the queen about the necklace?" Boehmer said, beside himself with joy. The sale might yet be made and the fortune he had invested in the piece recovered!

"I can promise nothing," the marquis replied, "but I will indeed speak to her about it."

❧

All that night, the Marquis di Sant'Angelo paced the floor, waiting for the dawn to break. If he could have wrenched the sun into the sky with his own bare hands, he would have done it.

Boehmer and Bassenge had gone to bed, but he remained in the mirrored salon, sometimes stepping out on its balcony, where the cold wind rippled the sleeves of his shirt and whipped his black hair into a frenzy. The barren branches of the old oaks creaked like hinges, and a pack of wolves, hunting along the banks of the Loire, howled at the moon. The sky was clear, and the stars twinkled as white and bright as the diamonds in the necklace he had been shown a few hours before.

But it wasn't the necklace that occupied his thoughts. The queen knew it had been made for her nemesis, du Barry, and for that reason alone, even if it were the most beautiful necklace in all the world, she would never buy it.

No, what occupied his thoughts was *La Medusa* . . . apparently adorning the greatest charlatan in France—a man who claimed to be three thousand years old. A patent sham, professing to know the wisdom of ancient Egypt.

How in the name of Heaven had he come by it?

And did he know—or had he discovered—its secret?

For over two hundred years, the Marquis di Sant'Angelo—as he had titled himself on the very night he left Florence—had searched for the glass. But ever since the day it had been torn from his neck by the Duke of Castro and handed over to the Pope, it had vanished without a trace. His spies at the Vatican had never been able to discover it, and the marquis had eventually assumed that, like so much of the papal treasure, and so many of his other great works, it had been melted down or dismantled . . . destroyed by someone who could never have guessed its latent power.

Caterina—his model, his muse, his love—had known. She had discovered it by chance . . . and to her great misfortune. But as a papal retainer had confided to him years ago—at the tip of Cellini's dagger—she had died in a shipwreck, fleeing the Duke of Castro's inquisitors. As proof, the man had shown him the ship's manifest and passenger lists, left in Cherbourg. She had changed her name, but Cellini recognized well her peculiar and barely legible handwriting. Reports of the ship's destruction had been widely circulated at the time.

Perhaps the sea had conferred a blessing upon her.

There were times when he wondered if he might not have been better off himself, inhabiting that tomb in the Basilica della Santissima Annunziata. Sleeping there, in silence, until the Second Coming.

But what reason was there to believe that Christ was going to return at all? What reason was there to believe in anything?

A hawk, with a rodent clutched in its talons, settled onto a swaying branch and proceeded to devour its screeching prey.

That was the way of the world, he thought. Every living creature was ultimately a banquet for some other. And no one had ever seen more of the grisly and unending spectacle than he had.

Over the centuries, he had uncovered secrets no other man had. He had delved more deeply into arcane matters than anyone else had ever done, even the learned Dr. Strozzi. And he had escaped death, a hundred times. But at what cost?

Life, he had discovered, knew its own limits. When the thread had been meant to be cut, it was cut . . . and all the time thereafter was only a hollow enactment of things never intended to occur.

Oh, he had lived on, but once he had reached his mortal span—seventy, seventy-five, whatever God had intended—his life had become as great a lie as Cagliostro's.

Was that, he wondered, why he had always harbored such hatred for the man?

He lifted his hands, still gnarled from his days as the great and applauded artisan, and wondered where, precisely, their genius had gone. On the night the old beggar had been buried in his tomb, it was as if his gifts had been buried then, too. He could sculpt, he could mold, but only as well as some rough, untutored apprentice in his shop might have done—as anyone with ten fingers and two eyes could do. He could not create works worthy of the artist he had once been, and so, over time, he had ceased to try. It was too painful, too degrading, to produce pieces of anything less than transcendent beauty.

The waters of eternity, he thought, the light of the ancient moon . . . united in the *Medusa*, they had granted him the gift he sought. But the gift they bestowed was an empty vessel. It was a life without purpose, and a destiny with no fitting end. He might have laughed if he were not the one who had been tricked.

Chapter 21

As the TGV pulled into the Gare de Lyon in Paris, David helped Olivia up from her bunk—"My head feels as if it's been hit with a hammer," she complained—and then wrestled their bags toward the door. When it whooshed open, he helped her out onto the platform while keeping an eye out in all directions.

The bald man and his accomplice, the one who had undoubtedly drugged their drinks, had to be somewhere in the mob disembarking from the train, and for all he knew they were still on the job.

David had slung the shoulder strap of the valise over his neck, and with one arm around her waist, shepherded Olivia to the cab stand, where he barged to the head of the line, pleading that his wife needed to get to a hospital. Once in the taxi, he directed him to the Crillon, where Mrs. Van Owen's very efficient travel agent had already arranged for their accommodations.

At the hotel, Olivia was sufficiently recovered to navigate through the lobby, and down the hushed corridor to the lavish two-bedroom suite with a bird's-eye view of the Place de la Concorde. Formerly known as the Place de la Révolution, its stones had once been awash in the blood from the guillotine; Louis XVI and his queen, Marie Antoinette, had been decapitated, like thousands of others, just a few hundred yards away.

"I need a hot shower," Olivia said, "and room service."

"What do you want?"

"Start with a dozen eggs, bacon, croissants, cheese, coffee—very black and very strong—and a gun."

"I don't think guns are on the menu."

"Just so long as I have something to kill them with, if I ever see those two again."

David placed the order, then quickly tried Gary again on his cell phone. This time the call went through, and even though it was the middle of the night in Chicago, Gary sounded wide-awake.

"I was planning to just leave you a message," David said.

"That's okay. I'm up."

"Where are you?"

"Right now, the den. I'm watching some old movie on TCM."

"How's she doing?"

Gary paused, before saying, "Okay, I guess. She goes in daily for treatments, but at least she's not living in the hospital. She doesn't have a nurse waking her up every two hours to take another blood sample."

"How's Emme holding up?"

"She's just happy to have her mom at home. For that matter, so am I."

"I wish I could be there to help out."

"Listen, you do what you have to do. Get that promotion. I'll keep you posted. But Sarah likes knowing you're out there, going to all those glamorous places. Which one are you in now?"

"Paris."

"Paris," Gary said, and David could picture him nodding in appro-bation. "I'll have to tell Sarah as soon as she wakes up."

"I'll send her a postcard," David said, "though I hope to be home before it gets there."

"That'd be great," Gary replied. "Emme's been practicing up on the Wii, and I think she wants to whip her uncle David at a game of tennis or Ping-Pong or something."

"Tell her I'm up for the rematch anytime."

Hanging up, David stared out the window, feeling the enormous distance between himself and his sister, and feeling, like a magnet, drawn back toward home. But what good would that do her? What good would that do anyone? Anything he could accomplish had to be done right here.

The bedroom door opened, and Olivia emerged in a plush bathrobe, ruffling a towel through her hair, just as the room-service cart arrived. Throwing down a cup of hot coffee before even touching the food, she asked, "So, I've been thinking about it. Do you think these two are the same guys who beat up Giorgio in my apartment?"

David had been considering that, too. "Even if they're not, I'd bet they're all good friends."

Olivia began to lift the silver salvers and inspect what was on the plates and in the bread basket. The aromas alone were overwhelming.

"I think so, too. Coffee?" she said, pouring a cup for David. The lapels of her robe gaped open at the throat, revealing skin as smooth as the butter she was slathering on her bread. David had to refocus his thoughts.

"I'm really sorry," he finally said, as she unabashedly dug into a plate of eggs and bacon.

"For what?"

As slender as a gazelle, she ate with the relish of a lion.

"For getting you into this mess," he said.

"What do you mean, for getting me into this mess? How do you know," she said, wagging a slice of crisp bacon in the air, "that it's not my mess?" She actually sounded a bit indignant. "It was my apartment they broke into. It was my old boyfriend they beat up. Maybe it's me they're after."

Oddly, David wished he could believe that—it would at least absolve him of any guilt—but he knew it wasn't true, and he knew that it was time he told her the truth. If she was going to assist him in his search, and be exposed to whatever dangers might lie ahead, she needed to know what she was getting into. He needed to make a clean breast of it.

"The woman who has given me this job," he began, "is named Kathryn Van Owen," and Olivia listened carefully as he explained what he knew of her. None of that was so hard to accept or understand. "But she believes," he eventually concluded, "in the power of *La Medusa*."

"She believes that it can actually grant immortality?" Olivia said, matter-of-factly. "I figured she did."

Olivia had read *The Key to Life Eternal*. She knew how the mirror had been made, and for what purpose, but still, David had expected more of a reaction than this. "You figured that?"

"Of course," Olivia said. "Why else would she go to all this trouble and expense?" She waved one arm around the lavish suite. "The real question is, do *you* believe it?"

Put on the spot like that, David hesitated.

But Olivia simply waited, and when he still didn't answer, she understood, and said, in a gentler tone, "Why?"

"I believe in it because I have to," he finally replied. As he told her about his sister, and his voice grew hoarse with emotion, Olivia got up from her chair, came around the table, and wrapped her arms around his shoulders. She smelled of bath soap and hot croissants.

"Do you remember what I told you in the back of the cab in Florence?" she asked.

David did not immediately know what she was getting at.

"I told you that we were alike. We do not do things for money. We do things for love. And now," she said, "at last I know the real reason for your search."

David felt a huge sense of relief, but at the same time he was still concerned for her safety. "If you want to return to Florence and go back to your normal—"

But she stopped him by putting a finger on his lips.

"Listen to me," she said. "Everything that has happened—including those men on the train last night—all of that has made me feel . . . restored."

"Restored?" David said. It was about the last thing he might have expected her to say. "How?"

"All my life," she said, slipping around from the back of his chair and insinuating herself into his lap, "I have spent holed up with my books and my papers and my theories. Sometimes, I would think to myself, what do they all matter? Who cares but me? But now I know that the truth does matter. Now I know—now I remember—that there are people who will do anything to suppress it."

"But they'll try again."

Olivia shrugged, and with one hand cradled his chin. "Let them," she said. "The truth always comes out in the end."

But when David started to protest one more time, she said, "If you are trying to get rid of me, it won't work." She shook his chin. "So will you stop?"

"I'll stop," he conceded.

"Good," she said, grazing his lips with her own before going back to her side of the table. "Now eat something. We need to go to the Louvre. The crown jewels are waiting."

Chapter 22

"How hard was it?" Escher said, as they approached the main court-yard of the Louvre. "You call yourself a doctor, you had one simple thing to do, and you couldn't get even that much right."

Julius's face scrunched up like he'd just had to eat something sour. "But I did do it right," he replied in a last-ditch attempt to defend himself. "If the dosage had been any higher, they'd have keeled over in the dining car."

Escher was sick of discussing it. He wasn't used to working with amateurs.

"Maybe it would help," Julius ventured, "if I knew what this was all about. First you run me out of Florence—if I go back to my place, some Turk is going to try to kill me—and now I'm in Paris, chasing after God knows what. Is there a point to all this?"

"The less you know, the better off you'll be." Escher knew, from experience, just how annoying it was to be told that.

"Well, then I should be in very good shape, because I haven't got a clue."

"Keep it that way," Escher said, "and wait here, out of sight, until I call you." He straightened his alpine, badger-bristle hat, and took the glasses and guidebook from his pocket. Now he looked pretty much like the other provincial German tourists who had just ar-rived, in a busload, at the museum. He left Jantzen standing by the glass pyramid erected in the forecourt and mixed in with the crowd.

David Franco and that friend of his, Olivia Levi, were just hurrying in through the main doors.

Escher, smiling benignly at the guards and the other tourists, passed through the security check and paid for his ticket while keeping a safe distance from his quarry. David had that damned valise slung over one shoulder, and though Escher fully expected the guards to force him to check it before going through the turnstile, he could see a conversation going on, in which Olivia seemed to be pitching in. A senior guard was called over, and after glancing at the contents, and exchanging some additional words, he spoke into his walkie-talkie, waited, then nodded.

A roll of tape was produced and wrapped twice in an unbroken string around the bag, sealing it closed. Then Escher could see the guard glancing at his watch, pointing up the main staircase, and off to the left. David and Olivia were nodding appreciatively before thanking the guards and heading off toward something that Escher saw was called the Galerie d'Apollon. He quickly consulted his own guide to see why.

∽≈≈∽

It had been several years since David had last been in the Louvre, but he hadn't forgotten how vast it was. When he'd been a student, traveling on his Fulbright, it had been an easy way to spend an entire day, simply wandering from one gallery or exhibition to another. You could do it for months and still find something new to see each time.

But today, there was no time to waste. He had an appointment in twenty minutes with the Louvre's Director of Decorative Arts—a close personal friend, thank God, of Dr. Armbruster at the Newberry. He'd put in a call to her office the night before, while it was still day in Chicago, and Dr. Armbruster had assured him she would pave the way. "If anyone knows where this *Medusa* might be, it will be Genevieve Solange. Go and see her, and good luck!"

In the meantime, he had an entire exhibition hall to check out.

Although the museum was thronged as usual, he and Olivia cut through the crowd like a pair of barracudas, climbing up the broad central stairs and heading for one of the most popular sites in the entire Louvre—the opulently decorated Gallery of Apollo, where the crown jewels of France were displayed.

Or what remained of them.

Over the centuries, what had once been a magnificent collection had been decimated by thefts, national fire sales, dismantlings, recuttings, and sheer disorganization, reflecting the turbulent history of France itself. Starting with the French Revolution in 1789, the crown jewels had been a bone of contention fought over by Royalists and revolutionaries, aristocrats and Communards, pretenders, conspirators, and kings. Even the imperial crowns, used in coronation ceremonies at Notre Dame de Reims ever since the cathedral had been completed in the late thirteenth century, had had their precious gems removed and replaced with colored glass. It was almost as if the nation feared that the royal jewels held some mystical power, that if they were allowed to remain intact, the monarchy—which had once been so ruthlessly expunged on the scaffold of the guillotine—might rise from the dead to reclaim them.

But if *La Medusa*—bequeathed to the French royal family—still existed, this might be its home.

David and Olivia split up on entering, in order to study the remaining trove that had been assembled around the room—and it was still enough to dazzle the eye and the mind. There was the golden, laurel-leaf crown commissioned by Napoleon Bonaparte, and from the Second Empire the glittering tiara of the Empress Eugenie. There were diamond and sapphire parures worn by Marie Amalie, wife of Louis Philippe, the last king of France, and an emerald-encrusted tiara for the Duchesse d'Angoulème, the only child of Louis XVI and Marie Antoinette to survive the bloodbath of the Revolution. (The heir apparent, little Louis-Charles, had died at only ten under the less-than-tender care of the National Assembly.) There were several of the world's most famous and priceless diamonds, including the shield-shaped Sancy, the peach-colored Hortensia, and the much-storied Regent, which over the years had adorned everything from an aigrette in Marie Antoinette's coiffeur to the hilt of Napoleon's coronation sword.

But there was nothing bearing the aegis of Zeus motif. And nothing so comparatively humble as a small, silver hand mirror.

Meeting at the far end of the gallery, David and Olivia hurried on toward the Richelieu Wing, where the Decorative Arts department was located. Passing through its discreetly marked doors was like passing from one century to the next, from the gilded excesses of a palace, which the Louvre had originally been, to a sleek, twenty-first-century office complex, with windowed cubicles aglow with computer screens. Madame Solange's office was at one end, overlooking an inner courtyard, and she greeted them warmly.

"Patricia and I studied together at Cambridge," she said, and it took David a second to realize that she was speaking of Dr. Armbruster. "It was delightful to hear from her again."

As David and Olivia sat down across from her neatly organized desk, she said, "And she tells me you have something quite remarkable to show me." She extended one hand toward his sealed valise.

"I do," he replied, handing it across the desk.

With practiced fingers and an X-acto knife, she cut through the sealed tape and allowed David to proceed. He carefully extracted the fine copy of the red-and-black sketch and laid it out in front of her. "It's called, as you can see, *La Medusa*."

He could tell, from her intake of breath, that she was impressed with what she saw. She whipped off her glasses, bent close to the paper, and studied the drawing. Finally, she said, "It's beautiful, but unsigned, I see. Do you know who the artist was?"

"Benvenuto Cellini," David replied.

"Cellini?" she said, surprised but not dismissive. "And how would you know this?"

"It's what we were told when the original was presented to the Newberry, and since then we have studied it extensively—from the handwriting to the paper and the ink. All the results indicate that it is authentic."

He reached into the valise and started to show her the lab reports, but she waved them away. "I will take your word for it, for the time being." She put it back on the desk, her hands idly twirling the ends of the Hermès scarf knotted around her neck. In Paris, David noted, even the museum curators were chic.

"Was it an early sketch for the *Perseus* in Florence?" she wondered aloud.

"No," David said, pointing out the view of its reverse and the annotations. "It appears to have been the design for a small hand mirror. Silver, with a niello finish."

Mme. Solange frowned and said, "I know of nothing like this from Cellini, or anyone in his workshop."

"Neither do we," Olivia interjected, "but that's why we're here."

"We found documents in the Medici archives that indicate the piece was given to the Queen of France in the mid-1500s," David explained. "We need to know if it might be part of the Louvre's collection."

Mme. Solange looked highly dubious but swiveled toward her computer screen and said, "We have such an extensive collection here that only a fraction can ever be properly displayed, but let's check." With rapid-fire strokes, she logged into what she explained was the Atlas database. "If there's anything fitting this description, Atlas will tell us."

With David hovering behind her chair, and Olivia perched on the edge of hers, she first entered Cellini himself, but apart from all the references to his most famous statue, there was nothing to match. Then she entered "Medusa" as a key word, and while several hundred objects showed up, everything from urns to coins to ewers, none was a mirror, or a piece of lady's jewelry. Switching to another database, with the improbable name of LORIS/DORIS, she entered the information again, in several different configurations, without coming up with a hit.

Leaning back, her fingers leaving the keyboard, she said, "I can't be the first one to suggest this, but the piece might be lost to the ages. Even if the monarchy still possessed it, it might have been stolen in 1792, when the royal treasury was burglarized."

"But the thieves were caught, weren't they?" Olivia said.

"Yes, they were—and before they were beheaded, one of them, named Depeyron if memory serves, admitted that he had hidden some gold and gems in an attic in the district of Les Halles. But a piece like this," Mme. Solange said, touching her fingers to the border of the sketch, "would probably not have been so appealing to them. You say it was only silver, and niello at that. They would have overlooked it."

"Even with ruby eyes?" David said.

"There's nothing about rubies in that sketch."

"I know," David said, "but in the records I read at the Accademia in Florence, it was mentioned."

"Oh well, in that case, there's always a chance it's in the mineralogical collection at the Paris Museum of Natural History."

"Mineralogy?"

"In 1887, when the government was afraid of an insurrection from the Bonapartists, the Finance ministry was instructed to auction off whatever crown jewels were still under its control. But if something was deemed a naturally occurring gem, it got a reprieve and was handed over to the Natural History Museum. They've got all kinds of things, from mesmerism crystals to some diamond and pearl pins that belonged to Marie Antoinette. For all we know, the ruby eyes might have saved this mirror. It's not very likely, but then again, who can tell?"

David glanced over at Olivia, who shrugged as if to say, it's worth trying.

"But let me look at their records," the director said. After a few minutes of rapid work at the keyboard, she exhaled in disgust, and David, glancing at her computer screen, read, in bold black type, "*Aucune approche disponible à ce temps.*"

"They are forever experiencing . . . what do you call them in the States?"

"Technical difficulties?"

"Yes, that would be it. Their records are not currently accessible online. I suggest you go over there tomorrow and ask for the director, Professor Vernet."

"It has to be today," David said, already slipping the sketch back into the valise.

"But they're closed today."

"Could you call him?" he said. "It's really very urgent."

"Urgent?" Madame Solange said, perplexed.

"I know Dr. Armbruster would greatly appreciate it," David said. "And so would I."

He was afraid he'd offended her, but after a pause, she said, "All right," and picked up her phone. "But when you get there, tell him I said that it was time he got his damn files up and running!"

Chapter 23

"Please tell Madame Solange, when next you see her, that I would be happy to fix the problem," Professor Vernet declared, as he flicked on the lights in the portico of the Galerie de Mineralogie et de Geologie. They were standing in a wide, high-ceilinged entryway in need of a good scrubbing, though one wall was adorned with an enormous wooden plaque, listing the Board of Governors in gilt letters. "In fact, I'll get to it just as soon as the Louvre releases some of its own government funding to its poor cousins like us."

David had the feeling he'd stepped into yet another territorial battle and elected to remain silent rather than risk saying the wrong thing. Miraculously, so did Olivia. Professor Vernet, wearing a white lab apron over a rumpled suit, looked as if he'd been disturbed in the middle of a rock-pounding session. A hammer stuck out of one pocket and there was dust and grit all over his sleeves. As a result, he kept his dirty fingers off the drawing as David showed it to him and explained what they were looking for.

"It's a very impressive piece," he conceded. "But I can also tell you that we have nothing in our collections that resembles it. With, or without, rubies."

"But with your database down—for the moment—how can you be sure? Maybe Olivia and I could help check?" David ventured, afraid of stepping on another set of toes but having no alternative.

"I already have."

David knew that couldn't be true. They hadn't been apart since arriving at the museum and just now showing him the Cellini sketch.

"It's all right here," the professor said, turning toward them and tapping his unconvincing copper-colored toupee. "And I can tell you we do not have such a thing."

He moved on into the dim gallery, closed to the public today. "Anything we retain of the crown jewels is exhibited in this room," he said, gesturing at a long and spacious hall, less opulent than the Louvre but impressive nonetheless. He nodded at a solitary watchman, who flicked on another bank of lights, and the glass cases suddenly came to sparkling life. In the center, under a separate light of its own, was a vitrine containing the incomparable Ruspoli Sapphire, a 135-carat, cube-shaped stone, bought by Louis XV. The size of a quail egg, it was the deepest blue David had ever seen.

Professor Vernet seemed gratified at David's, and Olivia's, appreciative gaze. "Over the years, many of the jewels were recut, to avoid identification when they were resold. But not, as you can see, this one."

After allowing them time to absorb its beauty, the professor moved on to a longer display case, where he showed them a collection of pins and rings and bracelets adorned with precious stones. "Some of these belonged to Marie Antoinette, some to the sisters of Louis XVI."

Studying them on their velvet place mats, brilliant and polished and refined as they were, David experienced a sinking sensation. What he was looking for in no way fit their style. A dull, silver looking glass in the shape of the Medusa's head? Marie Antoinette would no sooner have used such a thing than a wooden toothpick. He was beginning to think he had gone in the wrong direction, after all, and come, finally, to a bleak dead end.

But Olivia, who had wandered farther down the gallery, suddenly said, "Take a look at these."

The professor glanced in her direction and said, "Ah, the crystals. Far less valuable, of course, but marvelous specimens still."

David walked over and saw what looked at first like a display case in a geology museum of the Southwestern United States. There were quartzite crystals, sharp and angular, and lavender geodes split like cantaloupes, their two halves twinkling in the overhead glare. David didn't understand why Olivia had seemed so interested.

Then he saw her point at the placard on the display case.

"*Des possessions personelles de Comte Cagliostro, aussi connu comme Giuseppe Balsamo, environ 1786.*" From the personal possessions of Count Cagliostro (aka Giuseppe Balsamo), circa 1786.

"You are aware of Count Cagliostro?" Professor Vernet asked.

"Yes," David said. "We are." He remembered well the count's book of Egyptian Masonry that Olivia had pulled from the shelves of the Laurenziana—and now here he was again, smack in the middle of things. "But how did these wind up here?"

"The count used them in his demonstrations of hypnosis and magic. But when he had to flee Paris, some of them were left behind."

"Why the hurry?"

"Because of the Affair of the Queen's Necklace," Olivia interjected, and the professor nodded.

David had only a rudimentary recollection of that episode, and the professor seemed only too happy to provide a synopsis. David had the impression that the professor, at first annoyed at the intrusion in his schedule, had warmed at the enthusiasm of the comely young Olivia and enjoyed regaling her with his stories.

"The official court jewelers, two partners named Boehmer and Bassenge, had assembled a fabulously expensive necklace, in the hopes that Mme. du Barry, and later Marie Antoinette, would buy it. But neither of them did. Instead, a confidence artist, an attractive young woman named Jeanne de Lamotte Valois, managed to perpetrate a very great swindle."

"The greatest of its day," Olivia added.

"She persuaded an eminent, but unscrupulous, Cardinal to pay for it. He thought he was simply buying it on behalf of the queen, who would secretly reimburse him, but the queen did not know anything about the transaction. Nor did she ever receive it. Instead, the necklace was stolen by Valois and her confederates, broken up into pieces, and sold. And despite the fact that Marie Antoinette had never owned the necklace—indeed, she had pointedly refused to buy it on several occasions—the people of France never believed her. The necklace was often cited as just one more example of her extravagance."

"And Count Cagliostro was involved?" David asked, still feeling like the student who'd been left behind.

"Mme. Valois deliberately implicated him in the plot because she knew him to be a great favorite at court. The queen enjoyed his company, and had richly rewarded him with various tokens of her esteem. There was a trial, but after nine months in the Bastille, the count was finally acquitted. Still, he was smart enough to know that he had worn out his welcome in France and left Paris the next day."

"And look at these, down here," Olivia said, directing David to several amulets carved in the shape of scarabs and other foreign symbols. One was an amber gargoyle, grinning maliciously.

"Yes, those were the sorts of things the queen bestowed," Vernet explained. "She knew he had a taste for anything of an exotic or occult nature and I think he was afraid to spirit some of them out of France."

"Is it possible that *La Medusa* was one of the tokens of her esteem that he left behind?" Olivia speculated.

It certainly looked to David like the mirror might have been more to the count's taste than hers. "And these are all of his things, in the cases here?" David asked the professor.

The professor shrugged and said, "All but some of his papers. They're stored in the archives, next door."

"May we see them?" Olivia asked, eagerly.

The professor, who looked as if he could refuse her nothing, brushed some dust from the front of his apron and said, "For such a lovely young visitor, I don't see why not."

David felt distinctly *de trop,* but didn't care.

The professor led them out the other end of the gallery and down a long hall connected to an annex, talking all the way. "After leaving Paris, Cagliostro fled to Rome—unwisely, as it turns out—since the Pope found him guilty of blasphemy, burned his books, and imprisoned him in the Castel St. Angelo."

"Cellini's old home," David observed.

"From there, he was moved to an even more remote prison—the Castel San Leo," Vernet remarked, as they passed through the first of several security checkpoints, "where he survived for four years before being strangled by one of his jailers."

The professor opened a sticky steel-plated door and led them down a metal spiral staircase. They must have gone down three or four levels before he stopped and turned on a row of overhead lights.

Endless shelves, stacked with boxes, stretched as far as David could see, but Vernet appeared to know exactly where he was going, burrowing down one row, then turning into another before stopping and pointing to a large brown box on a top shelf.

"Could I ask you to take that one down?" he said, and David gladly obliged. A film of dust rose like a cloud from its top.

"And bring it over here," Vernet said, leading them to an equally dusty research table surrounded by some beat-up wooden chairs. David plopped the box down, and the professor said, "Every day that Cagliostro was imprisoned, he scrawled one sentence, with a sharpened rock, on the wall of his dungeon. Napoleon—who was also a great believer in the occult—later sent an aide to the cell where Cagliostro had died, with instructions to copy down all the words and images that remained." Tapping the top of the box, the professor said, "I'm afraid there are no amulets in here, but perhaps the information will guide you in your quest?"

David doubted it, but for want of any other lead, he was certainly prepared to follow this one. And Olivia looked genuinely elated.

"Normally, you understand, you would not be allowed to work here unattended," Vernet said, glancing at an old wall clock as it audibly clicked off another minute, "but I have some work to finish, and the archives are technically closed today."

"We'll be careful with everything," Olivia assured him, "and replace the box before we leave."

Vernet still hesitated, then said, "If mademoiselle would just be so kind as to drop by my office on her way out, I would like to hear how things went."

"Delighted," Olivia said, pouring it on.

And David couldn't resist adding, "I'll come, too."

The professor appeared not to have heard him, but before he'd rounded the corner of the shelves, David had popped the lid off the box. Inside, there were several plastic sleeves, each with its own typed label, many of them yellowed and peeling off. Olivia peered in, rummaged through, then grabbed one and plunked herself down in a chair on the opposite side of the table. David picked out another, this one marked *Documents originaux, C. San Leo, 1804.* These would be the first field notes from Napoleon's emissary, and he removed them with all the appropriate caution.

Written, or drawn, on paper as yellowed and crinkled as papyrus, and in an ink that had faded from black to gray, the entries were barely legible—and, as far as David could tell, they were all over the lot. Many of them were the traditional Masonic symbols—hammers and mallets, bricks and trowels—but others were crude facsimiles of Egyptian hieroglyphs. He recognized Anubis, the jackal-headed god of the underworld, and Isis, goddess of nature and magic, crowned with the curving horns of a bull. The aide had dutifully copied them down, as well as the sentences scrawled on the stone in Italian.

"The eye of the pyramid sees into all things," was one.

"The master of the Lost Castle possesses the secret of secrets," was another.

To David, they seemed like nothing more than the ravings of a man consigned to a dungeon.

But suddenly, one of them brought him up short.

"The immortal Gorgon belongs to Sant'Angelo."

The Gorgon . . . could this be a reference to *La Medusa*? And why would he say it belonged to a Roman prison? Had Cagliostro hung on to the glass when he fled France and run to Rome? Had the Pope relieved him of it, along with all his other blasphemous possessions? Or had he managed to hide it there, somewhere within the prison walls, before being taken away to San Leo? David focused all his attention on the pile of sketches and writing—whoever Napoleon had sent had done a thorough job of it—as he dug through them, front and back, but there was nothing more that seemed explanatory or revealing.

Still, it was a start, and it was only when he was about to tell Olivia about what he'd found that he realized she had fallen uncustomarily quiet ever since they'd opened the box.

When he glanced across the table at her, he saw that she had opened an envelope containing old black-and-white photographs, each one about eight-by-ten. Slowly, methodically, she was going over each one, then laying it on the stack in front of her.

"I think I might have found something," he said, relating the line about the Gorgon. "Sounds like it was too important to Cagliostro for him to leave it behind."

But Olivia, still absorbed in her own task, nodded absentmindedly, and said, "I think I've found something, too."

David reached over and turned one of the photos around. It showed the ruins of a fortress, atop a craggy cliff, and was captioned San Leo. So this was where Cagliostro had been imprisoned.

He turned another shot around, and this one showed a low dungeon door, with thick iron bars. The third picture was taken inside the cell, where portions of the stone wall had completely disintegrated and fallen apart. There were holes large enough to reveal fallen timber and rubble in the next cell.

"Something tells me Napoleon's crew didn't take these Polaroids," David said. "Who did?"

"Turn them over," Olivia replied, laying down yet another one on the pile.

David flipped the photo, and saw a faded black stamp on its back—two jagged lightning bolts, on either side of the words *Das Schwarze Korps*. The Black Corps. It meant nothing to him.

"*Das Schwarze Korps* was the official newspaper of the SS, Heinrich Himmler's personal mouthpiece," Olivia explained. "It was the place where all the racial theories, and occult underpinnings, of the Nazi regime were broadcast. According to the dates of entry in this file, the Nazis received permission from the Vichy government to access these files on June 15, 1940. That's exactly one day after they took Paris. You have to give them credit for one thing—they didn't let the grass grow under their feet."

"But if these photos were taken in Italy by the Nazis, how'd they wind up here, in the French files?" David asked.

"I would say that the investigator was compiling the complete dossier here. Why not? After all, he expected the Reich to be around and running the place for another thousand years."

"Who did? Himmler?"

"No, he was a little busy just then. But it appears he sent his right-hand man."

She showed him a letter from a French bureaucrat, summarily dismissing the previous administrator of the archives—Monsieur Maurice Weinberg—and cosigned, in a crabbed, precise hand, by the Reichsführer himself. The letter appointed in his place an emeritus professor of philosophy and theology at the University of Heidelberg. A man named Professor Dieter Mainz.

Dieter Mainz, whose name had appeared on all of those library request cards at the Laurenziana, too.

Olivia looked like she had struck gold. "I knew it!" she said. "They were tracking count Cagliostro all along."

But were they tracking him in search of *La Medusa*? David thought with horror. And what if they had found it? What if it had been but one tiny item in their massive plunder of Europe? So much of the treasure looted by the Nazis had been destroyed in the war, or lost. And plenty more was still stashed away in secret vaults, under aliases and forgotten code numbers, from Brussels to Buenos Aires.

"But do you want to know the best news yet?" Olivia said.

"What?" He could use some good news.

She held up her hand, covered with dust from the box and papers. "Nobody else has come this way in a long time."

It was a good point, and he was glad she had made it. This was a trail no one else had blazed, though whether it led anywhere was still an open question.

When they had completed their review of everything else in the box, which included several pamphlets printed in France and extolling the power of the magic Cagliostro had uncovered in ancient Egypt, they closed up the carton, replaced it, and threaded their way back to the museum director's office. It looked as if it had once been a large recital hall, and had a desk at one end and a long table covered with rocks and chisels and tools at the other. Professor Vernet was turning the handle on a vise, to crush a stubborn specimen, when Olivia said, "Thank you for your help."

The professor looked over his shoulder, turned the crank one more time, and said, "Happy to be of assistance, mademoiselle."

His eyes, David noted, never left Olivia.

Brushing the rock residue from his hands and removing his apron, he offered to escort her—them—to the doors of the museum. All the way, he engaged Olivia in a discussion of her work, where she had studied, how she liked Paris, while David followed along. In the portico, Vernet took her hand, and while assuring her again that he was available for consultation at any time—"Did I mention that I live quite close by?"—David idly surveyed the Board of Governors plaque. Several dozen names were listed, in no particular order, and while most of them meant nothing to him, some were famous from the worlds of French politics and finance.

And one, in gilded letters near the bottom of the last column, nearly bowled him over.

"Excuse me," he said, brashly interrupting an inquiry into Olivia's plans for dinner, "but it appears you have a Monsieur di Sant'Angelo on your board?"

"Yes, what of it?" Vernet replied, miffed at having his pitch cut short. "He has the best eye for gems in all the world. We often consult with him when something especially rare comes to our attention."

"He lives here?"

"Oh yes—in a grand old house in the Sixteenth Arrondissement, on the rue de Longchamp. Number 10. He has a business there, by appointment only."

Was it possible? David thought, his mind racing. When Cagliostro had written that the Gorgon belonged to Sant'Angelo, did he mean a *person* by that name, and not a place? Was he referring to an ancestor of this very man—perhaps a jeweler in his own day? Had the count left *La Medusa* in his keeping when he fled Paris one step ahead of the mob?

"Has the family lived there long?" David asked.

"Oh, as far back as anyone can remember. Long before the Revolution, that much is certain."

"And have they always been jewelers?"

"In a manner of speaking. Collectors as much as purveyors. Why do you ask?"

"No reason, just curious," David said, intervening to free Olivia's captive hand from Vernet's grasp. "I can't thank you enough for all your help, but we do have to go."

Olivia looked relieved to regain her freedom and allowed David to steer her toward the doors.

"Wait—if you are interested in Cagliostro and his practices," the professor said, in a last-ditch effort to lure them back again, "you might also like to see Franz Mesmer's iron rods. We have them in storage!"

"Next time!" David called out, as Olivia waved farewell, and they hurried down the steps of the museum and into the chilly dusk.

Chapter 24

Somewhere in the Sologne Forest, the Marquis di Sant'Angelo grew so impatient with the rate of progress they were making that he stopped the coach and exchanged places with the driver. The coachman was now reclining inside the carriage, while the marquis himself, wrapped in a hooded coat stitched from the fur of the wolves he had hunted on his estate, sat on top, cracking the whip over the heads of his four black horses.

He was determined to arrive at the palace of Versailles in time to see the queen at the evening meal and secure an audience with Count Cagliostro. The accompanying coach, carrying the royal jewelers and their priceless diamond necklace, had long since been left behind.

As the light began to fade from the winter sky, the carriage clattered into the village, which had sprung up solely to accommodate the needs of the ever-expanding royal court. Peasants were scurrying about in the cold, loading wagons with barrels of wine and wheels of cheese. They leapt out of the way as the marquis turned the coach into the broad avenue leading to the palace itself, rolling past the snow-covered parterres and terraces, past the empty orange groves and over the ornamental bridge above the Grand Canal. The palace itself loomed ahead, behind an immense forecourt, like a great white wedding cake of columns and colonnades. Lanterns and candles had already been lighted in several hundred of its windows in preparation for the night's festivities.

But then there were festivities every night.

Once, years before, the marquis had spent a good deal of time at court, keeping company with the previous king and his notorious mistress, Madame du Barry. Louis XV had been known for his debaucheries, but the marquis had found him frank and entertaining— and vastly preferable to the present king and his court of sycophants and dandies. The only reason he had spent time at Versailles in recent years was to visit with the queen. Marie Antoinette had touched his heart upon his first sight of her there in 1770.

The dauphine, as she was then known, had just arrived, like a gift-wrapped package from the royal house of Austria—a girl of fourteen with roses in her smooth white cheeks and a fall of fair blond hair. She was as skittish as a fawn, with wide blue eyes and a long, slender neck, and the marquis felt for her plight . . . a shy child who was comfortable speaking only German, deposited among a throng of jabbering Frenchmen—all of them vying for position and favor with the future Queen of France. Her fifteen-year-old husband-to-be, the dauphin, was a surly, fat sluggard the marquis wouldn't have trusted to clean his boots.

And now she was the most famous—and in some quarters vilified—woman in all of Europe.

When the marquis pulled in on the reins and brought the horses, foaming at their bits, to a stop, several liveried stable hands raced to open the carriage doors and the coachman stumbled out, pointing to the marquis and trying to straighten out the confusion. Sant'Angelo laughed, stepping down and leaving it to the servants to sort things out. Striding up the wide staircase, he entered the palace itself, which was buzzing like a hive with valets de chambres and ladies' maids scuttling to and fro, and headed straight for the chambers of the Baron de Breteuil, Minister of the Royal Household.

"I need to see the innkeeper!" the marquis exclaimed, bursting into the room, still in his wolf furs, where the baron was conferring with some elaborately coiffeured men. "I must have my usual quarters!"

The baron immediately broke away and, shaking Sant'Angelo's hand, said, "Of course, of course, Monsieur le Marquis, but we weren't expecting you!" In a lowered voice, he said, "I was under the impression that Messieurs Boehmer and Bassenge had gone to see you at the Chateau Perdu . . . about a certain matter."

Breteuil knew everything that everyone was doing, at any given moment.

"And so they have. In fact, they should be here soon."

"Then you've seen the necklace?"

Sant'Angelo shook his head dismissively. "A gaudy piece that the queen would never wear—especially since she knows it was originally made with du Barry in mind."

Breteuil frowned and nodded, as if this confirmed his own suspicions. "But the jewelers are so persistent," the baron said.

"In their shoes, I would be, too. They've got a fortune tied up in that piece. If they make it back to Versailles tonight, don't put them up anywhere near me."

"I understand," he said. "And I'll have your own rooms made ready immediately."

"Good," the marquis said, clapping him on the back, in part because he genuinely liked the baron, who also had the queen's best interests at heart, and in part because he knew such conduct was a gross breach of the elaborate court etiquette. At times like this, he missed the last king.

※

For Louis XVI and Marie Antoinette, life at Versailles was a life lived in public. From the moment they awoke in the morning to the moment they retired for the night, they were accompanied, assisted, advised, pampered, coddled, served, and observed. The marquis could not imagine living life as such a spectacle and he did not imagine that the teenage Antoinette had expected it either. Life at the royal Austrian palace of Schönbrunn had been, by comparison, restrained and secluded.

On one of her first duties after her marriage at Versailles—a wildly extravagant affair that drew six thousand of France's richest and most prominent citizens—she had been ushered into her private chambers (still shadowed by a substantial coterie of her retainers, including the Princesse de Lamballe, who was to become her close confidante), and shown the royal jewels. The marquis, in his informal role as arbiter of all things elegant and artistic, had been admitted to the august group, and he had watched as this slip of a girl, dwarfed in a dress of white brocade with enormous hoops on either side, was maneuvered into a chair for the ceremony.

At Versailles, if Antoinette so much as plucked an eyelash, it was a ceremony.

Two kneeling servants presented a red velvet box, six feet long and half again as high, with several dozen different drawers and compartments, all lined in pale blue silk. The bounty within was unparalleled, and the marquis could not help tallying it all up in his head as the dauphine removed and admired each of the many treasures. There were emerald earrings and pearl collars that had once belonged to Anne of Austria, the Habsburg princess who had married Louis XIII in 1615, a diamond parure, tiaras, brooches, diadems, and a pair of newly made gold bracelets with the initials MA engraved on clasps of blue enamel. The marquis even spotted in the inventory one or two pieces that he remembered from Florence, long ago, when they had adorned Catherine de'Medici before she had decamped to become the Queen of France.

But when the dauphine withdrew a folded fan, studded with diamonds, and tried to flutter it open, the leaves remained stubbornly closed.

The Princesse de Lamballe tried to lend a hand, shaking the fan herself, but her luck was no better.

Sant'Angelo knew why; the Parisian jeweler had consulted him on its design, and the marquis himself had suggested a hidden clasp, perfectly concealed in a circle of white diamonds.

"*Erlauben Sie mich,*" the marquis said, leaning close. Allow me.

The dauphine had flushed at his sudden proximity—and several of the courtiers reared back in shock—but when he took up the fan, undid the clasp, then, like a coquette at L'Opera, cocked his elbow and fanned himself with its silk leaves, the Dauphine spontaneously laughed—which gave the others permission to laugh, too. Continuing the joke, he said in a raised voice, *"Es ist unertraglich heib hier drinnen, denken Sie nicht?"*—It is insufferably hot in here, don't you think?—and Antoinette had beamed at him, grateful not only for the levity but for the taste of her native tongue. The marquis had spent many a year in Prussia, and the language was still at his command.

"May I know your name?" she inquired in German. "I don't believe we've been introduced."

"This, madame, is the Marquis di Sant'Angelo," the Baron de Breteuil hastily inserted himself to answer. "An Italian friend of the court."

"And a friend, I hope, to you, too," the marquis replied. Although many of those present could probably follow the gist of the conversation, the fact that it was conducted in German formed a special bond between the two of them. Glancing around at the deeply rouged ladies in attendance, Sant'Angelo had leaned in even closer than before and whispered, "Have you ever seen so many appled cheeks? It looks like an orchard in here."

Antoinette covered her lips and tried not to laugh. It was the custom at the French court to plaster rouge on the face like primer on a wall, and he guessed that the young girl would not yet have accustomed herself to the gaudy sight of the ripe red cheeks everywhere. Even the market women tried to copy the effect using grape skins.

"But it's the powder," she replied, sotto voce, her eyes straying to one of the more monumentally dusted wigs, "that makes me want to sneeze."

"That's what the fan is for," he said, fluttering it again, before showing her where the clasp was hidden and handing it back. He had

had a daughter, Maddalena, in a far-off time and place, and on the last occasion he had seen her she was about this same age. . . .

But that was another life, and, as he had learned to do over the years, he quickly shut the door on it.

Other gifts were presented, too, and some of these were intended for her attendants, such as a set of porcelain Sèvres for Prince Starhemberg. When the ceremony was over, the dauphine extended her hand again, and reverting to German a final time, said to the marquis, "I hope that we shall be great friends."

"I am sure of it, Your Highness."

"And I believe that I shall be in need of them here."

She was young, but perhaps not so naïve as he'd thought.

Over the next fifteen years she had learned fast, adapting to the rites and rituals, the pomp and circumstance, of the most refined court in Europe. He had watched her grow from an awkward girl to a confident, even imperious, woman. And tonight, when he saw her at the *grand couvert*—where the king and queen dined in solitary splendor, while dozens of spectators looked on—the queen raised her eyes above the gold-and-enamel saltcellar and nodded a greeting. If only she knew, he thought, that the saltcellar, commissioned by King Francis at Fontainebleau in 1543, was from his own hand.

Waving the Princesse de Lamballe to her side, she whispered in her ear, and moments later the princesse herself drew the marquis aside and said, "The queen invites you to join her at the Petit Trianon tonight. Count Cagliostro will be there, and she thinks you might like to meet him."

"Indeed I would," he said.

The Petit Trianon was the queen's private refuge—a separate, small palace on the grounds of Versailles, where no one was admitted unless by order of the queen herself. Consequently, invitations to her salons there were terribly coveted, and hard to come by; the marquis had once heard that even the king, despite the fact that he had given it to her, had to ask permission to enter its gates.

At ten o'clock, Sant'Angelo approached the neoclassical palace, so much less ornate and extravagant than its Rococo counterparts, mounted the steps, and passed through several rooms painted a distinctively muted blue-gray. From the main *salon des compagnie,* he could hear the strains of a harp and a harpsichord, playing a song written by the queen's favorite composer, Christoph Willibald Glück. He assumed that it was the queen herself, an accomplished musician, who was sitting at the keyboard.

And, as he entered, he saw that he was correct. Antoinette was playing the harpsichord, the Princesse de Lamballe the harp, while perhaps a dozen other members of the nobility were sprawled about on upholstered divans and gilded chairs, sipping cognac, playing cards, amusing themselves with one of the many Persian cats or small dogs that had the run of the place. The marquis, who had seen more than his share of imperial courts, had never known one to include quite so many pets. A parrot perched on the mantelpiece now, safely out of harm's way, while a white monkey, on a long leather leash, explored the underside of a marble-topped console.

The marquis waited at the threshold to be acknowledged by the queen, but she was concentrating so hard on the score that she did not see him. He recognized the Countess de Noailles, Mistress of the Household, sitting with her dreary husband at a faro table; the high-spirited Duchesse de Polignac, reclining beside a portly man in an open frock coat (frock coats, which were considered too casual for court, were encouraged at the Trianon), and a dashing young officer in a Swedish Cavalry uniform festooned with gold braid. This was the Count Axel von Fersen, emissary to the French court, and from all accounts the queen's lover.

When the piece was finished, Marie Antoinette looked up at the round of applause, and upon seeing the marquis, glided across the floor toward him. At Versailles, even the way women walked, their feet swishing across the floor as if barely in contact with it, was prescribed and artificial.

But there was nothing false about the warmth of her smile.

"It was such a wonderful surprise to see you tonight!" she declared. "I hope you will be spending many days with us!"

"I haven't made my plans as yet," he replied.

"Good! Then I'll make them for you," she said, taking his arm and introducing him to several of the guests he did not know. It was only here, at the Petit Trianon, that she could be so free-spirited and informal. She had made the place her private retreat, a refuge from all the stifling protocol and public display of the main palace; here, she had even arranged for the servants to be kept out of sight, and in her boudoir she had installed panels that could shutter the windows entirely with just the turn of a handle.

"Tomorrow," she said to the marquis, "we'll have a sleigh ride on the Grand Canal, then a performance at the theater. I'll arrange it all! And tonight, of course, Count Cagliostro will be demonstrating his powers of mesmerism and mind reading."

"I was hoping to find him here already."

"Oh, he is always very mysterious," Antoinette said. "He likes to make a grand entrance. But this gives us time to play something together!" she said, drawing him toward the harpsichord. "We keep your flute here always."

"I'm afraid I haven't played much lately," the marquis demurred, but Antoinette, pouting, said, "Not even for me?"

When the Queen of France made such a remark, it was never clear, even given their friendship, whether it was a request or an order. And when she suggested that they play "C'est Mon Ami," he knew she would brook no denial. The lyrics of the song had been written by the poet Jean-Pierre Claris de Florian, but the music was the queen's own composition, and she was quite proud of it.

The flute was presented to him, with an exaggerated bow and a sly smile, by the Princesse de Lamballe; he knew she sensed his reluctance. The flute itself had been a gift from Antoinette, a way to encourage him to come to the Trianon and accompany her, and now, as she launched into the tune, singing the words in a bright contralto, he had little choice but to bend his head and play the tune from memory.

"*C'est mon ami, Rendez-moi,*" she sang, her head erect, "*J'ai son amour, Il a ma foi,*" repeating the refrain. She was dressed in a gossamer peach chemise over a silk gown, with no hoops or stays, and in her hair she wore a simple aigrette of white heron feathers with a sapphire clasp. Her figure had filled out, and her Habsburg lip, with its unfortunate droop, had become more pronounced, but her grace and carriage were unchanged. Fersen, the Swedish count, watched her with a rapt gaze, and the marquis was glad that she had found someone to provide her with the passion that the king, a cold and ungainly man, with an equally dismal reputation in the bedroom, could not. (It was common knowledge that he had a physical deformity that made intercourse painful for him.)

They had no sooner finished the tune than the applause was abetted by the sound of clapping from the entryway, where a stout, swarthy man with smoldering eyes, rimmed with kohl, stood. His dark hair was swept back with pomade but no powder, and he was dressed all in black, his silk tailcoat adorned with white ivory scarabs and amber pins shaped like gargoyles.

La Medusa, on a silver chain, hung around his neck.

Even as Sant'Angelo's eyes were riveted on the glass, Count Cagliostro's were drawn to him. It was as if two predators had crossed paths while hunting and did not know whether to go their own way or lock themselves in combat.

The court jewelers, however, had been right—this Medusa was the same as the one on the marquis's ring.

And it did not bear the ruby eyes of the version he had made for Eleonora de Toledo.

This, then, was the glass that possessed the power, the one that the Pope had stolen centuries before. Sant'Angelo could not imagine by what circuitous pathway it had come down to Cagliostro . . . but he did know that he would reclaim it before the night was through.

"I am honored," Cagliostro said, approaching and bowing his head, "to make your acquaintance at last."

When he looked up again, it was with a soulful but piercing

gaze, and Sant'Angelo recognized that the man was taking his measure.

Just as he was doing in return.

"I have heard so much about you, in so many quarters, for so long," the count went on, in a voice that seemed purposefully mellifluous . . . and difficult to trace. There was the hint of Italian in it, but also an intonation that seemed deliberately Eastern. "Your eye for things of beauty is celebrated everywhere."

The marquis did not know if the count referred, obliquely, to the queen, or the famously orphaned diamond necklace. He suspected the confusion was intended.

"As are your powers in other spheres," he added.

Sant'Angelo had no doubt, however, what this last sally referred to. He had acquired a reputation, wherever he went over the years, as a master of the dark arts. No one else, it was said, could have had the courage to inhabit the notorious Chateau Perdu, or have acquired such wealth and position with no known forebears. It was rumored that the marquis could read minds and foretell the future. It was a reputation that he neither encouraged nor dispelled.

"And your reputation, Count, certainly precedes you everywhere," the marquis replied. "The queen tells me you'll be doing some of your tricks tonight."

A flash of anger crossed Cagliostro's face, which he quickly disguised. "I will, of course, do the queen's bidding, but tricks are the province of magicians."

"Oh," Sant'Angelo said, "I was under the wrong impression. I am so sorry if I have given offense."

"Not at all." His thick fingers touched *La Medusa* on its chain. "I can't help but notice that you seem intrigued by my medallion."

"I am," the marquis replied. "Where did you get it?"

He could see a quick calculation going on in Cagliostro's mind. "It was a gift," he then said, "from Her Majesty."

This news astonished the marquis. How had he known nothing of this?

"It was sent to her by His Holiness, Pope Pius VI," the count continued, plainly having decided that the truth in this instance did more for his status than any lie might have done, "on the birth of her son, Louis-Charles. To protect the mother and child from the evil eye."

"*Il malocchio*," Sant'Angelo said.

"You know our countrymen," Cagliostro replied. "The queen wore it to a reception for the Pope one night, purely as a courtesy, but had very unpleasant dreams and asked me to dispose of it the next day. But it was so beautifully wrought, I could not bear to do it."

"How fortunate," the marquis replied.

"Besides, the queen has no use for such superstitious baubles. She had already found a nearly identical trinket in the royal coffers, but this one had ruby eyes, and she had melted it down to make a silver buckle for her shoe. The rubies became a pair of earrings for a friend."

That anyone, even a queen of France, would make such use of his handiwork made Sant'Angelo's blood boil.

And as if Cagliostro knew that he was pricking the count, he languidly raised one hand toward the Princesse de Lamballe and said, "You see? She's wearing the earrings now."

Sant'Angelo struggled to betray no emotion. This was the fate, he knew, of so much of his work—to be unwittingly disassembled or pillaged for its precious elements. But to discover that not one, but both, of his amulets should have found their way to the same place—one by way of the Medici, one from the hand of a pope—was astonishing beyond measure. It was as if the two *Medusas* had been drawn to each other, across space and time, by a force as mysterious as magnetism and unstoppable as the tides. Magic, beyond magic.

He simply thanked God that this one piece had survived.

Raising it on its chain appraisingly, Cagliostro said, "Rumor has it that it's over two hundred years old—the work of Benvenuto Cellini, in fact."

"Really?" the marquis replied. He had quite purposefully taken off his identical ring and left it at the Chateau Perdu. He pretended to examine the piece more closely. "I wasn't aware that he worked in niello."

"Cellini worked in every form and finish."

He was right about that, Sant'Angelo thought; he had tried his skills at everything. But had the count unlocked *La Medusa*'s secret, he wondered? Of course he would have uncovered its mirror . . . but had he put it to its proper use? Sant'Angelo's hand itched with the urge simply to snatch the piece free, but he could hardly start a brawl in the queen's own palace.

"I'm so glad that you two have met," the queen said, approaching with her Swedish lover Fersen standing close at her side. "I can't think of two more accomplished men to add to our company tonight."

"Not three?" Fersen said, leaning in to her, and she laughed, batting at him with her fan.

"Remember," she confided to the marquis, "how you taught me to properly wield this weapon?"

After some cajoling from de Lamballe and Polignac, Count Cagliostro consented to display some of his powers—acquired, or so he declared, from the ancient adepts in Egypt and Malta, hundreds of years ago. But then he was full of such boasts. Reputedly, he claimed to have restored the library at Alexandria at the behest of his personal friend, Cleopatra, and to have wielded the dagger that killed her consort, Ptolemy. He had been traveling all over Europe for years, raising money and founding lodges to promulgate the lost wisdom of Egyptian Masonry. As far as the marquis could tell, however, the lodges were empty, while the count's pockets were full.

He obliged the company now with some of the standard conjurations, making images appear in a vase of water (done, the marquis knew, with chemical reactions familiar to any alchemist worth his salt) and silverware move (with lodestones concealed in his cuff links). But the pièce de résistance, for which the count was famous from Warsaw to London, was one of his mesmerism performances. In preparation, he asked that the lamps be dimmed and that everyone arrange their chairs or cushions to face in his direction. Fersen sat at the queen's feet, along with her other lapdogs.

Once everyone had done so, and a fair amount of nervous giggling had subsided, he asked for volunteers for the first experiment—and Mme. Polignac's hand went up in an instant. She came forward, grinning, and took a chair he set out. Cagliostro drew himself up to his full height (augmented, the marquis was convinced, by platforms in his boots) and carefully removed *La Medusa* from around his neck. Holding it up, he let it dangle in the air.

As the others watched silently, he instructed the young princess to attend only to the sound of his voice, and gaze only at the medallion, which he swung slowly back and forth, back and forth. Sant'Angelo had seen similar displays at the salons of Franz Mesmer in Vienna, and within minutes the suggestible young woman was under his sway.

"You are in a deep sleep," he intoned, "a deep and comforting sleep . . . but when I tell you to awake, you will awake, and you will rush to kiss the oldest man you see in the room."

For a split second, the marquis wondered if he would be unmasked.

But when the duchess came out of her trance, she glanced about, as if unaware that anything at all had happened, then scurried to a dignified old burgher, distantly related to the Habsburgs, and throwing her arms around his neck, kissed him.

The room erupted into laughter, and the duchess, blushing fiercely, stepped back, her hand to her mouth. The burgher reached out playfully, as if to claim another kiss, but Cagliostro called him forward instead. The man took the chair the princess had vacated, and once again the count placed him under his spell.

"And when you awake," he suggested this time, "you will stand on one leg and crow like a rooster anytime Her Majesty plays the refrain of '*C'est Mon Ami.*'"

A ripple of subdued mirth went through the room, and Cagliostro raised a finger to hush them. Bringing the burgher back to his wits, he said, mournfully, "Alas, your will was too strong for me."

"I could have told you that before you went to so much trouble," the old man huffed, proudly.

"I could do nothing to overcome it," Cagliostro said, as the queen crept to the harpsichord and began to play the refrain of *"C'est Mon Ami."*

Not even back in his own seat yet, the burgher suddenly lifted one leg and let out a trilling cock-a-doodle-do. Then, so surprised was he at his own action—and in front of the queen yet!—he tumbled, beet red, onto a velvet settee.

The marquis knew where this was going—the count was going to mesmerize everyone at once, then do something to leave the proof that he'd done it—removing and hiding all their shoes, for instance. Mesmer had once switched everyone's jewelry around. It was all just a parlor game, and Sant'Angelo knew that it depended upon the willing abdication of will on the part of everyone in the room . . . a phenomenon he knew could sweep over an intimate group quite readily.

So, when the count did indeed ask for everyone's attention, and insist that they all follow his instructions and his voice to the letter, he played along, lowering his own eyelids, then his head on cue. But his hands were folded in his lap, like an arrow, and his thoughts were directed, straight as a rapier, at the count.

Already, he could sense a hesitancy creeping into Cagliostro's words.

The marquis raised his eyes, and even in the gloom, he could see that the count was studying him.

Yes, I know every trick in your bag, Sant'Angelo thought.

And like a lightning bolt, a thought shot right back into his own head. *Every trick?*

The marquis rocked back in his chair, in shock. This so-called count had greater powers than he had ever imagined, powers that Sant'Angelo assumed only he possessed. The marquis knew nothing of the Egyptian Masons, with whom Cagliostro claimed to have studied, but it was clear that he had learned great secrets, nonetheless. What Sant'Angelo had divined from the ancient *stregheria* of Sicilian witches, the count must have imbibed from his Coptic priests. While heads drooped and arms hung listlessly all around the room,

Sant'Angelo and his adversary were wide awake, all their respective faculties focused on each other.

But you challenge the power of the pharaohs, my friend.

To Sant'Angelo's astonishment, the shadows in the room began to move and take on the shape of birds—fat black ravens—that swirled across the walls and ceiling, before ominously massing. The marquis's respect for Cagliostro's powers grew even larger as he braced himself for an attack.

Which came only seconds later.

In a silent horde, their wings spread and beaks open, the ravens swooped down and Sant'Angelo instinctively started to raise his hands to protect himself against them. But then he caught himself— if you gave in to the illusion, you only gave strength to it—and deliberately let his arms drop to his sides.

If you let your adversary alter your reality, you became his slave.

And Sant'Angelo was not about to let that happen.

The parrot on the mantelpiece squawked in alarm, and the white monkey screeched. The little dogs yapped and scuttled from the room, as the queen stirred in her chair, and Fersen muttered uneasily.

I know what you've come for, the count continued.

The marquis berated himself for allowing his desires to become evident.

So it must be more valuable than I know.

The candles in the chandelier sputtered, some blowing out, as a wind seemed to sweep through the garden and rustle the curtains.

Oh, how he had underestimated his opponent, Sant'Angelo realized. But then, so had the count.

The marquis took a steadying breath, and concentrated his mind. He could feel Cagliostro trying to batter his way in again, but now that he was aware of the count's abilities, Sant'Angelo was able to effectively shut him out. He imagined himself ensconced, surrounded, *protected*, behind the high walls of the Chateau Perdu.

A draft blew through the room, sending the sheet music flying from the harpsichord.

And then the marquis conjured an eagle, its broad wings and razor-sharp talons spread, flying into the flock of ravens, tearing their ranks into disarray. The ravens scattered, some plummeting from the sky with broken wings and loose feathers, others disappearing like smoke.

If a battle of conjurations was what Cagliostro wanted, the marquis would give it to him, in spades.

But even as his eagle wreaked havoc, another and more sinister figure arose on the wall to defy it—the size and shape of a man, it bore the long snout and high pointed ears of a jackal.

Sant'Angelo recognized it instantly.

It was Anubis, the ancient Egyptian god of death, rising up like an avenging angel.

Before his eyes, the creature expanded, its muzzle extending out over the ceiling, its jaws open, its teeth like the jagged edge of a saw. . . .

And even Sant'Angelo felt a momentary shudder. *Resist it*, he told himself.

The creature's paws seemed to extend along the walls, long nails raking the mantelpiece and window frames.

Terrifying as it is, it is just an illusion.

But then, even to the marquis's astonishment, the monster's claws knocked a vase from the mantel. It shattered on the floor, and Antoinette herself let out a whimper of fear.

My God, he thought—Cagliostro was the most formidable adversary he had ever crossed.

The back of his neck tingled with what felt like the jackal's hot breath, and even the drip of saliva from its slavering jaws.

"Do you surrender?" He heard the count's voice, echoing as if from the bottom of a well. *"Do you bend your will to mine?"*

And in answer—what use were further words?—Sant'Angelo conjured a lion, massive and ferocious, roaring with rage. It sprang up from the floor, taking shape as it rose, its mane bristling, its ragged claws taking wild, deadly swipes at the head of the rearing jackal.

A tremor rumbled through the parquet floor, and the Princesse de Lamballe, though still in a trance, slumped to the floor.

The lion rose on its hind legs, bellowing, and the jackal began to shrink.

Looking up, Sant'Angelo saw the count reeling back, his focus lost, his confidence shaken. *La Medusa* dangled limply in his hand.

But rather than easing off, the marquis pressed his advantage.

On your knees, he ordered. He formed his thoughts like musket balls and shot them directly into his adversary's mind. *Your knees, I say!*

The count faltered, then slowly sank down, his own will broken. The shade of Anubis dwindled to the size of a rat . . . and scurried off.

And hear only my voice. He sent the words like another volley.

Cagliostro shook his head, as if trying to rid it of a searing pain.

Down! the marquis insisted. *Down!*

And the count sank lower, sprawling on the floor.

Sant'Angelo rose from his chair, and wending his way past the tormented dreamers, stood above the count. Cagliostro's hands were pressed to his temples, as if his head might split open at any second; with one more, well-directed tap, Sant'Angelo thought, he could break it in two like a quartz crystal. Cagliostro groaned in agony.

La Medusa lay beside him on the floor.

Sant'Angelo bent down and picked it up, clutching it in his fist as if to never let it go.

You will *remember who overmastered you tonight, Count.*

Cagliostro writhed, his boots scraping on the wood. The white monkey, screaming in fright, tried to run past, but Sant'Angelo snagged its leash and looped it several times around his groveling foe's neck.

But you will never be able to speak of it. His mind, Sant'Angelo knew, would rot from within, like termite-infested wood.

Turning toward the queen and her guests, restive but still mesmerized, the marquis instructed them to awaken only at the tolling of the clock. It was one minute before midnight.

Then he gathered his wolfskin coat and left. He was halfway to the Trianon's gate when he heard—added to the shrieks of the monkey and the cawing of the parrot—the commotion of the queen and her guests shaking off their trance. There were shouts of nervous exultation, raucous laughter, voices babbling in shock and surprise.

But what, he wondered with some satisfaction, did they make of the prostrate magician, with a screaming monkey wrapped around his neck?

He did not look back. There was no reason to. As his boots clicked across the flagstones and he gazed down at the long-lost *Medusa,* now cradled in his hand, he felt more at peace than he had for centuries.

Chapter 25

Coming around the corner of the Rue de Longchamp, David and Olivia paused. On one side of the street, there was a large park, with a sign advertising a boating lake and concession stands. And on the other side, their immaculate façades perfectly aligned, there was a row of eighteenth-century town houses, three or four stories high, with blue mansard roofs. In several of them, windows were lighted, revealing luxurious jewel-box interiors. A party appeared to be going on in one of them, with a woman in a backless gown laughing and sipping from a champagne flute.

But the address David was seeking, the last in the row, showed no signs of life. It was surrounded by a black wrought-iron fence, enclosing a garden and a porte cochere; its windows were dark, the curtains drawn. Although he would have found it hard to say why, the white limestone house gave off a forbidding air, as if it were holding itself aloof from the others. Security cameras were discreetly mounted at either end of the fence, and there was another one above the door. One bright spotlight, apparently motion-sensitive, switched on as David studied the small, gilded plaque, which read, *"L'Antiquaire."* Antiquary. *"Consultations Privées sur Rendez-vous Seulement."* Private consultations by appointment only.

It was just past seven, and David lifted the heavy door knocker—fashioned in the shape of a lion's jaw—and banged it three times. Inside, he could hear the boom echoing around an empty foyer.

They waited a minute or so before Olivia pointed out a touch pad with an intercom, and pressed that, too.

David had the distinct impression that they were being watched, and he looked up at the impassive lens of the camera, with its tiny winking red light. He lifted a hand to indicate that he knew.

There was a click of static, and a gruff voice said, "*Que voulez-vous?*" What do you want?

"We would like to see the Marquis di Sant'Angelo," Olivia leaned forward to reply, her French being far better than David's. "It's important."

"He's out."

"When will he be back?" David asked, realizing that, in their scruffy coats and jeans, they probably made a far less favorable impression than most of the marquis's private clients. "We can wait."

There was a pause, the sound of a heavy bolt being thrown back, and the door opened. A scowling man of about thirty glared down at them.

"What do you want with him?" he said, doubtfully.

"A consultation," David said.

"About?"

"That's none of your business," Olivia interjected. "We have serious matters to discuss."

The man at the door looked unmoved—in fact, he looked ready to slam the door in their faces—so David jumped in to placate him.

"We're looking for an artifact that we believe the marquis may know something about."

"He knows about a lot of things," the man said, the door swinging more closed by the second.

"It dates from the Renaissance," David blurted out, "Florence probably, and it's a mirror."

Although the man said nothing, the door stopped closing. David could see him debating what to do.

"Come back tomorrow," he said.

And then the door closed, though David was sure they were still being monitored.

"I'm freezing," Olivia said, stamping her feet. "There was a restaurant on the boulevard. Let's get something to eat."

They were seated at a table in the window, with a view of the park, and ordered some hot sandwiches and coffee. The barren branches of the trees across the way were bending and swaying in the rising wind; the air smelled like rain. There were only a few other customers, bundled in their coats, trying to get the chill out of their bones. But David was feeling more optimistic than he had in weeks—he felt that he might finally be onto something, and the reaction of that man at the door only bolstered it.

For her part, Olivia was thrilled that by following her nose with Cagliostro, she had again picked up the trail of Dieter Mainz, and now she was rattling off more of the Third Reich's crackpot theories—"in 1937, a rocket engineer named Willy Ley broke away from something called the Vril Society and had the courage to openly speak about their aims in public."

"Which were?" David said, listening, really, with only half an ear. He could not get his mind off meeting this antiquarian Sant'Angelo, and his eyes stared past his own reflection in the window to watch the night grow more turbulent. A smallish man, in a bulky jacket and hat pulled low, was lighting a cigarette at the entrance to the Metro station across the street.

"The members of the society—and most of the Nazis' upper echelon, including the Führer, by the way, were members—believed that by pursuing esoteric knowledge and ancient teachings, they could awaken their latent vril."

"Their what?"

"It's a meaningless word, really, invented for a science-fiction story by Edward Bulwer-Lytton. The vril was supposedly an essence in the blood, a mystical power, that could grant them virtual immortality."

The waiter brought them more coffee, asked if they would like to see the pastry selections, and when David looked back at the window, he was surprised to see that the man with the cigarette was standing just outside the glass, studying them like fish in an aquarium.

And damned if it wasn't the same man who had doctored their drinks on the train.

"I can't believe it!" Olivia said on seeing him there, and they were both incredulous when he casually ground out his lighted cigarette, came inside the bistro, and, as if they were old friends, pulled up a chair at their table.

David thought Olivia was going to grab her fork and try to stab him, and he laid a calming hand on her arm.

"I don't suppose you expected to see me again," the man said, taking off his hat and calling for a glass of the house red. His curly hair was squashed down tight around his crown.

"No, I can't say that I did," David replied, automatically hooking his wrist tightly through the handle of his valise.

"But rest assured, I have no schnapps for you tonight. In fact," he said, taking his wine from the waiter's tray, "I have some advice I'd like you to take instead."

He sipped his wine, while Olivia stared daggers at him and David wondered why on earth he would think that any advice he offered would be taken seriously.

"I regret what happened on the train," he said. "I'm a doctor, and—"

"I thought you sold medical supplies," David interrupted.

"In a manner of speaking, yes. But I am a doctor, and as such I have taken an oath to help, not to harm, people. I know that you are carrying something precious," he said, nodding at the valise, "but I have not been told what it is. Frankly, I don't care. But other people do care, very much, and you have already met some of their . . . employees."

"Your friend with the knife?" In case he had had any doubts about that muddled night on the train, David had found the puncture wounds in his duffel bag when unpacking at the Crillon.

"Yes," he replied. "But there are others." The self-proclaimed doctor sipped his wine while David and Olivia waited. "My advice to you—and I tell you this at considerable risk to myself—is to drop your search immediately, pack your bags, and go home. Live a long and healthy life. Forget whatever it is you think you know because—trust me—you know nothing."

"Then why are you here?" David asked. "If we know so little, why would anyone be bothering to pursue us?"

The doctor sighed, as if weary of trying to explain himself. "Because you're like a couple of clumsy children playing with a loaded gun."

Olivia bridled. "I am no child."

"And when guns go off," the doctor continued, "there's no telling who will get hit."

"Then tell us who these people are," David demanded, "and what they want."

"They're people who have been playing this game a lot longer than you have. They have no scruples, they have no moral reservations, and they make their own rules. It doesn't matter what they want—they will get it in the end." He finished his wine in one big swallow and stood up, pushing his chair back. "That's all you need to know," he said, throwing enough money on the table to cover the entire bill. "Don't say you haven't been warned." He pulled his hat down low over his ears, and as he turned to leave, Olivia put a hand on his sleeve and asked, "Why are you telling us all this?"

"Because I can't have any more blood on my hands."

With that, he left, and David watched as the doctor ducked out of the café doorway, waited for a rusty old taxi to pass, and darted, like the white rabbit in *Alice in Wonderland*, down into the hole of the Metro station.

Chapter 26

❧

That's the second time I've seen that old taxi, Julius thought, as he waited on the train platform. And even here, he noted a couple of suspicious-looking travelers, one of them carrying a too-prosaic sack of groceries, the baguette sticking up out of the bag. Julius waited for the train to whoosh to a stop, got on board, then, just as the doors were closing, ducked out again. But no one else got out with him.

He had just taken a huge chance, back at the café. If word of his betrayal ever got back to Escher, or God forbid Emil Rigaud, he'd vanish as thoroughly as the Turks had. You didn't erase Rigaud's emissaries without, eventually, being called to account.

But damn them all, he thought, as he paced the platform. God damn the whole organization. He had been systematically sucked in, his career destroyed, his reputation shot. And all in the service of what? He was damned if he could even remember how Rigaud and Linz had ever sold him such a lunatic bill of goods. Blood-purification rituals, a mysterious essence called vril, endless cell rejuvenation. Not to mention the promise of untold riches and universal acclaim as the doctor behind it all. Lunacy, pure lunacy. And all he could muster, in defense of his own actions, was that he hadn't been himself back then. He had been writing himself far too many prescriptions, for a host of potent drugs. But still . . . what had he come to? A man of his gifts, reduced to traipsing after a couple of supremely naïve academics as they strolled, oblivious, through a veritable minefield. What a waste.

A train rumbled in on the opposite track, but after it left, the platform was empty. Julius looked around, but on his side the only other people waiting were a couple of Muslim women, their scarves tied tightly around their hair. Europe was changing, he thought. Perhaps he should consider emigrating. On the wall, there was a travel poster for New Zealand. Would that be far enough away to escape his past?

When the next train came, he got on, glad of the warmth, but still keeping a wary eye out. Ever since Escher had shown up on his doorstep, he'd had to keep looking over his shoulder. But after all the killing, brutality, and deception he'd seen over the past week, he'd finally done something to expiate the guilt. He had entered something on the other side of the ledger. He just wasn't sure if he'd gotten through to them. The girl had a combative streak, he could see that, and the man—David Franco—looked, despite his spectacles and scholarly demeanor, like a man on a mission. A mission, Julius thought, that could still wind up costing him his life if he didn't take the warning to heart.

At his stop, he got out quickly, scurried up the stairs, and out onto a seedy street in the Pigalle section of the city. Escher had checked them into a hotel where he was clearly a regular customer—the ancient lady at the concierge desk had given him a toothless smile while sliding a room key across the counter.

"Your usual, monsieur."

Escher had thanked her and slipped her some money.

Their room, on the top floor and facing the front, was furnished with double beds, threadbare carpeting, and a view of an alleyway. But as he approached, Julius saw that the lights in the room were on, which meant Escher had returned from his visit to the Crillon and would be awaiting word on what David and Olivia had been up to. Julius had not wanted to go too close to the town house—he could see a camera above its door—but he had texted Escher the location and address.

He plodded up the creaking staircase, already editing in his mind what he was going to say, and looking forward to a pot of hot tea, when he opened the door and saw Emil Rigaud standing between the beds, slipping a cell phone back into his pocket.

"We've been waiting," Rigaud said, and it was then that Julius took note of the young man with a scar across his neck—it looked as if someone had once tried to cut his throat—lurking just behind the open door. The man shoved the door closed with his foot, then stood in front of it like a sentry. Another man, in a white shirt and red tie, emerged from the bathroom, drying his hands on a towel. Julius could hear the water running in the tub.

"Monsieur Rigaud, what an unexpected pleasure," Julius fairly stammered.

"It is?"

"Of course, of course," Julius said, his heart hammering in his chest. Rigaud was seldom the bearer of glad tidings. "But what are you doing here?" Gesturing around the shabby room, he tried to make a joke. "As you can see, I am traveling budget class."

Rigaud didn't crack a smile. "I'll tell you why I'm here," he said, though Julius was still focused on that water running in the tub. "I came up to Paris to see why you and your friend have been making such a hash of things."

Rigaud was nearly fifty, but in admirable shape—taut, lean, wearing one of his hand-tailored suits. Only his hair—dyed a too-bright blond—struck a discordant note.

"I don't know what you mean," Julius said, his mouth going dry and his pulse pounding. He had a momentary thought of trying to bolt past the guard at the door, or even of getting out the window and onto the fire escape.

"Sit down," Rigaud said, slinging a wooden chair in front of the clanking radiator.

"If I may just take off my coat first?" Julius said, his mind racing, as he placed it and his hat on the end of one bed.

The tub was still filling.

Julius took the seat, the man at the door moving to stand just behind his chair.

"First there's that little mix-up in Florence, with Ahmet and his friends."

"What mix-up?"

"Please," Rigaud said. "This will go so much more smoothly if you just answer my questions."

"You mean, when he came by to make a pickup? The last time I saw him, he was—"

The back of Rigaud's hand slapped him so hard in the mouth that Julius heard a tooth crack on his ring.

"Understand that I am reconciled to his loss," Rigaud said, turning away and shaking his fingers.

Julius did not imagine that the loss had been very painful for him.

"All he had to do," Rigaud continued, "was persuade that Swiss errand boy to go back to the States and get out of our way. Schillinger should know better by now than to meddle above his pay grade."

Julius suspected that Schillinger had a hard lesson coming, too, if he hadn't already received it. But what difference did it make? Julius had far more pressing concerns than that.

"It appears that Ahmet got distracted. Is that what happened?"

Julius was torn between coming clean and sticking with the lie he'd already begun.

"Drugs can do that to a person, wouldn't you say?"

Julius knew that he wasn't really expected to answer that—and he knew now that the general outline of the incident was fairly well-known to Rigaud. He'd missed his chance to take the high ground and confess.

"But now that Ahmet and his friends have disappeared," Rigaud said, "it's like somebody's poked a stick in the hornet's nest." Waving his hands at his two helpers, he added, "You know how our Turkish associates like to stick together."

Julius dug his handkerchief out of his pocket and held it to his lips. To his shame, he felt a trickle of warm urine running down his leg.

"And then there was that embarrassment on the night train. How could you two have bumbled such a simple task so badly?"

Julius debated keeping silent, or speaking, and when Rigaud didn't add anything, said, "I did speak to them, in the dining car. As I'm sure you know." At this point, he was just trying to feel his way along, admitting to nothing that might get him killed but supplying whatever information seemed safe. "And I do believe I got a good idea of who they are."

"Yes? And who are they, exactly?"

The radiator clanked like a string of tin cans being thrown down a chute.

"A couple of idiots. Babes in the woods. They know nothing. The girl—Olivia—will be back leading tour groups, and Franco will be back at his library desk by this same time next week. I'm sure of it." Then, dabbing at his lip, Julius told him about following them to the Louvre, throwing in as many details as he could think of, whether they were relevant or not, in a vain attempt to seem utterly transparent. He mentioned how long they had stayed there, the precise time they left—"That's when Ernst went back to the Crillon, to see what he could find in their room"—their subsequent visit to the Natural History Museum, and their excursion at dusk to the town house in the Sixteenth Arrondissement.

"They were turned away at the door," he said, "and went off to a nearby café."

"What was it called?" Rigaud asked.

"The café?"

Rigaud waited, and Julius knew that he had come to the moment of truth—how much more could he divulge? And had he—despite his best efforts—been under surveillance when he went across the street to join them?

"I don't remember the name."

The man in the necktie went into the bathroom and turned off the faucet.

"And then what did you do?" Rigaud asked in a measured tone.

What could he say? If he went so far as to admit that he had joined them, he would have to come up with some plausible reason for having done so. But given his role in drugging their drinks on the train—a ruse that Rigaud would assume even these babes in the woods would have been bright enough to figure out by now—how could he say it had been an attempt to ferret out any more information? Even David and Olivia couldn't be presented as *that* dumb. His mind was racing, but getting him nowhere.

"Well?"

On the other hand, if he suggested he was trying to feel them out—perhaps for a bribe of some kind?—he would have to explain that the offer was of course extended as a sham. The seconds were ticking away, and with each one Julius knew that he was looking more suspicious.

"What did I do then?" Julius finally said, pretending as a last resort to be taken aback by the very question. "I left them there, eating I don't know what—should I have gone inside to see what they'd ordered?—and I came back here." He wiped his bloody lip again in a show of false bravado. "To this reception."

"Really?" Rigaud said. "So you haven't had your dinner yet?"

"No," Julius said, confused. "Not yet."

"No chance to drop into some little café or restaurant?" he said, his eyes still riveted on Julius, whose wet pants were sticking to his leg.

"It's all right," Julius said, "I'm not hungry. Just exhausted."

Rigaud, as if deliberating, ran a hand carefully over his blond hair—Julius saw blood glittering on the ring that had cracked his tooth—then nodded to the young man behind the chair. A gag suddenly dropped over Julius's head and cut into his mouth, stifling his scream, as the Turk in the necktie went into the bathroom to turn the taps back on.

Leaving Hamid behind to mop up and deal with Escher, Rigaud ordered Ali to drive him back to the Crillon. Although his quarry was staying there, too, that wasn't the real reason he had checked in. The Crillon, to his mind, was simply the finest hotel in Paris. The Gestapo had thought so highly of it, in fact, that they had made it their French headquarters during the Second World War, and what better recommendation could you get than that?

Rigaud sat in the backseat of the Land Rover, looking out at the busy streets of the city, and thinking about what he'd tell Linz, and that impossible-to-please wife of his, when he got back to the Chateau Perdu. On the bright side, he could tell them that he had eliminated any further problems from Julius Jantzen, and, shortly, Ernst Escher. They had both gone off the rails and proved to be more trouble than they were worth. He made a mental note to call Joseph Schillinger in Chicago and give him some cock-and-bull story about what had happened to his faithful hound, Escher. He'd undoubtedly see right through it, but wasn't that half the point? To scare him back into his usual compliance? And even if he wanted to protest, who would he do it to? Auguste Linz? Christ, the man was too scared even to say his name.

"Can I tell my cousins now?" Ali asked from the driver's seat.

"Tell them what?"

Ali turned his face so that the scar on his throat was especially prominent. "That it's done? That Ahmet and the others have been avenged?"

"Oh, yes, go right ahead," Rigaud said. He'd forgotten for a moment that one of the reasons for this little expedition was to quell the rebellion among the worker bees. All things considered, the Turks were a useful crew, content to ask no questions and, when paid on time, willing to do anything required. It was Linz who had first suggested enlisting them. "They're one step up from dogs," he had observed, "and they can be trained the same way." Rigaud might have differed in his assessment—he thought they were at least two steps up from dogs—but he never forgot that they were punctilious about their honor and their vendettas.

As for the librarian and his tour guide, there he was less certain of his estimation. So far, they seemed like a couple of industrious drones, who had managed, by some miracle, to hang on to their bundle of papers and whatnot. But were they a threat? Did they pose any real danger to Auguste Linz and his secrets?

Not for one second did Rigaud think that.

Nor did he think that their efforts would wind up revealing anything worthwhile to add to Linz's inventory.

That Palliser fellow, for instance, the one who'd once worked for the International Art Recovery League, he had been more of a problem. There was a mercenary streak in him that made his actions more unpredictable. That was why Rigaud had decided to nip that one in the bud. Palliser, like a couple of the other investigators before him, had been a pro . . . and as soon as he had shown signs of getting close to the center of the web, Rigaud, on instructions from Linz, had plucked him up, flown him by helicopter to the chateau. After a bit of casual interrogation, they had dropped him down the ever-reliable oubliette. It was all like a game of chess, and if removing Palliser was like taking the queen, dispensing with David and Olivia would be like eliminating a couple of pawns. They were less trouble alive than dead.

At the hotel, Rigaud and Ali surveyed the lobby, just on the off chance that the two young sleuths were there, then went up to their own suite. As Ali called room service, Rigaud, getting undressed, called out to him to order his usual—a Campari and soda, with a twist of lemon. Then he stepped into the shower and turned the hot water on full blast.

He let his head hang down under the spray, his ropy, well-muscled arms leaning on the wall, and thinking, not for the first time, what an empty game it all was. Linz already had what he wanted; his position was unassailable. But he always kept his guard up, always kept his network of spies and loyalists, experts and assassins, working for him. He lived for intrigue—what else was there?—and the possibility, however remote, that someone, somewhere, might stumble upon some dark secret or device that he had so far overlooked. Sometimes, Rigaud suspected that he did it just to keep his mind alive and his spirits engaged.

Linz could no more exist without an adversary than night could exist without day.

There was a cool draft as the bathroom door opened and closed, and a moment later, the door to the shower stall opened. Ali held out a glass of Campari, with a lemon twist clinging to the rim, and then, naked, stepped into the stall to join him.

Chapter 27

Marie Antoinette, Queen of France, Archduchess of Austria and Lorraine, widow of Louis XVI, who had been decapitated ten months before, had just been sentenced to death herself.

From the bedroom of his Paris town house, the Marquis di Sant'Angelo was awakened by the cries of exultation in the street. The lowly sansculottes, so named by the aristocrats because they wore pantaloons instead of the knee breeches fashionable at court, were running riot with joy. As the marquis wrapped a dressing robe around his shoulders and stepped out onto the balcony, he saw the revelers banging on the doors of the houses they passed, slapping back the shutters, waving their stocking caps in the air. A misty dawn was breaking, and it appeared that it would be a beautiful day for an execution.

It was October 16, 1793. Or, according to the new (and more "scientific") revolutionary calendar that had recently been implemented, the sixth of Vendémiaire.

"She's condemned!" a sweaty laborer shouted up at the marquis: he was wearing the tricolored cockade of the Republic on his cap. "The Austrian bitch gets the razor today!"

The national razor was one of the many colloquial names for the guillotine. Every week there was a new one.

The laborer remained there, grinning and waiting for Sant'Angelo to display his own revolutionary zeal, but he received no such response. The marquis knew that it was unwise to appear anything but pleased—he could be denounced and tried and executed himself—but he was not about to betray his true sentiments for even a moment. He glared down until the brute in the street, feeling a strange chill enter his bones, slunk away like a whipped dog.

Still, Sant'Angelo could hardly believe his ears. The queen had been kept a prisoner of the National Assembly for nearly two years thus far, and for all that time, the marquis had awaited some rational resolution of her ordeal. An American patriot then in Paris, a man named Tom Paine, had suggested that she be exiled to his own country, and many others were confident that the royal house of Habsburg would never let a member of its own family perish on the scaffold. They would either send an armed force to rescue her from her terrible captivity—their troops were stationed only forty leagues from the capital of France—or would make some diplomatic arrangement involving an exchange of hostages. (They held several members of the French Assembly as potential bargaining chips.) Failing that, there was always the possibility of a hefty ransom, which was the customary means of rescuing royalty suddenly stranded in foreign and hostile territory.

But nothing—none of it—had happened. For strategic reasons that the marquis could guess, and practical considerations that made any rescue attempt too dangerous to attempt, her allies had decided to remain idle. They were simply going to let this reign of terror that held all of France in its grasp devour the daughter of the Austrian empress, Maria Theresa. Every day, the marquis had listened in horror as the tumbrels rattled over the cobblestoned streets on their way to the Place de la Révolution, carrying the prisoners, condemned at the Palais de Justice, on their last journey. Most of the time, the marquis, whose house stood well back from the main thoroughfare, heard only the catcalls of the onlookers, shouting epithets and taunts, but there were times when he could make out the victims' sobs and screams, their pleas for mercy or prayers for deliverance, as the open carts rumbled on.

The procession seemed endless.

Indeed, so much blood had been spilled beneath the guillotine that deep trenches had been dug to channel the flood away.

And still the tumbrels kept rolling.

But ever since Count Cagliostro had revealed to him that the queen had not only owned the *Medusa* but spent a very unpleasant night before abruptly giving it away, he had prepared for this grim occasion. If, as he suspected, she had looked into its depths, if the moonlight had caught her reflection in the beveled glass, then the fate that awaited her now might be unthinkably horrifying. As the creator of the mirror, it was his duty to come to her aid, at any cost.

Throwing off his robe, he dressed quickly in the priestly black vestments he had set aside in the armoire and concealed the garland under his starched white collar; then he hung the *harpe*—the short sword with its distinctive notched end—beneath his robe and stuck a sack of gold coins in his pocket. Racing down the stairs with a letter and a breviary in hand, he passed Ascanio and warned him to have the carriage ready for a hasty departure to the Chateau Perdu later that day.

"Keep the horses in harness and the curtains drawn!" he bellowed, as he raced into the streets of Paris.

Although the queen had been interrogated for the past two days, the sentence of death had only been passed at four in the morning, and the whole city was abuzz. Everywhere, people were gathered at street corners, or in the doorways of shops and taverns, chattering away, laughing, slapping each other on the back, singing a few bars of "La Marseillaise." It was a holiday mood, and Sant'Angelo's heart sickened.

What did they truly know of the woman who had been sentenced?

He, too, had heard the vile stories that had been spread for years.

That she had purchased a diamond necklace with two million livres stolen from the national treasury.

That she and her loyal retainers Lamballe and Polignac had enticed the members of her Swiss Guard to join them in orgies at Le Petit Trianon.

That she had advised the starving peasants, who had no bread, to eat cake.

But all of the stories, he knew, were lies—lies designed to sell papers and pamphlets. Calumnies whose sole purpose was to inflame the mob and feed the fires of the Revolution—fires that needed constant stoking. For all of their talk of reform and revolution, the likes of Danton and Robespierre and Marat had plunged the country into even greater turmoil and despair, into war with neighboring countries and abject poverty at home. If these self-anointed leaders did not keep the people aroused with calls to preserve the Revolution, or to defend it from one imaginary foe after another, then the people might shake themselves awake from the trance they were in and begin to question the very men who had drenched their streets in blood and made France a pariah among the civilized nations of the world.

Even his clerical garb, with his broad-brimmed black hat shielding his face, made Sant'Angelo an object of unwelcome attention on the streets. Much of the clergy had been purged, and only those priests who had taken the constitutional oath were permitted to perform the customary ecclesiastical functions. Marie Antoinette had never wavered from her firm Catholic faith, and the marquis knew that she would never admit to her presence—much less make her final confession to—any clergyman who had sworn such an oath.

But he also knew that, once she saw his face beneath the black brim, she would understand that something else was afoot.

As he approached the Conciergerie, once a Merovingian palace, but now—along with the Tour de L'Horloge and the Palais de Justice—the hub of the Revolutionary Tribunal, he could feel its silent menace poisoning the very air. A Gothic fortress, it was recognizable from afar by its three towers—the Caesar Tower, named for the Roman emperor; the Silver Tower, so-called because it reputedly held the royal treasury at one time; and the third and most awful tower of all, the Bonbec, or "good beak." The name was inspired by the "singing" of the prisoners who were consigned to its torture chambers.

The marquis hurried along the banks of the Seine as it caught the full morning light, and across the old stone bridge. There was a strange heavy air in the courtyard, compounded of victory, revenge, and a vague sense of unease. Even the hostlers and guards, going about their usual business, seemed to feel the weight of what they were about to do. Killing the king had been bad enough; killing the queen, the weaker vessel, the mother of two living children and the last person who would ever sit upon a throne of France, felt, even to some of the firebrands among them, fundamentally ignoble.

In all the commotion and confusion—horses being tethered to the tumbrels, gendarmes reading out the lists of those to be executed that morning and corralling them into the waiting carts, lawyers searching for their doomed clients—the marquis was able to make swift progress toward the queen's own chambers in the inner courtyard. Looking up, he could see the narrow window of her cell, not only barred but partially blocked up. Two sentries stood at the door to the tower, and he brandished his letter of authorization from the Tribunal (which he had forged several weeks before, and signed in the name of Fouquier Tinville, the principal prosecutor in the case against the queen). He watched their worried faces as they debated its merits.

"Come, come," the marquis said impatiently, "the widow Capet is entitled to her last communion." The words—*the widow Capet*—were like ashes on his tongue, but that was how the court now referred to her. The ancestors of Louis XVI had borne that ordinary surname.

"But she already refused a priest yesterday," one of them objected.

"She wasn't on her way to the guillotine then."

"She says that any priest who's pledged his first allegiance to the Constitution is no priest at all."

"I'll hear that from her own lips," Sant'Angelo said, as the massive gong in the clock tower rang out. "Or would you rather explain to the prosecutor why the widow was late to her appointment on the scaffold?" He made as if to leave in a huff, when the sentries grudgingly let him pass.

Holding up the bottom of his black robe, he ascended the winding steps three at a time, waving the letter at two more guards, who were presently occupied with wrestling a condemned husband away from his sobbing wife, then up to another barred door. Here again he showed the letter, but once he determined that the jailer could not read, he quickly produced his purse and poured a cascade of coins into the man's weather-beaten hand.

Going ever higher, he passed several cell doors, where other prisoners of consequence were being kept. In the Conciergerie, there had always been varying levels of discomfort. For the wealthy and privileged, willing to fork over the necessary bribes, there were private cells with a bed, a desk, and even writing materials. For the less-well-to-do, there were *pistoles*, with a bunk and a table. And for the commoners—known as the *pailleux*—there were the rocky, underground caverns kept damp by the Seine, where matted hay, or *paille*, was strewn on the floor. In previous times, the prisoners there were simply left to die from malnutrition, or the infectious diseases that lingered in the gloomy vaults.

The queen, Sant'Angelo knew, was housed at the top of the tower, not out of any pity or concern but because it afforded the greatest security. There was only one staircase up, and at the door to her cell, another pair of gendarmes was waiting. The marquis slowed his step and approached with his breviary in hand.

"I am here for the prisoner to make her final communion."

"I don't know anything about that claptrap," one of them snapped. "You'll have to see Citizen Hébert; he's inside."

The marquis had not counted on this. Of all the bloodthirsty wolves of the Revolution, Jacques Hébert was the worst. Chief of the Committee of Public Safety, it was he who had published some of the most defamatory and revolting lies about the queen, and it was he who had declared, in his role as the champion of the sansculottes, "I have promised them the head of Antoinette! I will go and cut it off myself if there is any delay in giving it to me."

Apparently, he had decided to monitor the execution himself.

The marquis ducked his head to enter the cell (Hébert had had the doorway purposely lowered, so that the queen, whenever she came out to receive a visitor from the Convention, would have to bow her head to him), and found the chief and a couple of his minions from the Committee keeping vigil in the anteroom.

"Who are you?" Hébert demanded, wheeling on him. He was armed, as usual, with a tasseled rapier hanging at his side.

The marquis produced the letter and waited as Hébert read it. His eyes were close-set and red-rimmed, like a rodent's, and his jaw was constantly grinding. His dark hair, wet with perspiration, was tied back with the tricolor cockade.

"I've never seen you before," Hébert said suspiciously. "Which one of those corrupt orders do you belong to?"

"I follow St. Francis."

"And what makes you think the Capet woman will want to talk to you?"

"I don't know that she will," the marquis replied, affecting indifference. "But this privilege is still established by law."

He knew that the mention of the law was a cunning stroke; these assassins liked to pretend that they were only upholding justice— equal for everyone in the new Republic—and that their bloody acts were simply the seamless working of the state's machinery. Even the guillotine, now the dreaded symbol of the Revolution itself, had been invented as a swifter and more humane method of execution; in fact, however, it had become an indispensable means for conducting murder on an unprecedented scale.

Monsieur Hébert tossed the letter back at Sant'Angelo, and taking an iron key from his own pocket, unlocked the inner door.

"Be quick about it. She's had thirty-seven years to make her peace with God. I don't know how she can catch up now."

One of his minions laughed, and Hébert, too, seemed to enjoy his little jest. The marquis swallowed the anger that rose in his throat like a ball of boiling tar and went inside.

The room was nearly bare, with just a few sticks of battered furniture and a rumpled sheet strung on a line to conceal the privy bucket. With the window blocked, and the sun in another quarter, the tiny cell was as dim as it was chill.

Marie Antoinette lay on her hard pallet, with her hands folded under her cheek, her eyes glassy and staring at nothing.

Sant'Angelo would hardly have recognized her. He remembered so well the shy, sweet, and bewildered girl who had first arrived at court twenty-three years before . . . and, of course, the gay, beautiful woman that she had become, known for her finery and sophistication.

What he saw now was a haunted shadow of her former self, with wild, uncombed hair and a face that seemed an utter stranger to anything but sadness.

But had she truly aged? He drew a stool close to the bed, but even then he could not be sure. It was only a few years ago that the Pope had sent her the true Medusa, and the haggard expression she wore now could be nothing more than the natural countenance of a woman who had had everything in the world taken from her and was about to lose her own life, too.

"Your Majesty," he whispered, knowing that there was not a second to waste.

"I do not want you," Antoinette said, never bothering to raise her eyes past his black cassock.

"Look at me," he said. "I pray you, look at me."

Wearily, as if obeying yet another of her persecutors' commands, she raised her blue-gray eyes, then, after a second or two, understood that it was her old friend, the marquis, lurking under the brim of the priest's hat.

"How did you—"

"You must do exactly what I tell you to do," he said.

"You cannot give communion."

"I can do better than that."

She looked at him without any expression at all, as if perhaps unsure that he was really there at all.

"We can make our escape, if you will only believe me and do exactly as I say."

"My dear friend," she said resignedly, "it is over for me. I am only concerned now that you have placed yourself in such danger." She struggled to sit upright, and he held her by one delicate elbow until she had managed it.

Reaching under his collar, as if merely to remove the purple stole, he withdrew the hidden garland and held it low, between his knees, where it would be concealed by the breviary.

"I cannot ask you to understand this, but I can beg you to believe it. This wreath, placed upon your head, will render you invisible."

"Oh, now you sound like our old friend Count Cagliostro," she said, dismissing his words with a sad smile.

"His powers paled compared to mine," Sant'Angelo said. "Don't you remember that night at the Trianon?"

"Yes, of course I do," she said absently, "please take no offense. But even if I *could* escape, as you say," and she spoke, as if trying to reason calmly with a madman, "I would not do so. Not so long as my children were held here, too."

The marquis had assumed she would say as much. "But they are merely children," he tried to assure her. "They won't be harmed."

"Are you so sure?"

The marquis was not sure at all; the present barbarity knew no bounds. "But we can find a way to rescue them, too. For now, however, it's you, the queen, that these savages want."

"And if my death will satisfy them, then my children may be spared."

"Once you are safely away," Sant'Angelo urged, "there will be chaos and delay, endless recriminations and denunciations. They'll have Hébert's head on a pike, for one. And then I will come back—

I promise you—and spirit your children to a safe hiding place, too."

Placing a cold and frail hand on top of his own, she said, "It is enough that you have come to see me off. They have refused to let me say good-bye to anyone, or to receive any friend or family member."

"But if you will just let me put the wreath on your head, and keep you close behind me, I swear you will be able to walk out of here under their very noses."

"You don't think they would notice my absence?" she said, dryly.

"I will create such confusion that I'll have them believing a flight of angels just carried you off to Heaven."

"And where will we go instead?"

"I will take you to my house, where a carriage is already waiting. We can be at my chateau by dusk, and from there—"

But the look on her face told him not to continue. No doubt she was remembering the last escape plan, when her carriage had been delayed at the town of Varennes and the king had been recognized; the royal family was escorted back to the Tuileries in disgrace. Ever since that fateful night—June 21, 1791—their captivity had been complete; the family had been systematically separated and imprisoned in one place after another, each one more dreadful than the one before.

"I thank you," she said, "but now I only wish for all of this to come to an end. I wish to be with my husband, and in the arms of God." Bending her head, as if to make the present charade, for his sake, more convincing, she touched the breviary in his hand and murmured a prayer.

"Time's up," Hébert said, striding into the room. Right behind him, he had a barber, carrying a rusty pair of scissors. "Move along now, priest."

Shoving Sant'Angelo aside, he yanked away the muslin fichu draped around the queen's shoulders and said to the barber, "Start cutting." The barber gathered whatever he could of her hair and sheared it off as if she were a sheep.

"We don't want anything to impede the razor, do we?" Hébert gloated.

When the cutting was done, the queen was thrown a white linen bonnet, with two black strings to tie it behind.

"Stand up," Hébert barked, and the marquis could tell he took exquisite pleasure in every discourtesy he could show her. "Put your hands behind your back."

At this, even Antoinette seemed surprised, and said, "You did not bind the hands of the king."

"And that was a mistake," he replied, pulling her wrists back, then knotting a rope around them. Her shoulders were so sharp, it looked as if they might pierce the cloth of her simple white dress.

"Time to go," Hébert said, nudging the queen with his knee, the way one might nudge a turkey toward the chopping block.

With the Chief of the Committee of Public Safety in the front, and his minions on either side of her, Marie Antoinette was led through the anteroom and down the winding stair. For a moment, the marquis considered attacking them all right then and there, and dragging her off, but he knew that even the queen would resist him. She was reconciled to her fate and did not so much as look back at him.

But he would not—he could not—abandon her. Even the king had been allowed the company and solace of his own *abbé*, Edgeworth de Firmont, on the way to his execution. Marie Antoinette had no one. Alone in the cell, Sant'Angelo tossed the black hat in the corner, along with the breviary, and lifted the garland to his own head. Made so long ago, from the bulrushes surrounding Medusa's pool, twisted and gilded together in the solitude of his studio, he placed it on his own head.

But the effect, as he knew, was not instantaneous.

Rather, it was as if he had stepped beneath the cascade of water spilling over the lip of the Gorgon's rock. The top of his head felt anointed, then his face, and neck, and shoulders. Slowly, the sensation, like a trickle of cool water, worked its way all the way down his body, and even as he looked on, his chest, then his legs, then his feet too, disappeared. He was as solid as ever—something he sometimes forgot, when he banged into a doorframe or stumbled over a stool—but he was utterly invisible to the mortal eye.

By the time he had managed to get downstairs, carefully avoiding any contact with the turnkeys or the guards, the queen was being led toward a rickety tumbrel. Her husband, he knew, had been transported to his death in a closed carriage, safe from the howls and imprecations of the mob, but Hébert seemed determined to miss no opportunity to torment the widow Capet. Her steps faltered as she realized that this was to be the way in which she was conveyed to her death, and she had to turn to Hébert and beg him to untie her hands for just a moment.

Hébert nodded at one of his men, wearing a red stocking cap with a white feather stuck in it, who undid the knot, and the queen, desperately seeking some corner of the courtyard that might afford her some privacy, scurried toward a wall, and lifting her hem, squatted there, her pale face reddening with shame, meeting no one's eye.

As soon as she was done, Hébert had her hands retied and she was thrust back into the open cart. Stepping into it, she naturally sat facing the front, as she had always done in her coach, but the driver, not unkindly, directed her to sit with her back to the horses. This, the marquis knew, was to keep the prisoners from catching sight of the looming guillotine until the last moments of their journey.

And just as the cart jolted to a start, Sant'Angelo leapt up into it. For a second, the horses slowed, reacting to the added weight, but then plodded on, out of the Cour de Mai, where all was relatively silent and restrained, out of the Conciergerie, with its thick walls and lofty towers, and, finally, into the open streets of the city . . . where madness reigned.

The marquis had never seen a more frightening sight, even in the underworld.

As the cart lurched along the quayside and past the old clock tower, hundreds of people, their faces twisted with rage, shaking their fists, brandishing clubs and knives, pitchforks and bottles, poured toward them from every direction. The gendarmes accompanying the cart could barely keep them from overturning the tumbrel and tearing Marie Antoinette limb from limb on the spot. A famous actor, Grammont, rode in front, and attempted to divert the crowd by waving his sword in the air and shouting assuredly, "She's done for, my friends! The infamous Antoinette! Have no fear—she'll soon be roasting in hell!"

But that didn't stop the curses and the spittle and the rotten fruit from being thrown. The marquis could only wonder at the queen's composure. She sat erect in the cart, her head high, her chin thrust out, determined, it would seem, to emulate the sangfroid displayed by her late husband. Sant'Angelo did whatever he could do, blocking what projectiles he could without giving himself away, and once, when one of the savages tried to leap into the cart, kicking him in the face so hard his teeth exploded like sparks. The man, not knowing what had happened, staggered back into the street, blood gushing between the fingers he held to his stunned mouth.

The journey seemed interminable, and Sant'Angelo assumed that the driver had been instructed to take the more roundabout route in order to prolong the queen's agony. On the narrower streets, heads poked out of windows above the procession, and in one of them the marquis saw the painter Jacques-Louis David perched on the sill, hastily drawing in a sketchpad on his lap. On the rue St. Honoré, he saw a silent priest, nodding his head in a benediction to the passing queen. Only once did the mob thin, and that was as the tumbrel passed the Jacobin Club, where loitering was not allowed. Nearby, in the Maison Duplay, behind the shutters he always kept drawn, lived the ruthless mastermind of the Revolution, Maximilien Robespierre. But he was nowhere to be seen this day.

Even the heavy, slow-moving horses, called *rosinantes*, were meant to be an affront to the queen's dignity. These were not carriage horses, accustomed to city traffic, but lumbering beasts, used for drawing plows, and the driver had to calm them down and keep them from trying to bolt. Several times the queen was nearly toppled over by a sudden lurch, and the marquis put out a hand to steady her. But in her mind she was clearly so far away, her eyes focused on something no one else could see, that his touch did not even register.

And then the cart slowly turned into the rue Royale, where the sound of the waiting mob, tens of thousands of them gathered in the Place de la Révolution, swelled like the crashing of an ocean wave. The cart rumbled on, past the palace of the Tuileries, where the king and queen had spent so many happy times with their children. The marquis himself had given an impromptu flute lesson to their daughter, Marie Thérèse, in a music room off the mezzanine there. Marie Antoinette's gaze lifted at the sight of the gates and terraces and momentarily glistened with tears.

And above the roar of the crowd, he could hear the guillotine, even now going about its business. Prisoners were being dispatched with grim regularity, their demise signaled by a succession of distinctive sounds. First, there was the dropping of the *bascule,* the plank on which the victim was laid flat. Then, after the plank was slid into place, there was the bang of the *lunette,* the wooden pillory, which locked the victim's head, facedown, beneath the blade. And finally the swishing of the blade itself, as it plunged eighteen feet, then rebounded, splashed with blood and bits of flesh.

Depending on the notoriety of the beheaded, all of this was immediately followed by general exultation, as the executioner wiped his instrument off and his crew threw buckets of water on the platform to wash it clean.

Armed guards had to force a path through the mob for the queen's tumbrel, which gradually drew to the foot of the scaffold and stopped. Antoinette, who had barely even seen the sun or breathed fresh air for months, struggled to stand up, and Sant'Angelo quickly put an arm around her waist and helped her to keep her balance as she stepped from the unsteady cart. For a moment, she seemed bewildered at this strange sensation of assistance, and looked around, but he said nothing to give himself away.

Let her imagine it to be an angel at her side, he thought.

With her hands still bound behind her, and unknowingly supported by the marquis's unseen arm, she ascended the stairs, her plum-colored slippers sliding on the slick wood. Purely by accident, she stepped on the foot of the executioner.

"I am sorry, monsieur," she said instinctively. "I did not do it on purpose."

And then, as the marquis stood helplessly by, Marie Antoinette was laid on the plank and her neck was clamped into the *lunette*. Just below her, the eager spectators jockeyed for position, the better to dip their hats and handkerchiefs in her blood. Among them Sant'Angelo saw Hébert's companion, the man with the long white feather in his cap. He was dancing a jig in anticipation.

And then the executioner took a step back and released the gleaming blade. It hurtled down with a rattle and a crash. When the head was displayed—its mouth open, its eyes bulging wide—a cheer like nothing the marquis had ever heard before went up from the happy crowd.

Chapter 28

When Escher came up out of the Metro at the Pigalle station, he was more than satisfied with his day's work.

Breaking into the suite at the Crillon had been no trouble at all, and although David had taken his precious valise with him, both he and Olivia had done him the great favor of leaving their laptops in the room. Ernst had spent so many hours opening, downloading, and transmitting their various files that he had had to order up some room service. He'd had lobster, champagne, and a perfect lemon soufflé. Why not?

But what a strange haul it had been. Franco's files included everything from a gallery of Bronzino's portraits to treatises on ancient glassblowing techniques. And the woman's? Hers were even crazier, ranging from mythology to mesmerism, Egyptian burial practices to Nazi training manuals. Just like the bookshelves at her apartment. For Escher, who was usually forced to operate on a strictly need-to-know basis, it was nice to get a glimpse, however inscrutable, of what his quarry was up to, and what it was that Schillinger and his mysterious overseers might be after. He always liked to know more than his employers thought he did.

As he crossed the alleyway, he glanced up to see lights on in his room. Jantzen must be back. But when he came through the doors, the concierge furtively waved him over. She had just been eating candy, and her fingers were sticky with caramel. "You have visitors upstairs," she muttered.

"How many?"

"I'm not sure. There were three, but I think a couple left."

Escher certainly wasn't expecting anyone, and he asked the old lady to wait five minutes and then go upstairs to offer a turn-down service. Going back around the alley, he climbed the fire escape as quietly as he could. When he got to the top floor, he crept to the window and looked inside through a part in the curtains.

There was no sign of Julius, but a man in white shirtsleeves and a red necktie was sitting in a chair right between the beds. A man he didn't know, holding Escher's own gun in his hands.

God damn it. Escher, knowing it would have been confiscated at the Louvre security desk, had left the gun behind.

There was a knock on the door and the man stood up silently, holding the weapon steady, with both hands, in front of him. This was no amateur.

The concierge unlocked the door, and with fresh towels in her arms, came in. The man hastily slipped the gun under the bedclothes, and Escher could hear the old lady apologizing for the intrusion. While the gunman was distracted, claiming to be waiting for his friends to return, Escher slipped his fingers under the window and raised the frame a foot or more.

When the old lady left, the man tossed the towels on the bed and resumed his vigil.

Escher no longer had to guess what the others had left him behind to do.

It was only a matter of minutes before the gunman noticed the draft in the room, and the curtain billowing out. Escher could see him debating whether or not to get up, but then, putting the gun on the bed, he got up, stretched and rolled his neck. Escher flattened himself against the brick wall of the hotel and waited. A few seconds later, the curtain was pulled back, but instead of trying to close the window, the guy did Escher a favor and opened it wider. Escher's hand shot out and snagged his necktie, then yanked his head out the window. With his other hand, he clubbed him in the face. The man's hands groped at his assailant, but Escher twisted the necktie tighter. The guy was halfway out and already strangling when Escher shoved the window down on his shoulder blades.

The wind went out of him, and Escher used the moment to stand up and stamp on the back of his neck. There was a nasty crunch, and Escher stamped again. The body was twitching when Escher dragged it all the way out and rolled it, like a heavy bag of laundry, over the edge of the fire escape. It plummeted onto an array of trash cans, making an enormous crash, before slumping out of sight behind them. Escher held his breath, waiting for any reaction from a neighboring window or passerby, but it was a cold night, windows were closed, and in this neighborhood people knew better than to stick their nose in where it wasn't wanted.

Bending double, he slipped into the room, and quickly retrieved his Glock 9mm. The ashtray was filled with cigarette butts, one of those flavored Eastern brands, Samsun or Maltepe. He looked all around the room, and then, with his gun cocked, moved toward the bathroom door. It was ajar, and Escher could hear the drip of the faucet in the tub.

With one finger, he pushed the door open. The shower curtain was drawn, but even before he pulled it back, he knew what he was going to find.

Julius, his face scrunched up like a rabbit's, was lying in the water, fully dressed, with a sliver of white soap bobbing around his chin. His skin was blue.

Escher felt insulted. Not because he'd particularly liked Jantzen, or even trusted him. But it was an affront to him as a professional. Your partner, however incompetent, was not supposed to die.

Escher swiftly packed up his own things, along with anything that might identify Jantzen's body—most notably his cell phone and PDA. Who knew what kind of information—marketable information— might be on those? Then he climbed back out the window and down the fire escape. The body behind the trash cans had already attracted some curious rodents.

On the street, he drew no notice, and as he walked away from the hotel, he reminded himself to send the concierge, along with a few hundred euros, a box of her favorite caramels.

Chapter 29

After the blade had fallen, the head and corpse of Marie Antoinette were summarily tossed back into the tumbrel and taken to the Madeleine, an out-of-the-way cemetery on the grounds of what had once been a Benedictine monastery. Although the journey was less than a kilometer, the rue d'Anjou was unpaved and the wheels of the tumbrel sometimes became stuck. It was already midday by the time the cart got there, with the marquis, still invisible, trudging along behind it on foot.

The gravediggers, unwilling to interrupt their lunch, told the driver simply to leave his cargo on the grass while they finished eating. They had been working for weeks, digging trenches, packing them full, then applying a liberal dose of quicklime to dissolve the remains. As far as they were concerned, this was just one more customer, and she could wait.

The marquis kept watch from a safe distance, where the head lay on the grass, its white bonnet now encrusted with blood and plastered across its features. Standing beside a stone bench, left there by the monks who had all since been executed, he forced himself to think of happier times, when the young Marie Antoinette, uprooted from everyone and everything she knew, had eagerly accepted his guidance and support through the maze of the most formal court in the history of the Continent.

And though it was true that she had had her faults—she could indeed be frivolous and wildly extravagant, petty and jealous, fickle and unfaithful—he had yet to find any human being who did not. And her life, despite its outward grandeur, had also had far more than its share of loneliness, lovelessness, and despair. Born in a palace, she had died on a scaffold.

And at the last she lay a few yards off, dismembered and defiled, on a patch of dirt. When he was confident that the gravediggers were paying more attention to their apples and cheese than to the queen's remains, he ventured closer. Though any rational man would have thought him insane even to question it, he had to be sure that no magic had prevailed, that the queen was well and truly dead. He was just reaching down to brush away the cloud of flies and lift the bonnet away from her face when he heard someone shout, "I hope we're in time!"

Looking up, he saw Hébert himself, his rapier jingling at his side, and his two accomplices approaching the gravediggers. A young woman wearing a kerchief over her head, and carrying a heavy basket, struggled to keep up.

"Citizen Hébert!" the head gravedigger said, leaping up and brushing the crumbs from his shirt. "We've been waiting for you."

"The hell you have," Hébert said, "but it's just as well. Mademoiselle Tussaud has her work cut out for her." With a flick of his finger, he directed the woman toward the body of the queen, and Sant'Angelo flinched. What fresh desecration was this to be?

As the Chief of the Committee of Public Safety and his cronies bantered with the gravediggers not far off, Mademoiselle Tussaud knelt beside the remains and dug into her basket. The marquis stood stock-still, hardly daring to breathe. She looked vaguely familiar to the marquis, then suddenly he placed her; he had seen her at Versailles, giving drawing lessons to the king's sister, Madame Elizabeth.

And now, here she was, with a kerchief concealing her own shaved skull. So she was a prisoner, too, Sant'Angelo thought, one who had no doubt been given a reprieve by the Tribunal so long as she did their awful bidding.

With the efficiency any artisan would admire, she smoothed a patch of canvas on the ground, then arranged her supplies on it. As the marquis silently observed, she turned her back to the men and murmured to the head, "Please forgive me, madame. I wish you no harm." The tips of her fingers made a hurried cross on her own bosom . . . and then she peeled the soiled bonnet away from the queen's head and laid it to one side.

Peering close, the marquis was relieved to see no sign of animation. The eyes were closed, the mouth slack and twisted.

With a dampened sponge, Mademoiselle Tussaud wiped away the dirt and caked blood, dabbing at the drooping Habsburg lip.

"I am sorry to be so rough," she confided, as if she was accustomed to such conversations, "but they never give me enough time. A mask needs to be done right, or it shouldn't be done at all."

The death masks of prominent victims had been exhibited in Paris for some time now. The marquis had seen the mask of the butchered Princesse de Lamballe, for example, exhibited in a store window like the latest fashion. But this one, the marquis feared, would undoubtedly be the biggest draw of them all.

Then, with a handful of rags, the young woman dried the features of the face, and set the head upright.

"The barber really took a hatchet to you, didn't he?" she said. "Oh well, it doesn't matter. I will make you beautiful again."

Taking up her hairbrush, Tussaud pulled the bristles roughly through the tangled mat of hair, once, twice, but on the third stroke—just as Sant'Angelo felt sure that his worst fears had not been realized—the eyes of the queen flew open, in an expression of utter bewilderment and horror. It was as if she had been willing herself to remain in some dream, concealed by the bonnet, but now, with these constant ministrations, could no longer sustain her disbelief. The mouth opened, struggling to speak, but the only sound was a wet smack. Tussaud fainted away on the grass, as the famous blue-gray eyes flitted about the cemetery, lost, confused, in terror.

And the marquis—who knew now, without a doubt, that she had

looked into the glass of *La Medusa*—also knew what had to be done. And swiftly.

The mouth opened wider, as if to scream, the teeth stained pink with her own blood.

If he meant to save her from suffering for eternity, he would have to act quickly.

Running to the open grave, he grabbed the first woman's head he could find and plunked it down on the cloth. This one made no protest.

And then, with his invisible hands, he lifted the head of Marie Antoinette, covering her eyes with the bonnet as a final mercy, and said, "Be at peace." Then he dropped it into the copper-lined barrel of quicklime. There was a hissing and bubbling as the head sank, the caustic brew instantly working to dissolve the skin and devour the bone. In a matter of a minute, the flesh was gone and the skull had disintegrated. Only a few stray hairs stuck up out of the boiling stew.

"What's taking so long?" Hébert called out to Tussaud, who was just recovering her senses. "We haven't got all day." He was sharing a bottle of wine with his committee members—one of whom still sported the white feather in his cap. Its tip was now scarlet, and Sant'Angelo knew perfectly well how it had come by its color.

"Even now, this queen keeps everyone waiting," the man with the bloody feather quipped, and everyone laughed.

"We'll have to put that in the paper," Hébert said. "Make a note of it, Jerome."

The third man, with the ink-stained hands of a printer, said, "I won't forget."

The young Tussaud swallowed hard and looked at the head on the cloth, and even if she knew that this was no longer the head of the queen, she knew enough to say nothing. Bewildered, she draped the damp muslin cloth over the face, spread an even coat of plaster, and after allowing it to dry, pried the mask loose and laid it in her basket, covered with a scrap of cotton. Brushing her hands clean on her skirts, she stood up and said to Hébert, "I am done here, Citizen."

"It's about time," he replied, strapping on the sword he had laid on the grass. "I've got a newspaper to get out." He slapped his tri-cornered hat back on his head.

"Tomorrow's edition should be a sellout," the head gravedigger predicted, in his most unctuous tones.

"I'm going to write the whole issue myself," Hébert announced, snapping his fingers at Tussaud, who was struggling to gather up all her things. "Octave, go help her, for God's sake, or we'll never get back to the office."

When they had gone, Sant'Angelo waited, as silent witness and friend, until the gravediggers threw all that was left of the queen's re-mains into the open pit. Without the head, he was relieved to see, life was at last extinguished. Using the bottom of his boot, the head gravedigger tipped the barrel of quicklime over on top of the bodies, waiting for the brew to sizzle and hiss its way through the carnage. Then, as they started to shovel the dirt in after, the marquis turned and went to exact his revenge.

Sant'Angelo, like everyone in Paris, knew where *Le Père Duchesne* was published, and he waited outside for many hours, watching Hébert at a desk above the printing press, writing in full view of passersby. Page after page flew off his desk, written in the earthy, lewd voice of the titular character, depicted as an angry peasant with a pipe between his teeth. The marquis also caught glimpses of Jerome and Octave, setting type, cranking the press, reading proofs.

When the work was finally done, it was almost midnight, and they adjourned to celebrate at what was once the barracks of the Swiss Guard. But now that the entire Guard had been slaughtered in defense of the royal family, it was called the Tavern of the Guillotine, and it offered an unequaled view of the scaffold; on the back of the menu each day there was a list of the people to be executed.

The marquis, still wearing the garland, sat at a table outside, listening to their boisterous laughter as Hébert read aloud passages from the next day's paper.

"When the widow Capet saw that she had traded a coach-and-four for a dung cart, she stamped her pretty little foot and demanded that someone answer for it."

And then, "With the rudeness for which the bitch was widely known, she purposely trod on the foot of Monsieur Le Paris"—as the executioner was commonly known—"and would have thrown a proper fit if she'd only been able to keep her wits, and her head, about her."

It went on like that for well over an hour, but the marquis used that time to stoke his anger and resolve. He rested the *harpe*, an exact duplicate of the sword he had fashioned for the hand of his Perseus, against the knee of his cassock.

And when the Chief of the Committee of Public Safety—and publisher of the scurrilous paper—emerged, again with his two accomplices, Sant'Angelo followed them. They were going, he soon realized, to the Conciergerie, perhaps to select some more victims for the next day. The streets were dark and grew damp as they approached the banks of the Seine. The lower level of the prison, where the *pailleux* were confined like cattle in a pen, looked out, through a grating of iron bars, onto a walkway that ran along the river. It was the only air that penetrated the dreadful caverns. But the path was narrow and at that hour no one was around, except for the prisoners who saw Hébert through the bars. Most of them were silent as he passed—many had been denounced and sentenced by this very man—but a few could not restrain themselves and reached out their arms to plead for mercy or beg for a chance to argue their innocence one last time. Their frightened faces, grimy with sweat and tears, glistened in the torchlight from within the cells.

The marquis would not get a better opportunity. Moving up swiftly behind the printer Jerome, he whispered in his ear, "Wouldn't you like to wash that ink off your hands?"

The man whirled around and saw only the slick cobblestones

shining in the moonlight. But he shouted, "Who's there?" and Hébert and Octave, who was still sporting the bloodstained feather in his cap, turned around.

"What are you shouting about? Can't you see that these people need their rest?" Hébert said with a laugh.

An elderly prisoner called out to him, "Citizen Hébert—a word, I beg you—just one word!"

"There was someone right here," the printer insisted. "He just spoke to me."

"And what did he say?" Octave asked, smirking.

"He asked . . . if I wanted to wash the ink off."

And then, before Hébert or Octave could make some rejoinder, the marquis grabbed him by the scruff of his neck and dragged him, his boots scuffing wildly at the stones, to the stone parapet above the riverfront.

"Help me!" the printer screamed. "Help me!"

With a mighty shove, Sant'Angelo sent him toppling over the wall. There was a loud splash as he plunged into the Seine.

Octave and Hébert ran to the parapet, staring down into the swiftly flowing stream, but there was no sign of him. Octave drew a pistol from his belt, and Hébert pulled his rapier from its scabbard.

But they could see nothing, and no one, to fight.

The marquis slipped behind Octave. The sound of his boots was swallowed by the cries of the prisoners, many more of whom were now pressed against the bars, their hands clutching the grate, their eyes bulging with wonder. Whatever strange miracle was occurring outside their bars, they wholeheartedly approved.

"So, you like your souvenirs?" Sant'Angelo murmured as he ripped the bloody feather from Octave's cap.

He made the feather bob and dance in the empty air, until Octave took a wild shot at it. The marquis felt the heat of the bullet as it passed below his arm. Then he raised his sword and, in one fell swoop, sliced the man's hand off altogether.

Still clutching the pistol, the hand fell, and Octave didn't seem to understand what had just happened. He stood stock-still, looking down at his own spurting wrist, before suddenly howling in pain, wedging the stump under his armpit and fleeing down the concourse.

The prisoners, delighted with the show so far, banged on the bars with tin spoons and closed fists.

The chief backed away, his sword probing the darkness in every direction.

"Where are you?" Hébert cried out. "Who are you?"

But for this last act, the marquis did not want to be invisible. He wanted Hébert to know who was about to kill him. Taking off the garland, he slowly came into view, like an image coalescing from the moonbeams themselves.

"The priest?" Hébert said.

The black cassock whipped around Sant'Angelo's legs, blown by the wind from the river. The bloody sword glittered at his side.

"Guards!" Hébert shouted at the top of his lungs. "Guards!"

Wordlessly, the marquis moved closer.

Hébert swung wildly with his rapier, all the while retreating, but when a blow came close enough, Sant'Angelo parried it with the edge of his own sword. The clang of the steel rang out through the night air.

The prisoners shouted, "Kill him, Father! Kill him!"

Hébert's tricornered hat fell from his head and blew along the stones. His face was white with terror, and suddenly he found himself so close to the bars that the frenzied hands of the inmates were clutching at his sleeves and collar. He whipped around, slashing at the arms extended through the grate, then turned again to confront the marquis.

There was the clatter of hooves, as mounted gendarmes, aroused by the commotion, appeared at the end of the concourse.

"Who's down there?" the captain cried. "What's going on?"

"Shoot him!" Hébert called out to them. "I order you! Shoot the priest!"

Sant'Angelo saw a musket lowered, and a puff of smoke. The bullet whizzed over his head and clanged off the iron bars.

With a sweep of his blade, he knocked the sword from Hébert's hand, but a fusillade of shots suddenly ricocheted around him; the gendarmes were galloping down the concourse. Putting a hand on Hébert's chest, he thrust him up against the seething wall of fingers and hands, hundreds of them, all intent on tearing him to pieces. Like a pack of harpies, they grabbed hold of him, rending his clothes and ripping out his hair, scratching at his flesh, digging in their nails like claws. An old man gnawed ferociously at one arm. A hollow-eyed girl inserted a knitting needle into the back of his neck as delicately as if she were making lace.

Slipping the garland back onto his brow, and holding his arms out as if in surrender to the coming soldiers, the marquis left the prisoners to their deadly work. In seconds, he had melted back into the night.

And as the horses whinnied around him, and the gendarmes swung their muskets this way and that—"Where's the priest?" their captain cried, waving his sword, "Where did he go?"—Sant'Angelo turned toward home. The streets now were dark and silent, and most of the day's celebrants were asleep, or lying drunk in the gutter. For the moment, their bloodlust had been sated.

Chapter 30

As he had watched their mysterious stranger descend into the Metro station across the street, David's first impulse had been to run after him and force him to explain himself, to tell them something concrete about their adversaries. Otherwise, what use were these cryptic warnings?

But he sensed that the doctor—if that's what he really was—had already taken as much of a chance as he was willing to.

"So what's next?" Olivia asked. "We could camp out on the marquis's doorstep, which might get cold, or go back to the hotel."

Truth be told, neither of those was what David wanted to do; what he wanted to do was climb the wall around the town house, break in through the first window he could find, and scour Sant'Angelo's collection himself, from top to bottom.

Taking out his cell phone, he checked for messages, but there were none of any consequence. He tried Sarah, got her voice mail, then tried Gary and got his voice mail, too. Every time he called, or spoke to them, his heart was in his mouth, afraid that Sarah might have taken a turn for the worse. Although he hoped for the best, he was always—secretly, and to his own dismay—expecting the worst.

"The hotel," David conceded, as he pulled his coat off the back of his chair. "You can fill in some of the blanks on Cagliostro on the way."

Outside, the street was nearly deserted, but on the train platform he felt oddly exposed. There were a couple of men loitering near the tracks, reading papers, or studying their BlackBerries, and though there was nothing overtly menacing about them, David got a strange vibe. He was starting to wonder if the good doctor had given him the willies, or worse yet, dropped something into his drink again. But glancing at Olivia, he could tell she was feeling edgy, too.

"Maybe we should splurge on a taxi?"

"If we can get one," she said.

They had no sooner emerged from the station than a pair of head-lights approached them from down the street. David noticed that the light on the top of the cab suddenly went from Off to On, but it was only when it stopped at the curb that he saw it was a rusty old heap, the same one that had been cruising the block an hour ago. Inside, he saw a swarthy, foreign driver, with a string of wooden beads hanging from the rearview mirror, and caught the sweet scent of Turkish to-bacco.

Olivia had her hand on the door when David backed off and said, "No thanks."

Cranking the window lower, the driver said, "What's the prob-lem? Anywhere you want to go."

David tapped the door politely, and said, "Changed my mind. Thanks, anyway."

Olivia looked confused as the driver, sneering, pulled away from the curb and drove, slowly, toward the corner.

"What was wrong with that cab?" Olivia asked.

"Didn't feel right," David replied, and after all they had been through already, Olivia knew enough to respect a hunch.

David waited until the taxi was just out of sight, then took Olivia's hand, saying, "Let's take a walk," and ducking into the park. "We'll catch a cab on the other side."

It was a cloudy night, with almost no moon, but the pathway was marked every fifty yards or so by old-fashioned lampposts. The gravel crunched under their feet as they walked, and the wind stirred the barren branches of the great old elms. No one else was on the walkway, the green metal benches were empty, and the few concession stands that they passed were sealed up behind accordion gates. A separate path sloped down on their left, toward a man-made lake and a ramshackle boathouse. A wooden sign on a shingle advertised rowboats for rent.

Olivia pulled her collar up around her neck and stuck her bare hands deep into her pockets. David wondered if she was questioning his decision.

With the leather valise slung over one shoulder, he kept an eye out, looking into the shadows on either side and occasionally turning to stare into the darkness behind them. Even he was starting to wonder if he hadn't made the wrong call.

But then she surprised him, as she often did. "You know," she said, launching into what she'd actually been brooding over, "Cagliostro was said to have initiated Napoleon into the secret mysteries of Rosicrucianism, among other things. And after the count was murdered in 1795, legend has it that the Emperor ordered his soldiers to find the count's grave, dig up the body, and bring him the skull."

"What for?"

"A drinking cup."

"Sounds more like something Hitler would do."

"It does, doesn't it?" she said. "All dictators are madmen. But they shared something else, too. Napoleon was determined to uncover knowledge, in any form, from any source, and assimilate it into his growing empire."

"Like the Rosetta Stone."

"Exactly. That was why he sent scientists and scholars like Champollion off in the first place—to decipher the ancient wisdom of the East."

David saw a movement in the trees, and relaxed only when a fat gray squirrel came the rest of the way around the trunk.

"And even though his motives were less benign, Hitler did precisely the same thing. He sent zealots like Dieter Mainz to Paris to track down any arcane knowledge that might help him to erect the Reich."

The squirrel scampered across the pathway, which circled a classical fountain—a triton rising from the deep. While David listened to Olivia expound, he tried to gauge where they were in the park and how much farther it might be before they got to the other side.

"But I wonder what Dieter Mainz was able to make of those ravings that Cagliostro left behind? I'm no Champollion, but I'd love to show some of those hieroglyphs to one of my old professors in Bologna. Is there anyone at your library in Chicago who specializes in Egyptian texts?"

He didn't answer her.

"David?"

His attention was firmly concentrated on a figure in the trees, up ahead. All he could make out was the hint of a black leather jacket.

"There's someone in the trees on the right," David said, slowing his pace but purposely not stopping. He didn't want to let on yet that he'd seen him.

Olivia looked, too, and murmured, "Maybe this is the gay pickup spot."

Possible, David thought, especially as he could now make out a second man, even farther into the shadows, with the collar of a peacoat turned up.

"Do you want to turn around?" Olivia said.

And David wasn't sure—until the wind carried the faintest scent of cigarette smoke his way.

Sweet and aromatic.

"Yes," he said, stopping in his tracks.

The two men were moving closer together—for a hookup?—as David slipped his arm through Olivia's and steered them back toward the triton fountain. He resisted turning around for several seconds, leaning in like a lover, but when he listened hard, he could hear the sound of footsteps on gravel.

And when he did turn, he could see the two men casually sauntering after them. It was no time to take a chance.

"Run," he said, releasing Olivia's hand. "Run!"

They both took off, racing around the fountain and down the darkened path.

When David glanced back, he couldn't see the pursuers anymore. But he could hear the sound of twigs snapping, leaves crumbling, and footsteps pounding on the cold, hard soil near the trail.

Olivia, in her sneakers, was running at a good clip, and David made sure to stay close by her side.

But he had the feeling that the guys chasing them were loping along on either side, hidden by the trees and brush, and intent only on blocking their exit from the park.

"Where to?" Olivia panted.

And that was when David spotted the separate trail leading down to the boathouse and pointed at it.

Olivia abruptly veered off, down the sloping path to the lake, her arms spread out to maintain her balance, and David followed her. He didn't see anyone behind them, but he was sure that they would figure out what had happened in a few seconds—if they hadn't already.

A string of forlorn white lights dangled around the eaves of the boathouse, but the door was shut and the shutters drawn. A little wooden gate blocked the pier; Olivia vaulted it easily, with David hot on her heels. Three or four old rowboats bobbed in the black water.

"Get in the boat!" David said. "The one at the end!"

Without missing a step, Olivia ran down the wooden pier and jumped into the boat. As David hastily untied the rope, she straightened out the oars. He thought about untying the other boats and setting them adrift, but before he could do it he saw the man in the peacoat skittering down the hill, with something that looked suspiciously like a gun glinting in his hand.

"Row!" David said, and she had no sooner dipped the oars in the water than David leapt off the pier, landing with a thud and knocking her backwards off the thwart. The boat careened away from the dock with the two of them tangled on its floor.

David heard one of the men shout to the other.

Slinging the valise off his shoulder, he scrambled over Olivia, and grabbed for the oars.

He could hear the thumping of feet racing down the pier.

Bending low, he put his back into it, and pulled hard. The boat skimmed forward into the dark, the oars creaking in their locks. As soon as he'd managed to raise them from the water, he pulled again, starting to get the rhythm of it. The two men were shouting at each other, in a language he didn't understand, and although it was too dark to see what they were doing, he could hear the splash of a rope being flung into the water and the hollow clunk of a prow banging against the pier.

He dipped the paddles again, wishing he could somehow do it more quietly, and saw an orange spark ignite from the direction of the dock. A bullet plowed into the water near the stern. Olivia, crouching low, said, "David, keep your head down!"

Another spark ignited, with only the slightest *phht*, and this time a splinter of wood exploded off the rim of the boat.

David knew they were just shooting at the sound of the oars—out here on the lake, it was almost pitch-black—but if he didn't keep moving, they might catch up.

"David, what can I do?" Olivia said. "How can I help?" In her voice, he heard more anger than fear.

He didn't know what to tell her. He pulled again, but it was hard to row without sitting up and exposing himself to another wild shot. And no matter how carefully he dipped the oars, they squeaked in their locks and came up dripping.

There was another flash in the night, that one closer, and the bullet cracked into the back of the boat, flinging a powdery dust into the air. David wondered when they might lower their sights enough to put a bullet into the boat below the waterline.

"David, let me row for a while!" Olivia whispered. "I can do it."

But David shook his head and asked her if she could swim.

"Of course I can swim."

"Then take off your coat—it will weigh you down—and get ready to."

He let go of the oars—already his hands were starting to ache—fumbled in his pocket for his cell phone, and turned it on.

"You see the boathouse?" he said. From the lake, they were the only lights visible. "Swim back there."

But she paused. "Only if you will, too."

"I'll be right behind you. Get going!"

Dropping her coat and kicking off her sneakers, she rolled over the edge of the boat and into the water. Once he was sure she was well away, he bent double and quickly pulled the oars through the water three or four times, putting some distance between them and their pursuers.

The gun blazed again, and the bullet clanged off the oarlock with a shower of white sparks before ricocheting into the darkness.

He heard a laugh of exultation—the shooter must have guessed how close he'd come—and he prayed that Olivia would be able to slip past them unnoticed.

The white lights of the boathouse were still visible, but that was all. Thick clouds covered the moon and stars.

David dropped the oars, pulled off his shoes, and shrugged his coat from his shoulders. And then he groped for his valise under the thwart. He couldn't leave it behind, but he thanked God the original papers were still hidden away in Chicago.

The gunman shouted something that was plainly a taunt, and fired again. The bullet sizzled into the water by the bow.

David slung the valise over his shoulder, then bunched his coat on the seat and tucked his open cell phone on top of it, with just a hint of its light shining clear. *Let them follow that, like a beacon, farther into the lake*, he thought.

And then he slipped overboard.

The water was so frigid it took his breath away, but he put both hands on the stern of the rowboat and shoved it off as hard as he could. In seconds, it was invisible even to him.

Then, using the breast stroke to minimize any splashing, he started back toward the dock. His clothes, plastered to his body, were heavier and more cumbersome than he'd imagined, and the valise acted like a drag.

But when he heard the other boat come near, he stopped swimming altogether and let himself drift on the water. All he could make out was the shape of the boat, a black hulk moving through the black water, and the silhouette of a man hunched in the bow, who was talking—and no doubt issuing directions—to the rower whose back was turned. David was no more than five or six feet away, so near that the blade of one paddle almost smacked him as he ducked his head below the water. He felt the ripple of the boat's wake lapping the surface above him.

But once it had gone by, he raised his head, clenching his teeth to keep them from chattering, and started swimming in earnest, eager to get his blood pumping again.

But where was Olivia? He didn't dare call out to her, and he heard nothing at all.

He swam on, the lights of the boathouse glimmering fuzzy and white behind the lenses of his soaking glasses. What he wouldn't give right now for just a sliver of moonlight on the water, enough to give him a glimpse of Olivia moving safely toward the shore.

In the distance, he heard the *phht* of the silencer again, followed by the pop of something exploding—the end of his cell phone—and then a cry of joy. The shot must have caught the thing dead center and blown it to smithereens. They probably thought at least one of them, whoever had been holding it, was injured or dead.

He kept swimming, though it was increasingly hard to tell if his feet and legs were cooperating. His whole body was starting to go numb, and the valise felt like a millstone.

He took deeper breaths, cutting through the water as fast as he could, trying to keep himself in line with the lights of the boathouse while searching desperately for some sign of Olivia.

The bulky outlines of the tethered boats eventually loomed into sight, and he moved toward them, his arms as heavy as lead weights. But when he finally threw an arm over the side of one of them, he felt an icy hand clasp his own and pull him up.

"Come on, David! Come on!"

He looked up and saw Olivia's face, her dark eyes shining in what looked like a frame of frozen hair. Gasping, he hauled himself into the boat, banging his shins and elbows on the thwarts, but his limbs, blissfully, were too cold to feel the pain.

He hugged Olivia's shivering body to his own, but neither one of them had any heat to share.

"They'll be back," David said. "We have to get going."

He stood up shakily, then clambered after Olivia onto the dock. There was only one place he could think of going before they froze to death. Clasping hands, they ran back up the hill, down the path, and out of the park.

A car rolled by, with a couple of kids who saw them emerge onto the street, drenched and shoeless, and they shouted something derisory as they drove past.

But down the block, David saw that the lights were on in the house of the Marquis di Sant'Angelo.

"It's just a little farther," David said, and Olivia immediately understood.

On the doorstep, clutching each other against the cold, David felt the security camera taking them in, and he shouted, "You have to help us!" into the intercom.

The door flew open this time, and the servant stood back to let them in. They stumbled, still dripping and nearly frozen, into the marble foyer, where a man in elegant dinner clothes, his black tie hanging loose at his throat, was standing at the top of the stairs.

"Ascanio," he barked, "get some blankets!"

David nodded his thanks, his head quivering from the cold, his arms thrown around Olivia.

"I'm Sant'Angelo," the man said, leaning hard on an ebony walking stick as he descended the stairs. "You're safe here."

But David didn't know what safe felt like anymore.

Part Four

Chapter 31

Gary had seen David's last call come in, but for the first time he hadn't picked up.

Because for the first time, he hadn't known what he would say.

Sarah had collapsed the day before, keeling over in the laundry room, and now she was back in intensive care. Dr. Ross had been called, a whole host of new tests had been done, her condition had eventually been stabilized; but Gary had the impression that they had turned a terrible, and possibly final, corner. Until he was sure it was true, he didn't want to burden David with that news (even though David had always insisted on being told the truth, whatever it was).

Dr. Ross came into the waiting area, with a sheaf of papers and lab reports stuffed in a folder, and hard as Gary searched his face for any glimmer of hope, he saw none.

The doctor sat beside him, and for several telltale seconds, continued to burrow into the paperwork . . . as if even he was trying to postpone the inevitable.

"How's she doing?" Gary asked. "Can I go in and see her now?"

"I would wait a bit," Dr. Ross replied. "The nurse is still with her."

Gary nodded, watching the TV mounted from a ceiling bracket. In barely audible tones, a weatherman was announcing yet another storm on its way. Little white icicles on the map pointed down at Chicago like daggers.

"I wish I had better news for you," the doctor finally said.

It didn't matter that Gary had seen it coming; he still felt like he'd been punched in the gut.

"The new regimen isn't working. In fact, it's made the situation worse."

"But I thought she was rallying."

The doctor shrugged, and said, "That can happen, initially. But then the systems can't sustain it—her blood counts have been so bad for so long, her lymph nodes are all gone or lethally compromised—and one thing after another starts crashing. It becomes a cascade, and even when we're able to stop one organ failure, it's usually at the expense of another. At this point, the cancer has simply spread too far, too wide, and too deeply. The disease, I'm afraid, is in control, and all we can do is try our best to ameliorate its more painful effects."

Gary took some time to digest what the doctor had just said. In the background, he could hear someone on the TV offering advice about avoiding heart attacks while shoveling snow.

"At this point in time," the doctor said—and Gary, his mind battening on anything but what was about to come, thought, *Can time have a point?*—"it would probably be best to think about moving her to our Hospice and Palliative Care Center. We could make her a lot more comfortable there, for as long as necessary."

Gary certainly knew what this meant; it meant Sarah had reached the end of the line. But he still found it nearly impossible to make his mind go there. "I can't just take her home?"

Lowering his head and pursing his lips, the doctor said, "I wouldn't recommend it. It's going to be very hard at this stage, and right now, the hospice unit has room available. It's very tranquil, very quiet, and I can arrange to have her transferred there in a couple of hours."

"Does Sarah know about this?"

"She does. She's the one who first brought it up. No one ever wants to be in the ICU five minutes more than they have to, and I don't blame them."

Neither did Gary. It depressed the hell out of him just to visit there, and when he had brought Emme the day before, the old lady in the next cubicle had suddenly expired, and much as he had tried to disguise what was going on from his daughter, Emme knew. Gary and his mom, who had flown up from Florida the day before, had ushered her out into the waiting area, but Emme had broken down in terrified sobs. All that night, Gary had slept in the bed with his daughter cradled in his arms, and Gary's mom was back at the house right now, just trying to hold things together.

"Why don't you go on in now and talk it over with your wife? The nurse has given her a mild sedative, but she should still be fairly lucid. Decide what you'd like to do."

What he'd *like* to do? What he'd like to do was yank Sarah out of that damn bed and run for their lives.

"I know this is hard," Dr. Ross was saying, "the hardest thing you'll ever have to do in your life. But it's the right thing, for you, for your wife, and for your daughter. At least Emme can see her mother there in a much less frightening, and less clinical, setting. We have found it's a lot less traumatic this way."

Somehow, Gary was able to ask, without even looking at the doctor's face, how long Sarah would be staying in the hospice. It sounded, even to him, as if he was asking how many nights she'd been booked at a hotel.

"It's always hard to predict these things, but I'd say three, four days, at the outside. The hospice time is chiefly used to treat the pain and afford the patient a chance to say good-bye to loved ones." The doctor put a consoling hand on Gary's shoulder as the TV segued into a blaring car commercial. "It's been a long road," he said, "and I can't tell you how sorry I am that we have wound up here. But I think you'll be surprised. This stage of the journey can really be a very peaceful and healing one."

Gary could do without the New Age spin.

Giving his shoulder a gentle squeeze before continuing on his rounds, Dr. Ross said, "I've left word at the nurses' station. Once you've talked to Sarah, they can take care of everything."

Gary remained on the sofa. The TV anchors were reporting a multicar collision on the Dan Ryan Expressway. His hand mechanically fished his cell phone out of his pocket and he hit the speed dial for David. There was no excuse for delaying any longer; David would have to know what was up and get back to Chicago on the double. Standing up, Gary moved to the far corner of the room, where the TV couldn't be heard. As he waited for the phone to connect, he stared out the window at a view of a frozen parking lot. A guy was madly scraping the ice from his windshield. His call went straight into voice mail, and for a second Gary wasn't sure how to say what he had to say. Finally, he just told him that even though they were doing everything possible to keep Sarah pain-free, the situation looked very bad. "If you want to say good-bye, you're going to have to come back. Fast." Then, for good measure, he called the last hotel that David had reported in from—someplace called the Crillon in Paris—and left pretty much the same message on the automated service there.

Returning the phone to his pocket, he went back through the double doors into the ICU. This was one trip he wouldn't miss. Everywhere you looked, through parted curtains, you saw people in terrible trouble; every sound you heard was either a suction tube, a beeping monitor, or a visitor softly murmuring hollow words of encouragement.

Sarah's head was turned toward him as he came in, and he realized that he had forgotten to consciously compose his features, as he always tried to do, into a more upbeat expression. But what would that even look like now? he wondered. How did you put a good face on *this*?

As he drew the plastic chair to her bedside and closed his hand over hers—God, her skin was cold—Sarah said in barely a whisper, "You talked to Dr. Ross?" and he nodded. Her eyes, once as bright and brown as buttons, were sunken into the hollows of her face, and her eyebrows and lashes, as well as her lush brown hair, were long since gone. She reminded him, disconcertingly, of the Visible Woman model he'd had when he was a kid. She was so wasted away she was almost transparent.

"Good." She closed her eyes, took a shallow breath, then said, "I could use a change of scene."

Gary wondered if he would have been brave enough to be making a joke—any kind of joke—if he were the one lying in that cranked-up bed, with the IV lines running in and out of his arms.

"I hear it's nice over there," she said. "And I don't want this to be the last place Emme ever sees me."

"Then I'll tell the nurses we've agreed, and we'll get you moved."

Her head nodded almost imperceptibly on the pillow. At least that was settled.

"How's Emme holding up? Yesterday was awfully hard on her."

"Mom's keeping her busy. I think they went to a movie today. With Amanda."

Sarah nodded again. "As soon as I'm settled into the hospice, bring her over there. I hate having her see me like this, but I also don't want to just disappear into thin air, the way that they made my own mother disappear."

Gary knew that the loss of her mom had haunted her all her days. How could it not? Sarah had always felt that she had been kept in the dark for too long, and that, in a well-meaning attempt to shield her from some of the trauma, the medical establishment had wound up leaving her with a more unhealable wound.

"And besides," Sarah said, "I'm selfish."

"You're about the least selfish person on the planet."

"I want every second with her that I've got left." She looked as if she might cry, but her body seemed incapable of generating a tear. Every ounce of energy she had in her was being mustered in the fight for survival.

There was only one big question still hanging in the air, and Sarah finally asked, "Have you talked to David?"

Gary told her that he'd left him a couple of messages and expected to hear back any minute.

"Where is he now?"

"France."

"France," she said, with a wistful smile. "I'm glad one of us got there."

"He'll be home as fast as he can get here."

"Good. Good. But the longer it takes, the better."

Gary was confused.

"Because there's no way I'm going anywhere without seeing him one more time." She set her fragile jaw like a linebacker. "I don't care how long it takes. I'll wait."

Gary believed her.

"I'll wait," she repeated, before slowly drifting off into a drug-induced sleep.

Chapter 32

The papers from his valise were pretty much ruined. The only good news David could think of was that the originals were still safe and sound at the Newberry.

Still, the marquis had laid the documents out on his desk in the center of his salon with all the care and respect one would accord a newly discovered codex by Leonardo. They lay atop a layer of soft, absorbent linen, and even now he was dabbing at their edges with a dry sponge.

The pages of the manuscript, *La Chiave Alla Vita Eterna*, might as well have been glued together; they would have to be dried out slowly over the next few days, their leaves delicately separated by scalpels and tweezers.

But it was the sketch of *La Medusa* that had immediately drawn Sant'Angelo's full attention. Professor Vernet at the Mineralogical Museum had said the marquis was an expert in these matters, and the fact that he had instantly focused on this remarkable sketch only confirmed it. He was smoothing out its wrinkles as tenderly as a father would handle his infant child.

The man himself was like no one David had ever met. He wore an imperious expression and, beneath a prominently hooked nose, a luxuriant dark moustache. To David, he looked like a throwback to some earlier era. And despite his pronounced limp, he bore a powerful physical presence. Still wearing his formal clothes, the black tie dangling loose around his neck, he brooded over the papers. His pleated white shirt was fastened, David could not help but notice, with glittering sapphire studs and matching cuff links.

"In future," he said, "you should really keep things like this out of the water."

"In future," David replied, "I hope to avoid being shot at."

David had filled him in quickly on how they had come to show up at his door, soaking wet and out of breath, but when Sant'Angelo had asked who would be chasing him so intently, and why, David had been unable to supply the answer.

"They wanted that," Olivia had jumped in, gesturing at the drawing.

"This?" Sant'Angelo said. "It's just a sketch—and a copy at that."

"They want the actual object, the looking glass," she said, glancing at David to make sure he was okay with her being so forthcoming.

David nodded his acquiescence. Like Olivia, he was sitting in silk pajamas and a velvet robe supplied from the marquis's own wardrobe. They had changed in a sumptuous bedroom suite upstairs and come down to steaming cups of hot chocolate.

"A little mirror, made out of what?" Sant'Angelo said skeptically. "Silver?"

"But by a great master's hand," David replied.

The marquis nodded. "Ah, so you do know. Cellini's hand is always unmistakable, is it not?"

David shouldn't have been surprised. He had the sense that this man knew far more than he was letting on.

"I have a client, and she has commissioned me to find it," David said. "At any cost." As a dealer in these things, the marquis would surely be intrigued by that mention of a commission.

"She has, has she? May I ask her name?"

"I'm not at liberty to divulge that," David said, feeling that it was best to keep at least one or two cards close to his vest, especially with someone as cagey as Sant'Angelo.

The marquis nodded, no doubt accustomed to people keeping the names of their employers to themselves. But he wasn't nearly done with his questions—and David wasn't done with him, either. It was all a matter, David knew, of who divulged what and in what order.

"But what brought you to me in the first place?" Sant'Angelo said, leaning back in his chair, his fingers steepled in front of him.

David saw no harm in answering this one directly, telling him about some of their discoveries at the Mineralogical Museum. "Cagliostro seemed obsessed with someone by the name of Sant'Angelo, then, there it was—your name, in gold leaf, on the plaque listing the Board of Governors."

The marquis acknowledged as much.

"So I have to ask," David said. "Your family has apparently been in Paris for many generations, and working in this trade. Did one of your ancestors come into possession of *La Medusa*?"

Sant'Angelo didn't even hesitate. "Yes."

Olivia nearly leapt out of her chair, and David felt like the wind had been knocked out of him. Here was the most concrete proof yet that the thing had existed, not to mention some indication of where it had been. He was almost afraid to speak again.

"You don't, by any chance, have it in your possession now?"

"No."

"But you know where it is?" Olivia said, perched on the front of her chair.

This question, however, did give Sant'Angelo pause. "Yes," he finally admitted.

David hastily drained his china cup, then placed it on a corner of the desk, well away from the drying papers. "Where?" he asked. "Where is it now?"

But Sant'Angelo clearly had given as much as he was prepared to give; now it was his turn, and he leveled his gaze at David.

"First, tell me why you—or your client, excuse me—wants it so badly."

"It's extremely valuable, as you know anything from the hand of Cellini would be."

The marquis waved the comment away like a buzzing fly. "If you don't speak honestly, we are done here."

"Tell him," Olivia said.

But David was hesitant, afraid that once he launched into the whole story, Sant'Angelo might think him as mad as his mysterious client.

The marquis waited.

"She believes that the Medusa holds a secret power."

"Of what?"

And when David paused again, Olivia said, "Immortality."

But if he thought the marquis would react badly, he was again mistaken. He sat stock-still, absolutely inscrutable.

"And you?" he said to David. "What do you think? Do you think it holds the power of immortality?"

"I have to."

This response did surprise him. "You have to? Why?"

"A life is at stake."

"Your client's?"

"My sister's."

As the marquis listened raptly, David poured out the rest of the story. Hang the consequences, he thought. He didn't have time—more importantly, *Sarah* didn't have time—for him to play games. As he recounted the furious search he had so far undertaken, Olivia occasionally broke in with various asides, but if David worried that her mentions of the Third Reich, and Hitler's own fascination with occult objects like *La Medusa,* would distract Sant'Angelo, or put him off in some way, he soon saw that he should have no fear on that score. Indeed, there was no part of the story that seemed to unduly surprise, appall, or even astound him. He was either the most trusting man in the world, or he knew that what they were saying was true. Though how it could be the latter was still a total puzzle to David.

When the narrative had finally drawn to a close, Sant'Angelo had a faraway look in his eye, and when he got up from his chair and walked, slowly, leaning on his cane, to the fireplace, he put one hand on the mantel and stood there, staring into the flames. He spoke without turning around.

"I once knew a woman," he said, "years ago, and in another country. She was lost at sea, or so I was told."

The logs crackled in the grate, an orange spark exploding onto the fire screen.

"To my knowledge, she's the only one in the world who would know—and believe in—the power of *La Medusa*."

David and Olivia exchanged a glance, but kept silent.

"She was very beautiful—famous for it, in fact."

David felt a little chill run down his spine.

"There were painters who tried to convey her beauty on canvas, but none of their works have survived. And though sculptors tried their hand at it, too, marble and bronze were ill suited to capture her most remarkable feature."

"What was that?" David asked, knowing in his very bones what Sant'Angelo was about to say.

"The color of her eyes," he said, turning from the fire to look at David. "They were violet."

David knew that the expression on his face had just told the marquis exactly what he wanted to know.

"It would not be safe for you to go back to your hotel tonight," the marquis said. "You will stay here, and in the morning I will tell you where to find what you're looking for."

Then he turned back to the fire, his head down and his ebony cane glowing like a branding iron.

❧

In their room upstairs, unseen hands had turned the bedclothes down, drawn the curtains, and turned the lamps low. For David, it was hard to believe that just the night before he had been defending his life in a cramped train compartment, and now he was ensconced in the luxurious bedroom of a Parisian town house . . . with Olivia, in a pair of vastly oversized pajamas, climbing up into the four-poster bed.

Pulling the down-filled duvet up to her chest, then patting the mattress, she said, "It is big enough for two, you know."

David took off his robe, tossed it on a chair, then sat down on top of the duvet.

"Do you think he meant it?" David asked. "That he knows where to find *La Medusa*?"

"I do," Olivia said. "But I know it will have to wait till morning." She pushed the pillows to one side and shoved the coverlet farther down.

David had not been able to check in with Gary or Sarah for the past twenty-four hours, and now that his phone had been blown to pieces and Olivia's drowned in the lake, he looked around for a phone in the room.

"There's no phone in here," Olivia said, reading his mind. "I checked."

"Maybe I should find one downstairs," he said, starting to get up, but Olivia drew him down again.

"David, it can wait for a few hours. She was doing all right the last time you called, yes?"

"Yes."

"Then stop thinking about it just for one night. Think about yourself," she said, drawing closer. "Think about us."

She reached up with one hand and took off his glasses. She laid them on the bedside table and turned the lamp off. The only light in the room filtered through a crack in the curtains, which opened onto the street . . . and the boating park beyond.

"Can you still see me?" she joked.

"Sort of."

She leaned forward, kissing him. "Now do you know where I am?"

"I have a very good idea."

She laughed and slunk down into the bed.

"Come find me."

David lifted the duvet enough to scoot himself under it and felt the warmth of Olivia's body against him. Her eyes were shining in the dark, her black hair was spread out on the plump white pillow. Propped on one elbow, he bent his head to kiss her.

"Umm," she said, "you taste like hot chocolate."

"I thought that was you." He kissed her again. "Yep, it's you." He reached around her slender waist, pulling her closer. Her own arms went up and around his neck.

"Maybe that day, when you wandered into the piazza?" she said.

"Yes?"

"Maybe that was fate."

David, who would never have even considered such a thing a few weeks earlier, did not dismiss it. His world had been cracked wide open and suddenly allowed for a million possibilities.

If Olivia was his fate, he thought, as their bodies came together under the coverlet with a natural but urgent ease, he was all for it.

Chapter 33

Alone at last, the marquis threw another log into the fireplace and stared into the rising fire.

Was it possible? Could Caterina still be alive? Could she have been alive all these centuries?

He felt at once an agony in his heart, the agony of all those lost years, and a kindling of hope, a kindling like nothing else he had felt for ages. The expression on David Franco's face had conveyed the truth more eloquently than any words could do.

While Sant'Angelo could see now that the public accounts of his own death and burial must have persuaded her that he had indeed left this world, how could he have been so misled himself?

What foolishness, what insanity, what melancholy dolor had allowed him to believe the accounts of her demise? He could see that the sources of the story had all had their own reasons to say what they had said, to swear to what they averred. And he lambasted himself for his gullibility, his blindness, his despair. Had he believed in her death because he could not bear the thought that he had condemned her to the destiny he had endured?

And now, she wanted the mirror back. She wanted *La Medusa* back, at all costs. But why? To work its magic on someone else? Or, to see if, in its destruction, she could undo the curse she had brought on herself that fateful night in his studio?

He drew a chair closer to the fire—it was at that time of night that his legs always gave him the most trouble—and sat down. He must think, he must make a plan. He must rouse himself to fight for a future. Tonight he had learned that there was more than a reason to exist—there was a reason to *live*.

He put his head back, his eyes closed, and felt the heat from the fire wash over him.

But first he would have to confront the greatest defeat of his life, the one from which he had never fully recovered. He would have to conquer a dread that even he, the immortal Cellini, felt in the very marrow of his broken bones. Only once in his life had he confronted a foe so powerful, and in command of such dark resources, that his own abilities had paled in comparison. For decades, he had been content to observe a stalemate with this evil adversary, a stalemate that his enemy appeared content to observe, too. Sant'Angelo imagined them like two prizefighters, mauled beyond recognition, but still respectful and wary of the other's power. Each of them knew the gift that *La Medusa* bestowed, along with the mighty cost it exacted, but so long as the marquis remained aware of his enemy's whereabouts, and sure of his limitations, he was willing to bide his time.

Now, that time was up. If by acting at last to reclaim the mirror, he could reclaim the greatest love of his life . . . if he could share his sentence with the only woman in the world who would understand it . . . then the stalemate had to be broken. It was fate that had sent him into the Colosseum that night with Dr. Strozzi, fate that had taught him how to create *La Medusa*, fate that had shuttled him like a spinning top from one country to another, for hundreds of years. Now, it was fate that had sent these two young adventurers to his door, each with his or her purpose. But the main purpose they would fulfill would be his own. They would have to go into the lion's den itself, a place where his own broken legs could not take him and where his very essence could trigger the alarms. Once there, they would have to defeat a creature more bloodthirsty than any Gorgon that had ever haunted the underworld, a creature whose reputation was still so fearsome that it was the one thing he dared not reveal.

He pulled the black tie loose from his collar and let it drop to the floor, as, in his mind's eye, he recalled the summer of 1940 . . . and the caravan of armored cars that had snaked up the private road leading to the Chateau Perdu. He could still hear the rumble of their engines.

He had been out hunting with his gamekeeper, old Broyard, when they heard them wending their way along the long drive that led to the castle. Quickly, he'd climbed higher on the ridge, then, trading his rifle for the pair of binoculars Broyard was holding out, swung himself up into a tree. Brushing away the leaves with one hand, he caught a glimpse of a quartet of armored cars, followed by a long black Mercedes, racing through the woods. Nazi pennants rippled over the front fenders of the limousine.

"Germans?" Broyard asked nervously.

"Who else has petrol?"

So it had come, he thought. It was inevitable. The Nazis had invaded France in early May, taking only a few weeks to breach the Maginot Line and, by the fourteenth of June, their tanks had been roaring in triumph down the Champs-Élysées. It had only been a matter of time before the marquis received just some unwelcome deputation as this.

"How many?" the gamekeeper asked, as Sant'Angelo climbed down. He said it as if he were contemplating how many rounds he'd need to shoot them all.

"Too many," the marquis replied, clapping a hand on the man's aged shoulder. He shared his sentiment, but knew he had to be more cautious than that.

"Come on," he said, slinging his rifle across his shoulder.

As swiftly as the old gamekeeper's legs allowed, they scrambled along the top of the ridge, with the dense forest on one side and the river Loire far below on the other. As they came closer to the chateau, a vast field opened up on the hillside, a sloping meadow where sheep had once grazed, but from which, the marquis feared, they might be more easily spotted by the intruders still motoring up the drive. Keeping close to the ground, he ran toward a large and circular stone pit. Built by the Norman knight who had erected the chateau in the fourteenth century, the pit had once been used to bait animals—bears, wolves, boars. A set of stone steps descended several meters into the ground, where it was joined to a barred cage. Sant'Angelo grabbed the rusty handle and pulled hard, opening the cage. It still bore a telltale animal scent. Lowering his head, he crept inside, then groped along the moss-covered wall until he found an identical iron handle in the seemingly solid stone. Pulling with all his might, he was finally able to unseal the hidden door there, and, doubling over, duck inside.

"Keep a lookout from the ridge," Sant'Angelo said, "and don't do anything to set them off." Broyard nodded, before closing the stone slab behind the marquis.

The darkness was absolute, but the marquis fumbled in his pocket and found a pack of matches. Apart from a tunnel that led down to the riverbank, there was only one way to go from there. Lighting one match after another, he inched along, hearing only the squelching of his boots and the occasional squeak of a rat. The tunnel—the knight's secret escape route—went even deeper than the moat, and its rock walls still held the rusted chains where prisoners had once been kept.

But when the marquis felt his boot stub against an iron grate, he knew that the oubliette, into which the condemned had been hurled, lay just below him. The lucky ones died from the fall, the others died a slow death from starvation.

Sant'Angelo stepped carefully around its edge before eventually coming up against the back of a towering old wine rack. He pushed it to one side on creaking hinges, and emerged, blowing out his last match, into the wine cellar.

Celeste, a pretty young housemaid, was so startled that he had to clap a hand over her mouth to keep her from screaming. She was passing dusty bottles to Ascanio.

"I was wondering where you were," Ascanio said crossly.

The marquis removed his hand, and Celeste fell against Ascanio's chest with relief.

"How many of them are there?" Sant'Angelo asked, brushing the dirt and cobwebs from his hunting jacket.

"Ten or fifteen. All SS."

"More," Celeste said, her eyes wide.

"What do they want?"

"Right now, they want wine." Ascanio tucked another bottle under his arm. "I was trying to decide which bottles had already turned."

The marquis smiled, and said, "Don't do anything rash."

"You mean like killing them?"

"I mean, anything that will bring the whole Third Reich crashing down on our heads." Then he mounted the back stairs up to his rooms, where he changed into the houndstooth jacket and trousers of a country squire—a fashion he had adopted when he lived in England—before descending the grand escalier to the main hall . . . where confusion reigned.

SS soldiers, in pea green uniforms, were poking the muzzles of their machine guns everywhere, ordering the marquis's staff to open every door, empty every drawer, and pull back every curtain.

In the center of the entry hall, overseeing it all, stood a man recognizable from every newsreel and newspaper in Europe: Heinrich Himmler, the Reichsführer, Hitler's second-in-command and head of the dreaded Gestapo. In person, he was an even more spindly creature than he appeared in the carefully contrived news footage. He was wearing a dove gray uniform, with boots that came all the way up to his knees; the fearsome *Totenkopf,* or death's head, gleamed above the black visor on his cap. He was wiping his wire-rimmed spectacles clean with a handkerchief when the marquis approached.

A soldier immediately interposed himself, but Himmler waved him away with the handkerchief.

"Herr Sant'Angelo?"

"*Oui*," the marquis replied, staying sufficiently distant that any handshake could be avoided.

"You know who I am, no doubt," he said in German, slipping his spectacles back on.

"*Ich mache.*" I do.

"But I doubt you know my adviser."

A big man with a squarish head stepped forward. He was wearing a green loden coat, far too warm for the weather, decorated with the War Merit medal and the requisite Nazi armband; he carried a bulging briefcase under his arm.

"This is Professor Dieter Mainz, of the University of Heidelberg."

Mainz bowed his head and clicked the heels of his boots.

"He has been eager, as have we all, to make your acquaintance."

The marquis expressed surprise. "I live a quiet life, here in the country. How could I have come to anyone's attention?"

"I will be happy to explain," Mainz said, in a voice that sounded as if it would be more comfortable booming out in a lecture hall. "We have reason to believe—good reason, based on my own research— that your ancestor, from whom your title descends, was a man of extraordinary talents."

"How so?" Sant'Angelo replied, knowing full well that this ancestor stood before them at that very moment.

"My investigations," Mainz confided, "suggest that he was well versed in many of what are commonly—and unwisely—dismissed as the occult arts."

Sant'Angelo again feigned ignorance. "I come from a long and distinguished family, but I can't say I know much about that. Are you sure you've come to the right place?"

"Quite," Mainz said. "Quite sure."

Himmler was squinting at him closely. "Apart from your servants, do you have anyone else here at present?" he asked abruptly.

"No. I have no family."

"No guests either?"

"No."

"No woman?" he asked, with a tilt of his pale, anemic face. "Or man?"

Sant'Angelo took his meaning, but he didn't deign to answer.

"Then you won't mind," the Reichsführer went on, "if we continue our inspection." Without waiting, he barked some orders and half a dozen of the soldiers charged up the two sides of the staircase. All of them, Sant'Angelo could not help but notice, were tall, blond, and blue-eyed. He had heard that Himmler, the architect of the Nazi breeding programs, liked to handpick his recruits.

Ironically, Sant'Angelo thought, the Reichsführer could never have met his own criteria.

An adjutant whispered something in Himmler's ear, and the two of them retired to the adjoining *salle d'armes,* or armor hall, where Sant'Angelo could see that a command post of sorts was being hastily assembled. The medieval weaponry that lined the walls was overwhelmed by the flood of modern communications equipment—radio sets and decoding machines and rickety antennae—strewn around the room. One soldier was standing on top of the refectory table to loop a wire over the chandelier, while another had opened a casement window to affix a receiver to its frame.

"I'm dreadfully sorry about the inconvenience," Professor Mainz leaned close to say, "but they have so much to do just now." He said it as if he were talking about some local burghers who were preparing for a visit from the mayor. "Tonight, as you may be aware, is the summer solstice."

True enough, the marquis thought, *but what of it?*

"It's one of the ancient celebrations that we have reconsecrated," Mainz offered. "It takes the place of all that Judeo-Christian claptrap. In fact, I've written a book on the subject, *Arische Sonne-Rituale.*" Aryan Sun Rites. "If you like, I would be happy to send you an inscribed copy for your private library."

Sant'Angelo nodded, as if in gratitude.

"I'm a devoted bibliophile myself," Mainz confided. "My house is so full of books, my wife says I'd fill the bathtub with them if she'd let me."

Ascanio and Celeste walked by, with several glasses and a wine bottle on a tray.

"But you must have inherited quite an impressive collection yourself."

Sant'Angelo shrugged, to suggest he didn't bother himself with such things.

"Oh, don't be so modest. Books make the house, don't you think?"

"I've heard that said."

"But where do you keep your library?" Mainz asked, looking around as if he might have missed it somehow.

Ah, so this was where it had been going.

"I'm afraid you'll be disappointed," Sant'Angelo replied.

"Oh, let me be the judge of that. I may be able to share with you things about your ancestors that you never knew. In fact, I believe that when I have told you about the arcane knowledge acquired by your forebears, you will be pleased and astonished. Now," he said, taking his host by the elbow and steering him back toward the grand escalier, "perhaps you can show me those books, yes? Upstairs? In one of the towers? I thought most of these pepperpot turrets were truncated in the sixteenth century? I wonder how these were spared."

Sant'Angelo deftly removed his arm.

"Perhaps a bit of your ancestor's hocus-pocus?"

They were halfway up the stairs when the marquis heard the first explosion outside.

He stopped and was about to run back down, but Mainz said, "Just a safety precaution. No serious damage will be done. Now, let's go see that library!" It wasn't a request but an order.

Sant'Angelo guided the lumbering professor past several salons and corridors, lined with faded tapestries and furniture, and into the main library of the house—a cavernous space with shelves from floor to ceiling and a wooden ladder on wheels to help reach the books on top. There, the marquis kept an extensive collection, everything from Marcus Aurelius to Voltaire, all in fine bindings, their titles lettered in gold on their spines. Most of the books he had purchased while traveling the world, and as a result they were in many languages—Italian, English, German, French, Russian, Greek. The professor placed his own bulging briefcase on the center reading table and strolled about the room, whistling under his breath.

"Fantastic," he said. "Simply fantastic."

Many times he stopped and lovingly removed an ancient volume from a shelf. "The complete histories of Pliny the Elder," he said in wonderment. Leafing through another volume, he said mournfully, "The Philippics of Tacitus. My copy was lost in a fire in Heidelberg." Once or twice, Mainz seemed so immersed that Sant'Angelo thought he might simply be able to steal away and not be missed. Another round of dynamite exploded, and Sant'Angelo could hear huge trees toppling over.

But after perusing a couple of dozen books, even inspecting the volumes on the higher shelves, Mainz stopped, and from his perch atop the ladder, looked down at the marquis and said, "But this is not where you do your own work."

"Work?" Sant'Angelo replied, assuming a touch of haughtiness. "I'm not sure I know what you're referring to."

Mainz waved his hand around the room. "There's not a book missing from a shelf. Not a paper or pen on the table. And these," he said, gesturing at the thousands of volumes on display, "are not the kinds of books I know you own."

He stepped down from the ladder, and with an icy smile, said, "I want to see the private collection."

When Sant'Angelo didn't reply, Mainz went on. "You can show it to me yourself, or I can have the soldiers find it, even if it means breaking down every door in the place. Come on," he said, again in that comradely tone, "how often do you meet someone like me, who can appreciate the true worth of such stuff?" He walked on toward the door, turning only to say, "Which way do we go, marquis?"

Sant'Angelo began to wonder if Ascanio had not been right about killing them on sight. But there was little he could do now, with

Himmler himself and the SS dispersed all over the chateau and its grounds.

He led the way back down the corridor, then up the winding staircase to his private study high in the eastern turret. It had never been wired for electricity, and with dusk falling, the marquis had to stop to light the gas lamps in sconces along the walls. The room was stuffy, too, and he threw open the French doors to the terrace and stepped outside to see what destruction had been wrought to his estate.

There was the smell of scorched wood in the air, and when he walked to the end of the parapet and looked toward the sheep meadow, he saw that the Germans had blown up the old oaks that ran along the ridgeline and were now using their armored cars to push the splintered trunks off the cliff.

Before he could think why they were doing it, he heard Mainz inside the study, exclaiming over something.

"Like me, you are a Renaissance scholar!" the professor said, when Sant'Angelo stepped back inside. He was holding a copy of Cellini's autobiography in his hand—the original printing, done by Antonio Cocchi in 1728. "But you have this book in half a dozen other languages, too! Along with his treatises on goldsmithing and sculpture. Then you must admire him as much as I do?"

"Yes, I suppose so."

"Then you know, too, that he was not just a great artist. He was also a great occultist. Surely you remember his account of conjuring demons in the Colosseum?"

"He was given to tall tales, I think."

But Mainz shook his head vigorously. "No, it was not a tall tale, as you call it. In fact, it was not the full tale—I am convinced of that. In the 1500s, it was simply too dangerous to tell the whole truth about such things. One day," he said, slipping the book lovingly back into the shelf, "I will find the rest of the story."

Then he simply looked around the room—a pentagon, with cherrywood bookcases alternating with floor-length mirrors—and said, "I envy you this aerie." He shrugged off his loden coat, revealing a white shirt stuck to his body with sweat, and laid it across a chair. "At home, just to get some peace and quiet, I must work in a pantry!" He wandered around the room, touching the books—their subjects ranging from *stregheria* to astrology, numerology to necromancy— and seemed transported. This, his expression advertised, was what he'd been looking for. His stubby fingertips trailed over the edge of the writing table, where a gilded bust of Dante, his head surmounted by a silver wreath, stood in pride of place. Sant'Angelo was careful not to let his own eyes linger on the piece.

"I regret that my Italian is so bad," the professor said. "The infinite charms of *The Divine Comedy* are sometimes lost on me."

"That's a pity. He was the greatest poet the world has ever known."

But Mainz laughed. "You would say that, wouldn't you? Judging by your name, you're an Italian. And yet your family has lived in France for centuries. Why is that?"

Sant'Angelo shrugged, and said, "Ancient history."

The professor paused, then went to his briefcase and unfastened the leather strap. "Ah, but ancient history is my specialty." He began to root around inside, pulling out a stack of papers. "Only last week, we turned up some interesting information at the National Archives." He pushed the bust of Dante to one side, nearly displacing the wreath around its brow, to make some room on the table. "I took the photographs myself. I think you'll find them quite interesting."

They were meticulously done photos of handwritten and handdrawn pages, the text in Italian.

"The scribe who made the original drawings and notes worked for Napoleon. The words were taken down from the walls of a cell in the Castel San Leo, outside Rome. We went there, too, of course, but nothing much remained. So all we have left is these transcriptions."

Sant'Angelo suddenly understood why the Nazis were there.

"I assume you can guess the occupant of the cell," Mainz said.

"Count Cagliostro." What use was there in playing dumb anymore? The words themselves, accompanied by Egyptian symbols and signs, were gibberish, but several times they made mention of Sant'Angelo and a lost castle. The Chateau Perdu. The old charlatan might have been constrained from uttering a word about what he knew, but apparently it had not kept him from writing about it. In the end, he might as well have provided the Nazis with a road map.

"So you can see why we wanted to make this call. Reichsführer Himmler has a great interest in the more arcane sources of knowledge. Wherever we go, we root it up, like truffles," he said, snuffling like a pig.

Sant'Angelo was well aware of the Nazis' predilections. The swastika itself was an ancient Sanskrit symbol of peace, now turned back on its axis to suggest something else entirely.

"Obviously, the count—the master of the Egyptian Masonic lodges—was well acquainted with your predecessor," Mainz said, smiling coldly. "But I wouldn't go so far as to say they were friends. Professional rivals, I would call them. Wouldn't you?"

The marquis stifled an impulse to retort that the powers of the count had been vastly overrated.

"Cagliostro seemed to think that the Chateau Perdu contained some powerful secrets."

"That may be," Sant'Angelo replied, "but in that case, they're still undiscovered." He might have said more, but he noted that the professor's attention had been diverted; his ears had pricked up, like a hunting dog's, and now the marquis could hear it, too—the low thrum of an airplane engine in the distance.

"Come," Mainz said, hurrying out onto the balcony. "He's coming!"

Who's coming? Sant'Angelo thought, following him out. Dusk was falling, and from the west, he saw the red wing lights of a small plane, racing toward the chateau as if it were fleeing from the setting sun. It was going to come in low, just above the ridgeline, and he understood why the soldiers had felled the oaks; they had been clearing a runway approach. All down the sheep meadow, he saw that the armored cars had been placed in parallel lines with their headlamps on, and soldiers with flags and flashlights were positioned on the field.

The wheels of the plane touched the grass, bounced up, and touched again as the ailerons were deployed to cut its ground speed. Even from the parapet, Sant'Angelo could see the Nazi insignia on the fuselage, along with the number 2600—the number that the Führer believed held some mystical power, and that he insisted be placed on all his private aircraft.

Hitler himself had come to his chateau?

The soldiers waved their lights like fireflies as the plane jounced along for the entire length of the meadow. It was only as it was about to run out of room and go crashing into the dense forest that it came to a halt, so abruptly that the nose dipped and the tail end rose up like a scorpion's stinger.

When the engines were cut off, two SS men ran to the port-side door, just aft of the wings, and helped unfold the stairs. The others—Himmler among them—stood at attention in a single line, facing the plane.

In the descending gloom, the marquis saw a figure appear in the door. He was wearing a mustard-colored field uniform, with breeches, boots, and a visored cap. And even from the balcony, his face, with its doleful eyes and toothbrush moustache, was unmistakable.

Sant'Angelo suddenly realized that the professor standing beside him, like all the SS men on the field, had raised his arm in the stiff-armed Nazi salute.

It was returned with a desultory flip, from the elbow alone, by their master, who was already strutting toward the main gate of the chateau, trailed by several officers and attachés.

"You are being granted a great honor," Mainz said. "The Führer will be spending the night under your roof."

Sant'Angelo's mind reeled.

"So let's have something to show him!" Like a schoolboy giddily awaiting a visit from his sweetheart, Mainz hurried back inside and began to riffle through the photos.

"For instance," he said, flourishing a photograph and proffering it to Sant'Angelo, "on this one Cagliostro has scrawled 'The little palace' and drawn this hieroglyph beside it." It was a raven with its wings spread.

"It looks like a raven."

"Of course it does," Mainz said impatiently. "And the three short vertical lines beside it indicate a flock of them. But does it *mean* anything to you? Is such a motif present anywhere in this chateau, or in a family coat of arms, perhaps?"

The little palace—no doubt he meant Le Petit Trianon, Sant'Angelo thought, though he did not share that insight with the professor.

"And this glyph, placed below it," Mainz said, showing another photo, one depicting a jackal, but with its head thrown back, as if its neck were broken.

"He has written, 'The master of the lost castle prevails.' But prevails over what? Over Anubis, the Egyptian god of the dead?"

Sant'Angelo remembered well the psychic battle in Marie Antoinette's hideaway. Apparently, the good count had remembered it, too, even as madness overtook him.

Mainz laid out several more photos of the transcriptions. Even though he had not understood the meaning of what was recorded on the walls of the cell, the French scribe had made fine and accurate renderings. But the marquis sensed that the professor was expecting greater help in deciphering them.

"And then there's this," he said, delicately removing a yellowed sheet of paper—this one was no photograph—done in gray charcoal and what might have once been red wine. "Although I have a great reverence for the French National Archives," Mainz said, "I felt that this was art, and needed to be more widely seen in the original."

It was a powerful sketch of the Gorgon's head, suspended as if on chains. The caption read, "*Lo specchio di Eternità, ma non ho visto!*" The glass of eternity, but I did not see! The professor pulled the damp collar of his shirt away from his thick neck. "As it turns out, the count was a fairly good draftsman. But have you ever seen anything like this, a mirror perhaps, or an amulet, with the face of the Medusa on it? I suspect it belonged to your ancestor."

Sant'Angelo's mind was racing. The glass, as always, was hanging under his very shirt.

"Cagliostro appeared to put great stock in it," Mainz added. "For four years, he wrote on the walls of his cell with a jagged stone, or a lump of charcoal. But this picture he daubed on the only sheet of paper he had, using his own blood."

So it was blood, not wine . . . and the count had finally figured out the value of *La Medusa*. Judging from his inscription, however, he had not fathomed its secret until he had lost it to the marquis, and by then, of course, it was too late. Was the bitterness of that knowledge what had driven him insane?

"Come now," Mainz cajoled, "let's not pretend that you are a neophyte in these matters. This library alone confirms that you are a student of the dark arts. Perhaps you are even a master. Why don't we put our heads together? There's probably a lot we could teach each other."

Oh, yes, there were any number of things that the marquis would have liked to teach him, right then and there, but the professor had turned away again, his face suddenly flushed. Voices echoed up the stairs, followed by the clomping of heavy bootheels. Mainz whirled around, and, despite the warm night, put on his green, bemedaled coat again.

The first ones to enter the study were a pair of SS guards, the jagged sig runes that looked like thunderbolts glittering on their epaulets. They quickly moved aside to make room for Himmler, holding a wineglass in one hand, as he calmly surveyed the mirrored walls and the packed bookshelves, the gleaming table with its bust of Dante, the photographs from the French archives. He actually sniffed the air, as if to detect any potential menace—or latent powers?—lurking in the room. The marquis had the impression that he was doing a final security check before permitting his master to venture inside.

But he barely glanced at Sant'Angelo.

"What have we learned?" he said to the professor.

"We've really just begun," Mainz replied. "I've been showing the marquis —"

Himmler snorted at the mention of the title.

"—some of the material we've recently acquired."

Himmler took the sketch from the professor's hand, studied it, then held it up between pinched fingers in front of Sant'Angelo.

"Ever seen this?"

"The *Medusa* is one of the most common images from antiquity."

"But this one is a dead likeness of one that was done by the necromancer Cellini, as a design for a Medici duchess." Himmler rudely shoved the bust of Dante aside so that he could sit on an edge of the desk, and in so doing, knocked the garland loose. To Sant'Angelo's relief, no one paid any attention as it rolled out of sight under the desk chair. "And in what godforsaken spot," Himmler asked Mainz, "was it that you found that other drawing?"

"In the Laurenziana. Among the papers of the Medicis."

"Ah, yes—in Florence. I don't understand it myself, but the Führer is oddly fond of that town. He likes the old bridge."

The collar of his Gestapo uniform was too big for his scrawny neck, Sant'Angelo noted, and the service medal that was pinned to it only made it gape more. His gray tunic was festooned with other military ribbons and pins.

"It's hard to believe that such a storied object—one that Cellini made, Cagliostro captured, and Napoleon coveted—could simply have gone missing," Himmler said, his eyes—small and pale and mean—glimmering behind his spectacles.

It was then that Sant'Angelo decided . . . *I could kill him.* Or, better yet—*I could wait for my chance and kill his master. Strike the serpent at its head.* He wished he had his harpe at hand; he could have used it, like Perseus, to chop off the head of the monster. But there were other ways. He had reduced Cagliostro to a weeping, craven coward, and in the centuries since, even as his artistic powers had withered, his occult faculties had become more refined. Like a fine wine, they had matured. And despite the risk, when would he ever have a better chance than this to deploy them?

"The sketch," Himmler continued, "suggests it might have been worn like a necklace." His bony fingers caressed his own medal. He cocked his head at one of the guards, who promptly came around the table unholstering his gun, and then roughly pressed the muzzle to Sant'Angelo's temple.

"Open his shirt," the Reichsführer told the other guard.

The second one, a towering blond oaf, yanked the marquis's shirt open, sending the button flying, and then, spotting the chain, lifted it over his head.

"You see?" Himmler said to Mainz. "Direct action is always best."

The guard placed *La Medusa* in Himmler's hand, where he let it dangle from his fingers. "It doesn't feel especially powerful," Himmler said, weighing it up and down. "Is it?"

Sant'Angelo prayed that he could retrieve it before the Nazis ever had the chance to gauge its full potential. But the Luger was still grazing his skull, and he hardly dared to breathe.

"You can put that down now," Himmler said, and the guard immediately obliged, stepping back a few feet, but with the gun still in his hand. "We don't want anyone's head exploding while there's still something worthwhile in it." A wintry smile creased his lips. "Now," he said to Sant'Angelo, "answer the question."

"It's simply a good-luck charm that has been in my family for many years."

"Has it worked?" Himmler asked in a doubtful tone.

Before Sant'Angelo could summon a reply, there was a sharp cry—"Heil, Hitler!"—from the bottom of the steps, and he could see a long shadow playing on the wall of the stairwell . . . and rising up into the turret.

Himmler quickly got off the desk and the guards went rigid at attention. Mainz mopped the sweat from his forehead and wiped it on his sleeve.

The shadow grew larger, nearer, and the mirrored walls of the study suddenly seemed as if they were closing in. Even the marquis felt the imminence of something powerful . . . and evil.

"Who can breathe in here?" he heard the Führer complain as he entered the room. "Open those doors all the way."

The oafish guard leapt to the French doors and threw them back.

The Führer's eyes darted around the room, taking in everything without turning his head more than a few degrees. His field uniform was more modest than Himmler's, decorated with only the red armband and, on his left breast pocket, an old-fashioned Iron Cross, the one engraved with the year 1914 and given out to veterans of the First World War. Surveying the many mirrors, he said, "Vanity is a weakness. A weak man worked in here."

No one contradicted him.

"And why, even this high up, is there still no breeze?"

Sant'Angelo had the impression that they were all being blamed for the lack of air.

Taking off his hat, adorned with the gold Imperial Eagle, he placed it on the desk upside down, then smoothed the back of his head with a trembling left hand. His eyes were an icy blue, and his brown hair was shorn oddly close along the sides. In the front, it fell in a heavy sweep from a parting on the right. Only his bristly moustache was tinged with gray. Noting the Medusa in Himmler's hand, he said, "You hold that bauble as if it were significant."

"It is, Mein Führer."

"Given the trouble you've put me to, it had better be."

Hitler took it in his right hand—Sant'Angelo noticed that he had placed the left one behind his back—and took an interested, but skeptical, look. First he studied the glaring face of the Gorgon, then he turned it over and grunted when he saw its black silk backing. With a thumb, he removed it, uncovering the mirror.

Sant'Angelo prayed that he would stay clear of the moonlight just beginning to show on the terrace outside.

"So it's a lady's looking glass," he said, looking away from the mirror. "And not a particularly good one. The glass seems flawed."

Sant'Angelo hoped he would put it aside; but instead, he distractedly wound the chain in and round his fingers, the *Medusa* herself cupped firmly in his palm.

"We believe there is more to it than meets the eye," Himmler said, though with great deference.

"Yes, yes indeed," Professor Mainz blurted out. "I believe that a manuscript exists, perhaps in this very chateau, which will explain how it was made—and the powers that it can bestow."

Hitler flicked his eyes toward Sant'Angelo. "Well? Can you speak?"

"I can."

"Then do so. I haven't got all night."

"You have already taken the measure of the thing quite accurately," Sant'Angelo replied, in a deliberately timid tone. "It's simply a little mirror, poorly made, without a single precious stone to distinguish it."

"Ah, but that's exactly it!" Mainz said, unable to restrain himself. "The things that have the greatest power always disguise themselves!" As he went off on a fevered disquisition of the occult and its physical phenomena, the marquis gently folded his hands together, in an innocent gesture, and lowered his eyes. He knew that he had been dismissed—judged and found wanting in Hitler's eyes—and that was just what he hoped for.

He focused his thoughts entirely on the Führer . . . focused them, as he once had done years ago, on a sham Italian count. If he was going to break this monster's mind, he first had to find a way inside it.

The discussion went on all around him, Mainz rambling on about a Spear of Destiny, Himmler babbling about an ancient king named Heinrich the Fowler, but Sant'Angelo tuned them out, as if adjusting a wireless set, and concentrated on a single signal . . . the one coming from the Führer himself.

But no sooner had he found it, loud and clear, than he felt as if a wintry wind had just blown through his very bones. Even in that stifling room, he felt a glacial chill. Rather than being able to marshal his own thoughts, he found them scattering in all directions, like dead leaves drifting across a field of rubble.

Concentrate, he told himself. *Concentrate.*

But it was like loitering on a battlefield, after the slaughter.

He gathered himself together, trying to erase the desolate scene, and tried again. With every ounce of energy that he could muster, he burrowed into the Führer's brain.

And this time—this time—he saw Hitler's head snap backwards. The palsied left hand—was the man diseased?—brushed the back of his hair again, in what was plainly a nervous tic.

He had found his point of entry, and now the marquis bored in deeper, harder. His own temples throbbed with the effort. The Führer's shoulders seemed to droop, his knees to bend.

"Of course we haven't even begun a proper interrogation," Himmler was saying, as if Sant'Angelo weren't there to hear it. "This so-called marquis cannot be as ignorant as he claims."

Sant'Angelo was careful not to move a muscle, or call any undue attention to himself, as he continued about his work.

"But in my estimation, the entire chateau is a source of power," the professor added. "I felt it the moment we passed the gatehouse. We must look under every stone."

The blood drained from the Führer's face, and he wavered on his feet. His hand shook more violently, and Himmler suddenly took note.

"Mein Führer," he said, "are you all right?" He motioned for the desk chair—an ornately carved throne—and one of the soldiers carted it around the table as if it were made of toothpicks and slapped it down behind him. Himmler guided their shaken leader onto its velvet seat.

"Go get the doctor!" Mainz cried, and the soldier standing by the door bolted down the stairs.

Beads of sweat dotted Hitler's brow.

The marquis concentrated even more. Like a mole, he was tunneling into the deepest recesses of the monster's brain, and there, once he was at the very core, he would brew a storm so great that the Führer's eyes would go blind, his ears go deaf, and his blood would boil beneath his skin. To the Nazis in the room it would look like a stroke—a fatal stroke—the kind that might suddenly afflict any-one . . . even the master of the almighty Third Reich. And no one would be the wiser.

But then the jolt came. The counterattack.

Sant'Angelo had never felt such a powerful blast. It dwarfed Cagliostro's powers.

The Führer, whose chin was nearly resting on his chest now, whose whole left arm was quivering, showed no emotion, but the shock wave came again, rocking the marquis so hard he nearly lost his balance. He was amazed that no one else had felt it.

Recovering himself, he leaned forward, his hands on the desk to brace himself, but now he saw Mainz, kneeling by the chair, glance up at him suspiciously.

"What are you doing?"

Sant'Angelo couldn't reply—he needed to focus all his attention. Hitler slumped in his chair, as Himmler stood helpless by his side.

"Answer me!" Mainz stood up, fists clenched, the veins bulging in his neck. "What are you doing?"

Sant'Angelo summoned all his strength, whipping the storm in-side the Führer's head to an absolute fury, a raging tornado of puls-ing blood and engorged vessels, of electrical discharges and chemical surges . . . dragging him toward the brink of a fatal seizure or stroke. He didn't care which.

But Mainz had figured it out, and he was grabbing at the marquis, wrestling with him.

"Shoot him!" he shouted at the oafish guard. "Shoot him in his fucking head!"

As the two men fall to the floor, struggling, the marquis felt an-other shock of retaliation, as powerful as a hammer blow to his chest.

The Führer's power was greater than anything he had ever encountered, as if he were channeling the devil himself.

The guard was trying to get a clear shot, but Sant'Angelo and the professor were so entangled that it wasn't possible.

And that was when the marquis was able to reach under the table and snare the garland.

Mainz's heavy hands were grappling at his throat, but Sant'Angelo banged a fist under the man's chin, so hard that the back of his head smashed against the bottom of the table. While he was absorbing the shock of the blow, the marquis was able to crawl free . . . and settle the silver circlet around his brow.

He was crouching on the floor, framed between the open French doors, when the band took its effect. The marquis watched in the mirrored walls as his own image rippled, faded . . . and then disappeared. A bullet from the guard's gun shattered the glass behind him, as Hitler's head came up, his hooded, bleary eyes searching out his enemy. His face had the demonic glow of a furnace.

Himmler, who had spent his whole life in search of just such magic as the marquis had displayed, stood slack-jawed, while Mainz and the soldier, gun still raised, froze in place, not knowing what to do.

Before they could gather their wits, Sant'Angelo sprang to his feet and moved to one side.

"Shoot where he was!" Mainz screamed, and a second later the woodwork exploded in splinters.

"Block the door!" Himmler cried, and the remaining soldier jumped to block the stairs.

There was only one way to go, and even as Sant'Angelo realized it, so did Mainz.

The marquis ran out onto the balcony, and was about to climb over the railing and down the vines, when he felt the professor's hands, groping wildly in the air, catch hold of his collar. Sant'Angelo squirmed out of his grip, but Mainz seemed to have a sixth sense about where he was, and snagged him again.

"I've got you now, you bastard!" Mainz crowed, his hair sopped in blood, his lips flecked with foam, as he pulled him back from the balustrade. "I've got you!" he spat at the night air.

And Sant'Angelo took hold of his loden coat and swung him around so violently that he tripped over his own feet, struggling all the while to hang on to his invisible prey.

"I've got you!" he rasped, as the marquis swung him around one more time, before suddenly letting him go. Mainz careened toward the balustrade, teetering there for just an instant, his arms spread wide, before the invisible marquis shoved both hands against his burly chest and sent him plummeting over the rail.

"Shoot everywhere!" Himmler shouted, and the soldier emptied his Luger in an arc, hitting nearly every spot on the balcony.

"Alive!" the Führer croaked. He had lurched up from his chair and was leaning hard against the doorframe, his left arm shaking uncontrollably. "I want him alive!"

A dozen soldiers charged up from the stairwell, rifles at the ready.

And that was when Sant'Angelo, perched like an acrobat on the balustrade, leapt into the embrace of the closest oak. Crashing down through the boughs, his legs twisting and breaking as he fell, he was finally, miraculously, suspended, as if by a celestial hand. High above the ground, in the blackness of the night, he was sheltered among the thick branches and leaves.

But the pain in his legs was nothing compared to the pain in his heart. In one fell swoop, he had lost his chance of assassinating the Führer . . . and he had lost *La Medusa,* too.

Chapter 34

When David woke up, he didn't know which was more disorienting—finding himself in a canopied bed in the Marquis di Sant'Angelo's house . . . or finding Olivia asleep in his arms.

Their clothing, dry and laundered, was neatly set out for them on a wooden rack, along with several new items—shoes and coats, most notably.

And someone was knocking, again, on the door.

David pulled the sheet up over Olivia's shoulders, and said, "Come in."

A maid, carrying a breakfast tray, entered and without even a glance in their direction, left it on a table by the window. Opening the curtains, she revealed a lovely view of the park . . . and its now-placid boating pond. "Monsieur Sant'Angelo," she said, before closing the door on her way out, "will see you in the salon when you're done."

When the door closed, Olivia opened her eyes. "So this is real?"

David could hardly believe it himself. "I think so." But Olivia's naked body, her head nestled against his chest, was definitely real. The bed was big and soft, and their two bodies had made a deep, warm indentation in the mattress. He felt her slender fingers graze his shoulder, his arm . . . and much as he hated to interrupt, he knew that he had to.

"Can I take a rain check?" he said.

"What is that?"

"It means, hold that thought. I need to find a phone."

Grabbing his robe off the back of a chair and a cup of coffee from the table, he went out into the hall—he had hardly seen anything of the upstairs the night before—and bumped into the maid again. "Is there a phone?" he asked, and she pointed him into a sitting room filled, as was much of the house, with antique statuary. David felt sure he recognized one bust as being that of Cosimo de'Medici, and another, judging from its skullcap and regalia, as a Renaissance pope.

His first call was to the Hotel Crillon, where Gary had indeed left a message. "Call me, anytime, as soon as you get this." It was the middle of the night in Chicago now, but David wasn't about to wait. He called Gary's cell and Gary picked up on the second ring.

"Sorry if I woke you," David said, "but your message at the hotel said to call."

"You're not checking your cell?"

"I lost it," David said. "What's going on?"

He could hear Gary stirring in his bed, gradually waking up. But David was already calculating. How bad could it be if Gary hadn't said anything yet?

And then he did speak.

"David, you need to come home."

His heart stopped in his chest. "Why? What's happened? I thought Sarah was responding so well to that new therapy."

"Not anymore," Gary said, his words coming slowly, and with great deliberation. "She had a bad relapse, and they've stopped it altogether."

David waited for word on what they were going to try next . . . but it didn't come.

"Sarah's been back at the hospital," Gary said, "but she's been moved."

"Where?" David asked, dreading the answer.

"The hospice unit," Gary said, as if he didn't want to say it any more than David wanted to hear it. "But it's really not a bad place.

They're making her as comfortable as they can, and Emme was able to come by for a pretty decent visit. Sarah's got her own room, with a view of a little rock garden with a pond, and the staff has been great."

David was still waiting for it all to sink in.

"But I'm afraid that Dr. Ross doesn't think that she'll be there for very long."

"How long does he say?" David asked.

They both knew what they were really talking about.

"A few days, at the outside. That's why you need to get back home as fast as you can. Sarah said she would wait for you—and you know how it is when she makes up her mind to do something," Gary said, starting to break down. "But this is just too much for her—she's not going to be able to hold on much longer."

When they hung up, David sat on the sofa, staring blankly at another bust, this one in the center of the mantel. It was a woman with a haughty expression, her face turned to one side and a mane of luxuriant curls falling onto her bare shoulders.

His immediate thought was to call the airport right away and book the first flight back to the States. With luck, he could be back in Chicago in eight or nine hours.

But to do what? Kiss his dying sister good-bye? To tell her that he had failed in his mission to save her—and right when the answer was nearly in his grasp? If the journey he had been on had taught him anything, it was that the world was a far stranger place than he had ever imagined. His eyes strayed again to the bust on the mantel, and for some reason, even now it captured his attention. He found himself rising from the sofa to inspect it more closely.

And that was when it struck him, just as it had when he'd come across the sketch of Athena in the pages of *The Key to Life Eternal*. There was a real-life model for this antique bust, and he had met her.

"I carved that myself," came a voice from the doorway. It was Sant'Angelo, in a silk smoking jacket worn over a pair of dark slacks and a crisp white shirt with billowing sleeves. "Ascanio bought the marble from Michelangelo himself." He came into the room, studying David for his reaction. "Does she remind you of someone?"

"She does."

"She should. I first met her at the court of the French king, and she was my muse from that day on. Her name was Caterina." He touched the stone. "What does she call herself now?"

"Kathryn." What was the use of concealment any longer?

Sant'Angelo, the tip of his cane grazing the floor, nodded. "It's just like her to have kept her name like that all these years. She was always stubborn."

"And you?" David said, hardly believing that he had entered into this conversation at all. Could he actually be speaking to his boyhood idol, the legendary Benvenuto Cellini? "Weren't you famously hard-headed, too?"

The marquis tipped his head to one side in agreement. "We were alike in that. I'm no more likely to give up the name Sant'Angelo. It's the prison from which I was reborn, and I will never forget, or deny, that." Taking a seat in a chintz-covered armchair, he waved at David to sit opposite. "May I say what a relief it is, after all these years, to have encountered someone who so readily . . . understands."

David did not reply. He would not have known what words to use. But he noticed that Olivia, still in her robe, was standing silently in the doorway. How long had she been there? he wondered. What had she overheard? The marquis glanced her way, and said, "You may as well join us."

She sat beside David and reached out to clutch his hand.

"May I assume that there are no secrets here?" the marquis asked.

"You may," she answered, and David nodded his confirmation. Sant'Angelo's shoulders relaxed and he settled more deeply into the chair.

"That call you just made—it was to your sister?" Sant'Angelo remarked to David, as if resuming a perfectly ordinary conversation.

"Her husband," David answered.

"And?"

"She has only a day or two left."

"Oh, David," Olivia lamented, and squeezed his hand in sympathy. "I am so sorry. You must go to her, right away."

Sant'Angelo nodded thoughtfully, then lifted his head and said, "You could do that. By all means. You could return to her as quickly as you can, only to stand at her bedside helplessly and watch her succumb to the inevitable." He let that dreadful option sink in for a few seconds, before gripping the head of his cane with both hands, and saying, "Or you could fight!"

The words hung suspended in the air. David knew what a sensible librarian at a well-respected institution like the Newberry would do.

And he knew what the fearsome Cellini would have done. The choice was as clear as day, and he made it.

Before he could even speak, he noted his host's lips curving into a subtle smile of victory. "I knew you had it in you," the artisan declared, his dark eyes flashing. "And now, it's time you knew the rest," he said, removing a silver garland from the pocket of his smoking jacket.

Chapter 35

It had been many years since Ernst Escher had tried to cram himself into such a tiny car, but the beige Peugeot was all that the rental agency had left—and besides, it was a good car for surveillance purposes. Easy to park, and utterly inconspicuous. And Escher was pretty much living in it now.

After leaving the hotel the night before, he hadn't dared to check in anywhere else. Who knew how many desk clerks might be on the take from those murderous Turks? He'd parked down under one of the bridges, slept for a few hours, and after looking over the last photos and text that Julius had sent him, he'd driven to the quiet street across from the boating park.

The town house was impressive, with a walled garden and a driveway on one side. Escher had slowly cruised past, then turned around and parked fifty yards up the street. The rearview mirror was positioned to show him anything that happened at the house. This was the last place Jantzen had tracked them to, and when Escher had done some checking at the Crillon he discovered that Franco and his friend Olivia had not spent the night in their room.

Chances were they'd spent it in the town house, with what was apparently some very well-heeled friend.

When his own phone rang, he saw it was the ex-ambassador Schillinger, calling from Chicago for his regular progress report. But

Escher, who'd been circumspect all along (omitting any mention, for instance, of that bloody fracas in Florence), was even less inclined to tell him much now. He no longer knew whose side anyone was playing on.

"Where are you?" Schillinger complained the moment Escher picked up.

"Still in Paris." He wasn't about to be any more specific than that.

"With Jantzen?"

"No."

Schillinger sighed. "Don't tell me you've had a falling-out with him, too? Julius is no fool. He might be able to help you."

Escher knew that Schillinger had no great regard for his intelligence, but then, he was happy to return the compliment.

"Have you made any progress at all? Or, more to the point, has Franco? I'd dearly like to know what he's up to. That information could be very important—and valuable—to certain people."

"Would one of them be me?"

"When have I ever not rewarded you for a job well done?" Schillinger snapped.

"The job is getting done all right," Escher replied, keeping an eye on the rearview mirror, "but it has gotten a lot more complicated." He'd checked the morning newspapers, but so far the murders in Pigalle hadn't made it into print.

"What's that supposed to mean?" Schillinger said, losing what little patience he had ever had. "Please don't tell me you're trying to renegotiate the terms of your employment? I have sometimes regretted my generosity as it is."

"I'm way past that," Escher said, leaning back in the seat with one eye fixed on the rearview mirror. As far as he was concerned, he wasn't even working for Schillinger anymore. He'd been a fool—a lackey working for a lackey. Now he was a freelance bounty hunter, and if this Franco character turned out to be carrying anything of real cash value, then Escher was going to take it to the highest bidder. Schillinger might be out to score points and kiss ass, but Escher was simply out to make a score.

"Oh, Ernst," Schillinger said condescendingly, "it sounds to me like you are about to make such a grave mistake."

Escher could picture him slowly shaking his shaggy white head.

"By now, even a man of your limited imagination should have been able to figure out that it's not only me you're working for. I'm just a functionary, if you will. The organization is more extensive than you know. And frankly, I'm the best protection you've got."

"That's funny," Escher replied, reflecting on the two most recent attempts on his life, "but I'm not feeling particularly well protected these days."

"Why, did something happen?" Schillinger asked, and Escher couldn't decide whether to believe him or not. More and more, he'd come to suspect that he was caught in the middle of a cross-continental rivalry—a bitter and deadly contest that Schillinger, an old fool marooned in Chicago, would surely lose.

And Escher didn't like being on the losing side of anything.

In the rearview mirror, he spotted a sleek, silver Maserati pulling up to the side door of the house. A tough-looking guy in a black windbreaker—he looked like a tradesman, Italian or maybe a Greek—tossed some duffels and backpacks into the open boot. Then the girl, Olivia, came out of the house—wearing a black coat, different from the day before—and slid into the backseat. David followed, and got in the front on the passenger side. He was dressed all in black, too. They looked like a troupe of mimes, or second-story men.

"Ernst? Are you still there?"

"No," Escher replied, snapping the phone shut and turning on the ignition. He felt like a falcon that had just flown free.

The boot was slammed shut, and the driver stopped to exchange a few words with a formidable-looking man, well dressed, leaning on a black walking stick. The lord of the manor, Escher assumed.

The Maserati—a car that Escher knew cost no less than ninety thousand euros—purred out of the driveway, and as it passed the stubby Peugeot, Escher slumped down in his seat, waited for a delivery van to get between them, then promptly pulled out. The street was quiet and serene, with the park on one side and the row of elegant town houses on the other, but soon the Maserati had entered the thick, late-morning traffic of the city. The congestion actually made it easier for Escher to follow unnoticed; for all its horsepower, the Maserati couldn't get through the honking horns and red lights and stop signs any faster than anyone else.

Still, he wished he'd had the chance to attach a transponder under its bumper. Technology always helped in situations like this.

He especially regretted it when the car rounded a busy traffic circle and signaled a turn onto the ramp leading to the A 10, a major motor route heading southwest into the Loire Valley. Once they got out onto the highway, where the speed limits were 130 kph and enforcement, even of that speed, was virtually nil, it was going to be a struggle for his little Peugeot—which wasn't exactly a new model to begin with—to keep pace, much less without being spotted.

And Escher didn't doubt that David and Olivia had wised up enough to check if they were being followed. They might be naïve, but they weren't stupid.

Schillinger's crack about his limited imagination came back to him, and before focusing again on his driving, Escher entertained a brief fantasy of retribution, stuffing the old man's mouth with whatever precious papers were in that valise. The Maserati had flown down the entry ramp and merged seamlessly with the swifter highway flow. Fortunately, this close to Paris, there were still plenty of other cars and lorries and tour buses—dozens of the buses, in fact, packed with tourists setting out on the chateau circuit—to impede its progress. But that wouldn't last long.

Escher checked his gas, and at least he was still running on a virtually full tank.

Within a half hour, however, the buses had all moved to one lane, and the other traffic had sufficiently thinned that the driver of the Maserati could start to step on it. And he did. The silver car zoomed ahead, and Escher had to put his foot to the floor of the Peugeot just to keep it in sight. The cabin whined with the sound of the engine and the doors rattled, as, on both sides of the road, fallow fields and barren vineyards flashed past. The car was going so fast that Escher, who had to keep one eye on the Maserati at all times, barely had a chance to read the little blue-and-white signs marking each town and tourist site they passed. Several times, one bus or another would peel off, but the silver car stayed in the passing lane and barreled straight ahead like a bullet.

Escher adjusted himself in his seat, and kept both hands tightly on the wheel. But he was afraid that if he kept up this speed much longer, the motor might die, or something else might go wrong. He berated himself for not having gone to some other rental agency and getting a better, more powerful car.

And then, just as he was sure he was about to lose the Maserati altogether, it suddenly, and without warning, cut across the traffic lanes, causing one truck to swerve wildly and another to hit its brakes, before shooting toward the exit ramp for a couple of towns called Biencie/Cinq Tours. It was standard procedure for losing a tail, and Escher wondered if he had actually been spotted, or if the driver was just doing what came naturally.

But with only seconds to react, Escher simultaneously flipped on his flashers and his turn signals, and navigated as fast as he could toward the right side of the road. Other cars blasted their horns and one driver flew by giving him the finger. But he was too far along to make it down the ramp, and it was all he could do to stop the Peugeot on an overpass a hundred yards ahead and jump out of the car.

With the roar and the wind of the traffic rushing by, he ran to the guardrail. Below him he saw empty fields, a white farmhouse, and a two-lane blacktop going north and south. The Maserati was sitting at the crossroads, plainly waiting to see if any other car came down the exit behind it. Escher instinctively ducked lower, and watched as the car sat there for a full minute before turning to the right, where a blue arrow pointed toward the town called Cinq Tours.

Chapter 36

The moment Ascanio swept the car across the traffic lanes, and gunned it down the exit ramp, Olivia had let out an involuntary scream and David clutched the walnut trim on the dashboard so hard his knuckles turned white.

"Are you crazy?" Olivia cried.

But Ascanio was looking in the rearview mirror as the car descended the ramp, and at the bottom he stopped abruptly, letting the car idle there. It was a lonely spot, with brown farmland and a white farmhouse off in the distance, and it took David a few seconds just to release his grip on the dashboard.

"I had to be sure we had no company," Ascanio said.

"Well, I think we've settled that question," Olivia said. "But next time, could you at least give us some warning?" She muttered an oath in Italian, and Ascanio smiled.

Then, he turned the wheel to the right, toward the town called Cinq Tours. The road there, part of the Route Nationale system, was older and narrower, and it meandered through scenic but now-barren fields and forests. In a grove of old oaks, David saw a pack of wild boars, pawing and snuffling at the hard ground.

"A local specialty," Ascanio observed with a tilt of his chin. "In his day, the marquis was a very good hunter."

"But not so much anymore, I'd guess." David had been wondering how to ask the indelicate question, but this was as good, or bad, a time as any. "How were his legs injured? In an accident?"

Ascanio waited for a tractor to lumber over an old stone bridge, then maneuvered around it. "An accident of history," he replied. "It happened during the war."

The war. David almost laughed at the absurdity of it. Which one? It could be almost any war at all, from the Napoleonic campaigns to the Second World War. The marquis might have been a field marshal at Waterloo, and Ascanio his aide-de-camp. It was an alternate reality that David was working in, but since that was also the only reality in which some hope for his sister survived, he was not about to challenge it.

A few kilometers on, they came to a cobblestoned town square, with a white stone cross in its center, a few shops, and an inn—L'Auberge Sur le Carré—bearing the green and white *Logis de France* imprimatur. Ascanio parked the car right outside, close to a lone gas pump.

"We can get something to eat here," he said. "They do a good rabbit-and-mushroom stew."

But David didn't want to wait, much less for rabbit stew. "Why don't we just keep going?" he said. "It can't be much farther to the chateau." He still had every intention of getting on a plane to the States that same night.

Ascanio opened his door and got out. Poking his head back in, he said, "We have to wait till it gets dark, anyway. And I like stew."

Slamming the door shut and heading into the inn, he left them, still in their seat belts, in the car. David turned around and Olivia, unsnapping her belt, said, "He's right. We have to eat. Come on."

They found Ascanio in a wooden booth in back. Only one other table was occupied, by a couple of farmers in overalls. The owner, a cheerful, chubby woman wearing a soup-stained apron, brought them a bottle of the local wine and took their orders—three rabbit stews.

By the time she returned with the food, Ascanio had already taken out some papers, a map among them, and was explaining the rest of the plan first laid out by the marquis. Glancing down as she made room for the plates, the woman said, "Do you need directions?" But Ascanio, laying his hand across a rough diagram, said, *"Non, merci.* We have a GPS in the car."

She flicked a hand at the notion. "My husband has one of those, too, and it never works right." She looked to make sure they had everything they needed, then said, *"Bon appétit,"* and went to get the farmers another round.

David ate, with no more relish than a machine taking on fuel, and listened as Ascanio further elaborated on the deeds that lay before them. For David—a man who was given to rumination, a man who spent most of his working hours in the company of old books, a man whose biggest challenge was usually determining the arcane meaning of an obscure quotation—this had all been a rude and rough awakening. He felt like a spy might feel on assuming a new identity.

But there was also something—how could he put it?—*invigorating* in it. Something that stirred his blood and energized his will. In the modern world, action—physical action—was so seldom taken. Disputes were resolved in courtrooms and arguments in therapy sessions. The focus was always on emotions and interrelationships and reaching consensus.

But with Ascanio and Sant'Angelo, David felt none of that. He was dealing with the certainties of another age. In Cellini's day, a difference of opinion led straight to a brawl. An insult could result in a sword fight to the death. According to his own autobiography, Cellini had killed three men in duels, and countless others in battle. Had it not been for his present infirmity, David was sure he would have been participating in the assault that lay ahead.

When Ascanio had shown them the diagram of the chateau, expertly done in the marquis's own hand, and outlined the course of action he was proposing, it was like listening to a fantastic tale out of the *Arabian Nights*. But this was a tale in which David and Olivia were to play a vital part! It was only when Ascanio told Olivia, while mopping up the last of his stew, that she would have to stay back with the car while he and David went to reclaim the *Medusa* that she objected.

"Without my help, you would not even be here! Who was it who knew enough to follow the trail of Cagliostro? This is just the same old paternalistic bullshit. Who has more of a right than I do to join this fight?"

But an angry look crossed Ascanio's face. He rolled up the map and papers, threw a wad of bills on the table, and said, "Come with me."

He strode out into the square and stopped in front of the white marble cross. David and Olivia quickly caught up, and even though it was getting late in the day and the light was starting to fade, David was able to read the plaque that said the monument had been erected to commemorate the villagers executed, on this very spot, by the Nazis on June 20, 1940.

"The marquis himself donated this monument."

There were perhaps a dozen names inscribed on its column.

"They were the household staff of the chateau. They were killed in retribution for the marquis's escape." His finger ran along the letters of one name—Mademoiselle Celeste Guyot.

"I never had the heart to tell him," Ascanio said, "but it should have said Madame."

"She was married?" David asked.

"The night before," Ascanio replied, and from the expression on his face—great sorrow and implacable rage—David did not have to ask who her husband had been. Nor did Olivia contest his instructions again.

Ascanio went to the gas pump, slipped in a credit card, and refueled the car. Then he filled a couple of gallon jugs, and put them in the boot, too. David didn't ask why. He drove the Maserati out of the square, where amber-colored lights were just coming on in some of the storefronts, then out onto the road leading to the Chateau Perdu.

The road was so narrow it essentially became a single, unlighted country lane. Posts with red reflectors atop them were positioned every fifty yards or so, but often they were obscured by the overgrown shrubbery and trees. For the first time, David began to see how aptly the chateau had been named—this was a lost region, a place that showed no other signs of human habitation. For the next few kilometers, nothing but dark woods lined both sides of the road. The moon hung low in the sky, peeking out from behind a scrim of fast-moving clouds.

"The gatehouse," Ascanio finally said, dimming the headlights, and David, peering through the side window, detected a stone house, covered with vines, squatting like a toadstool among the overhanging trees. No lights were on inside, and it looked as if it had been untenanted for years. Ascanio drove past slowly, long enough for David and Olivia to take in the high iron gates, and a driveway on the other side that disappeared into the blackness.

"So where's the chateau?" Olivia said, and Ascanio replied, "Right where it's been for eight hundred years. On the cliffs."

Only when they were well past the gates did Ascanio turn the headlights back on. A rubblestone wall, five or six feet high, ran for a long distance along one side of the road, and even when it ended, massive old oaks formed an impenetrable barrier.

"How do we get back there?" David said, and Ascanio pointed to a break in the trees, where a rusty chain had been looped around two trunks, along with a sign that read PRIVATE PROPERTY—NO TRESPASSING. To David's surprise, he nosed the grill of the Maserati up to the chain and pressed on the gas. There was a screeching sound of metal on metal, a crack and a pop and a flash of white light as one of the headlights blew out, and the chain snapped in two.

With only one light remaining, he maneuvered the car along a bumpy, overgrown track that wound through the trees before eventually opening up to a view of the river. There was an old, cracked, concrete loading dock, and a long wharf beyond that extending into the rolling waters of the Loire. To David, it looked as if this place, too, had been unused for many years.

The moment Ascanio stopped the car and turned off the engine, they were swallowed up by the night. The boot of the car popped open, and Ascanio got out without a word and began to hand David his supplies—a backpack loaded with gear, a flashlight, and one of the plastic jugs of gasoline. He pulled a matching pack over his own shoulders and, like some pirate, he took the *harpe*—the short sword with its fearsome notched end—and slung it, still in its scabbard, onto his belt. Grabbing the other gasoline jug, he said to Olivia, "Turn the car around, then just wait for us. If we're not back in a few hours, drive back to Paris."

"I'm not leaving you here!"

"You won't be," he said. "We'll be dead."

David's blood froze in his veins at the casual manner in which Ascanio said it, but he felt as if it were a test, too. Ascanio looked at him, waiting to see him quail, but David would not. He hadn't come this far to give up now.

Not when Sarah's life hung in the balance.

Ascanio said, "Come on then," and took off into the trees. Olivia plucked at David's sleeve, kissed him hard on the lips, and said, "I will be here."

David turned, and lugging the plastic jug, picked his way with the flashlight through the dense forest. All he could see of Ascanio was the other flashlight beam, held close to the ground, and he had to struggle just to catch up. There was still no sign of a chateau, but Ascanio was leading them down toward the riverbank. There, they marched along, while the ground began to rise above them into sheer cliffs. David's boots squelched in the muddy soil, and the gas sloshed in the jug. After several minutes, the clouds passed away from the moon, and high above them, David could see, like the fingers of a giant grasping hand, five black towers.

"I see it," David said, and Ascanio simply nodded. Waving his flashlight back and forth across the base of the cliff, he revealed a series of caves and crevices worn into the limestone over many millennia.

"Look for five vertical cuts," he said, making a slicing motion with the hand holding the flashlight.

David trained his beam, too, onto the cliffs and stepping carefully over the rocks and rubble, was the first to find the deep incisions, like hashmarks, chiseled above a cave entrance no bigger than a wagon wheel.

Ascanio shifted his backpack higher onto his shoulders, ducked his head, and vanished into the hole. David quickly followed and found himself at the bottom of a shaft, with steps only four or five inches wide, carved out of the stone. Ascanio was already wending his way up them; David could see the glow of his flashlight, and loose pebbles and dirt skittered down from above. David had to keep his head bent low, his shoulders tucked in, and his feet positioned sideways on the steps in order to get up them. It would have been a difficult climb under any circumstances, but because he was toting the jug in one hand and the flashlight in the other, it became a precarious balancing act, too. One missed step and he could find himself tumbling head-long all the way down the winding passageway.

The air was damp and foul, and every breath felt as if it were being inhaled underwater. Ascanio was coughing, too, but the light from his beam continued to ascend. They were burrowing up through the earth, and by the time Ascanio had stopped and David had managed to catch up to him at the very top, they were both short of breath and drenched with moisture. Ascanio's flashlight and jug lay on the ground, and he gestured at a round slab of stone.

"We have to move that," he said, so David put his things down, too. They were in a space only a few feet square, and it took a minute just to figure out how to divide the labor. As Ascanio pushed on one edge of the slab, David pulled on its upper rim. It rocked a few inches, then settled back into its age-old groove.

"Again," Ascanio said, and that time the slab rolled to one side, just enough for Ascanio to slip through. The scabbard of his sword scraped against the stone. "Quick," he said, extending his arm back through, "hand me my pack." David did, then handed his own through, too, before scrunching down, as if trying to worm through a rubber tire, and into a rocky tunnel. A string of lightbulbs, all of them off, dangled along the roof. Ascanio was already removing the cap of his jug, and motioning David to move past him.

As soon as David had, Ascanio bent over and, walking backwards, began sloshing the gasoline in a long trail along behind them. They moved steadily down the tunnel, David leading the way now, until Ascanio's jug was empty. They were standing above an iron grate, and when David directed his flashlight beam into it, he could see a steep fall, and hear, at the bottom, the ebb and flow of river water.

Ascanio tossed his own empty jug aside, opened David's, and they continued on, with Ascanio dribbling gas behind them all the way. Wine racks rose on either side, until they came to some steps leading into an old-fashioned scullery; beyond that, in the kitchen, they could hear the sound of a radio playing. Ascanio put a finger to his lips as he reached up with the *harpe* and cut the cord that connected the lightbulbs strung the length of the tunnel.

Then, creeping behind the last of the racks, they peered out between the bottles to see a woman with her gray hair in a long plait bustling about the kitchen, tidying up. She wiped the counter clean, put some stray dishes in the dishwasher, then turned it on.

Surveying her domain before closing up for the night, she said, "*Que faites-vous vers le haut là?*"—What are you doing up there?—to a kitten with its paws up on the center table. She flicked off the radio, put on her overcoat, and deposited the kitten into one of her voluminous side pockets. Then, tying a scarf under her chin, she left, leaving the room illuminated only by a night-light above the stove and the red glow from a wall clock advertising Cinzano.

The clock continued to tick, the freezers—two of them— hummed, and the dishwasher gently rattled its plates, but there was no sign of further activity. Finally, Ascanio crept out from behind the rack, and after glancing out the kitchen door, came back and began to shake the remaining drops of gasoline onto the floor. When the jug was empty, he tossed it out of sight under the sinks. He stashed his flashlight in his backpack, then, gripping the hilt of the *harpe*, he whispered to David, "*La Medusa?*" It was as if he was asking him if he wanted a beer.

"Yes," David said, relieved to discover that his own voice was firm and determined. He wiped the grime from his glasses and looped the wire sidepieces firmly back behind his ears. "*La Medusa.*"

Chapter 37

There had been no sign of the Maserati on the lonely country road, but several times Escher had come to junctions and turnoffs, and at each one he had to stop and look for fresh tire tracks. Once or twice, he followed what turned out to be dead ends—spurs that ended in vineyards or empty barns.

But whenever he came on a small store or gas station, he pulled in and asked if anyone had seen his friends go by, in their brand-new silver Maserati. Fortunately, it was the kind of car they were likely to remember. At one station, a teenager working the register said it had gone by about an hour ago and pointed toward the town of Cinq Tours.

Escher had purposely looked puzzled, as if he'd forgotten something, and said, "What's in Cinq Tours?"

"Fuck if I know. You want to buy anything?" he said, anxious to return to his video game.

Escher bought a pack of Gitanes and got back in the car. He fished his flask out from under the seat, had a shot of whiskey to restore his spirits, and headed on. Twenty minutes later, he had to pull over to let a flock of sheep amble by. When he asked the shepherd about the car, the man said not a word, but jerked his staff toward Cinq Tours again. It was getting late, the sun setting, and none of this was going to get any easier after dark.

Escher drove the little Peugeot over an old stone bridge, past a millrace, and thought, *This is just the kind of picturesque crap tourists love.* Give him a city anytime. Up ahead, he saw the lights of a town square, with a white cross in its center. There was an inn on one side, with a couple of muddy trucks parked in front, but no Maserati. He pulled in next to the gas pump and got out.

There were a bunch of locals inside, in woolen shirts and work boots, and a TV was mounted on brackets over the bar. The evening news was on, but no one was watching. Escher went straight to the bar and asked the bartender about the car, and whether or not two men and a woman had recently stopped in together. The bartender said, "I just came on, but the owner's been here all day." He called back into the kitchen, and a harried woman, wiping her hands on an apron, popped out.

Escher repeated his question, and she said, "Oh yes, your friends were here, oh, maybe an hour or two ago. They had the rabbit stew—it's very good tonight," she added, cleaning a spot on the bar where she could serve him and setting up a wineglass with the other hand.

"Thank you," he said, "but I need to catch up with them. They forgot something important. Do you have any idea where they were going from here?"

She shrugged, fast losing interest. "They had a map. Maybe the chateau, though God knows why."

Escher had seen no signs for a chateau, nor any tour buses.

"Of course," he said, nodding. "How would I get there?"

She was already halfway back to the kitchen. "Keep going. A few more kilometers. Pierre!" she hollered at someone inside. "What's burning?"

Escher charged out to his car, sorry to hear that they had such a lead on him, but relieved to know that they had so little idea they were being tracked that they'd actually dawdled over bowls of stew. He steered his car around the monument and onto the road leading out of town, which he discovered was even worse here than it was coming in.

Night had fallen, and the moon was going in and out of the clouds racing in from the west. He followed the road, but wondered why there were no signs for the chateau that the innkeeper had mentioned. There were no signs for anything, in fact—just reflectors, popping up like red eyes in the darkness every so often. But at least there were no other turnoffs or intersecting roads they might have taken, and before long he spotted a gatehouse, where he stopped and got out of the car. There was no one in the house, no chateau as far as he could see, and a massive padlock on the gates. Getting back in the car, he continued on, hoping he might come across another entrance, but all he saw was a long stone wall that didn't look easily breached. Just when he had decided to go back and take one more look at that gate—how hard would it be to shatter that padlock?— he noticed that the wall had given out, and in a space between two trees, a broken chain was lying on the ground. When he stopped and got out, he could see bits of a broken headlight, too. His own headlights didn't penetrate very far into the woods, but he could see that there was some kind of old driveway here. *Is that where they went?*

But why?

He drove his car far enough into the trees to be unseen from the road, turned it around, and left the key in the ignition for a quick getaway if he needed one. Then he got out with a flashlight in one hand and his Glock 9mm in the other. It was easy enough to follow the worn old trail, but he was careful to make as little noise as possible and to keep his beam close to the damp leaves and soil. Eventually, he could hear the sound of the river, and he could see something gleaming in the intermittent moonlight.

And damned if it wasn't a silver Maserati. He hadn't lost his touch, after all.

Crouching low, he crept up on the car and peered inside. There was no one in it.

But when he looked down toward the river, he saw a platform of some kind, like an old loading dock, and a wooden pier—at the end of which someone was smoking a glowing cigarette.

As he moved closer, he could see that it was the girl, Olivia, huddled in her dark coat, her hair tucked up under a knitted cap. This was too good to be true. Looking all around, he saw that she was alone. A sitting duck. If he'd had a reason to eliminate her, he couldn't have asked for a better chance. But he had no such reason— not yet, anyway—and something told him that she might wind up being a valuable bargaining chip before the night was over.

Stepping softly onto the dock, he called out, "Catch any fish?"

She whirled around, the cigarette flying from her fingers.

He raised the Glock just enough for her to see it, and said, "Keep your hands out of your pockets and walk toward me."

She hesitated.

"Now." He raised the gun higher.

With her arms held away from her body, she walked toward him, and when she got close enough, he said, "Where are your friends?"

"What friends?"

"Please don't spoil things. We've been getting along so well."

"They're . . . gone."

"And they left you here, alone, in the woods?"

He was considering his options, and they were all good. She was completely at his mercy, and if he played his cards right, he might even be driving back to Paris in a new Maserati.

"Come on," he said, waving her on with the gun. "Back to the car."

She moved slowly, her body tense. She was thinking, he could tell, of sprinting into the woods.

"Don't even think about running," he said. "I was the best marksman in my class."

When they reached the car, he told her to open the boot and stand back. When she did, he played his flashlight over the interior. But there weren't any weapons there, nor did he see that damn valise David Franco had always been carrying. Of course, if it had fallen into his lap that easily, he might have thought a trap had been laid for him.

"Okay," he said, closing the lid, "get in the car."

He waited until she got in on the driver's side, then slid into the passenger seat, with the gun still trained on her. "This could all have been avoided," he said.

"If we'd let you steal the valise on the train?"

He gave her a cold smile. "Nice to know I'm remembered." He opened the glove compartment and rummaged inside. "So, what time are David and your driver due back?" To encourage an honest answer, he touched the muzzle of the gun to her cheek.

"Get that thing out of my face," she said with a snarl.

He had to give her that; she had guts to go along with her looks. "What time?" he repeated, glancing at the dashboard for the clock. There were so many goddamn dials and knobs and temperature controls that he couldn't even locate it.

"Who are you, anyway?" she said. "Your accent sounds Swiss."

"Swiss Guard," he said, still proud of the credential, even if he had been dishonorably discharged.

Olivia scoffed. "You're not working for the Pope tonight."

"No," he admitted, "I'm self-employed."

She twiddled her fingers atop the steering wheel, as if she were waiting for a bad date to end, and Escher decided to move the car farther into the trees. When David and his friend came back, he wanted them to have to walk out into the clearing where he would have the drop on them.

"Tell you what," he said. "I know a better place where we can wait for your friends. Put the car in gear, and drive out . . . slowly. If you touch the horn, I'll kill you where you sit."

❧

Olivia did as she was told, her mind racing a mile a minute. She started the car, and the seat-belt warning bell began its rhythmic chime. She buckled up, and said, "You do it, too, or that damn thing will keep on ringing."

A plan was already forming in her head. But could she possibly pull it off?

Without taking his eyes off her, Escher reached over and slung the seat belt across his chest.

Olivia fumbled around, pretending to look for the headlights switch. The car was already facing the road, as Ascanio had earlier instructed her to have it positioned. But the delay allowed her to hit the button on her armrest that lowered her own window, and then hit another that clicked the doors locked.

"Stop fucking around," Escher said, flicking the gun barrel up from his waist.

"Give me a break," she said. "I've never driven this thing before."

She glanced up at the rearview mirror, tilting it to get a good look at what was right behind her.

And it was the loading dock and the wooden wharf beyond it.

As she took hold of the gearshift, Escher sat back in his seat, the gun down, and said, "Steer toward those trees up ahead." Discreetly, and with one foot still on the brake, she put the car into reverse and undid her own seat belt. The chime started ringing again.

"Why is that damn bell ringing?" he said, but then his whole body jerked forward as she took her foot off the brake and slammed it down on the gas pedal, pushing it all the way to the floor. The car rocketed backwards. She held the wheel firmly to keep it on course, but the bumpy ground bucketed them around as the gun went off with a deafening blast, blowing a hole in the dashboard. She was barely able to steer the car across the dock before, with a stomach-dropping sensation, she felt it hurtle off the end of the wharf and into the empty air.

The splash, a second later, rocked the car like a seesaw, as water gushed in through her open window.

But Olivia was already scrambling out of it. Escher was struggling to unfasten his belt with one hand and jerking madly at his locked door with the other.

She was almost clear when she felt his hand groping at her legs, trying to drag her back inside, but all he got was one of her shoes.

The Loire was cold and the current was strong, but Olivia was able to wriggle free of the car as it spun slowly downstream. Its lone headlight was still shining in the water. As she squirmed out of her sodden coat and let it sink, she saw the panicked Swiss Guardsman, still entangled, gasping behind the windshield. The interior was almost filled by now.

The river was carrying her downstream, too, and she had to strike out hard for the riverbank. By the time she made it, she was several hundred yards from the wharf. She clambered up onto the rocks with one foot bare, shivering wildly, and looked back at the water. There was no sign of a swimmer, anywhere. All she could see, in fact, was the silver roof of the Maserati skimming along the moonlit surface, leaving a trail of bubbles in its wake.

And then, like a submarine smoothly diving, even that disappeared.

Chapter 38

Entering the *salle d'armes,* David felt as if he were surrounded.

All along both walls, gleaming in the moonlight, there were standing suits of armor, some holding pikes or lances or swords. A battle-axe and a mace were crossed above the great stone hearth, a crossbow and arrows above the door. It was an amazing display, David thought, enough to rival any museum's collection.

As quietly as he could, he followed Ascanio, who knew the chateau well, out into a vast entry hall with a grand escalier. The marble stairs swept upward like a pair of angel's wings, and Ascanio, like David dressed all in black, moved stealthily up the right-hand side.

But they had gone only a few steps, shielded by the balustrade, when they suddenly heard footsteps on the floor above, and the clicking of a woman's heels. If she chose to come down their side of the steps, there'd be nothing they could do to avoid exposure. Hunching down low, they waited, until they heard her call out, "Monsieur Rigaud? *Où êtes-vous?*"

But thankfully she did not start down the steps. Instead, a voice answered her from somewhere on the same floor.

"*Je suis ici,* Madame Linz." A man was approaching her.

David wished that he could simply melt away into the marble stairs he was flattened against.

"That business in Paris then?" the woman was saying. "It's all taken care of?"

"Yes, I took care of it myself," he said, though David thought he detected the slightest lack of conviction in his tone.

"You're sure?" she said.

So she'd noticed it, too.

"Quite, Madame. I have already given a full account to Monsieur Linz."

Through the balustrade, David could just catch a glimpse of this man Rigaud, with close-cropped hair, dyed an unnatural shade of blond, and an erect, military bearing.

She scoffed. "You can tell *him* whatever you want. But you had better not ever lie to me." She took a step away, and David saw that she was young and pretty. "You've made the rounds?"

"I have."

"It's been a long day, and Auguste's stomach is bothering him again. We are going to bed."

"I hope he feels better in the morning."

"Leave a note for the cook, will you? He'd like cream of wheat for breakfast."

"I'll let her know."

"Good night then," she said, the sound of her heels clicking away.

"Sleep well, Madame," he replied, before returning to wherever he'd been.

David realized that he had not taken a breath the whole time. He took one now, and after a few seconds, Ascanio gestured toward the top of the stairs. There, they saw light spilling from a doorway at the far end of the hall, and Ascanio quickly led David in the other direction and up another staircase.

This floor was as gloomy as the rest. Wall sconces, with dim bulbs, provided the only light, and there were cords and wires running along the baseboards of the hallways and salons they moved through. It was as if the place hadn't been renovated in sixty years. But everywhere David looked, he caught glimpses of old oil paintings hanging forlornly over velvet sofas, and antique sculptures tucked into forgotten corners. It was a total hodgepodge—in one room alone, he saw what appeared to be an Italian fresco, a Ming vase, a Dürer etching, and a framed Egyptian papyrus. Who was this Auguste Linz?

Again, they rose, checking every room but encountering no one else. Ascanio, crooking one finger, led David into a salon, where he closed the door quietly behind him. Only then did he take out his flashlight and shine it around the room. At first, David didn't understand what he was seeing—images were repeated, fractured, distorted—but then he saw that the salon had five sides, and they were all mirrored. An unlighted crystal chandelier hung directly above an ornate desk covered with papers and books and a bronze bust of the composer Richard Wagner. Ascanio stopped to train the flashlight beam on the blotter, where a notebook was open. In it, Linz had been scrawling something in a crabbed hand, in German, but so forcefully that the pen had indented every letter.

"This was once the marquis's private study," Ascanio whispered, taking a few seconds to absorb the room, as if for the first and the last time, but David's attention was riveted on the notebook. Though his command of German was poor, and the handwriting hard to decipher, one thing jumped out at him as if it were in letters a foot high.

It was his own name.

"No," David urged, as Ascanio started to move the flashlight beam away. "Look!"

He pointed to his name, and from what little he could read at a glance, he saw something about a search—*die Suche*—and an *Italienisch Mädchen*, no doubt referring to Olivia.

"We don't have time!" Ascanio said. "Come on!"

But David wasn't about to leave this behind. He slipped the journal into his backpack before turning to see Ascanio probing the edges of one of the floor-length mirrors with his fingertips.

❦

Rigaud was almost done with his exercises, and admiring his own bulging biceps—he could not understand how other men his age could let themselves get so badly out of shape—when Ali offered him the hash pipe again.

"If you want to relax," Ali said, lying on the bed in nothing but an unbuttoned pair of jeans, "this will do a better job than that." The pale scar on his throat looked whiter in the lamplight.

Rigaud did two more reps with the barbells before placing them back on the rubber mat in the corner of the room. Straightening up, he put his hands to the small of his back, where the T-shirt was stuck to his body, and wearily exhaled.

Ali took a hit off the pipe, then through clenched teeth said, "You still look pissed."

"She talks to me like I'm some gaddamned butler," Rigaud said, sitting down beside him on the bed. "She forgets I was a captain in the French army."

He took the pipe, held a lighted match to the bowl, and inhaled deeply.

"Screw her," Ali said, putting a consoling hand on his arm. "You don't work for Ava. You work for her husband."

Rigaud nodded, knowing he was right. But it was still hard to take. He had accepted this job because it felt like a cause, a mission, but over the years he had begun to have his doubts. What was he really doing? Whatever powers he once thought had been at Linz's command, they seemed to have deserted him. He was a frustrated, impotent man—in every sense, if Rigaud could judge from Ava's mood—and the tasks he set for Rigaud were increasingly redundant and defensive. Rigaud longed to go on the offensive for a change; but every time he even suggested as much to Linz, however obliquely, the man flew off the handle and went into one of his foaming, arm-waving, apoplectic fits. If he didn't know better, Rigaud might have thought he was going to keel over on the spot.

Ali was rubbing his shoulders, and Rigaud took another long drag on the pipe. He kept his windows open to let out the smoke and the aroma. Linz, he knew, would not approve. But the master suite was far off, at the top of the eastern turret. And good God, why was someone of his age, and former rank, having to worry about such stuff? "Lie back," Ali was saying. "I'll give you a massage."

"I still have work to do."

"So do I," Ali said, rising up on his knees and kneading the kinks in his back.

Putting the hash pipe on the bedside table and pulling off his sweaty T-shirt, Rigaud rolled over onto the bed. The hash was very pure, and all the trials of the recent days—most notably dispatching Julius Jantzen—began to recede. It was highly annoying that a man like Ernst Escher was still running loose, but the Turks would eventually track him down again. They weren't good for much—and Rigaud had often argued with Linz to replace them with a more professional bunch—but Linz liked them for their single-mindedness and overall lack of curiosity. Even Rigaud appreciated their unslakable taste for revenge.

Ali's fingers were working their magic on the knots in his back and shoulders and Rigaud allowed himself to drift away. Soft music was playing, that Eastern stuff that Ali liked, but right then it sounded good even to Rigaud. He remembered that he had to tell the cook, who arrived with the other servants at six in morning; that Linz wanted cream of wheat for breakfast. But then, just as promptly, he forgot all about it.

Chapter 39

Ascanio pressed the gilded border of one of the mirrors, and it opened out to reveal a spiral staircase that rose toward the top of the turret. Then, raising one finger to urge absolute silence, he slipped onto the staircase, with David right behind. The steps wound upwards for twenty or thirty feet before coming to an end behind what looked like a heavy flap of cloth. It was only on closer inspection in the flashlight beam that David could tell, from the complex threadwork, that what they were standing behind was an immense, hanging tapestry.

Ascanio flicked off his light, and ever so gingerly pushed an edge of the cloth to one side. Over his shoulder, David could see that they were in a kind of anteroom, with a reading chair and a marquetry table holding crystal decanters and a brass lamp. A master bedroom was just beyond it. He could hear classical music playing, a shower running, and voices.

Linz and his wife.

"Ava, bring me the pills."

"How many of these are you going to take?"

"Just bring them."

David saw Ava—completely nude—saunter out of the bathroom with her palm open.

All he could see of Linz were his legs, in a pair of black silk pajamas and scuff slippers on his white ankles.

"Put something on," he scolded, "for decency's sake."

"I was just about to take a shower. The water's finally hot."

He took the pills, and she strolled back out of sight with an athlete's casual grace. David heard the bathroom door slam shut.

Ascanio crossed himself, then put his backpack on the floor and opened it. Then he withdrew the silver garland.

David had witnessed its powers only hours before, in the privacy of Sant'Angelo's home. And as much as anything else he had seen, or been told, that demonstration had convinced him of the marquis's claims. If he had had even a scintilla of doubt, watching the marquis disappear before his very eyes had erased it.

Fixing his eyes on David, Ascanio settled it squarely on his own head.

And within seconds, he had vanished.

The flap of the tapestry lifted, then fell back, as Ascanio slipped out from behind it. David wiped a vagrant spiderweb from his glasses and stared intently . . . but what was there to see?

Linz's slippers were twitching in time to the music. But suddenly, as if he had heard something no one else could, or sensed some menace no one else could have detected, his slippers stopped. He sat bolt upright on the bed, rolled to one side, and fumbled in the drawer of the bedside table. In an instant, he had drawn out a gun and fired it into thin air.

There was a cry—it was Ascanio!—and a billow of blood exploded like a balloon in the empty air. Linz shot again, and the second bullet ripped through the tapestry and lodged in the wall above David's head.

A moment later David saw Linz suddenly topple backwards off the bed, as if he'd been hit by a freight train. David rushed out, only to see Linz, in a red robe, wrestling on the floor with his unseen assailant.

But that was when he also saw, swinging against Linz's bare chest on a silver chain, *La Medusa*.

His hand was still clutching the gun, but it was being banged repeatedly against the bedstead, and blood from an invisible source was spurting onto the carpet. Linz was struggling to hold on to the pistol, and when he swung the arm free, David saw the butt of the gun plainly collide with something solid. A second later the garland rolled free, spinning on the floor like a plate.

"It's around his neck!" Ascanio cried to David, as he shimmered back into view. "Get it!"

But the muzzle of the gun was pointing right at him, and David ducked just as the next shot blasted the ceiling light, raining shards of glass. He was grappling for it when he heard a hellish scream and wet feet squishing across the floor. A naked body, lithe and strong, leapt on top of his back, the legs wrapping themselves around his waist, the arms folded across his throat, choking him.

David staggered back, catching a glimpse of himself in the bureau mirror—with Ava's snarling face, teeth bared, over his shoulder—as he tried to shake her loose. But her grip was too tight, and he was stumbling backwards, barely able to stay on his feet at all. His glasses hanging from one ear, he crashed up against a heavy armoire. He heard her grunt, the wind knocked out of her, and he threw his head back, catching her chin. He ran a few steps away from the wardrobe, then rushed backwards, slamming her against the cabinet again.

"Bastard!" she gasped through bloodstained teeth, but still managing to hang on like a Harpy.

With what breath he had left, David reached behind his head, trying to grab her hair and pull her off his back; but she bit at his fingers and hands. He whirled around and threw himself, as if he were on fire, backwards onto the floor. Her arms loosened their grip, he took a breath, then rammed an elbow back into her face. He felt her nose shatter, and her whole body went limp.

Shaking free, he crawled to his feet, only to be bowled over again by Linz as he ran from the room, the tails of his red robe flying.

"Go after him!" Ascanio said, collapsing against the bedpost and holding out the sword. "I'll never catch him!" His pants were torn, and blood was coursing down from a bullet wound in his leg.

David staggered up, hooking his glasses back on, as Ascanio pressed the *harpe* into his hand. "Now you know who he is!" he shouted, staring deeply into David's eyes. "Don't you?"

But David, reeling, simply nodded in confusion. His mind could not process something so enormous . . . and so terrible.

There was a crash from the anteroom as the table and lamp toppled over.

"We should have told you! But it's up to you now, to finish the bastard, once and for all!"

David felt his fingers gripping the handle of the sword as if they belonged to someone else entirely.

"Go!"

David turned and ran toward the anteroom door—it had been flung open and the carpet runner in the hallway was rumpled from Linz's headlong flight. David could hear his feet tearing around a corner toward the staircase.

He took off after him, vaulting down the stairs three at a time, then through a suite of dark, cluttered rooms, where the curtains rippled from Linz's flight and furniture had been overturned to block his pursuit.

Linz was heading, David now knew, for the grand escalier, and bloody footprints on the marble floors confirmed it.

As did his rasping cry from below—"Rigaud! For Christ's sake, Rigaud!"

But when David ran past the hall where Rigaud had last been seen, his door was firmly shut and there was no light emanating from under it.

At the top of the staircase, David caught a glimpse of Linz's black slippers, racing around the bottom of the stairs and off toward the armor hall. He was still trying to call out, but his voice was hoarse and barely carried.

David lunged down the stairs, nearly losing his balance on a smear of wet blood, before skidding into the entry hall and pivoting.

He couldn't see Linz anymore, but he knew which way he'd gone, and he ran after him, the short sword still clutched in his hand, as something long and sharp suddenly grazed his shoulder and thwanged into the wooden frame of the door.

Linz was standing halfway down the hall, doubled over from throwing the spear, huffing and puffing with his hands on his knees. But his face was contorted with rage, his eyes bulging, and his thatch of brown hair, shorn close on the sides, sweeping low over his forehead. His left arm was shaking, as if from a palsy, and David had the ghastly impression that he had indeed seen this face before.

And Ascanio had said: *You know who he is, don't you?*

Linz cursed and whirled around, grabbing a battle-axe and shield from the wall. His robe flapping open, and the Medusa swinging on its chain, he was done with running and advanced on David.

"Sie denken, sie können mich toten?"—You think you can kill me?— he challenged, as David deftly dodged the first swing of the axe. David backed up, and the next swing crashed into a suit of armor, knocking it off its pedestal and sending the pieces careening across the floor.

David tried to parry with the short sword, but Linz banged it aside with a shove from the shield. By the moonlight pouring in from the windows, David could see the fury in his eyes, and the manic gleam . . . of pleasure.

"Niemand kann mich töten!"—No one can kill me!—he exulted.

Linz rushed at him, the shield raised, trying to knock him off his feet, but David dodged the attack and the axe crashed into another suit of armor.

The man was breathing hard, the weapon was heavy, and David stepped back as Linz turned again, like a maddened bull, searching for his enemy.

"Ich will tausend Jahre leben!" he exploded—I will live a thousand years!—and the very marrow in David's bones froze.

It was the voice he had heard in newsreels, scratchy and amplified and bursting with hate. It was the face, with its blazing eyes and chin raised in defiance, that had inflamed a nation and engulfed the world in war. The madman who had conjured up the fires of the Holocaust.

In that instant, David understood just what creature had managed to slink from its bunker in Berlin to claim the gift of immortality. And why, for fear that his courage might fail him, or his belief might falter, he had not been told.

But now he knew, and he felt as if an electric current had suddenly coursed through his veins, down his arm, and into the very blade he held. When the monster charged again, his hatchet raised, David nimbly stepped to one side, and before the man could turn he swung the razor-sharp edge of the sword into the back of his neck.

The monster crumpled, a geyser of blood erupting, but the chain of the Medusa had kept the sword from cutting clean through.

Finish it, David heard in his head. *You have to finish it.*

Pulling the sword free with one hand, and yanking the head back with his other—even now, the eyes were boiling with rage and hot spittle was flying from the lips—he chopped again. But the head still clung to the body.

Finish it.

Clutching the head by a thatch of its blood-slick hair, he hewed at the stump as if it were an unyielding branch. And though he wielded the sword, it felt as if the blade was acting on its own, hungry to complete some ancient labor. Another blow, and the body at last collapsed in a heap.

David felt as if time had stopped. All he could hear was the pounding of his own heart, booming like a bass drum. His breath burned in his throat. His gory prize—mouth open, eyes agog—dangled by its hair from his hand. Gradually, he came back to himself, like a man emerging from a trance. The sword clattered to the floor. And then the head dropped, too.

Stooping, he retrieved from the expanding pool of blood the thing he had come so far to find. Looping the Medusa around his neck, he stood up again, like Perseus astride the slaughtered Gorgon, and went to rescue his companion—and tell him it was indeed finished.

Chapter 40

Once she was sure that the car had been swallowed up for good, Olivia had stumbled, soaking wet and missing one shoe, up the muddy bank. But she knew that if she didn't find some dry clothes or some cover fast, she'd freeze to death while waiting for David and Ascanio to come back.

She didn't even allow herself to think that they might not return.

She made her way across the cold, hard ground to the cement dock, then back to the spot where the Maserati had been parked. Unless her attacker had followed them on foot, he must have left a car hidden somewhere nearby. But the woods were dark, and it was slow going over the rough, uneven terrain. Her blouse and pants were still dripping, and her one shoe kept her off-kilter. She followed the trail as well as she could, taking advantage of every spot of moonlight to plot her course, and eventually she spotted the back bumper of a car hidden among the trees close to the road. She started to run toward it before realizing that there might be an accomplice inside.

Wiping the wet hair back from her eyes, she inched forward, keeping among the foliage, until she was close enough to see that it was a little, beige Peugeot, with no one in it. It was pointed out toward the road, just as she had done with the Maserati. Everybody, she surmised, had been preparing for a quick getaway.

Now if only it was unlocked.

And it was, with the key still sitting in the ignition. She turned it on and started the heat going at full blast. Then she surveyed the interior, which looked as if somebody had been living in it. Cigarette butts crammed the ashtrays, cardboard coffee cups littered the floor, and clothes were spilling out of an open duffel bag on the backseat. She quickly rummaged around in it and found a heavy fisherman's knit sweater. Peeling off her wet blouse, she pulled it on over her head, then a pair of woolly white socks that came halfway up her shins. The heat was going strong and she had stopped her shivering altogether.

But her curiosity was greater than ever. Who was this man who had been so relentlessly tracking them? She popped open the glove compartment for the car registration papers and found instead a brochure from the rental agency, with his completed application inside.

"Escher," she read, "Ernst Escher." The name meant nothing to her, and though he'd paid with a credit card from a Swiss bank, he listed his address as a post-office box in the States. Chicago, in fact—where David, of course, was from.

Had he been following David's trail all the way from America? On his own? Or at someone else's behest?

On the passenger seat, there was another rucksack, which she quickly unbuckled. This one looked like a doctor's bag inside, stuffed with prescription pills and bottles, along with a BlackBerry and a burgundy Austrian passport, with its distinctive gold coat of arms.

She flipped the dog-eared passport open. The pages bore dozens of stamps, for every place from Liechtenstein to Dubai, but the picture in front was of a weaselly-looking little man named Julius Jantzen. The same man who had drugged their drinks. He was thirty-eight years old, five-foot-six, unmarried, and although his current address was Florence, Italy, his birthplace was listed as Linz, Austria.

Hitler's hometown, she thought.

She wondered if this Jantzen character wasn't still out there in the woods somewhere. She tossed the passport back into the bag, steering the Peugeot out of the trees and back toward the dock. She parked it out of sight again, with the motor off and the lights out.

And was surprised to find that her hands and feet were becoming numb. Inside her, despite the warm interior of the car, she felt a cold and hollow spot growing. She was going into shock, she dimly recognized. While she'd been fighting for her life and struggling to find safety, she had been operating on sheer survival instinct and adrenaline. But now, now that she was temporarily—and provisionally—safe, now that she was warm and dry and no gun was grazing her cheek, her heart was still racing, her breath was coming in short, shallow bursts, and her mind was grappling with the trauma she had just undergone.

She had escaped dying by the skin of her teeth.

And she had killed a man in the process. Not a good man, not some innocent, but a man, nonetheless.

She had killed him—and nearly died herself.

Her thoughts were flying back and forth between those two poles, like a shuttlecock, and the cold spot in her gut was only getting colder. She had a whole pharmacy in the bag beside her, but she had no idea what to take. She began searching the glove compartment, the storage slots in the doors, and under the driver's seat, where she finally found what she was looking for. It was an old, dented flask, but she unscrewed the top and took a whiff of what smelled like good Irish whiskey. She took a gulp, then another, and felt the warmth of the alcohol blooming like a rose inside her. She closed her eyes for a second, willing herself to breathe more slowly, and let the feeling diffuse. An owl hooted in the trees, reminding her of her own Glaucus back home. Her cluttered little apartment in Florence had never seemed so appealing.

And then, glancing at her ashen face in the rearview mirror, she shook her head, as if to physically dismiss all the fears from her mind, and pinched her own cheeks, hard. She could not afford the luxury of a breakdown at that moment. Not while David and Ascanio were still out there. Not while the job was still undone. She knew David. She knew he would not give up. His sister's life was at stake, and even in the short time they had been together, she had seen what a fierce and unbreakable bond that was. She took another sip of the whiskey, and even though she was not a religious woman—for her, churches were places to tour, not worship—she found herself praying all the same. Not to Jesus or Mother Mary. But to the miraculous powers of the universe, the benign and unseen forces in which she *did* believe. Olivia's mind had always been open, and as she stared into the darkness of the trees, she prayed, with a fervency she had never felt before, that she would see David emerge again, safe and unscathed. It would not be fair, she thought, for something so wonderful, something that she had waited so long for, to come to such an abrupt and awful end. A wave of indignation came over her—not an uncustomary sensation for someone of her temperament—and it felt good. She felt like she was coming back to herself. Indignation, in her opinion, was very underrated.

Chapter 41

In the bedroom at the top of the turret, David found Ascanio tying a tourniquet around his leg to stop the bleeding; he had snapped a leg off a chair and made a rough splint to hold the broken bone straight.

On the bed, David saw the shape of a body, wrapped tightly in a blood-soaked sheet.

Ascanio's eyes went straight to the Medusa hanging from David's neck.

"*Bene,*" he said, nodding his approval. He glanced at the bloody sword that David had returned to his belt. "You finished it?"

"Yes."

"He's dead?"

"Yes."

Ascanio gave him a long look, wanting to be sure.

"You should have told me . . . everything . . . before we came."

Ascanio nodded, as if in agreement. "We did not think it would be necessary. It could have been too much to hold in your mind."

"Never underestimate me again," David said.

"I won't," Ascanio replied. "You can be sure of that." Tucking the garland into the backpack, he threw an arm around David's shoulder for support, and said, "Now let's get out of this damn place." Limping alongside him, they descended from the tower, all the while keeping an eye out for Rigaud.

As they passed through the armor hall, Ascanio stopped above the decapitated body of Linz, which lay in a sticky pool of coagulating blood. The tails of the robe were spread out like a bat's wings. "Heil, Hitler," he muttered, kicking the axe away.

Then, before stepping around it, he asked David, "But what did you do with the head?"

"I let it fall," David said.

"Where?" Ascanio said.

"Right here," David said. But it wasn't there now. Ducking to look under the refectory table, he didn't see it there, either.

Which meant that someone—Rigaud?—must have removed it.

"Come on," David said, looping a strong arm around Ascanio's waist and helping him to hop from the room. From the grimace on Ascanio's face, David could tell that each step was excruciating, but he knew that there wasn't a second to waste.

Once they'd made it to the kitchen, Ascanio plopped onto a chair, sweat dripping from his brow.

"We have to keep going!" David said. "We can't rest yet!"

Waving at the stove, Ascanio said, "Quick, turn on all the burners."

"What?" David said. "Why?"

"Just do it, David!"

And he did.

"Now, blow out the pilot lights."

David blew them out . . . and suddenly understood. It was another little detail that Ascanio had not shared with him.

Ascanio struggled to his feet, wincing with pain, and threw his arm around David's shoulders again. The sweet, subtle smell of gas had already begun to permeate the room.

They hobbled down the stone steps to the old scullery, past the dusty wine racks, and into the hidden escape route carved by the Norman knight. It was too narrow there to walk side by side, so David had to let Ascanio support himself by leaning against the walls. David took out his flashlight to show the way while glancing over his shoulder for any sign of Rigaud.

The pungent aroma of the gasoline they had poured on their way in wafted up from the floor. When they had reached the oubliette, its scent was joined by the dank river water sloshing at the bottom of the shaft.

They were only yards from the side tunnel leading down to the Loire when David heard noises coming from the scullery. He flicked off his flashlight and urged Ascanio to hurry.

"Someone's coming!" he whispered.

Ascanio pressed on, dragging his splinted leg, while David crouched low right behind him, staring back over his shoulder into the darkness.

He heard the sound of racks being shoved aside, wine bottles smashing, and boots crunching across the broken glass.

And then he saw the pinpoint white light of a flashlight beam, searching high and low.

They were far enough away that it had not reached them, but it was coming closer all the time.

"Who's in there?" a voice called out. Rigaud's. "Stop where you are!"

The tip of David's sword suddenly scraped against the stone wall.

"Stop now, or I'll shoot!"

"It's here," Ascanio murmured, ducking through the hole in the wall.

"I said, Stop!"

The flashlight beam danced toward them, like a firefly, and in the reflections off the wall and ceiling, David saw Rigaud, holding something in the crook of his arm and running toward them.

Ascanio's arm suddenly extended out through the hole, holding a pack of wooden matches. "Light the pack and throw it!"

David dropped his flashlight, and grabbed the matchbook. But the gasoline trail was several feet behind him now, and he had to creep toward Rigaud, all the while trying to strike a match in the dark. The first one broke in two, the second one was too damp.

Rigaud had undoubtedly heard him by then, and his flashlight swung directly onto David's face as the third match caught fire and David touched it to the gasoline on the floor. A ribbon of blue flame shot down the tunnel, and in its light he saw Rigaud drop his flashlight and fumble for his gun.

But what David truly remembered, just seconds before the blast nearly threw him through the hole, was the severed head Rigaud was cradling beneath his arm. David could have sworn that the mouth was twisted in a silent scream and the steely blue eyes were furious . . . and alive.

A fireball had hurtled down the length of the tunnel, then out of sight around the corner, where it collided with the cloud of gas in the kitchen, sending an earthshaking explosion up through the very rafters of the chateau. David and Ascanio, scuttling down the chimney to the river, feared the cliff itself would collapse around them. Dirt and dust filled the air, choking them, and the steps quivered under their stumbling feet.

At the bottom, they crawled out, coughing and sputtering, onto the rocks and mud of the riverbank. David, after catching a breath, turned to look up at the promontory. Bright orange flames were licking up at the sky, as fire burst like streamers from the windows, and the towers, one by one, crumbled and fell.

A burning timber caromed off the cliff top and, turning end over end, splashed with a boiling hiss into the Loire.

"Let's get out of range!" David said, helping Ascanio up and back toward the old loading dock.

They climbed along the bank, then into the woods, but just where David hoped to see the Maserati, he saw nothing. For a second, he thought he'd lost his bearings, but then a pair of headlights flashed on from the neighboring trees, and he heard a car door fling open.

"David!"

Olivia was running full tilt, in a bulky sweater and a pair of white socks, with her arms out.

"Help me," he said, and Olivia threw a supporting arm around Ascanio's waist. Together, they deposited him, as gently as they could, in the cramped backseat of the Peugeot.

And then they held each other close, rocking silently in the moonlight. In the distance, David could hear the crackling of the flames, punctuated by the crash of timbers and stone.

"So you got it," she said, touching *La Medusa* as tenderly as one would touch the crown of a baby's head.

"Yes," David replied, holding her more tightly. "Now I have everything."

"Can we get the hell out of here?" Ascanio growled. "It's a long way back to Paris."

Olivia slipped behind the wheel and, after taking another gander at the splint, handed the bag of drugs to Ascanio. "I'm sure you'll find some painkillers in there. I'll find the closest hospital."

"No!" he objected. "I told you, we're going straight back. I'm not having some hick doctor meddle with my leg."

As she pulled the car back onto the trail, she glanced over at David to see what he thought, but he appeared to agree with their passenger. "Paris," he said, resolutely. "As fast as we can get there."

"But I'll still need to know something," Ascanio said, popping open a vial of pills and hastily swallowing several of them dry. "If you traded the Maserati for this piece of shit, you will please have to tell me why."

Part Five

Chapter 42

Olivia drove the little Peugeot straight into the hospital emergency entrance, and David had hoisted Ascanio halfway out of the backseat before he protested and grabbed for the Medusa hanging under David's shirt.

"That belongs to Sant'Angelo!" he said, his words slurred by the Percocets he'd taken. "Give it to me!"

But David pulled back and let the emergency workers running out of the hospital strap Ascanio to a gurney and wheel him inside. It was clear he had lost a lot of blood, and the makeshift tourniquet was all but falling off. One of the doctors was asking David a battery of questions about what had happened and who the man was, when David—pleading that he spoke no French—bolted back to the car and told Olivia to gun it.

"Wait!" the doctor shouted, running down the drive as the Peugeot pulled away. "You can't do this!"

But David watched the hospital recede in the rearview mirror, as Olivia headed back into the Paris traffic. Even she looked uncertain about what to do next.

"The airport," he said.

"You don't want to call the marquis? There's quite a lot you should tell him, no?" While Ascanio, knocked out by the drugs, had snored in the backseat, David had filled her in during the long drive from the

Loire Valley, and it was a miracle that she had been able to keep control of the car the whole way. He could think of no one else in the world who would have been able to do the same.

"Maybe the marquis could help?" she added.

"No," David said. "Just drive."

Using the BlackBerry from the doctor's bag, he hastily dialed Gary's number in Chicago.

"It's me," he said, the second Gary picked up. "How is she?"

"Hanging on. Where the hell are you?"

"On the way to Orly Airport." He had not wanted to have this discussion with Ascanio in the car—snoring or not.

"You're not on a plane yet?" Gary said, sounding downright angry.

"I'll explain later. I'm coming as fast as I can."

He heard Gary blow out a breath in disgust. "Maybe I didn't make it clear enough, David. There's not much time. Emme was here all afternoon, and for all I know, that'll be the last time she ever gets to see her mom. Sarah's waiting for you, David. She's *been* waiting for you. But there's only so much she can do."

"I know," David said, his fingers automatically feeling for the *Medusa*. "I know."

"Christ," Gary said, "no promotion is that important."

That hurt, but David knew where it was coming from. Gary didn't understand the delay—how could he? And what could David have ever said that would have persuaded him? "Please, just tell her I'm coming. I'm coming!"

When he hung up and the car had to stop at a traffic light, he felt Olivia's eyes on him.

"You don't trust Sant'Angelo?" she asked.

And David admitted, "No, not completely." He turned to look at her. "He thinks the mirror is his."

"It is, isn't it?"

"But he's not the one who sent me to find it. And he's not the one who promised to save my sister's life with it."

"What if he said he would let you?"

"What if he said he wouldn't?" he replied. "Can I take that chance? Now?"

The light changed, and Olivia took off again. David set his jaw and tried to gather his thoughts. Everything had been moving so fast, and there was no letup in sight. But in his gut he knew that returning to the marquis's town house could cause anything from a fatal delay to the loss of the *Medusa* altogether. No matter what he did, he would be forced to betray someone—Mrs. Van Owen or the Marquis di Sant'Angelo. He'd had to make a choice, and with Sarah's life hanging in the balance, he'd done the only thing he could possibly do.

Now he just prayed that the instructions in *The Key to Life Eternal* would work. He knew every word of the text by heart—he had read them a hundred times—but putting them into effect would be another matter altogether.

As they neared the airport, the traffic slowed. Buses and taxis vied for space with thousands of cars, and the lanes were narrowed for random security checks.

"Try Air France," David said, thinking it would probably be his best bet. If not, he could always run to another terminal.

Olivia jockeyed the car to the curb, cutting off a rental van with only inches to spare, and abruptly stopped.

They turned to each other and she said, "You're going to make it, David. I can feel it."

David wished he felt the same way. Reaching out to her, he held her close, kissed her, and said, "Stay safe. I will come back as soon as I can."

A cop waved his baton, urging them to move along.

"I love you," he said.

She smiled, kissed him back—her warm lips lingering for just a second—before pushing him toward the door. "Tell me that in Firenze."

And then, with his backpack slung loosely over one shoulder, he ran into the Air France terminal. With no luggage to weigh him down, he headed straight for the first-class ticketing section and asked when the next nonstop flight to Chicago would be.

"Flight 400 is leaving in thirty-five minutes," the clerk said, as David slapped his passport and credit card down on the counter.

"One ticket," he said, "one way."

"But I'm afraid," she said, consulting her computer screen, "it's full."

"I'll take anything. Coach, the cargo hold, you name it."

She smiled nicely, but he could tell he had already made her nervous. And why wouldn't he? There were scratches all over his face, he was dressed entirely in black, he hadn't shaved, he was buying a one-way ticket. For all he knew, she'd already pressed the security button hidden beneath the counter.

"Listen," he said, in the most reasonable tone he could muster, "my sister is very ill, and I have to get home. Can you help me?"

"Our next flight to Chicago," she replied, her fingers clicking over the keyboard, "doesn't leave until this evening, but if you wanted to fly to Boston, and connect there with . . ."

But by then David had already decided what to do, and taking back his passport and card, he loped down the corridor, studying the Departures list for Flight 400. It was already boarding at Gate 23. Dodging around the other travelers, he headed for the gate, but saw a long line of people already waiting to go through the security check-in.

And behind him, out of the corner of his eye, he spotted a blue-uniformed cop in a white kepi following briskly in his wake. Another one was hustling to catch up.

He ducked into a coffee bar, then out again on the other side, and into the first men's room he saw. He went to the last stall on the end, latched the door, and rooted around in his bag, pushing aside Auguste Linz's journal and pulling out the silver garland. Quickly buckling the bag again, he slipped it back onto his shoulders.

Then, with a silent prayer, he settled the garland on his brow.

He waited, stock-still, but felt nothing. My God, he thought, had he done something wrong? It wasn't working. Had Sant'Angelo and Ascanio deliberately failed to tell him something? And what if he got all the way to Chicago and found out that he was missing some crucial step with *La Medusa,* too?

But then, just as the panic was rising, he noticed something strange—a sensation like cool water being poured over the top of his head. He actually touched his hair, thinking it would feel wet, but it didn't. It felt just the same. But the sensation continued, and it had descended to his face and neck, then his shoulders and chest. He kept patting himself, but his body was completely and palpably there.

And then he saw something strange. Reflected in the back of the steel door, he saw his own murky image—only his upper body was no longer part of it. As he watched in shock, the rest of him, too, began to vanish. He slapped at his thighs, feeling a surge of terror, but his thighs felt the blow, and his hands felt the flesh. Still, staring in amazement at the back of the door, he could see that his legs were also invisible.

And when he looked down at his feet, he watched as they, too, boots and all, disappeared. He stamped them on the floor—he felt the hard tiles, he heard the thump—but he couldn't see anything there.

Nothing at all was reflected now, however blurrily, in the back of the stall door.

He could twitch every finger, curl every toe—they felt just the same as always—but he also felt weightless, the way he imagined an astronaut might feel in zero gravity. He reached out to touch the latch on the door and found it oddly difficult to do. Without being able to see his own limbs and watch where they were in space, he discovered that it was very hard to coordinate his movements. Even something as simple as unlatching the door took a concentrated effort, and he suddenly understood why Ascanio had resisted wearing the garland until the last moments of their mission. It was too easy to make a fatal blunder.

He had just stepped out of the stall when the two cops burst into the men's room, and he froze in place. It was a long, narrow space and they moved quickly to check for feet under the stalls. Several were occupied, and the men at the sinks, seeing that something was up, made hasty departures.

With the end of his baton, one of the cops knocked on the closed doors and said, *"Ouvrez la porte, s'il vous plaît. C'est la police."* The other, unfortunately, had moved to block the exit.

David stood, not four feet from the cop with the baton, holding his breath, as toilets flushed and the doors, one after another, obediently opened. Looking into the wall-length mirror, he saw the cop, he saw the row of stalls, but not a sign of himself. It was positively unnerving.

The cop glanced in each compartment, looking increasingly perturbed, before turning to his companion and saying, *"Où est-il allé?"* He threw up his hands in confusion. As the other cop came over to see for himself, David slipped out the exit.

Zigzagging among the crowd, who occasionally reacted to his proximity with a sudden flinch or quizzical turn, he ran straight to the security check, where the line was even longer than it had been. But between the *Medusa* still hanging under his shirt and the garland and flashlight still in his backpack, he doubted he would ever be able to go unnoticed through the metal detectors. He scanned the people at the front of the line, and one of them was a teenager with his ankle in a cast and aluminum crutches under each arm. David slunk in right behind him, and when, predictably, the alarms went off, David scooted around one side of him and took off down the corridor.

Gate 23 was off on his left, but he could already see a flight attendant bundling up the tickets she'd collected, while the other was kicking loose the doorstop to the boarding ramp. He scooted past them—they both raised their heads at the errant breeze—and was halfway to the hatchway when he saw that that, too, was being closed.

"Hold it!" he shouted without thinking, and the steward stopped, looking all around to see where that voice might have come from, but it provided just enough of a delay for David to breeze onto the plane. The hatchway was pulled shut, and David breathed his first sigh of relief.

Looking into both cabins of the plane, however, he could see that the ticketing clerk had been right. Not a single seat was empty.

But then, how could he have sat in one, anyway, without somehow giving his presence away? All it took was someone hearing him breathe, or tripping over his invisible legs on the way to the bathroom. He couldn't even hide out in one of the stalls without eventually drawing attention to the *Occupé* sign that never went out.

The plane taxied away from the gate, and then, to David's anguish, lingered on the ground for what seemed an interminable time. He glanced at his watch, before remembering that he couldn't see its face anymore. Several times, the pilot came on to apologize, and to explain that a storm front moving east had slowed down all traffic heading west. But David heard a lot of unhappy muttering among the passengers and crew before, having idled on the ground for at least an hour or two, the plane finally took off.

Once it had settled into its cruising altitude, he found as much of a sanctuary as he could—a corner of the little space between the front and back cabins, under the porthole window of an emergency exit. If he scrunched down with his knees drawn up tight, and his back against the vibrating wall, and stayed aware of any steward who occasionally came through to retrieve something from one of the storage bins, he just might be able to make it all the way unnoticed. He'd be stiff as a board when he arrived, but he'd get there.

The flight time, he knew, had been posted as nine hours. But he wondered, given the weather conditions, how much time it would really take.

There was no way he could call Sarah or Gary to see where things stood . . . but he knew that Sarah had said she would wait for him, and they had never let each other down yet. *Wait for me*, he muttered under his breath, *wait for me.*

Chapter 43

When the Marquis di Sant'Angelo burst into the hospital room, trailed by a nurse pulling on his sleeve, Ascanio was just awakening from the anesthesia.

"You are all right?" the marquis said, leaning over his bedside. He had certainly seen him looking better, but he had also seen him looking worse.

"Monsieur," the nurse was complaining, "these are not visiting hours, and the patient is still in recovery. You may come back when —"

But Sant'Angelo brushed her aside and clutched his dear friend's hand. One leg was in a formidable cast, but all in all, Ascanio looked as if he would come through the ordeal intact.

"I'll be fine," Ascanio said, groggily, as he squeezed the marquis's hand to reassure him. "But a fine pair we'll make," he added, gesturing at the marquis's ebony walking stick. "A couple of gimps."

"Not for long," Sant'Angelo said. "The doctors tell me they got the bullet out fine, and you'll be walking perfectly well in a few months."

Ascanio nodded, and the nurse, after checking his blood pressure and offering him a sip of water through a straw, left the room, throwing one more murderous glance at the marquis.

Opening his fur-collared coat, Sant'Angelo drew a chair to the bedside, and said, "Tell me what happened."

"David didn't tell you already?"

"Franco? He told me nothing. He called, said you were here, and hung up before I could ask him a thing. I thought he would be here, in fact." A look crossed Ascanio's face that worried the marquis. "What did he *not* want me to know?" Sant'Angelo said.

Ascanio pointed a finger at the water, and the marquis held the straw to his lips again. And then, haltingly, Ascanio told the story of their assault on the chateau, of their final battle with Linz, and the ensuing fire and destruction. But when he was done, the marquis was still awaiting the one piece of information Ascanio had seemed to scrupulously elide. He only hoped it was an effect of the anesthesia.

"*La Medusa,*" he prompted, his eyes actually flitting about the room. "Where is *La Medusa*?"

Ascanio looked away, and Sant'Angelo pulled his chair so close to the bed it was scraping the rail.

"Where is *La Medusa*?" he said, his voice taking on an edge of steel. "And where, for that matter, is David Franco?" He hardly needed a map anymore to put the two missing pieces together.

And that was when Ascanio told him that David had made off with it. "I was in no condition to chase after him," Ascanio pleaded. "They dropped me at the hospital, and that girl drove them off like a bat out of Hell."

Hell, Sant'Angelo thought, was where he'd send them, if he didn't get back what belonged to him. Hadn't he told this Franco everything he needed to know? Hadn't he revealed to him secrets that he had told no other man? And this was how he was to be repaid?

"He's on his way home," Ascanio said. "To save that sister of his! I'm sure of it."

Sant'Angelo was sure of it, too. He had foreseen something like this happening. It was why he'd had one of his minions trace the call David had made from his home, and cross-check the name of hospice patients in that immediate vicinity. David's sister, he'd learned, was named Sarah Henderson, and she was in a place called Evanston, just outside Chicago. In spite of everything the marquis had done for him, it was clear to Sant'Angelo that David had more important priorities right now than returning his property to him. First, there was his sister. Not unexpected. And ultimately, there was his loyalty to the woman who had sent him on this mission to begin with.

Plainly, the librarian was not as innocent as he'd seemed. That, or he had had some iron injected into him by recent events. Either way, Sant'Angelo had to grudgingly admire the man's nerve.

But the time had come for the marquis to put aside all subterfuge. At long last, he had done away with his nemesis at the chateau—that black stain on the soul of the world—and now it was time for him to reclaim what was due him—*La Medusa,* and his long-lost love in the bargain.

"Tomorrow," Ascanio was saying. "I'll be able to go after him tomorrow!" He actually tried to rise in the bed, as if he could throw off the traction wires holding the leg in place and the IV line connected to his arm.

The marquis put a hand on his shoulder and pressed him back against the pillows.

"Rest," he said. "You've done well. I can take care of things now." And then, jabbing his cane at the floor as if he were impaling an enemy with each strike, he stalked out of the room, nearly knocking over the nurse, who had returned to chase him out.

Not two hours later, he was on his own private plane, taking off, in the teeth of an oncoming storm, for the United States. His pilot had begged him to reconsider, but when the marquis offered the flight crew a ten-thousand-euro bonus, all complaints ceased and a new flight plan was entered that would take them over Halifax and around the worst of the weather.

The marquis sat back in his plush leather seat, staring out the porthole window and wondering just how far behind this Franco he was. He understood why the man was in such a hurry, but the marquis had never intended for *La Medusa* to slip from his grasp again. Nor had he intended for it to be used, willy-nilly, by whoever found it. Only he, the marquis, and his faithful servant Ascanio, were to possess its powerful secret. Look whose vile hands it had fallen into for decades.

No, the marquis would not rest until it was back in his own safekeeping, and this time for good.

The plane hit a patch of turbulence, and the pilot came on to apologize. "Sorry, sir, but we may have to divert another hundred miles or so north."

To the marquis, it felt as if Nature itself were trying to thwart him.

But then, to calm himself, he remembered the way David's eyes had battened on the bust atop his mantel. Caterina, he was all but sure, lived on—and in the most unlikely place of all.

That the great, and only, true love of his own long life, could have been swimming beside him through the sea of time—and without his ever knowing it—was almost too much to bear. The thought of the years that they might have passed together, sharing this strange fate, tugged at his heart; but the prospect of amending it was enough to fill him with a purpose and hope he had not felt for centuries.

When he had first perfected *La Medusa,* crafting the mirror from such unholy stuff, he had never suspected the toll it might exact. He was a young man then, and what did he know of life? All he wanted was eternity . . . and it never occurred to him that eternity could be the loneliest destination of all. He could not have guessed what it would feel like to walk among mortal people, to form attachments and forge relationships, in the full knowledge that your friends and loved ones would wither and die before your eyes—if you lingered long enough to witness it—while you soldiered on. He remembered the many occasions he had seen puzzlement, then a kind of fear, gradually creep into his friends' and lovers' eyes, as they noted how time had continued to ravage them while sparing Sant'Angelo entirely. And he had known, on those occasions, that it was time yet again to move on, to start over, to begin the slow withdrawal of his affections. Burdened with a secret no one other than Ascanio could believe or understand, he had become a nomad among men, a traveler in the solitary regions of infinite time.

The flight attendant was at his elbow, asking if he would like something to eat or drink. He requested she bring him his customary hot chocolate.

The storm was battering at the plane, and the pilot was still trying to maneuver around it.

Sipping the soothing chocolate, he put his head back and stared out at the red lights flashing on the wing, and the blowing snow and sleet glazing the window. There was so much he missed, from open and honest love to the skills his hands had once possessed. The greatest artisan in the world. At one time, there was no one who could have challenged him for that distinction. His works had been the marvel of their day, and he had lived to see some of them—not many, but enough—endure. What he had not understood, however—and wasn't that the way of all magic?—was the price.

Eternal life, but at the cost of his genius.

It might just as well have been buried in the basilica, along with the pauper who occupied his tomb to this day.

He had imagined himself creating miraculous works forever, refining his talents, perfecting his arts.

But that, he had learned, was not the way it worked.

Only Providence knew how long you had been allotted, and once you had exceeded that secret span, you lived on sufferance. You became a walking shadow of your former self, bereft of all the gifts that had made life sweet and fruitful and worth prizing in the first place.

Cellini, the cleverest man of his day, had been outwitted.

The plane, buffeted by another strong gust of wind, banked its wings, and the chocolate lapped into his saucer. The attendant, on unsteady feet herself, brought him a fresh cup and another linen napkin.

The artisan who had never made an untrue object in his life had been lured into a trap of his own design. With greater skill than even a Leonardo or Michelangelo, he had fashioned for himself a destiny with no purpose, no shape, and no end.

Chapter 44

"Where is David?" Sarah murmured, as Gary took a seat beside her bed in the hospice. "I need to see David. Where is he?"

Gary wished he knew, and he wished he knew what to tell her. He had been waiting for his cell phone to ring any second, telling him that David had at least landed in Chicago. But so far, nothing. "Soon," he said, for the hundredth time, "I'm sure he'll be here very soon." He'd even tried reaching him on the last cell-phone number David had called from, but he'd gotten a mysterious message, in Italian yet, saying that Dr. Jantzen was not available. Or at least that's what he thought it had said.

He glanced out the window at the rock garden, with its ornamental pool—now frozen—and its white-barked birch trees. He could see the lighted windows on the other side, too, occupied no doubt by other dying patients. The late-afternoon light was even more attenuated by the cloudy skies and the oncoming storm. He was terrified that David's flight—whichever one he was on—had been delayed by the weather.

Sarah's eyes closed again, and her head twisted on the pillow. Gary wondered if he should call the nurse and get her some more painkillers. "What do you need?" he asked.

"My mouth," she whispered. "It's so dry."

He reached into the plastic cup for a chip of ice and put it on her tongue. It seemed as if she didn't have enough strength even to suck on it, and the chemo had left her with mouth sores that refused to heal. But when the ice was gone, he picked up the tube of Vaseline and gently rubbed some of it on her parched lips. Her eyes took on that faraway look again.

"Maybe I should make a meat loaf," she said, in one of the typical non sequiturs brought on by the medications.

"That sounds good."

"David always likes it."

"So do I."

"And chocolate pie for dessert," she said. "It makes Emme so happy."

Emme was home now, with her grandmother. She'd come by a few hours ago, but Sarah had been seized with a feverish bout of pain and nausea, and the scene had suddenly gotten so awful that Gary had had to take Emme out to the car and rock her in his arms until she was able to stop crying.

Much as he hated for that to be her last view of her mother, he wasn't sure that there'd be time for her to come back again. He'd told his mom to put her to bed early and try to get her to go to sleep.

Gary hadn't had more than three hours of sleep in a row for days.

But there was a faint smile on Sarah's face now, which meant that she was probably imagining herself back in her own kitchen, preparing that meat-loaf dinner. *Just as well,* Gary thought. When she was conscious, she was fretful and wore herself out asking about David, or worrying about what should be done to help Emme through the trauma once she was gone. When the morphine was kicking in, she was off on a cloud, but untroubled.

Gary slumped back in the chair, yawning and scrubbing his face with his hands. Dreadful as it was to be there, at least this place wasn't as dismal and antiseptic as the hospital. Each room was private, and done up in neutral colors, with indirect lighting and soft, soothing music. You weren't even allowed to use your cell phones except in the main lounge area. That, plus the view of the outdoor garden, gave the hospice a peaceful, even comforting, atmosphere.

A flock of sparrows landed in the garden, pecking at the ground between the tufts of snow and ice. Gary picked up a piece of the dried toast from the meal tray that Sarah hadn't touched, left the room, and went down and around the corridor. A door there opened directly into the garden, and he stepped outside.

The cold air was a shock, but a bracing one. He took a few steps on the little winding path that circled the fountain, and the birds nervously flitted up onto the branches of the birch trees. He tore the bread into tiny pieces and threw them on the ground.

"Go for it," he said, and once he'd taken a step back, the birds swooped down.

He looked up at the gray sky, getting darker by the minute, just as an airplane, its red lights flashing, passed high overhead, heading toward O'Hare Airport. And he prayed—he *prayed*—that David was on it.

Chapter 45

O'Hare was tied into one big knot.

David's plane, like dozens of others, had been forced to circle the airport, flying out over Lake Michigan and then in again, as the controllers tried to safely land all the existing traffic before the wind and snow got any worse, or made any more of the runways inoperable.

The FASTEN SEAT BELTS sign had been on for nearly the entire hour, as David had huddled, invisible and anxious, against the emergency exit, occasionally peering out through the porthole at the turbulent clouds scudding across the night sky. Would the storm abate, or would it increase to such an extent that the moon was completely obscured? From everything he knew about the Medusa—first from his study of *The Key to Life Eternal*, the rest from the mouth of Sant'Angelo himself—the moonlight was as essential to his enterprise as the mirror itself. As he had translated the text himself, sitting in the silo of the Newberry . . .

> "The waters of eternity,
> Blessed by the radiant moon,
> Together stop the tide of time
> And grant the immortal boon."

If his plan was to succeed . . . if the magic was to happen . . . he would need all the elements to come together.

And even then, what were the chances?

When the plane was finally cleared to land and David could hear the wheels coming down, he breathed a sigh of relief. There were still a dozen hurdles to go—on a night like this, just getting out of the airport was going to be tough—but oh, how he longed to get his feet on the ground. For that matter, he longed simply to *see* his own feet again. Being disembodied felt alarmingly close to feeling nonexistent.

It was a bumpy landing as the wheels skidded on the runway and the crosswinds tore at the plane's wide wings; without a seat or seat belt to hold him in place, David was buffeted from one wall to the other. But with one invisible hand, he made sure he kept the wreath on his brow. His head ached from its grip, but now was no time to be discovered and hauled off to airport security as an undocumented passenger.

"S'il vous plaît séjour posé jusqu'à ce que nous soyons arrivés à la porte," the intercom announced, and the few impatient passengers who had already tried to retrieve bags from the overhead compartments dutifully sat back down. David used the opportunity to slink silently up the aisle and position himself directly behind the main hatchway. Getting the ramp in place created another delay, but as soon as the door was thrown back, David breezed past the flight attendant, who seemed to sense his presence somehow and put a worried hand to the base of her throat, before skirting a waiting wheelchair, running up the ramp, and out into the terminal.

Following the signs for Customs, David hurried along the endless corridors and escalators, and though a luggage cart was trundled over his foot and a baby carriage was shoved into his shin, he was able to pass through the automated doors without trouble by following close on the heels of a bulky businessman.

At the Customs desks, David looked around to see which officer was already occupied riffling through someone's luggage, then shimmied past the girl whose guitar case was being given the once-over—

"Yeah, I packed it myself," she was reciting, "and it hasn't been out of my sight"—and then raced down the concourse, past the big plate-glass windows where people were waiting to spot their visitors, and out toward the taxi stands.

The line was interminable, passengers huddled against the biting wind, stamping their feet to keep warm as the cabs were slowly motioned forward by the dispatchers, loaded up, and sent on their way.

But David had no time to spare on this, and renting a car would take even longer.

Across several lanes, in the section reserved for unloading private car service clients, he saw a maroon Lincoln parked, and the driver—a young guy with a soul patch—was helping an elderly couple to wrestle their bags onto a trolley. David loped across the lanes, dodging the cars that of course could not even see him, and while the driver was settling up, he slipped into the backseat and took off the garland.

For a second or two, as nothing happened, he feared he'd done himself some irreparable harm. But then, he felt a tingling in his toes, the same feeling he'd get when he'd been out skating too long and the blood had slowly started to return. His boots reappeared, drumming on the floor of the car. Then the sensation coursed up his legs, and they, too, gradually became visible.

But the driver got in sooner than David had expected, jumping into the seat to count his bills.

David prayed he wouldn't look into the rearview mirror yet.

Reaching for the radio mike, he said, "Car 6, calling in."

"Hey, Zach."

"I've just made the drop-off at Air France."

David felt the rippling sensation moving up his torso. Glancing down, he saw his coat coming into view, and then his chest. His arms prickled, as if each hair was standing on end, and he flexed the muscles gratefully.

"You got another pickup for me?" Zach asked.

"Looks like it," the dispatcher replied. "Alitalia."

"Cancel that," David interrupted, and the driver whipped around in his seat. David hoped that the crown of his head wasn't still missing.

"What the *hell*?" the driver said, dropping the mike. "Where'd you come from?"

David held up a fistful of bills. "Do it, and they're all yours."

Zach looked very confused.

"Hey, Zach," the radio dispatcher said, "let me give you the name."

"Tell 'em you're busy," David urged.

"Those are euros," the driver mumbled to David.

"Zach, you still there?"

"True," David said. "That means they're worth more than dollars." He leaned forward and handed over the whole wad of them.

"I do know that," Zach said, as he thumbed through the bills. "I'm in grad school."

"Then you can figure out how to get to Evanston hospital."

Satisfied with the windfall, Zach pleaded engine trouble over the radio, then shut off the mike for the breakneck trip to the suburbs.

David fished Jantzen's BlackBerry out of his pocket again, called Gary, and got his voice mail. "I'm in a cab," David said, "and on the way." Hanging up, he simply stared blankly at the phone. What if he was already too late? Nothing he had read suggested that the *Medusa* could reanimate the dead. It could bestow eternal life, but it could not return it to those already gone. He reached into his shirt just to feel its presence on his chest. The silver was cold, the silk backing slick. That was strange, he thought. It did not absorb any of his body heat. It remained unaffected, oblivious to its surroundings, as if in a vacuum of its own. His fingers traced the contours of the Gorgon's face. He knew every tendril of its hair, every furrow of its snarling brow, but for the first time since acquiring it, he feared it, too. What great transgression was he about to attempt?

The cab slowed down, and David said, "Can't you go any faster?"

"Not on the ice," Zach replied, "and I'm not about to total the damn car."

But something told him that Sarah was still alive. Some intuition, some sixth sense. The bond they had was so strong, and had always been so unbreakable, that if it had been severed, he'd have known. He'd have felt the break, no matter how far away he'd been, like a punch in his stomach.

Little cyclones of snow were whipping across the highway, and the wind was battering at the windows. Automated signs warned of delays up ahead and a maximum speed of twenty miles per hour. A Hummer, its warning lights flashing, had slid right into a traffic divider.

"Get off at Dempster," David said. "It'll be faster."

Zach did as he was told, and David steered him toward several shortcuts to get to the hospital complex more directly. But every time Zach tried to engage him in conversation, David shut him down. He didn't want him talking, he wanted him driving.

At the hospital complex on Central Street, David quickly scanned the various driveway signs and arrows for the one leading to the Hospice Care Unit. It turned out to be a separate one-story building, with a broad, covered driveway in front.

"Good luck, man," Zach said, as David charged out of the limo, his backpack hanging from one hand, and into the revolving door; it was one of those doors that turned at its own speed, but David was shoving at the bar, anyway.

A nurse behind the counter looked up as he arrived, panting, and said, "Whoa there, partner. Slow down. This is a hospital zone."

David dropped the backpack, and said, "Sarah Franco."

The nurse looked uncertain.

"Sorry. I mean Sarah Henderson."

"Oh, yes," she said, her voice now taking on a more solicitous tone. "She's down the hall, in Room 3. And you are?"

"Her brother," David said, already moving on.

"Hold on," the nurse said, as one hand reached for the phone. "I have to notify her caregiver. She might be sleeping."

What difference did that make? He was here to wake her up.

Outside her door, he saw Gary, in a flannel shirt and jeans, pacing the hall.

"Thank God," Gary said. "I had my phone on vibrate, and just picked up your message."

"How is she?" David said.

"One of the nurses is in with her now." He looked at David with enormous relief, tempered with a bit of reproach. "She's been waiting for you. I told you she would."

"I was counting on it," he said, even as he swiftly circumvented Gary—who looked startled—and headed straight into Room 3.

"David, you might want to wait a minute!"

But that was the last thing he wanted to do.

The nurse, an African-American man with gray hair and a gentle face, was just adjusting an IV line. He turned and said, "You must be her brother. She's been waiting for you. I'm Walter."

But David's eyes were fixed on Sarah, or what was left of her. In the time he'd been gone, she had changed from a woman hanging on to life, however weakly, to a woman already in the embrace of death. Her hands on the blanket were mottled and blue, her cracked lips were slick with Vaseline, and her face was a hollow mask. Even on seeing him, she showed none of the joy he had expected; her expression, instead, was querulous and uncertain. He wasn't even sure she recognized him.

"We just upped her Halperidol," Walter said, sotto voce. "In a few minutes, she may be more lucid."

David had thought he'd been prepared for anything . . . but now he knew that he hadn't.

"Can we be alone?"

"Sure," the nurse said. "I'm here if you need me."

David dragged a chair to the bedside and took her hand in his. The skin was cold and the fingers felt like twigs.

"Sarah, it's David. I'm here."

But she didn't respond. Her eyes were glassy and staring off into space, her bare skull covered by a paisley silk scarf.

He waited, wondering what to do next.

"Remember that day at the skating rink?" he finally said. "When you told me you'd give anything, anything at all, for the chance to see Emme grow up?"

A humidifier hummed quietly in the corner.

"I'm going to give you that chance."

Whether he was imagining it or not, her fingers seemed to stir in his grasp.

But how, he wondered, was he going to get this done?

The wind howled at the window, and it was then that he noticed the birch trees outside, in the little garden, and the frozen pond . . . glimmering dully in the moonlight.

He jumped from his chair. A wheelchair was folded up in the corner of the room, and he quickly opened it. He had to move fast, because he knew that if Gary or the nurse came in, they would surely intervene. He pushed the chair to the side of the bed, and tucking the blanket all around her, he lifted Sarah into it. She weighed so little, it was like lifting a bundle of rags.

Glancing out her bedroom door, he was glad to see that Gary and Walter had moved down the hall, toward the reception desk and its big silver coffee urn. In one swift motion, he steered the chair out her door and then out of sight down the hall. Now he just had to find his way into that garden.

In his haste, the first door he tried turned out to be a utility closet, the second one a dispensary. But the third, with a metal crossbar across it, looked more promising, and turning the chair so that he could press on the bar with his own back, he felt a rush of cold air. While he was dragging the wheels over the bump of the threshold, a corner of the blanket got caught in the closing door, threatening for a second to pull Sarah out of the chair altogether. David had to stop, bend down, and wrench it free.

When he looked up at her face, he thought he saw a glimmer of recognition.

"David? Are you . . . really here?" she said, her voice murky and slow.

"Sure looks that way," he said, tucking the blanket back around her.

"Where are we?"

"We're getting some fresh air," he said, his breath clouding, as he pushed the chair out into the garden.

"Cold," she said. "It's cold."

"I know that," he said, his fingers scrabbling under his shirt to retrieve the *Medusa*. A gust of wind plucked the scarf off her head and blew it onto the frozen pond. "I just need you to do something for me," he said, as he lifted the amulet over his own head, and brushed aside the black silk backing that concealed the mirror.

"Are we in the backyard?" she asked. "I bet Emme's waiting for you upstairs—you should go and surprise her."

"I will," he promised, "I will." He put the *Medusa* into her palm and helped her to raise her hand. "But right now I want you to look at yourself in this mirror."

She seemed confused, and irritated. "No, I don't do that anymore. I don't look at myself in mirrors anymore."

"You have to, just this once." He glanced over his shoulder, past the roof of the hospice, to gauge where the moon was in the sky. A dark cloud was just drifting past it.

He angled the mirror to be sure to catch the emerging rays.

"The mirror," he repeated. "Look in the mirror."

Frowning, she did what he asked. "I can't see a thing," she said.

"You will in a minute," he said, humoring her, as he bent low to see if the mirror was being held in the right spot. Its convex surface gleamed, like a shiny dark scarab, in the moonlight. He could see his sister's reflection, hovering in the glass as if it were staring *out* rather than *in*, and he braced her hand so that the pose would be held. The waters of eternity, captured behind the glass, were receiving their blessing from the radiant moon.

But how long did it take?

He was startled by a thumping sound—a palm flatly smacking against a window—and he glanced back into Sarah's lighted bedroom where he could see Gary, his shocked face pressed close to the glass, banging again and again.

"Keep looking," David urged his sister, "just keep looking." Any moment, he expected Walter to come barreling outside to rescue her.

But the hand holding the mirror suddenly dropped into Sarah's lap and her head snapped back against the wheelchair, as if she'd suffered a seizure.

Had it worked?

David snatched the mirror out of her lap, wondering if he would actually feel any difference in it. Would it be hotter? colder? *charged* somehow?

But it was his own face he was seeing . . . his own eyes staring back at him from the bottom of its deep, dark well . . . and before he knew it, a jolt like electricity had sizzled through his limbs. His jaw clenched shut, his head went back, and his knees nearly buckled; if he hadn't been holding on to the wheelchair, he'd have collapsed on the spot.

The courtyard door flew open, as Gary and the nurse came running toward them.

"Are you out of your mind?" Walter said, pushing the helpless David away from the handlebars of the chair.

David staggered backwards, his arms dangling loose, his legs shaking. He leaned, reeling, between the birch trees, afraid that he might pass out.

"What the hell is *wrong* with you?" Gary barked, as he snatched her scarf from the icy pond.

Walter whirled the chair around and headed back through the door. Gary, following him in, was so mad he didn't even bother to look back at David.

And David didn't blame them. He knew how insane this looked.

A bank of clouds obscured the moon, casting the courtyard into darker shadow.

Through the window of her room, he could see Sarah being lifted back into the bed, extra blankets being piled over her again. And he could only imagine what was being said about her distraught, but deranged, younger brother.

But none of it mattered. Not any longer. He had done what he had set out to do . . . and no one—no Greek hero, no Florentine artisan—could have achieved anything more. Come what may, he was at peace with what he had done.

Chapter 46

Kathryn Van Owen was staring out the windows of her penthouse aerie, watching the moonlight glint off the obsidian black surface of Lake Michigan, and wondering, for the thousandth time, what had become of David Franco. Had he found *La Medusa*, or had he, like Palliser and so many others before him, fallen into the spider's web, never to emerge again?

In the next room, she heard the phone ring, and Cyril pick up. She could not make out what was being said, but a few moments later, he rushed in and said, "It was the receptionist at the hospice."

Kathryn, who had been keeping close tabs on David's family, had already taken the trouble to bribe her for any news of his return.

"David Franco is there right now."

Kathryn's heart leapt in her chest. She knew all about Sarah's grim prognosis. But had David rushed back to save her, or simply to say good-bye? Kathryn was already moving toward the door, and Cyril, close behind, was grabbing her coat and gloves. And while she usually waited for him to bring the limo up, tonight she went down to the garage with him, opened her own door, and virtually jumped inside.

He pulled the car out of the garage, onto Lake Shore Drive, and into traffic made worse by the weather. Kathryn cursed the winds that gusted the snow across the lanes, slowing the other cars, and she cursed the cars themselves for impeding her progress.

How long had David been back? Why hadn't he called her the moment he returned? Was it because he could not admit his failure?

Or was it because he was concealing his success?

Oh, she could have warned him not to try his own hand at magic. She had feared that he might. But she also knew her admonitions would have fallen on deaf ears. After all, wasn't it his sister's critical state that she had been banking on all along? She knew that any doubts he might have entertained—doubts any rational man would of course have had—would be subsumed in his desperate search to find a cure. He had needed to succeed on this mission as no other searcher for the *Medusa* ever had.

Could that have made the crucial difference?

On one side of the limo, she saw the twinkling lights of the Chicago skyscrapers and apartment buildings. On the other, the emptiness of the vast and freezing lake.

But one thought alone—had he found the damned thing?—kept coming back to her. Would she finally hold the *Medusa* in her hand again? Would she be able to undo its sinister power? Over the years, how many times had she cast her mind back to Benvenuto's studio, and the night when she had removed the iron box from its hideaway . . . perused its mysterious contents . . . and awakened on the floor, naked, her hair white, with Benvenuto bending over her and asking in mournful tones, "What have you done? What have you done?"

Even now, centuries later, the words echoed in her head as if they had just been spoken.

Cyril turned the car off the wide, lakeshore highway and onto the less congested city streets. And by the time they pulled into the harsh white lights of the hospice driveway, she was already perched on the edge of her seat like a skydiver about to leap.

Without waiting for Cyril to come around and open the door, she threw it wide and, with her fur coat flapping open around her, flew into the building.

The receptionist took one look at her and instantly said, "Room 3. Down the hall, turn right."

She marched down the hall, the carpet muffling her steps, trying to compose herself. Vivaldi was playing over the speaker system, the lights were low and recessed.

She saw a burly man in a flannel shirt, urging a cup of hot coffee on an exhausted David Franco, who was slumped in a chair. His head hung down, his shoulders sagged, but only one thing truly startled her. And that was his hair.

It was dead white.

My God. He not only had the glass—he had looked into its depths himself!

When she stood before him, his eyes slowly came up to meet hers. She could not read his expression. It wasn't triumph, and it wasn't defeat.

It was uncertainty.

"Give it to me," was all she said, holding out her empty palm.

"Excuse me," the burly man said—surely Sarah's husband—"but who are you?"

"A friend of your wife's," she replied, without even looking at him. "The best friend she's ever had, in fact. Wouldn't you say so, David?"

Her hand was still out.

"Gary, could you give us a minute?" David asked.

"Sure, sure," Gary said, moving off warily. "But I'll be in with Sarah if you need me."

When he was out of earshot, David said, "How do I know if it's worked?" and Kathryn brushed his question aside like a gnat.

"Look at you," she said. "You can't be serious."

"But Sarah?"

"Enough of this," she said. "Another word and I'll think you're trying to renege on the deal."

"I would never do that."

"Good," she said, withdrawing a sealed envelope from her pocket. "You know what this is, right?"

David looked at it vacantly.

"Most people would be glad to get a million dollars."

A lanky man with a badge that identified him as Dr. Alan Ross came out of the room, noting something on a chart and saying, "David, can I have a word with you?"

He acknowledged Kathryn, but didn't say anything more until David explained that she was a family member and the doctor could speak freely in front of her.

"In that case," the doctor said, "I'll say I'm stumped."

"Stumped?"

"Your sister says she feels great, and trust me, she shouldn't."

"But is she?"

"I'll know a lot more tomorrow when all the tests can be done. I'm certainly not releasing her tonight. But for now? I don't know what's going on, but she's rallied in a way I've never seen before. All her vital signs are back to normal, and I just called down to the lab and the blood test we took is clean as a whistle. They thought I must have mixed up some samples." He shook his head in wonderment. "She even looks a hundred percent better. Gary said she just called the house and told Emme to get out of bed—and this is a school night, mind you—and come right over. I've never seen a remission like this. I wish I could claim I'd performed some miracle here, but I didn't."

"Maybe someone else did," Kathryn said.

"Maybe so," he admitted. "Maybe so." Shaking David's hand happily, he said, "Whatever happened, it's great news. I'll be back first thing in the morning." Then, glancing at David's shock of white hair, he said, "When did you decide to do that?"

"It was kind of . . . impulsive."

Still in a rollicking humor, the doctor said, "Next time you get an impulse like that, talk to Sarah. She was always the sensible one of you two."

He sauntered off, snapping his fingers at his side, and Kathryn tucked the check into David's breast pocket. Without another word, he fished *La Medusa* out from under his collar. It turned slowly on its chain, the Gorgon's glare catching the light.

But the moment it landed in her palm, she snapped her hand shut like a trap. "A pleasure doing business with you," she said before turning back down the hall. She was squeezing the amulet so tight her knuckles hurt.

But she had it, she had it at last!

She had just gone through the revolving door and into the cold night air—snow was swirling off the concrete—when a black Mercedes sedan, its headlights casting a bright blue glow, tore up to the driveway, skidding to a stop at the icy curb.

She stepped back, signaling to Cyril to bring her own limo around, when the back door of the car opened and a long, black walking stick descended onto the cement. It was followed a moment later by a man with a coat draped over his shoulders, in the Continental style. He had strong features, with a prominent Italian nose, a thick moustache, black hair dusted at the temples with gray . . . and a scowl that might have scared a legion.

Kathryn stopped where she stood, so suddenly that he almost collided with her. Apologizing as he passed, he momentarily glanced back.

And that was all it took.

Disbelief gave way to dawning amazement. She saw his eyes searching her face, his lips moving to form the right word.

"Caterina?" he said, as a nimbus of snowflakes whirled above their heads.

It was as if the world had stopped turning. All the strength had left her limbs.

"Benvenuto," she replied.

Dropping the cane, the coat falling from his shoulders, he snatched her into his arms, so violently that the *Medusa*, clutched in her hand, slipped through her fingers and landed with a sharp crack on the pavement.

"My God!" she exclaimed, looking down as its glass shattered into a thousand tiny fragments. A thin rivulet of pale green water trickled out, sizzling on the ice like acid. Before she could even consider the consequences, she felt a rush of hot blood pounding in her veins, and a flush filling her cheeks. She gasped in shock and saw that her lover was reeling, too. A light was blazing in his face, and his breathing was labored. Their eyes locked, and though they said nothing, they didn't have to. Both of them knew what the other was thinking, and feeling. Both of them had imagined this release for centuries.

Still holding her in his arms, he glanced down at his fallen cane. But she could feel his back straightening, his legs growing stronger under him. She could sense an even greater power than before surging through his body, just as it was doing through her own.

"*Il mio gatto,*" he said, a wide smile lifting the ends of his moustache and his strong arms buoying her up. "Still causing trouble, I see."

But she was too overwhelmed to reply.

He kissed her hard on the lips, then threw back his head in exultation. Snowflakes stuck to his eyebrows and moustache. He let out a loud, braying laugh that cut through the night and reverberated off the walls of the hospice before being carried away on the gusting wind.

"You know what it is, don't you?" he shouted, in joy. "You know what it is?"

But he didn't have to tell her. She knew. It was the power of time starting afresh, of life beginning anew. The clock that had stopped, nearly five hundred years before, had started again. The hands that had been frozen in place were ticking. He lifted her off her feet and swung her around, laughing. And though he was holding her so tight she could barely catch her breath, she laughed, too. Cyril, and a couple trudging into the hospice, looked on in amazement. Who would have thought that in a place like this, where death and sorrow reigned, mortality itself could have been so celebrated and embraced? And when her feet touched the ground again, Kathryn—no, Caterina now, Caterina for as long as she lived—felt the pieces of the broken mirror crunching under the sole of her shoe.

Chapter 47

For a January day in Florence, it was unseasonably sunny and bright. As David approached the Piazza della Signoria, he could see not only tourists but locals, too, out enjoying the clear skies and brisk air. Several vendors tried to sell him maps and souvenirs, and one even offered to be his personal tour guide.

But he already knew the best guide in town. An *Italienisch Mädchen*, as Herr Linz had put it in the notebook David had stolen from the Chateau Perdu. He had read it in its entirety on the flight back to Italy. Filled with elaborate sketches and directives, it was the monster's plan for the greatest art museum in the history of the world, to be built one day—no surprise—in his hometown and namesake of Linz. But far from being a tribute to mankind's noblest endeavors, the Führermuseum was to be a grandiose testament to Hitler's own ruthless ambitions. With its five-hundred-foot-long façade and rows of towering columns, it was designed to trumpet the victory of the Reich and show off its master's hoard of stolen trophies. Everything, apart from his greatest, and most secret, acquisition—*La Medusa*—was to be on display.

But as David now knew—from Sant'Angelo's lips—its like would never be seen again. The glass was gone, its magic was done. For those who had fallen under its spell, the spell was over. What was left in its place was simply life—ordinary life, starting up again where it had left off . . . though clean and unencumbered.

And that was enough. Sarah was fine and healthy. It was as if the disease had never struck. Dr. Ross wanted to make a casebook study of her, and he'd even stopped by the house to plead his cause. But Gary had put a stop to that in no uncertain terms. "Sorry, Doc," he'd told him as David stood silently by, "but we've had all we can stand of hospitals. No offense, but we hope we never see you again."

Dr. Ross had understood and taken it well. And when he'd gotten back in his car and driven off, Gary had turned to David on the front lawn. Putting a firm hand on his shoulder, he'd said, in a voice filled with gratitude, "I don't suppose you're ever going to tell me what really went on that night, are you?"

"It's a long story," David said, "and you wouldn't believe me even if I did."

Gary nodded slowly, and said, "You're right." Then, glancing at David's hair, he said, "You know, it's starting to come in brown again."

"It's a big relief."

"I'm sure that girl you told me about—Olivia Levi?—will be relieved, too. That Andy Warhol look wasn't working for you."

David had been well aware of that, and to spare her a heart attack when he surprised her in the piazza, he had put on a hat.

Right now, she was off near the loggia, shepherding a group of seniors to the base of the *Perseus*. He was far enough away that he couldn't hear what she was saying about it, but he could see her standing on the steps, arms waving with a flourish as the gray-haired men and women on the tour huddled close to catch every word.

By the time he'd crept up to the rear of the group, he could hear her asking them if anyone knew the story of Perseus and the Gorgon.

A professorial type in front said, "Perseus was tricked into promising the head of the Medusa as a wedding gift. But one look in the Medusa's eyes could turn a man to stone. He had to call upon the gods for help."

Several others in the group nodded their appreciation of his expertise and, emboldened, he went on. "Hermes gave him a sword, and Athena gave him a polished shield, so he could catch the creature's reflection. By looking only in the shield, he was able to kill the Gorgon without looking directly into her eyes."

Olivia, wearing the purple iris on her lapel, applauded. "And the man who made this magnificent statue? Who can tell me that?"

Before the professor could pipe up, David called out, "Benvenuto Cellini!" Everyone in the tour group turned their heads to see who the interloper was.

Olivia, shielding her eyes from the sun, said, "That is correct," and after spotting him in back, started down the steps. "And who commissioned it?" she said, deftly maneuvering her way through the crowd.

"Cosimo de'Medici."

"And why?" she asked, as David made his own way toward her, too.

"It was a symbol."

"Of what?" she said, as they at last embraced.

"Of perseverance. Perseus was always able to beat impossible odds to get what he wanted."

And then they were done talking. As he bent his head to kiss her, he could hear the members of the tour group speculating among themselves about who this guy was . . . and then, only seconds later, starting to grumble about the unexpected delay in the tour.

Finally, the professor in front decided to pick up where he'd left off. "I used to teach art in Scranton," he said, and the group seemed to breathe a sigh of relief. "So I know that if you look at this statue from behind, you'll see just how ingenious it is. The face of its sculptor is hidden in the design of the helmet," he said, while the tour group dutifully followed him around to the back of the statue.

"These tours," Olivia murmured to David, "they are not free, you know."

"So what do I owe you? As the newly appointed Director of Acquisitions at the Newberry Library, I have an expense account now."

"Really? Then I will think of something."

He kissed her again, holding her so tight her purple flower was crushed flat and his hat fell off. When she finally pulled back enough to see his two-toned hair, she looked puzzled and said, "What happened here? You did not tell me you had dyed your hair."

"I was saving that part." In point of fact, he had spared her all the details of his own experience with the mirror. It was enough that she knew it had saved his sister.

"This was not a good idea," she said, frowning and ruffling his hair with one hand. "Don't do it again."

"I'm certainly not planning on it."

"But what else have you been keeping from me?" she said, and then, her tone abruptly changing from playful to serious, added, "Your sister—she is still doing well?"

"Yes," he replied, "she's doing just fine. And she's looking forward to meeting you very soon."

"I look forward to it, too," Olivia said. "But what does she remember, about what happened that night at the hospital?"

"Not much." David considered it a blessing. "And what little she does remember just seems like a bad dream to her."

"*Un miracolo*," Olivia said with a knowing look, "that is what I would call it."

"Whatever you call it," David said, "it isn't something that will ever happen again."

Olivia nodded, sagely. "So *La Medusa*—it is truly gone? Forever?"

"Gone. Mrs. Van Owen even insisted that the silver be melted down and made into a pin."

"A pin," Olivia said, a note of regret in her voice. And David understood her sadness at the loss of such a miraculous device. True, it had fallen for a time into the worst hands imaginable, but now, no sooner than it had been recovered and restored to its rightful owner, its magic had been lost again for good.

"This statue represents the apogee of Cellini's career," the professor from Scranton was declaiming, and quite happily. "In the long and prolific career of this magnificent artist—one of the greatest masters of the Renaissance—it remains his single greatest achievement."

And though David and Olivia might easily have disputed that last contention, neither one of them said a word.

Chapter 48

"At this time the duke left with his entire court and all his children, except for the prince, who was in Spain. They went through the marshes of Siena, and by that route they went to Pisa. That bad air poisoned the Cardinal before the others; so that after a few days he was attacked by a pestilential fever that quickly killed him. He was the apple of the duke's eye: a handsome and good man, and his death was a tremendous loss. I let a few days pass until I thought their tears had dried; and then I set off for Pisa."

The marquis put the ancient manuscript down beside his cup of chocolate. Outside, he could hear a siren wailing on the Paris streets.

He had written these words, the last of his published autobiography, in December of 1562. Then, he had lost heart. Over the centuries, he had occasionally written down further scraps, but then consigned them to the vault deep beneath his town house. What was the use of telling his story, he'd thought, when it was necessary to withhold the darkest and most critical secret that lay at its core?

And what could be the point of telling a story that would never have an end?

But he had noticed a change in himself of late. It was as if his hands had found their talents again. He had sketched a design for a statue, and he had been pleased with it. He had even ordered a block of marble for the first time in ages. And he felt an accompanying urge to pick up the pen and resume his fantastical tale, regardless of whether or not it would ever be published—or believed.

"Benvenuto, it's almost midnight," he heard from the doorway. "Why don't you come to bed?"

Caterina, her long black hair spilling over the shoulders of her white silk nightgown, was standing like an apparition in the shadows.

From her intonation, it was more than sleep she was suggesting.

He smiled and said, "I'm having my hot chocolate. Would you like some?"

Ascanio had left the silver pot on a tray by the desk.

"That's what keeps you awake at night."

"I like the night. Don't you remember how I would try to rig my studio with torches, so that I could work until all hours?"

"I do," she said, holding up a hand to conceal her yawn.

"And how the neighbors would complain about the incessant hammering?"

"And yet you still managed to be late with every commission. I sometimes wondered why the duke didn't have you hanged from the top of the Bargello."

"Because then he would have been stuck with that numbskull, Bandinelli. Why, when I think of that atrocity he committed in the Piazza della Signoria . . ."

Caterina refused to take the bait; she'd heard it all before, countless times.

"I'm going to sleep," she said, coming to his side and bending down to plant a kiss on his brow.

But before she could get away, he threw an arm around her and pulled her into his lap. "Remember the night I first saw you, on the arm of that fop at Fontainebleau?"

"Yes—though I was the one who saw you first. You were busy telling the French king that he needed a new fountain."

"I was right."

"You were bold—that's what I liked."

"I liked your eyes." Indeed, they were still as violet and inviting as they had ever been.

"What's this?" she said, turning the pages of the manuscript on the desk. "Ah, I see. Are you planning to pick up where you left off?"

"I was considering it."

"You have an awful lot of ground to cover, don't you think?"

"But an awful lot to tell, don't you think?"

"No one would ever believe you."

That much he would concede. But who cared? An artisan did his best work without worrying about what his audience might think or believe.

They kissed, her arm around his broad shoulders, and then she squirmed out of his grasp, saying, "You know where to find me."

Benvenuto drained his cup, then turned off the desk lamp. He was still wide-awake—she was probably right about the chocolate—but he had an itch to read over the old papers that had been gathering dust in the vaults. He was feeling oddly inspired tonight.

He made his way down to the main floor, then down another flight of stairs to a ponderous steel door, heavy as the door on any bank vault. Pressing his finger, then his eye, to the biometric scan, he turned the wheel and the door swung open. The lights automatically went on and the fans began blowing.

There were several interconnecting vaults, holding bronze statues, oil paintings in gilded frames, antique tapestries, and cabinets filled with priceless gems. An Ali Baba's cave, if ever there was one. But he didn't stop until he came to the deepest and farthest recess of them all. Although the overhead light fixture there was the same wattage as in all the other vaults, for some reason that corner always seemed darker, as if some other force were struggling against the light. Even the marquis had never liked to linger in that spot. Against the farthest wall of rough-hewn rock stood the squat, black safe in which his most valuable treasures were kept. Lowering his head to the lock, he entered the combination, then turned the handles and opened the double doors.

On the bottom shelf, the *harpe* nestled on its black velvet cushion, right beside the silver garland.

In the middle, the manuscript pages rested in a cracked leather binder, which he removed and placed on top of the safe.

And in the shadowy confines of the topmost shelf, the iron strong-box glinted as silently and dully as a crocodile's eye.

He was already closing the safe again when something made him stop. It had been years since he had last opened the iron box—first made to contain the looking glass—and even then he had sworn to himself that he would never do it again.

But at present, for whatever reason, it beckoned to him. His curiosity was aroused, and he found himself drawing the box far enough forward that the circular dials on its lid were revealed.

The combination, of course, was as simple as Caterina's nickname, and he turned the circles one by one, carefully, until he heard the tiny click of the lock unlatching.

He paused, wondering if he wanted to go on.

But his fingers, as if possessing a will of their own, were raising the lid and pressing it back on the hinge.

The cold, white light of the vault pierced the black hollow of the box. For a moment, there was no response from the trophy resting inside. But then, as the marquis kept his eyes firmly fixed on the mirror affixed to the underside of the lid, it awakened to the sudden glare. Bewildered and unfocused at first, the yellow eyes quickly assumed a desperate cast. The snakes that made up its hair waved in the air, their tiny teeth snapping in vain. The mouth opened in its habitual snarl, as if struggling to cry out.

But even if it could shriek in fury, who besides the marquis could ever have heard it?

He met its gaze in the mirror, trying not to flinch, as the severed head assumed an expression of impotent fury, of seething and inexpressible rage. *Even now*, he thought, *the Gorgon remains the indestructible embodiment of madness, death, and desolation.* To behold her reflection was to stare into the abyss. He had thought, many times, of simply consigning his gory prize to the flames. But each time his hand had been stayed by some mysterious impulse. To destroy it would seem a sort of perverse sacrilege. Glad as he was that his own life once again moved forward like anyone else's, he was not prepared to eradicate this last living proof of immortality. Life and death, good and evil, were all part of some unknowable cosmic plan, and though he was forever done with his interfering, he was not done with his sense of wonder.

Pressing the lid down until he heard the lock catch, he slid the box backward on the shelf. Then he shut the safe and swiftly retraced his steps through the vault. He swung the heavy door closed, turned the wheel to seal it, and then, clutching the manuscript under one arm, mounted the narrow stairs. The whole way he felt as if there was something right behind him, ready to plant its claw on his shoulder, spin him around and petrify him with its baleful gaze. Only when he had reached the top did he stop and turn around and, after flicking off the lights, stare defiantly into the inky darkness. Nothing stirred, and he slammed the door to the staircase shut with a bang loud enough to awaken the whole arrondissement.

Then he stalked off to his study to continue his story where he had left off so very long ago.

Acknowledgments

Without a doubt, my first debt of gratitude must be to Benvenuto Cellini himself, whose engaging and memorable autobiography I read many years ago. It made such a great impression upon me, in fact, that I decided to write this novel. In the course of composing the story, I have incorporated certain elements from that book—incidents from Cellini's life, people he knew, works of art he did indeed create—while inventing many others. *La Medusa* is, of course, one of those inventions, as are some of the events and characterizations, based on fact, that appear throughout the book.

The two editions of Cellini's memoirs that I have relied upon are the celebrated translation by John Addington Symonds, and the brilliant new translation (and notes) done by Julia Conaway Bondanella and Peter Bondanella (Oxford University Press, 2002). In addition, I regularly turned to the beautifully illustrated and authoritative study *Cellini*, written by John Pope-Hennessy and published by Abbeville Press is 1985.

For the sections of the novel dealing with the French Revolution, I found Antonia Fraser's *Marie Antoinette: The Journey* (Nan A. Talese, Doubleday/Random House, 2001), to be indispensable.

I would also like to acknowledge the Newberry Library in Chicago, a fine and venerable institution to which my brother Steve introduced me. But again, while much of what I have to say about it is true, there's a lot in this novel that isn't. Most notably, the library does not possess Cellini's *Key to Life Eternal*. I made it up. If it did exist, it would make a fitting addition to their renowned collection of medieval and Renaissance materials.

I have taken similar liberties with several other well-known institutions, including the Louvre, the Natural History Museum in Paris, the Biblioteca Laurenziana, and the Accademia di Bella Arti in Florence, Italy. While much of their history is reliably reported, some is of my own creation—the less laudable items in particular.

Finally, this book would never have come to pass without the encouragement of my agent, Cynthia Manson, and the hard work of my eagle-eyed editor, Anne Groell. (Any mistakes are my fault.) Thank you both for helping to see me across the finish line.

ABOUT THE TYPE

This book was set in Monotype Dante, a typeface designed by Giovanni Mardersteig (1892–1977). Conceived as a private type for the Officina Bodoni in Verona, Italy, Dante was originally cut only for hand composition by Charles Malin, the famous Parisian punch cutter, between 1946 and 1952. Its first use was in an edition of Boccaccio's *Trattatello in laude di Dante* that appeared in 1954. The Monotype Corporation's version of Dante followed in 1957. Though modeled on the Aldine type used for Pietro Cardinal Bembo's treatise *De Aetna* in 1495, Dante is a thoroughly modern interpretation of that venerable face.

Blood and Ice

'Stunning . . . will chill you to the bone' Lisa Gardner

A force stronger than death awakes from the
frozen depths . . .

When journalist Michael Wilde is commissioned to write a
feature about a remote research station deep in the frozen
beauty of Antarctica he is prepared for some extraordinary
sights. But on a diving expedition in the polar sea he
comes across something so extraordinary to be almost
unbelievable – a man and woman chained together, deep in
the ice. The doomed lovers are brought to the surface but as
the ice begins to thaw the scientists discover the unusual
contents of the bottles buried beside the pair, and realise
they are all in terrible danger . . .

'The ingredients of vampirism, doomed romance and
Antarctic adventure are too seductive to resist. Masello has
written a winner, made for Hollywood'
The Times

'If H.G Wells, Stephenie Meyer and Michael Crichton co-
wrote a novel the result would be *Blood and Ice*'
USA Today

'This big, meaty, supernatural thriller . . . spans centuries
and continents from Victorian England and the Crimean
war to modern America and Antarctica . . . Gripping'
Guardian

Available in Vintage paperback and ebook